The Jewels of January

Julia Heart

ALL IS WELL
ALL IS WELL
ALL IS **NOT** WELL

Library of Congress Cataloging-in-Publication Data

Names: Julia Heart, 2023 - Author.

Title: The Jewels of January: a novel/ by Julia Heart.

Cover Design: Julia Heart & Lindsey Karnuth

Description: Paper back edition. | 2023.

Identifiers:
Paperback, LCCN 2023907679 | ISBN 978-1-7376129-0-2
ebook, LCCN 2023907927 | ISBN978-1-7376129-2-6

www.juliaheart.com

Content Guidance Letter

When I began writing this book, my intention was for it to be mainly upbeat and even funny. I quickly realized that it was challenging to fully portray certain thoughts and feelings without occasionally diving deep into sensitive topics. As a result, the story touches on certain subjects that may be challenging or unpleasant for some readers.

As a person that struggles with PTSD and Anxiety Disorders, I wanted to provide some guidance and context, for those with similar sensitivities. I have created a chart on the following page that outlines these sensitive subjects and how they are represented in the book. Please be aware that this list may contain some spoilers.

I offer this warning with the utmost respect and sensitivity to those who may find these topics distressing. I want to ensure that readers are informed and able to make the decision about whether or not to proceed with the story.

I'm happy to say I was able to leave all the irony and cheeky bits intact.

Warmly,
Julia

Content Warning List

Content Warning	How Depicted
Emotionally Abusive-Relationship	Mentioned, depicted, described, shown
HIV/AIDS	Mentioned, depicted, described, shown
Anxiety	Mentioned, depicted, described, shown
Bullying	Mentioned, depicted, described, shown
Cult	Mentioned, depicted, described, shown
Depression	Mentioned
Divorce	Mentioned from character's perspective
Hostage	Mentally, as in Stockholm Syndrome
PTSD	Mentioned as a possibility, described
Rape	Mentioned; NOT depicted or discribed
Suicide	Mentioned

The Jewels of January

Julia Heart

Chapter 1

She Sells Sanctuary

James

Something about driving up to Tulips made me feel dirty before I even got inside. I sat in line for the valet and wondered what would make this building look more like a house of ill-repute rather than a fancy bunker.

Maybe windows, and then, in my head, I heard my mother's voice say *topiaries*. She said *topiaries* to any outdoor decorating problem. I bet she'd also agree that painting the building a color besides beige would be another step in the right direction. Other topless bars around town had decent curb appeal. Even The Cock Pit out by the airport had an inviting entrance, and that place was a shithole.

Despite my familiarity with the topless bars of Austin, I didn't actually come to Tulips that often. I was here tonight to celebrate my friend Brad's birthday. The guys I was meeting were all bartenders at various clubs on 6th Street in Austin. Most of the downtown bars were only open from Tuesday to Saturday, so the people who worked there went out on Sunday and Monday nights. Because of this, the best places to get a drink with your guy friends were topless bars. Usually, I went to a place called the Candy Store about a mile away.

The booming bass pouring out of the building overpowered The Bell Biv Devoe song playing on my car radio, so I turned it off as I pulled up to first place in line to park. The muggy September air stuck to my face the minute I stepped out.

"Hey," I said to the valet as I handed him my keys, "don't park it too far away. I won't be staying long."

The attendant nodded, the smirk on his face suggesting he'd heard this often.

A car horn sent a violent noise through the already chaotic parking lot, and I snapped to my left. Brad, the birthday boy, was flipping me the bird from inside his car.

"Holy shit, you startled me!" I shout-laughed in his direction.

I'd met Brad at the University of Texas. I'd been in my new dorm room, tacking up a poster of Einstein sticking his tongue out. Brad had barged in the door, tossed an oversized duffle bag, and hamper full of athletic shoes on the empty bed, and asked, "Do you have any beer?"

"No," I answered, a grin spreading across my face, "but I know where we can get some."

My first priority for attending college was to get a solid education. My second was to have copious amounts of fun. Beer, girls, and parties were on my list of things to do as much as possible. We enjoyed living with each other so much we remained roommates for all four years.

"Don't be such an old man," he said, now standing next to me. "I'm the one getting older today."

I stood back upright and reached out to shake his hand while I used my other to give him an exaggerated bro-hug.

"Happy birthday, dude; you look good for forty."

"You're such a dick," he said with a laugh, "you know I'm only turning twenty-seven."

We moved the short distance to the entrance and went inside. As we walked through the heavy oak door, the vibration of the music thumped my chest cavity. The black lights illuminated my white polo shirt and gave my skin a deep bronze glow.

A door-girl in a skintight mini dress and teased out, over-bleached hair bent across the counter. "I need to see your identification, please, and five dollars for the cover charge," she said in a honey-toned voice.

I handed her both. She looked at Brad and said, "You get in free, birthday boy."

"Thank you!" he said as he hugged her. "You're the best."

"Oh my God," she said, bobbing her head from side to side with a smile. "You're so sweet."

Brad had been dating a dancer here named Ripley for the past six months, and in typical fashion had become a trusted friend to every other employee in the building.

She pointed behind her, still smiling at Brad. "Ryan and the guys are down at the front bar waiting for you, and I think Ripley's going to be on stage soon."

Our friends lifted their drinks in the air, waving us over.

"Go on," I said, giving Brad a friendly shove. "I'll be right there."

A large, half-empty tip jar sat next to the register. I dropped a couple of bucks inside while she checked my ID.

She batted her mascara-laden eyelashes at me as she gave my license back. "Thank you!"

I hadn't been here in a while, so after I moved past the counter, I took in the room before joining my friends. This interior looked similar to other topless clubs. The walls were all covered with black fabric and large mirrors. There were three stages, each one with its own lighting system and a stripper pole. It was one big rectangle with a bar in front and another in the back. Two-thirds of the floor plan sat a couple of feet higher than the rest, which helped the space look larger.

"James!" said a waitress walking in my direction, one hand under a tray full of drinks and the other wrapped around three longneck beers. "It's good to see you," she continued as she whizzed by me. "I saved you guys a table up by the main stage. I'll be there in a minute to take everyone's order."

I rushed out a "Thanks," but I think she was already out of earshot.

My eyes trailed back to the front bar when I noticed a dancer on the stage closest to me staring in my direction. She was holding onto the pole, looking me straight in the eye. I squinted a bit to get a better look. Did I know her?

There was a disheveled girl-next-door quality to her appearance. She didn't have that "big 80s hair" that was still holding strong even though it was 1991. Hers went just past her shoulders and, though tousled, didn't look like she used an ounce of Aqua Net.

Maybe she thought I was someone else?

She offered me an amused smile and turned away, strutting up the cat-walk-shaped stage with nothing on except a thong and a pair of suicide-high heels. Her stride was languid and teasing, as if she had nothing better to do than let people admire her. I rushed down the stairs and over to the stage to tip her. I must already know her.

She spun around without warning as I approached. I stopped jogging, pasted a goofy grin on my face, and continued walking up to the stage. She bent her knees and gracefully lowered herself to the floor. As she crawled over, I got a better look at her face. She had a soft Eastern European quality to her features, with dark brown almond-shaped eyes and full pouty lips. Being a bartender, I met a lot of women, but I didn't forget many faces, especially those I considered beautiful. I definitely didn't know her—but I sure wanted to.

Her seductive hooded eyes conveyed a desire I wanted to get lost in. Why was I so taken with her?

She took her messy blond head, starting at my left shoulder, and dragged it teasingly down the side of my body. She stopped for just a second at the top of my shorts. From there, she moved across my belly button.

The places where her face and head touched me burned a trail of heat through the button-down I was wearing. A slow rolling ball of energy picked up speed inside me. The hairs on my arms pricked to attention, and a twitch-inducing shiver climbed up my spine.

As she traveled back up, I let myself enjoy the view of her muscular back and heart-shaped bottom. There was an intimacy to the way she touched me, like we were the only two people in the bar and didn't have anything—or anyone—holding us back.

She dragged her head up the right side of my chest. "Thank you for the tip," she whispered into the most sensitive place on my neck.

She sat back on her knees and smiled at me, coy and demure. I melted a bit as I tried to understand my attraction. Her eyes drifted from my face to the middle of my chest. I followed her gaze, only to realize she had somehow unbuttoned my entire shirt.

I tossed my head back and laughed when I heard Brad say, "Ah, I see January indoctrinated you."

Her smile turned from coy to mischievous as she held out the side of her panties and waited for me to tip her.

"Looking good, January," Brad said. "We're celebrating my birthday tonight. Come over when you have time."

January nodded and smiled as she watched me button my clothes back up. Then she strutted away to get a tip from another guy.

Brad nudged me. "You okay, dude?"

"Any chick can be hot," I said. "But to be hot, playful, cunning, and devilish in eleven seconds takes talent." I wondered, what had just happened back there? Why was my pulse thrumming in my ears? Who was this girl?

When I swallowed, the back of my throat felt dry and tight; I needed a drink.

I went to the bar and came face to face with a friend. "Rich, I didn't know you were still working here." I shook his hand. He and I only saw each other in establishments that served liquor. One of us was always serving drinks, and the other was drinking; we never did either together.

His face lit up with genuine excitement. "I was totally quitting, but then I started dating a girl here." He tossed his hands up in a state of surrender. "Now I may never leave."

I smiled at him but wondered if I could simultaneously date and work with a dancer. I could see the benefit of knowing she was safe. But watching your girlfriend dance almost naked for a bunch of drunk dudes every night would be challenging.

I asked him for a Budweiser, and as he took my money, he said, "I see you met January."

"Yes, I have." I adjusted my wide smile into a cocky grin and continued. "She's the kind of amazing I think I should get more acquainted with."

"Dude," he said with a laugh, "you can't have that one."

I knitted my brows together. Just as I was going to ask what he meant, a waitress walked up and yelled out an order. I turned my back to the bar and my face toward the stage. January scooped up her clothes and headed to a table with three men in business suits.

I set my curiosity aside and went to find my friends. You can't have that one rolled through the places in my mind January had just awakened. It wasn't so much that he'd said it; it was the conviction in his voice, like he would have bet money on it.

Another thing was still on my mind too: how in the hell had she *undone my shirt*?

I walked around the cat-walk-shaped stage and up a set of stairs to get to my friends. I paused and gazed back once I'd made the climb. There were three sets of stairs in the bar, not including the sets the girls had to go up to get onto the stages. How do they do this all night—in heels?

I sat down, took a sip from my beer, and watched everyone unwind from their busy workweek. I'd take a bullet for most of these guys, and I was stoked to be here for Brad's birthday, but something was missing. Or perhaps too repetitive? As much fun as going out was, I was ready to be a grown-up. I wasn't saying I wanted a house in the 'burbs with a wife and family. But I thought I'd be more accomplished by now, more like an adult.

I was on my second beer when January finally showed up. Brad stood to say hello and hugged her. Her smile beamed across the table as she greeted everyone.

"Happy birthday!" She held his arms and, taking a step back, tilted her head to the side, assessing him. "Gosh, you look great; not a day over forty!"

"What the hell!" He wiggled out of her grip and pointed in my direction. "Did he put you up to that?"

My mouth dropped open to protest, but I was also shocked she had given him the same loving shit-talk like I had in the parking lot.

She looked over at me and then back to Brad; her brows climbed up her forehead, trying to figure out what he meant, "Ha, no, what? Did he bust your chops too?" She hugged him as he pretended to get over his wound; then she sat down—three people from me. Three people too far away.

Alex handed out a fresh round of drinks and placed a tall glass of plain water in front of January. I rubbed my hand down my chin; I can't remember the last time I'd seen a stripper drink water.

She was there about ten minutes before Brad asked her to dance for Parker, who was sitting right next to me. As she began her dance, I rolled my chair slightly towards the stage, away from them. It pained me not to watch;

I knew by the way she took my tip earlier that she would give a sensual lap dance. But giving them privacy was the polite thing to do.

"No More Tears" by Ozzy Osbourne oozed out of the sound system. I watched the girl on stage climb the pole and then drop into the splits from about seven feet up. She probably did every night, but I still pulled my eyes away just in case it killed her. Half the guys sitting in our section did the same; the other half applauded and tipped her generously.

I was contemplating the ridiculous behavior of men when I felt something hit my lap. It was January's shirt; her bra came seconds later. I could feel the warmth still in them. They smelled like an exotic concoction of lilac, sweat, and men's cologne. It reminded me of how she rubbed her face all over me, and the tips of my ears warmed. I folded her items and placed them on my leg, hoping she would have to interact with me once the song finished.

Midway through the dance, I caught Parker and January's reflection in one of the many mirrors surrounding the stage. I covertly watched as she turned her back towards Parker and gently pulled her micro shorts off her body. As before, she tossed them in my direction. I saw it happening thanks to the mirror and caught them in midair.

Was she flirting with me? Of course she was; it was her job. Flirt, tease, connect, and get you to buy a dance. I folded her shorts and placed them on the pile. The sum of her entire wardrobe took up less room on my lap than my handprint.

I was looking forward to asking her for a dance before I left, which was going to be soon. I still wasn't planning to hang out very long.

When Parker's dance ended, I rolled my chair back towards the table. Parker handed her a twenty, and she gave him a quick hug and a peck on the cheek.

"Thank you for the dance," she told him and then looked at me. "I'll be right there to get my things." She leaned across the table and grabbed her glass of water. After taking a healthy drink, she skirted around a couple other dances that were taking place and moved in my direction. She didn't seem to care that she was almost naked, and—obviously—neither did I.

"Aw, you folded them for me," she said, setting her glass on the table. The tone of her voice was half-sweet, half-condescending. She bent over and took her bra from the pile I had made. I watched her clasp the back together and maneuver the cups to the front. She then threaded her arms, one at a time, through the straps and inched them up and onto her shoulders. Her simple reverse striptease held my imagination hostage.

"How come I've never seen you in here?" she asked, while reaching for her shorts. "I know most of these other guys, but I've never seen you."

My eyes twitched as I forced myself to keep eye contact with her and not stare at her body. "I usually go to the Candy Store on Sunday nights."

"Oh, I see," she said, holding my attention with her probing stare. "Hanging out with the competition?"

"They have superb steaks over there," I volleyed.

"I hear the fish is good too," she said with a quick wrinkle of her nose.

A smile crept across my face as I realized she was saying the women there were smelly. All the local topless bars—and the Hooters—had long-standing rivalries with each other.

January took the last remaining item off my lap, her little half-shirt, which left a cold spot once her clothes were gone. I smiled in her direction, but she was already looking toward Brad. He gave her the international sign language for "he's next." January returned his request with a nod and a thumbs up.

She grabbed her water. "Thanks for taking such good care of my clothes. They're not used to being treated so well."

"You're welcome." I said, but the song changed, and she was already walking away.

I moved my chair closer to Parker and we settled into talking about sports, girls, and work; I wasn't really paying attention; all I could think about was what Rich had told me. You can't have that one. I liked this girl; I was going to have to prove him wrong.

January went on the main stage, which was an unexpected delight. But it didn't make up for the disappointment of not getting a table dance from her. I looked at the number of empty beer bottles on the table and then at my watch. It was late, and I had stayed much longer than intended.

"Another beer, James?" Alex asked me.

"No, thank you. How about an enormous glass of water and close my tab?"

She nodded and loaded up her tray with most of the empties.

"Did you have fun tonight?" a soft familiar voice asked me.

I spun my head around to see January standing there. The hairs on my arms stood at full attention.

"Yes, yes, I did," I said, sitting up straight and holding her eye contact.

Without asking, January spun a chair around and sat down. She leaned back and closed her eyes, leaving a quiet smile on her face. I wondered how she handled this much strenuous activity. I'd seen her do at least twenty table dances as well as rounds on all three stages. That was the physical equivalent of running a ten-K—in heels.

"Are you watching me?" she asked without opening her eyes.

"I've been watching you all night."

She lifted her muscular legs off the floor and placed them in my lap. The second they touched me, heat radiated through my body. This was much better than getting a dance from her. What was happening now felt more genuine than a performance.

Alex appeared with a water and my check. "Don't you two look comfy?"

January pointed to the chair next to her. "Join us," she said. "How's the movie going?"

Alex plopped into the seat, placing her tray on her lap. "So far, every scene I've done has ended up on the cutting room floor, and the producers hate the dailies."

"That sounds harsh," I said. My face contorted as I tried to imagine how difficult being an actor must be. "I wish I could help more, but if you come into Over Ice this week, I'll buy you a couple of drinks."

With what felt like a good enough excuse, I placed my hand on January's shins. "You too."

Her legs were as smooth as butter. I wanted to run my hands and face all over them.

Alex smiled, "I'd love to. How about Wednesday?"

"Yes, that night's perfect. You should bring Harris with you."

Alex and her boyfriend were the quintessential "it couple" of the downtown bar scene, she being an up-and-coming actress and he a bona fide music producer.

"Did I hear two bands he's working with are going to play that new music festival, South by Southwest?"

"Yes!" She looked up at me while counting her money. "He's stupid excited about it, says it's going to change the music industry."

"Yeah, a couple of event organizers came into the bar a while ago to see if we could be a venue. We're just not set up for it."

"How about you?" I asked January again while giving her leg a quick squeeze. "What night are you coming to see me?"

Her legs tightened a bit as the air around us stilled. Her guarded expression formed into a halfhearted smile as she answered me. "Someday soon."

"I have to cash out," Alex said, after an awkward pause. "See you Wednesday night, James."

January and I said goodbye in unison.

"Just for one drink?" I pressed, hoping she would change her mind.

She slipped her legs out from under my hands and placed her pretty feet back on the floor. "I don't drink."

"How about lunch?"

She made an exaggerated frowny face. "I don't eat either."

Ah, we were back to bantering. "We could go to a movie?" I tossed out.

"I work every night." Her eyes sparkled. "Besides," she said, as she walked backward toward the dressing room door, "do I look like the type of stripper that hangs out with customers?"

"I'm not a customer," I said, objecting to such a classification.

"Oh, but you are," she said. "You tipped me five bucks when you got here."

I went to protest, but she opened the door and slipped into the back part of the club. I stood there, delightfully bemused, as I watched her walk through the DJ booth waving goodbye.

Chapter 2

Blue Monday

Jewels

Despite the less than four hours of sleep I got last night, my body jerked into motion when I heard Frank's voice. He was checking on the girls on the other side of the house. I sprung out of bed, heading to the bathroom, dragging my blankets halfway across the floor.

Jodie had folded her futon bed from the bottom to the top. Her bedspread, identical to everyone else's in the house, was laid over it and tucked underneath the edges. She was twenty years older than me and one of the few women who didn't work at the club.

The rest of us were new to dancing. We used to work as house cleaners, massage therapists, personal assistants, just about anything for cash. That all changed when Frank discovered how much money we could make being strippers.

Our room was a rectangle-shaped en-suite. A make-up vanity sat between our bathroom and closet. Everyone here had a futon bed and a small shelf with doors. You could have a lamp, approved books, and an alarm clock visible. Knickknacks, memorabilia, or personal photographs had to go inside.

"We keep our house void of unnecessary clutter," Frank had told me the first night I moved in. "Clutter clogs the brain and fosters an anxious mind."

Clicking on the bathroom light, I looked for the note Jodie often left me. Today's purple post-it read, *"Keep on the Sunny Side,"* a song she used to sing while we cleaned windows together.

After I plucked it from the mirror, I sat down to pee.

Frank's voice boomed through our room. "Where's my Jewels?"

I forced a cheerful attitude out of my exhausted body and said, "I'm in here."

"Come downstairs when you get done. I want to talk to you."

"Okay, be right there." I couldn't tell if he was in a good mood or upset. Why would he want to see me? Had I left any of my chores undone? Was I keeping up with my daily affirmations?

I peed as fast as possible and put on one of the house dresses he liked us to wear. It was a simplistic tank-styled dress with a full-length panel skirt on the bottom. The fabric was washable thin, smooth-flowing silk; it was like wearing a whisper. We purchased them in bulk in several sizes, in the only three colors Frank allowed in the house: fuchsia, purple, and the occasional aqua blue.

Usually, I took these stairs two at a time when Frank wanted to talk to me, but today I was hiding an attraction to a customer I'd met last night, so I used the extra seconds to go over the key components to centering myself. I needed to be prompt but not rushed, precise but not rigid, and thoughtful without being in my head.

I willed myself to look innocent and opened the door. Frank's six-foot-tall wide-shouldered frame took up most of the recliner he was sitting in. There were several other chairs and a love seat in the room, but he asked me to join him and pointed at the floor. I did as he asked and sat with my legs crossed beside his chair.

This house was set up as a new-age adult learning and therapy school; Frank was our teacher, our guru, who'd helped me through one of the lowest parts of my life. His teaching style could best be described as tough-love; he believed the biggest hindrance to personal growth was the ego. "People would rather be right and stuck in their pain than change their perception and feel better," he often reproved. Embarrassing or yelling at you in front of your peers was a tactic he used often. He'd do anything in his power to get your ego to submit; our group and individual therapy sessions could get quite intense.

His fingers were loosely entwined on his lap, making him look approachable, but I'd seen dogs quietly lick their paws right before biting someone.

This was Frank's personal living quarters. It had a large bedroom, bath, and this living area. The only television in the house was down there. He allowed us to watch it with him on special occasions. The aroma of patchouli, sandalwood, and dragon's blood from the Nag Champa incense hung in the air.

I had been Frank's girlfriend for three years and used to live down here with him. But not too long ago, I was moved upstairs, and Dylan took my place. Frank treated her like a princess. He bought her nice things, talked to her for hours, and took her to lunch, all the things he did with me before they met.

At first I hated her. But Frank helped me see that jealousy was the problem, not Dylan. I was projecting my low self-esteem and fear of being replaced onto her. It took a lot of individual therapy sessions with him to integrate the change and accept the new situation.

I was running my newest mantra through my head. *All is well, all is well*, when he finally tipped his chair back up, looked me square in the eye, and said, "You've been working a lot, Jewels."

Crap, he was going to ask about work. I felt guilty as my pulse quickened as a split-second flash of the cute bartender shot through my brain. I was so busted.

"Are you trying to avoid being at home?" Frank continued, his voice an octave deeper.

I did my best to swallow without making a sound. *Concentrate*, I told myself. *You're in his crosshairs*. I gave him my best Mona Lisa smile, the one that was hopefully the hardest to read. "I'm not avoiding being here. I think I'm just in a routine and hadn't noticed the number of days adding up."

Hadn't noticed. Had I said that out loud? What a rookie thing to blurt out. I gave him all the ammunition he needed if he intended to bust me for something.

He leaned toward me. "Do you think it's a good practice to be rolling through life, not noticing what you're doing?"

It almost looked like he enjoyed watching me calculate the landmines around our conversation. He had me, and he knew it; if this were a game of chess, I'd already be out.

My mind flipped through all the responses I could have given him to get out of this situation, something from one of the many new age books he had us read or an affirmation he had us write.

I steadied my expression, and as I opened my mouth to answer, several lines of sweat ran down the side of my body. He knew I was thinking about that guy. *All is well. All is well.*

"No, that would be a bad idea," I began. "Right now, the universe is blessing me with abundance, so I thought I'd show my appreciation by being available to receive it."

I focused all my energy on keeping my face calm and my eyes neutral while waiting to see if my answer was good enough. Another drop of traitorous sweat rolled down my side.

"How much did you make last night?"

He was looking for another angle to apply pressure, testing for places I had gone astray.

"Four hundred and ninety dollars," I replied while smoothing the front of my dress. A small ripple of excitement stirred my stomach. He couldn't have asked me a better question. I exceeded my usual two to three hundred dollars a night, thanks to Brad's birthday party. I danced for several people at that table, everyone except the one I kept thinking about, the only one I'd wanted to dance for.

"How much have you made this month?" He was still testing me. We were to know our finances down to the penny. Frank often asked us, "How can you expect money to flow into your lives if you're not giving it the respect and attention it deserves?"

We had to keep meticulous track of our finances to tithe adequately. Ten percent of everything we made went directly to Frank. He also collected cash for other things, but this percentage was what he called our anointed portion. Our offerings supported Frank; we became his full-time job. With this system, he could give us therapy around the clock whenever we needed it.

I forced my face to relax. "Six thousand, three hundred dollars." That sounded like a lot of money. But it was only an average of two hundred and twenty-five dollars a day, and since I had worked twenty-eight days in a row, it was right on track.

Being a stripper was different from other industries where your income came from tips. The more you worked, the more you made was true across the board, but for a dancer, it compounded exponentially. The more you worked, the more people wanted a dance from you. Even guys who didn't like you would eventually get a dance just to see what the fuss was about.

Frank lifted his hand. "Six thousand dollars! That's my girl!"

Nothing made Frank happier than money.

I wanted to smile all the way to my eyes; I knew I was in the clear. But that big of a smile would have shown I was relieved. He would know I was hiding something, and the questioning would continue. Instead, I allowed my mouth to curl up just a touch on the sides.

"Okay," he said, his tone lighter, "you're doing very well, Jewels. You're going to be a great teacher someday. You'll find your to-do list over on the table."

These niblets of praise gave me hope and kept me going. If Frank thought I was doing well, someday I'd be able to help people the way he had helped me.

I stood up and did my best to keep my right arm close to my body so he couldn't see the sweat lines that had soaked through my dress. I grabbed the list and headed for the door.

"Ah, yes," he said, "One more thing. I want Dylan to start working at the club. I'm putting you in charge of training and keeping her safe."

I willed my mouth not to drop open. "When would you like her to start?"

He leaned back in his Lazy-Boy. "As soon as you finish that list."

Checkmate. Frank won again. Nodding, I hurried away.

It wasn't that I didn't like Dylan; I didn't know her very well. But she was one degree of separation from Frank, which made her the second most powerful person in the house. Something I knew well, from three years of experience.

Fuck.

Once I was back in my room, I checked the list. Frank had a habit of being encouraging but then assigning you a task that would be very challenging. He didn't believe in idle time; he'd often tell us that personal growth didn't happen while you were sitting on your ass.

The list didn't look bad, about four different stores, if they carried exactly what he wanted. Two of the places were for photography equipment. One was a clothing store, for the Egyptian cotton t-shirts he preferred to wear. And the last stop was for herbs, specialty supplements, and other things he needed to help treat his allergies.

Cedar fever was the popular name for the ailment that struck thanks to the onslaught of pollen that coated the central Texas air from December to the beginning of February, and Frank was one of its annual victims.

I walked into the closet, scratching my head. He seemed fine right now. But my job wasn't to question what he wanted; it was to get it done.

"You never know when doing exactly what I tell you could save your life," he had said one night at dinner. He was right, I had found a certain amount of comfort in following directions and doing what I was told.

I opened the drawers with my world clothes, things we could wear outside the house that would help us blend in better and not attract unnecessary attention. Frank told us the more enlightened we were, the brighter our light would be, which made us more easily detectable by evil. Dressing in trendy clothing would help camouflage us when in public. I was comforted with the idea of hiding from evil, but I wasn't a big fan of the current trends that were going around. I was preppy by nature and liked simple clothing. Big shoulder pads, bright neon-colored t-shirts, and Swatch watches were popular at the moment—and not my idea of subtle.

On one of our special shopping trips, he made me try on a pair of pink L.A. Gear high tops; they were hideous and I didn't hide my opinion about them. He educated me in the middle of the store about what it meant to let go of the self.

"Your ego has an unhealthy bond to your style," he'd said. "You have to learn to use clothing as a way to blend in with your surroundings. These are tools to use. Let go of the crumbs so that you can have the cake."

That was the first time I consciously chose his teachings over my identity. He offered me new trendy clothing in exchange for my button-fly Levi's, Ralph Lauren Polo shirt, and Bass Weejun loafers my grandfather had bought me. The confused woman working at the store shot me a questioning look when Frank handed her my old clothing to throw away. I nodded yes to her and cried myself to sleep that night.

I remember thinking, if this is what it took to feel better, I would do it. I would do anything Frank told me to if it would get rid of my anxiety attacks.

I pulled a t-shirt and jeans out of the drawer. I'd grown a lot since I had first gotten here. Both in my belief system and my relationship with the people I lived with. I had a special connection with all the women here, but Liz, Tracy, and I were about the same age and had a lot in common.

I was getting dressed when Liz, who danced as Victoria, came into the closet. "How was work last night?" she whispered, joining me on the floor. Frank preferred that we didn't talk about work at the house, so we didn't do it often or in his presence.

"It was great."

Her shoulders dropped. "I wanted to work, but Frank told me to manage food prep and logistics for last night's class. But it was very nice to be of service," she added, maybe so I wouldn't think she was contradicting Frank's lessons.

Classes were how most people found their way to Frank's teachings. I found my way here working with a guy at a clothing store who'd attended the Prosperity Class. After seeing me pass out from anxiety attacks a couple of times, he'd thought maybe Frank could help me. Some of the people that attended these classes, such as myself, were also interested in going deeper with the work and becoming part of the core group. I went from barely surviving to living in this beautiful house surrounded by people working on their enlightenment journey.

Initially, I'd felt guilty about losing contact with my friends and family, but now I had a life with purpose. Frank said he understood and that he, too, had to make similar difficult choices when he began doing the work.

"It's impossible to move forward in life," he'd once told me, "when everyone around you wants you to stay the same. When you're healed and strong, you'll be able to let them back into your life. You just need a little buffer from them right now."

"I don't suppose you saw Kevin?" Liz asked about her best customer.

"I sure did," I said, pulling a t-shirt over my head, and her face fell. I gave her a little nudge with my foot and said, "He told me he wouldn't stay if you weren't there and that he would come back tonight."

Everything about her began to glow. Good customers were like gold, and made learning prosperity a pleasure.

"What a sweet guy," she said under her breath. "I can't believe he didn't give his money to someone else."

She said this with a dreaminess we weren't allowed to have. I bet my face looked that way when I thought about the bartender; I wish I knew his name. *No, no, I don't*. I had to stop thinking about him. He wasn't part of my therapeutic journey, which made him a distraction as well as a potential pitfall. Since he'd mentioned that he rarely came to our club, I doubted I'd ever see him again—problem solved. My ten-hour crush on him was a minor glitch in my mental discipline journey. I forgave myself for being attracted to someone who could pull me off my path. I had seen the errors of my thinking; he was no longer in my mind or life. *All is well*.

The only man we were allowed to have feelings for was Frank. We projected our feelings of love and romance onto him so that he could work through them with us.

"Hey," Liz said, changing the subject, "I forgot to give you this." She reached into her pocket and handed me a flattened fortune cookie.

"Where did this come from, and what ran it over?"

"One of the new people didn't know we offered food before class and brought Chinese take-out. His order had five extra cookies, so I saved one for you. Sorry, I accidentally sat on it."

A breathy laugh came out of me while tearing open the wrapper. "What did yours say?"

"Your pet is planning to eat you."

"WHAT?"

"Who knows? Let's see if yours is just as silly."

I pinched the tiny piece of paper, wiped the crumbs off, and read it aloud. "The antidote to fear is trusting yourself."

"Well, that wasn't funny at all, what a buzz-kill," I said as I folded the fortune and stuck it in my drawer.

"You did well last night?" Liz asked, breaking the silence. "Did one of your big spenders show up?"

I laid back on the floor and pulled up my jeans. "No, but the Sixth Street crew came in and partied pretty hard. It was Brad's birthday."

"Is he the grumpy one?" she asked, scrunching her face.

"No, he's the sweet one, the one that has a crush on that chick, Ripley."

Liz looked up at the ceiling, thinking.

"You know the gorgeous one, always dances to New Order and Depeche Mode?"

She snapped her fingers. "Oh yeah, with the long blonde hair and perfectly straight bangs."

"Yep, that's her. I'll never know how she takes her bra off, hanging upside down on the pole."

Liz was in the middle of saying "for real" when she lifted her finger sharply in a "wait a minute" position. We both stopped breathing, staring at each other while we strained to hear who was in my room.

"What's on your list today?" she asked, no longer whispering. "There are a couple of kitchen items we need, is the grocery store one of your stops?"

"No," I said, pushing my feet into the pink high-tops. "But you can ask Frank if I can add it."

"No, that's OK; I'll pick it up later."

"Shit, I gotta get out of here, or Dylan and I won't make it to work on time."

Her eyes doubled in size as her lips mouthed, *Already?*

With the sun slowly setting and humidity hanging in the air, Dylan and I climbed into my little Mazda pickup truck and headed for Tulips. I wanted to ask her how she felt about having to work at the club, but I had to be careful. Because Frank was our group and individual therapist, he made it clear we were not to discuss our problems with anyone other than him. He was the most advanced and best-equipped to help us.

I kept my face towards the road but almost made myself dizzy, trying to read her expression through my peripheral vision.

What if I asked her how she felt, and she had an emotional meltdown? Or, even worse, she chickened out and asked me to take her home? Both possibilities would get me in trouble with Frank.

Instead, I started with something that hopefully couldn't lead to any trouble. "Do you have questions about the club you'd like to ask me?"

She looked at me but said nothing.

"Frank asked me to guide you and keep you safe at the club," I continued. "Questions you have about work would be fine for me to answer."

She screwed up her face.

"Which part do you think will be the most challenging?" I asked, hoping she would open up.

"I'm not sure I'm pretty enough to do this," she said.

"Of course, you are," I said, shocked. Dylan was beautiful. She had luminous light olive skin and bright blue eyes. Her wavy hair was thick and reached down to the middle of her back. Like mine, it was much blonder than her natural brown color. "But being pretty will only get you so far. The girls who make the most money are great at talking to men."

A warmth spread through me, thinking about some of my favorite customers and how kind they were when I started dancing.

"Every guy that walks into the club has a different reason for being there. Your job is to figure out what they want."

"What they want?" she repeated, a suspicious tone in her voice.

"Some guys are lonely, others are looking for a distraction, and some just want to drink a cold beer without being nagged by their wives."

"Doesn't it help if you have a perfect body?" she pressed. "What about mine? It's nowhere near perfect."

I stopped at the stoplight and put on my blinker. She was picking at her cuticles.

"I promise you don't have to be perfect," I said. "Perfection is an illusion, like control. Think of it this way. What's perfect for one guy is plastic to another. One guy will think a girl is chubby, and the guy next to him will think she's voluptuous. More than what they're looking at, most guys want to be seen."

She shifted her body, so she was facing me more. "Seen?"

"Yes. Look them in the eyes and ask them questions. I like to ask them about hobbies first; people love to talk about things they're passionate about, and want to share their excitement."

I lifted my hand to make a point. "I stay away from questions about their jobs or families, just in case those are the things they were trying to avoid."

She nodded her head, like she understood, but then placed her hands over her face and made a cute squealing sound. "Oh God, what about the going onstage part, the table dancing part, the acting sexy part?"

I turned into the club and pulled into a parking space. The bright neon sign of two perfect pink tulips bathed the lot in a warm glow.

I placed my hand on Dylan's forearm. "You're under no pressure to do any of those things tonight. We're just going to put on makeup, get dressed in sexy clothes, meet some friendly people, and see where it goes from there."

The muscles under her shirt sleeve relaxed as her shoulders dropped.

"I promise it's going to be fine," I said, smiling at her. "Let's go inside."

I opened the door to get out of the truck. The smell of warm rolls and chicken-fried steak filled my nose. We weren't allowed to eat refined flour, processed sugar, or red meat. We only ate the food Frank suggested, things like couscous, tabbouleh, cruciferous vegetables, and fish.

I took in a couple of deep, longing breaths and went to close the door when Dylan stopped me.

"Wait, Jewels, you forgot your makeup."

I ducked my head to look back into the truck, grabbed my Caboodles case, and winked at her. "Thank you, and until we get back to the house, call me January."

Chapter 3

Whisper to a Scream

James

As I worked the bubbles into a lather, I ticked off the things I wanted to get accomplished today. For starters, I was going to the Secretary of State's office to file a Doing Business As (DBA), for the club I was trying to open.

I'd love to skip this step, but registering that document allowed me to call my bar something other than my personal name. We already had a high-end steak house in town named Sullivan's, and I didn't want to call my bar James. I also need that paperwork to open a business checking account. So, the bank was the second place on my list to visit. I also had clothes to drop off at the dry cleaners, run by the post office to buy stamps, pop into the grocery store, January...

January? Uh, not January. A couple of days had passed since we met, but I couldn't stop thinking about her flirtatious smiles, how she doled them out to me as little gifts.

I grabbed the shampoo bottle and reminded myself that I didn't think about women when I wasn't with them. Sitting around thinking about someone who was not a current part of your life was a ridiculous use of time. It was a lesson I learned the hard way with my last serious girlfriend, Gracie.

January would not be an exception to my rule, but I was curious about her. I also couldn't stop wondering why Rich said I couldn't have her. Was she in the witness protection program? A member of the Illuminati secret society? Maybe she was married? But I think Rich would've mentioned that.

I finished showering and opened the bathroom door to let the steam out of the room. Was it always this dark in the mornings? The last time I woke up this early was the first night I slept here, the morning after I moved in.

When Brad and I moved out of the dorms, I told him to keep most of the stuff we had accumulated over the years, and I started over. I placed some mix-and-match dishes, a couple of towels, and a cutting board I made in junior high into the passenger seat of my 1983 Datsun 280z and began my new adult life. Except for my Sony Trinitron TV and king-size bed, everything else I had in my apartment came from garage sales or thrift stores. The bed filled up my entire room, but women seemed to appreciate sleeping on it, rather than a mattress, on the floor.

I grabbed a pair of my darkest colored blue jeans from the dresser and wished I had a suit. My mother made sure I always had a couple when I lived at home. I had taken my last one from high school to Goodwill last year, since I'd grown a couple of inches and filled out a lot since then. I didn't replace it because I didn't like suits and working as a bartender never required one.

Stepping into my loafers, I moved my collection of polo shirts across the wooden rod and contemplated my choices. I went to grab my favorite light-blue shirt and then reconsidered. If I couldn't wear a suit, I should at least wear a crisp, white, well starched button-down. If I don't get approved for a loan, I'd have to get a J.O.B.

I'd told my father after I graduated that I had no plans to use my degree shuffling paperwork or working in a cubicle farm. He wanted me to make my living in a stable environment. When he talked about it, the disdain in his voice would make the hairs on my neck twist, but I wasn't backing down.

"What about IBM?" he'd asked over dinner one night. "Now, *that's* a steady company. They have a huge office complex in Austin. You'll move up the ladder quickly there."

"I don't want to work for someone else." I'd tried to tell him I wanted to be an entrepreneur, but he'd start rolling his eyes before I could get the entire word out of my mouth.

"You're not going to be the next Henry Ford or Dale Carnegie," he would say with his mouth full of corn and condescension.

"Good, I was thinking of being more like Phil Knight of Nike or Steve Jobs."

"Jobs!" he'd barked out. "He got forced out of his own company. I wouldn't use him as an example."

"How about Michael Dell?" I'd shot back. "He dropped out of Med School and started Dell Computers in his dorm room. Now you can't go anywhere in Austin without someone saying his name or talking about their stocks doubling."

My mom had eaten her dinner, watching us quarrel back and forth. She loved a well-argued debate.

"Fine," he'd said, "become a computer sales guy. I'd prefer that over a bar owner. At least it won't embarrass me to tell my friends what you're doing with your expensive education."

I grabbed a shirt, tore off the dry-cleaner plastic, and held it up. Yes, this shirt would make me look like a man who knew how to run a profitable bar.

If I failed at getting my bar opened, I'd do what my father wanted. Until then, I would do everything I could to make my dreams come true, including letting him think I was actively looking for a job.

Checking myself in the mirror, I saw a fairly responsible guy. I grabbed my bag of clothes for the dry cleaner and headed out the door.

The four-story majestic building that housed the Secretary of State's office already had a line out the door. I took a number and looked at the clipboard; I was twenty people down the list.

"It won't take that long," said an employee behind the counter in a monosyllabic tone. "Down the hall, second door on your left, research your business name and make sure no one else has it, but don't get lost. We'll only call your number once; then we'll move on."

The room she mentioned was easy to find. It was full of mismatched metal tables pushed against every wall. A piece of laminated paper hung above each table, with letters written on them in black magic marker.

I went straight to the table with the letter G above it and started sifting through the ugly, dot-matrix books. The slightly putrid, metallic smell of fresh ink hung in the air. They must have printed these books once a week to keep up with all the changing business names. I found the one that said GE–GEN and flipped it open. My throat went dry as I ran my fingers down the page. *Please don't be here, please don't be here*. It wasn't! I rechecked; the name I wanted to call my business wasn't registered to anyone else. It was mine for the taking. I closed the book with a victorious thud and hurried back to the main room.

I tapped my foot against the chair, listening for my number, worrying about my father's inevitable disappointment. It wasn't my sole ambition to rebel against him, but I couldn't take his paying for my education as a promise to follow his dreams instead of my own.

The woman assigned to help me was cornbread-butter-sweet, but not as fast as I wanted her to be. She had a thick southern drawl and referred to me as one baking ingredient after another. I wasn't about to be disrespectful, but she was slow as molasses. I counted the ceiling tiles while she placed individual pieces of black carbon paper between the three different colored pages so she could type in triplicate.

"Here you go, honey," she said, handing me a pile of thin pink papers that had Petitioner's Copy embossed across the top.

"Thank you, ma'am. Is there any chance someone else could still get the name I just picked?"

"Well, sugar, there's always a chance, but it's very slim. You see, I'm just going to run this upstairs, but everyone else has to mail theirs in."

I thanked her profusely and headed to the bank.

I was looking at an image of great white sharks when I heard a woman with a timid voice. "Mr. Sullivan?"

I dropped the *National Geographic* on the table, grabbed my things, and followed her down a paneled hallway. The tinny sound of elevator music followed us through the building. As we passed the other offices, I discreetly wiped the sweat from my palms onto my jeans. She stopped at the doorway and gestured me into the room.

"Thank you," I called to her as she walked away.

"Come on in, Mr. Sullivan."

I turned to see a middle-aged man extinguishing his cigarette. He stood as I crossed the room and reached out to shake my hand. His gruff voice continued, "I'm Bob Bennett. I hear you're interested in opening a business account."

"Yes, sir," I said, straightening my back and shoulders, hoping to hide my inexperience so he wouldn't confuse it for immaturity.

"Please have a seat."

We both sat, and he began looking through the papers on his desk. "I have a commercial account form in one of these stacks," he mumbled.

I watched him for a couple of seconds. "I'm also interested in talking to someone about financing a building on Sixth Street I'd like to purchase."

He stopped shuffling through the papers and looked at me. "A building?" he asked, his eyebrows pitching upward. "There are a few buildings for sale right now; which one are you interested in?"

"The one at 606 Trinity Street."

"Ah, the bookstore." The corners of his mouth bent into a smile. "A blacksmith originally owned that property until the 1920s, when it became a fancy woman's dress shop." He held up a two-part form at arm's length and squinted. "I think it was the depression that eventually put them out of business. It became a pharmacy for decades and then the bookstore."

He set down the form and rooted around in the drawer in front of him for a moment. "Aha, here's the form we need."

I blinked twice. "Wow, that's a lot more information than my real estate attorney knew about the place."

"I'm a bit of a history buff regarding downtown Austin," he said, his chair protesting with a loud squeal as he leaned back. "I've also thought it was interesting how that property has a Trinity street address, even though the front door is on Sixth Street."

I nodded. "I wondered about that as well."

"That's not a detail that will appear on a title search. Chances are, it has much more to do with the Post Office than actual ownership."

"I have some paperwork for you, some things my attorney gave me. I just registered for the DBA, and have the initial comparative market analysis, building specifications, and a business plan I put together."

He rocked forward, holding his hand out. "A business plan?"

As he was thumbing through its contents, I used his mid-century furnishings and puke-avocado décor to distract me from thinking about how good January's head felt dragging down my shirt the other night.

"Well, James, it looks like you've done your homework. The building's price tag is around a million dollars, so you'll need about twenty-five percent as a down payment."

I cleared my throat, "Yes, sir."

"Please call me Bob."

"Yes, Bob. I've been saving for the past five years, but I'm nowhere close to having three-hundred-thousand dollars. I was thinking of getting investors to fill the delta."

He lifted his eyebrows while he nodded. I knew that some banks didn't like dealing with the paperwork it took to raise capital in smaller increments.

"Yep," he finally said, "getting investors is one way to get it done. What about your parents? Would they be interested in co-signing a loan for you?"

"No," I objected, repositioning myself in my chair. "My father isn't interested in this direction as my career choice. He wants me to be a company man, and I'm sure he doesn't want any more of his money tied up in my life."

Bob squinted back down at my paperwork. "Okay, I'm going to have my assistant type." He stopped himself and then went on. "Input is what they're calling it now. She will input your business plan into our fancy new Wang word processor. They say it's the wave of the future." Looking down at an open drawer, he pulled out the form he was looking for. "Do you have a personal account with us?"

"I do," I replied. "I've been with this bank most of my life. My father opened savings accounts for my sister and me as kids, and I opened my checking account right before I started college."

"Here in Austin?"

"No, sir—no, Bob," I corrected myself. "I grew up in Dallas."

"I like Dallas," he said. "Not as much as I like Austin, but it's a pleasant city. I worked in our downtown branch for several years."

I nodded in full agreement. Austin was way better than Dallas.

After I signed the preliminary paperwork, I ran my errands and put my groceries away. A montage of January putting her clothes on and bantering with me ran through my head as I ate a bacon-lettuce-tomato sandwich for dinner.

The only way I was going to stop thinking about her was to see her. I'd been in this situation before, where I thought a chick was pretty cool, but then I got to know her and realized we weren't a good fit. Maybe that pretty smile, bold confidence, and sense of humor were momentary distractions. Perhaps I drank enough to think she was incredible when really she was only so-so.

I also needed to ask Rich what he meant by *you* can't have that one.

Like a repeat performance of the last time I was here, I paid the door girl and showed her my ID. After adjusting to the light, I glanced toward the catwalk stage to see if January was up there. She wasn't. I scanned the rest of the club and the other two stages.

I turned to grab a beer at Rich's bar and there was January, staring right at me—again. Her expression jumped from happy to distressed in a nanosecond.

I walked toward her stretching out my fingers, attempting to relax. *Chill out, James, she doesn't know you're here specifically to see her.*

"What a nice surprise," I lied, while opening my arms and giving her a quick hug. "I didn't know you were working tonight."

She returned my hug and gave me a nervous smile.

"I'm shocked to see you too. I didn't think you came in here very often. I thought you liked the other club better," she said, rambling.

Well, shit, maybe popping in like this wasn't a good idea. I guess I misread our playful banter the other night. She really wasn't into me.

I rocked back on my heels to begin my awkward exit, but she put her hand up.

"I'm sorry, that all came out very weird," she said, giving me one of the many smiles I hadn't been able to get out of my head for the past two days. "Let's start over. It's *so* good to see you. And, to answer your question, I work almost every night."

"Every night, wow. Are you saving up to buy a car?"

"Yeah, something like that," she said, while spinning a tiny purse by its gold metal strap. She motioned towards the center of the club. "So, you hanging out for a while? I've got some time to burn before I go back onstage. Want to sit down?"

I nodded, and we walked to a table close to the middle stage. January situated her chair so we'd be facing each other knee-to-knee.

"Hello, James," Alex said. "How's it going?"

I thought about standing up to give her a hug, but there was no way I was going to disrupt the proximity of my current seating arrangement with January. I liked how close she was to me.

"I'm great. How about you? You and Harris still coming in tomorrow night?"

She grabbed a couple of unsteady beer bottles off her tray with her free hand. "Oh yes, we'll be there. Be warned, he's going to talk your ear off about the music industry. Are you drinking Budweiser tonight?"

"How about a Michelob Light instead?"

She spun around and headed for the bar. I glanced quickly at January.

She put up both her hands to stop my concern. "It's okay, Alex already knows what I want to drink."

"Are you sure?" I asked as I reached up and playfully grabbed her hands.

"Holy shit, your hands are cold," I said, folding them into mine. I rolled my chair a couple of inches closer to her and lowered our hands onto the virtual table our closely-knit legs had just made. A wave of heat spread down the back of my neck.

If I were on a date sitting this close to a girl, I would think she was very into me. But at topless bars, personal space was harder to define. For her, this could be business as usual.

"Are your hands always this cold?"

"Yes, they are. My feet and nose as well. They're all usually several degrees colder than the rest of my body." She shivered a little. "I never get ice in my drinks. If it were up to me, I'd drink hot water from an oversized mug all night."

I sat there nodding at her like a dork. I wasn't sure what to say, so I started with an obvious assessment. "You seem quieter than you did the other night."

She gave me a wry smile. "Quieter than I was at your table. I was all rowdy and in a party mood because that's what you guys were doing. The next table I went to was very subdued, so I adapted my energy level to match theirs." She gave her eyebrows a quick twitch. "I do that all night long."

I considered this for a second. I didn't have to do that for my job. Everyone that came into Over Ice was there to party. I didn't have to adjust my mood back and forth to get more tips; I just had to smile and not be a complete dick.

"Where'd you grow up?" January asked me.

"Dallas," I said, giving my head a little jerk to the North. I opened my mouth to ask her the same question, but she got her next question out faster than I did.

"Any siblings?"

"Yes, I have a sister."

"Here you go, kids," Alex said, with my beer and a glass of water, no ice, for January. "I'll be back in a few to check on you."

We let go of each other's hands and took a sip from our drinks. A momentary pang of disappointment worked its way through my brain until she offered them to me again. I put my beer down in a rush and covered them before she changed her mind.

"You were saying about your sister."

"Oh, yes, she's a couple of years younger than me. Do you have..." I almost got it fully out of my mouth.

"How many times have you been in love?"

"Just once but she moved away. How about you?" I asked, hoping she would take the bait.

"Did you and..."

"Her name was Gracie."

She cocked her head. "Southern belle?"

"No, British."

"Fun. Did you and Gracie date a long time?"

I took a sip of my beer and used the time to decide how to answer the question. Gracie and I hadn't dated for long, but I'd fallen hard for her. When she'd left, I'd had a difficult time adjusting to her absence. I'd thought we were going to have the perfect life together; we would finish school, travel the world, start a business, get married someday.

I wiped my lips with the back of my hand. "About a year."

January's face melted into what looked like a sympathetic smile. "I'm sorry. Too much? I realize this is none of my business."

"It will never be too much," I reassured her. "Anyway. Her mother became ill. She returned home to England to help take care of her. Long distance is a beating. The phone company charges $2.00 a minute to call the United Kingdom."

"She never came back?"

"She came back to school a couple of years later. But she said her goals in life had changed. She was looking for a partner that wanted a real job and career." I eyed her. "Are your hands warmer? Do you have any siblings?"

"Yes, thank you," she said with a giggle. "They haven't been this warm since I walked into the club." She took one more drink of her water. "I have a half-brother and a half-sister from each of my parents, but I didn't get to live with either of them very long."

She studied me for a moment. "So, if you're not going to have a real job, what are you going to be when you grow up?"

"I want to open a bar."

"That sounds like a real job. What are you going to call it?"

A smile broke across my face. She was the first person to ask me this question. Most people just gave me the side-eye and started with a list of why they thought it was a bad idea.

"Gellhorn," I said proudly. "I filed all the paperwork this morning."

She pinched her brows together. "Save me a trip to the library, what's a Gellhorn?"

I laughed, "It's not a what, it's a who."

"Now I really feel like a dork," she said as her cheeks flushed pink. "Who's Gellhorn?"

"Martha Gellhorn was the third wife of Ernest Hemingway. She was one of the best war correspondents of the twentieth century."

January looked puzzled. "You're going to name your bar after a woman?"

"I am," I said. "I like women. Why does it surprise you I would name my bar after one?"

She shrugged, and I took another sip of my beer. "I'm used to the way men and advertisers use women to sell products, not to celebrate their contributions to society."

I hadn't considered this. I was assuming that as a pretty woman, she was not only more aware of it but also more susceptible to it.

"How did you learn about her?"

"My father told me I could major in anything I wanted, as long as it was what he wanted. So, business was my first major. My second major, the one I did for my own interests, was journalism."

She lifted her hand to her mouth and rubbed her lip. For the first time since I'd been here, she looked a little self-conscious. "Um, I'm curious. If you like journalism, why didn't you go that direction as a career?"

Boom! Another brilliant question, one that no one ever asked me, not even my father. "I enjoyed learning about journalism, but it's one of the hardest jobs out there. I'd have to deal with deadlines, demanding editors, the pressure of coming up with fresh stories and worst of all, I'd have to get up early."

She asked with a smile. "Not a morning person?"

"No, not at all."

"Where are you going to open your club?"

The more questions she asked me, the softer and more relaxed she became. It wasn't until I saw this side that I realized how compressed her other side was, how controlled she had been, like an inner layer of stress was taking up half of every breath she took.

"Downtown, close to Ivory Cats." Her expression was blank and an almost apologetic way. "Do you know where that is?"

"Is it on Sixth Street?"

"Yes, that's right," I said, but thought that if she was asking me if it was on 6th Street that she might not really know.

"I work a lot, I don't go downtown often," she said, wringing her hands.

"Trust me," I said, taking her hands in mine to calm their anxious motion. "If I didn't work down there, I wouldn't go to Sixth Street very often either. It can get a little…" My mouth fell open as my train of thought fell away. "I can't believe your hands are this cold again!"

"I'm telling you," she said, pressing them harder into mine, "they're always cold."

"The building I want to buy is on the corner of Sixth and Trinity. It's currently a bookstore called Liberty Books." I checked her expression to see if I'd put her to sleep already.

"Go on," she said, squeezing my hands.

"Yes, well, they've been interested in selling and moving their store to South Lamar, but no one has offered them the right price." I stopped and took in a full breath to slow down my heartbeat. "The location is phenomenal; I think it's the best in town. It's caddy-corner from Paradise Cafe and across the street from Maggie Mae's. Both those bars do very well and have different clientele, so there will be a good crossover of university, artistic and businesspeople."

"January, Kat and Bobbie, you're next on stage," the DJ boomed over the PA system.

She slumped. "Looks like it's back to work for me. It's been nice talking to you."

I didn't want this to be the last time I saw her. "So, I'm not going to make the mistake of asking you out again, but would it be okay if I came in once in a while to say hello?"

She appeared to mull it over for a bit. "I think that would okay."

It wasn't exactly a date, but it almost felt like she wanted to see me again. "How about next Friday? I'll come in before I go to work."

She blushed. "Okay, Friday night it is." She let go of my hands and stood up.

"January," the DJ bellowed across the microphone. "Come pick your music, or I'll make you dance to Lawrence Welk!"

Right before my eyes, she changed back into what looked and felt like the woman I met on Sunday night. She might have just shown me a part of herself very few people got to see, yet I still knew almost nothing about her. I came here to find reasons to dislike her, but now I liked her even more.

Chapter 4

Every Rose has its Thorn

James

I parked my car in front of the portable marquee sign outside El Arroyo. Today's message read.

Soulmate, that was a concept I'd not thought of in a while. Were there people on the planet we fit better with than others? Was there one person that fit us the best, our other half? Maybe that was why I was so into January, why I was instantly attracted to her, why I felt so comfortable around her. Maybe Ryan would let me change the sign to say.

> **MY SOULMATE IS OUT**
> **THERE SOMEWHERE,**
> **SWINGING**
> **ON A STRIPPER POLL**

I took the keys out of the ignition and headed inside.

"Hey dude, how's it going?" Ryan asked as I walked through the door.

A muted love-stricken mariachi song and freshly baked tortilla chips hijacked my senses. I beamed at him. This guy and this food were definitely my soulmates.

"Doing great, my friend." I gave him a half-hug and a firm pat on the back. "It's good to see you."

Ryan was a couple years older than me and the sage of our group. He was the first to adopt what he called the you can't run my life by paying for my education principle.

Back when we were all at UT, he had popped over to the dorms and told Brad and me he was dropping out. While helping us scarf down a pepperoni pizza, he had said, "My parents have a stranglehold on my education. The worst part is I unwittingly gave them this leverage by letting them help me financially. When I'm not living up to their standards, I get the as long as we're paying your tuition speech." He had wiped his mouth on his shirtsleeve, muttering, "Fuck it, I'm going to quit."

"Dude," Brad had said, not bothering to swallow first, "are you sure that's what you want to do?"

"I'm not busting my ass getting a degree for a job I don't want, in an industry I can't stand, just to make my parents happy." He had leaned back, grabbed a Coke from the mini-fridge, and continued. "Maybe I won't quit, but I'm not staying in law. It's eroding my soul."

I could relate. The thought of clawing my way up to middle management had given me acid reflux. But I hadn't been brave enough to quit school. With a year left, I had told myself, get your degree; then your father would respect and be proud of you.

I had been wrong. I'd received my degree and I had still felt like a constant disappointment to him.

Ryan didn't end up quitting school. Instead, he changed his major to psychology and cut his class-load in half so he could pay for it himself. He only had two more semesters left.

I took a closer look at the restaurant. "Did a bomb go off in here?" Every flat surface was full of dirty dishes. I grabbed an empty bus tub and started helping him clear multi-colored stoneware and half-full glasses into the bin.

"We've been slammed for the past three hours." He glanced down at his watch while he straightened each chair. "You're a little early this week."

"I'm meeting up with a chick before work."

A shit-eating grin took over his face. "What chick?"

I wiped the table down and shoved the condiments to the middle of the table as heat spread across my cheeks. "Just a regular chick."

"Wow, she must be quite a woman to make you blush like that. Do I know her?"

The cowbell above the door clattered out a dull thud. "Holy shit," he said.

I turned to find a pack of bright-eyed kids decked out in maroon Austin High hoodies bounding through the door.

Ryan waved his towel to get the attention of the kitchen staff. "Dile a las camareras que vuelvan a entrar."

"What's wrong?" I asked him.

"The waitresses are in the back taking a break."

I gave him a quick nod. "You get the door; I'll keep clearing the tables until they return."

"Thanks, buddy." He handed me his towel. "What do you want to eat?"

"The usual, with an iced tea. I'll sit at the bar."

Shortly after I took a seat, the cook brought out my BBQ chicken enchiladas. I ate my dinner and watched the news from a small TV that sat over the bar. Peter Jennings, who I often reminded my father was a high school dropout and did not get a college degree, was sharing the sad news about another famous person who died from AIDS. This time it was Brad Davis, an actor in two of my all-time favorite movies, *Midnight Express* and *Chariots of Fire*. It was nice that the press had finally stopped calling it Gay Cancer. But the social stigmatism around AIDS was ever present. There was still no cure. The last I heard, you only had six months to live after diagnosis.

I left money and a generous tip at the bar, waved bye to Ryan, and slipped out of the restaurant.

"Have fun tonight," he yelled as the door closed behind me.

"Oh, I plan to," I said into the cool night air.

"Hey," I said to a guy behind the bar, "Does Rich have the night off tonight?" I was going to ask him what he meant by "you can't have that one." I couldn't get to the bottom of it the last time I was here because January was next to him the whole time.

"No," he said, "he's in the back cooler tapping a new keg. What can I get ya?"

"I'll have the Samuel Adams, Boston Lager, please."

I put off my question yet again and walked over to the stairs separating the club's upper and lower levels. January was on the main stage, pouring her heart and flexible body into the song "Suicide Blond."

"She's something else, isn't she?" a guy with a hideous floral golf shirt said to the dude sitting next to him.

A spark of pride expanded through my chest, knowing they were talking about my January.

The dude slouched back into his chair. "She's spectacular; too bad she's one of the cult girls."

I snapped my gaze to January and back to the guys. I must have heard them wrong. *Cult girls?*

My mind poured through everything she and I had discussed; her being in a cult did not ring a bell. But she had been asking all the questions, and I didn't know anything about her.

Those guys must be smoking crack. There's no way she was in a cult. My eyes darted around the club as his words bounced around my head. Girls, as in, more than one? A couple? Several? A plethora? If she was one of them, who were the others?

The enchiladas I had for dinner turned in my stomach, and my beer was empty. I headed to Rich's bar, scrutinizing every woman I passed, wondering if she could be one of them too.

Rich was on fire, but asked me if I wanted another beer. I couldn't extract the word from my mouth or the energy to nod yes. With the grace of a professional, he sidestepped the necessity to ask me twice and handed me another cold one. I took it without hesitation and threw it back, hoping it would wash everything I heard out of my mind.

I looked back at Rich and tipped my head slightly. "Cult girls?"

Rich glanced from my perplexed face to the main stage and back, all before I even registered my next breath.

His mouth moved as his face contorted into a pained expression; he spat out a single word: *Yes.*

"How many?"

"Eight—no, another one just started. Nine altogether."

"January?"

"Yes," he said, his expression full of pity.

"And that's why you said I couldn't have her."

January's second song ended, and I knew she would be dancing on the stage right next to us in a couple of songs. I needed a little time to digest all this new information; I wasn't ready to interact with her.

I looked down at my almost emptied, backwashed beer and put it on the bar. I tossed Rich a twenty and walked out the door. I gave the valet five bucks and asked for my keys.

"You don't have to bring it up for me, I can see it from here." I jogged over to my car and headed home.

Once in my apartment, I walked over to the bar area, which separated my kitchen from the dining room, and grabbed a bottle of Jack Daniels. I put it down right away. I didn't want to become the kind of person that used alcohol to cope unless I was at work—then it'd be medicinal.

Instead, I got a glass of water and sat on the couch in the dark. What the hell was wrong with me? Why was I weirded out about this girl? I was a bartender in a very popular bar. I had seen and slept with some of the most beautiful women in Austin.

If Rich hadn't told me it was true, I never would've believed it. I'd not seen most of those girls more than once. I wouldn't have spent a Friday night in a tailspin about them. But dammit, I already had a lot of feelings for her—talk about a blind side.

I paced my apartment like it was a cage. Certainly, I couldn't be mad at January for not mentioning she was in a cult. Who would do that? Who would flat-out say, "Hey, I think you're totally cool, but I'm in a mind-controlling cult and will never be able to hang out with you."

Could I be mad at Rich? I mean, he was rather obtuse with his innuendo. I thought he was challenging me, not warning me! He could have been more upfront and said, "Dude, that chick is in a *cult*; you can't have her. Go find lower-hanging fruit."

I had calmed down enough to know it wasn't anyone's fault, and nothing anyone would have said would have stopped me. I liked January; I still wanted her.

All I needed was a plan. But what kind? Most of my plans that involved me spending quality time with a woman included charm, flowers, dinner, and maybe a little wine. If I was going to spend quality time with January, I might have to add top-secret extraction to the list.

But did she want or need extracting? Looking back at the nights I'd seen her, my assumption would be no. There was nothing about her that suggested she needed anything from anyone. She didn't have that vacant look in her eyes like the cult girls that followed Charles Manson. She was confident, thoughtful, and funny, not a brainwashed zombie.

Weren't cults illegal? Maybe the FBI would help me. No, they would eventually want to know if any laws had been broken, and I would have to admit I was just trying to safely date one of the members.

I put my glass in the kitchen sink and looked at my watch. In all this excitement, I'd lost track of time; I had to be at the club in twenty minutes.

My phone rang as I opened the door to head out. I grabbed it off the cradle to answer it, just as I heard my father's voice leaving a message.

"James, I'm calling to see how the job search is going. Do you need some help with your resume? I saw in the paper this morning that 3M is hiring."

I gingerly set the phone back on the cradle, afraid it might accidentally connect the call. I was not in the headspace or mood to deal with him right now.

When I walked into the club, it was already door-to-door crowded. We had a buck-fifty longneck special until ten that drew in tons of frat boys on the weekends. I think Brad saw me from the entrance because he waved me over like he was on fire.

"I'm so glad you're here!" he said, bouncing up and down. "I have to take a leak."

"Why didn't you go earlier?"

"I've been the only one here since 6:30." He ducked under the bar flap, running toward the bathroom.

I opened the door and walked into the twenty-foot circular bar, placing myself in the middle of the throng staring down the multitudes of barely old-enough-to-drink people, ready to party.

"Who's first?" I asked everyone all at once. I knew it was a little perverse, but I loved to watch them all jump into action at once. I recoiled as if their reaction surprised me. It always made me laugh.

Men usually wanted a beer or hard liquor served neat. Women always wanted hard-to-make, complicated drinks like Long Island Iced Tea or Sex on the Beach which all had lots of ingredients and took forever to make.

"What would you like?" I asked a guy in front of me.

He started to give me his order when a girl with perfectly manicured fingernails and shiny hoop earrings yelled in my direction while slapping a platinum American Express card on the bar. "I need two top-shelf bloody Mary's ASAP."

"Darling," I said, as I set my brow, "you can have anything you want if you wait your turn and pay cash. I jerked my hand up, pointing to a sign above the cash register. Sorry, we ONLY take CASH! "Daddy's platinum doesn't work here," I added with a grin.

Taking plastic meant filling out a transaction form, manually running it through a card machine, and getting a signature. We were always too busy for that, even when we were slow. She turned up her brand-new nose job and walked away.

I pointed to the original guy. "Sorry about the interruption; what did you want to drink?" As I'd hoped, he asked for a couple shots of Jim Beam.

In the state of Texas, all alcohol sales were regulated by the TABC (Texas Alcohol and Beverage Commission), and every bottle in our bar had a numbered registration label. When emptying a bottle, you either cut off its label or destroyed the bottle itself. Everyone had their preferred method in the matter. Tonight, I enjoyed whipping the bottle against the side of the metal container and hearing it shatter. It was a safe way to let out my current frustrations about January, the girl I liked but definitely couldn't have.

What a circus this place could be. When I'd started working here, I enjoyed watching the pretty girls try to get me to serve them by acting sexy. They mustered up their best supermodel pose, and the nerdy guys standing close by would hit on them.

Though it was mildly entertaining, it was getting a little old. My bar would cater to a more diversified clientele, so I wouldn't have to deal with the younger crowds and entitled attitudes.

Brad tucked back into the middle and pulled me aside. "See that confused-looking girl with the red hair and greasy bangs?"

I looked over the crowd and found the one he was referring to.

"Don't serve her, she's wasted. I just saw her pissing in the garbage can next to the open door in the girls' bathroom."

I choked out a laugh. "What the hell."

When we were busy, there was always a line for the girls' john. Most of the time, they just started using the guys' bathroom.

Larger bathrooms were on my wish list for Gellhorn's.

Brad started serving people on the other side of the long cooler in the middle of the circle. It was a suitable setup. You could find everything you needed on either half of the circle, so we didn't have to go from one side to the other.

I took a couple more orders and met Brad in the middle when I went to grab some Miller Genuine Drafts for a couple of guys.

"Here ya go," Brad said, handing me a shot of whiskey.

It was customary for us bartenders to start our shift with a shot. It took a little alcohol to put up with stupid drunk people all night. He also placed two highball glasses on top of the cooler divide.

"Yours is the one on the left," he shouted over the music and lifted his shot to toast me.

"Drink up and be somebody." I threw the shot down my throat and recorded our unsold alcohol on the "spill sheet."

About ten minutes later, I got my first phone number and placed it in the glass he had pointed out as mine. We had been playing this silly game since we started working together five years ago, where we competed to see who could get the most phone numbers in one shift. People got more and more entitled as the night continued. The only way to keep doing your job well was to keep being nice; if you were nice, they almost always gave you their number.

The first time he suggested doing this, I thought he was an idiot. But Brad and I were always game for a healthy competition—plus I noticed the difference in my attitude and increased tips.

I made drinks and uncapped beers, collected numbers, and neutralized all January thoughts that popped into my mind. She was sweet and beautiful, but I had many of those girls in my life already—and a glass full of phone numbers to prove it.

Chapter 5

When Love Breaks Down

Jewels

I hefted my dance bag and makeup case out of my truck and placed my hand on a sudden flutter in my stomach. Was it just butterflies about seeing James or my old friend, anxiety

I'd not had an anxiety attack since joining the group. I hadn't thought about boys since then, either. I was sure they were related, but I was not ready to stop thinking about him quite yet. I'd do that after I talked to him tonight. This would be the last day I'd allow my mind to veer off my spiritual practices.

I'd met a lot of men at the club. None of them gave me butterflies or cared that my hands were cold. I dodged around the cars and a couple of catcalls from drunk customers, remembering how he talked to me like a person and not a blow-up doll.

By the time I'd gotten into the club, that nervous energy had risen from my stomach to my chest. My heart skipped a beat; that stopped me right in front of the door-girl.

"You OK, January?" she asked while adjusting one of her shoulder pads.

I swallowed down my nerves. "I'm fine. I thought I left my favorite outfit at home for a second.

She gave me a rushed smile and turned to greet a group of guys coming in behind me.

Maybe I should have at least stopped thinking about him until he actually arrived. Right now, I needed to concentrate on what I was doing; I was here to help Dylan become a great dancer. Correction, I was here to teach her how to make money; dancing had very little to do with it.

When I first joined the group, it was about learning how to eat right and meditate and how forgiveness was key to personal growth and happiness. Now, it felt like most of our energy was spent making cash and trying not to upset Frank. It might be a deeper level of learning. Like when I used to play Asteroids with my friends—the better you got, the more challenging it became.

"Hey, girl, how's it going?" Sean, the DJ, asked me.

The black lights from the club were making all his teeth glow except for the one he said he knocked out skateboarding as a kid. Sean had always been a little different than the other DJs. Whoever taught him how to talk to women deserved a medal. He would never look me up and down and say, "You look hot in that dress." Instead, he would make eye contact and say, "That dress makes you look confident and powerful."

This was my favorite place in the building. It was more of a pass-through that connected the club to the dressing room rather than an actual booth. The soundboard was on one side, facing into the club, close to the stage. Directly across from it to my right was a wall of records, cassettes, and a new shelf for compact discs. A CD player had been installed a couple of weeks ago.

"I'm doing great," I said to his profile while he tweaked the lights and adjusted the music for the girl on stage.

"You sure?" he asked, turning to look at me. "You looked a little wobbly coming in the door."

"Wow, you don't miss much."

"Not from here I don't. I keep a close eye on everything happening in the club. I need to ensure none of the customers are harassing you ladies."

"Not from here I don't. I keep a close eye on everything happening in the club. I need to ensure none of the customers are harassing you ladies."

I shrugged. "I had a jolt of what might have been fear rip through me when I came in. But I'm sure it will pass soon."

I signed my name to the list that determined the evening's set rotation, and pushed through the heavy black curtain into the dressing room. My nose burned from various body lotions, hair sprays, and perfumes as I squinted into the bright fluorescent overhead lighting. The stools on my right were full of girls putting on or touching up their faces for the evening.

"Oh shit, I'm sorry, I didn't mean to step on your bag," I told one of the many girls by the lockers to my left, day-girls, packing up and leaving for the night.

"No problem," she said.

Once I walked past that initial tight space, things opened into a wider area. There were several floor-to-ceiling mirrors, and directly across from them was the entrance to the stage. This was everyone's favorite spot to bend over and ensure all your business was tucked into your t-back before heading out to the stage. Down a couple of stairs, and I was in the lower part of the dressing room. It was triangle-shaped and much bigger than the upper section.

There was shit everywhere! Micro miniskirts, halter tops, bras, and t-backs hanging half out of dance bags. It looked like a Fredericks of Hollywood had blown up in here.

"Is that Candy?" I asked, pointing under the counter.

"Yes," answered another one of the day-girls as she exhaled a plume of smoke and stubbed out her cigarette. "Don't wake her up. She's drunk and pissed at her ex-husband. She'll sleep it off and go home later."

I nodded in agreement and walked over to Dylan and Victoria; they had an empty seat waiting for me.

I plopped my bag on the floor and tossed my makeup case on the counter next to a bowl of stale popcorn.

"Look what I got!" Dylan said before my butt hit the chair.

She pulled a brand new, six-inch pair of black patent leather heels out of a box. "Wow, those are beautiful, your first break-neck pair."

She beamed. "They're so shiny. Look how pointy the toe is."

"Are you ready for this high of a shoe?" I asked her.

"Probably not. It's not just the height; the size of the heel is freaking me out, it's smaller than a pencil eraser."

I smoothed my hand over the side of the pump, flipped it over, and tried to press my thumb nail into the sole.

"Is it hard?" Victoria asked.

"Extremely. It's going to take gravel.

"Gravel?" Dylan squeaked out. "Gravel for what?"

Victoria nodded. "That's what I thought. I'm also a little worried about the shiny leather."

Dylan looked at me, puzzled. "Did I get the wrong shoes?"

"There's no such thing as wrong or bad shoes," I reassured her. "Have you started doing the splits on stage yet?"

Her face lit up like a kindergartener, full of shiny new pride and excitement. "I did the first one yesterday!"

It was hard for me to believe I used to be jealous of her. I was so worried she would replace me, but now I considered her a friend, someone I wanted to get to know better.

"That's great, we just need to tweak the shoes before you wear them..." I paused for dramatic effect. "...especially before you wear them on stage."

"Once you get dressed, I'll take you outside. There's a great patch of sandy gravel you can twist on, to help take the slick off the balls of the shoes," Victoria said.

"Ahhhh!" she slowly whined. "What are you doing to my beautiful shoes?"

Victoria let out a knowing giggle. "She's fixing them for you." She continued reassuring her. "Patent leathers and the stage don't mix well. When you do the splits, the shoe will stick to the polyurethane and stop you hovering a foot off the floor until you fall on your ass, and it won't look very sexy."

"But," I added to get her eyes to stop bugging out, "don't worry. If that happens, the guys will feel sorry for you and come up and give you a tip. I've met some of my best customers during my most embarrassing moments."

"Like that time your shoe flew off and hit that guy in the back," Victoria said, slapping her knee.

"Yes, he was great. I got my first hundred-dollar tip on stage from him," I said while using a nail file to scratch off a half-inch of the leather on the instep of her shoe, just below the big toe.

I grabbed the marker off the counter, filled in the newly inflicted scar and said, "A lot of prep work goes into making sure a new pair of heels doesn't kill you."

I loved these stolen moments with the three of us. It would make a great MasterCard commercial.

Hoochie outfit: $43.00
Stripper shoes: $37.95
Time spent with people on the same spiritual path: PRICELESS.

"Tada," I said, swallowing down a thickness in my throat. "There you go!"

"Won't the place you marked with the Sharpie rub off or fade?"

"Yes, eventually. I recommend buying a marker and keeping it in your makeup case; they come in handy."

She didn't look satisfied with my instructions, and held her stilettos close to her chest. "You defiled my brand-new shoes."

Victoria laughed and said, "Don't get too attached, you'll be replacing them in a couple of months."

Dylan's eyes bugged out, "Noooo, why would I do that?"

"Because," I said with a silly grin on my face, "that's how long it takes for the sides to bust out and the smell to creep in."

Some nights at the club everything popped at once; every good customer walked in the door, and every pretty girl was working, like when South by Southwest, Aquafest, and training camp for the Dallas Cowboys hit town.

I was sure none of those things were going on this evening, but it was still packed. Three waitresses greeted me when I walked down the four steps to get off the third stage.

"Please, January, that guy over there told me he's very interested in you," a newer waitress said with a fevered pitch.

I tossed my dress over my shoulder and started picking my crumpled tip money out of my t-back.

"I think my guy's a great tipper," interjected a girl with thick eyeliner who always wore Doc Martin boots and a flannel shirt tied around her waist. Those boots were becoming increasingly popular. I wanted to ask her if she was into the new grunge music I kept hearing about, but I was too busy. "You've sat with him once before. He's a little handsy, but he gets lots of dances."

I folded up my money and put it in my purse, nodding to let her know I was listening, and started putting on my dress. Just as I got my head through the opening, Alex took a step closer.

"I will pay you ten dollars to come to my table," she said. "He's buying Dom Perignon and gave me twenty to come and get you."

I cocked my head and pulled my dress down over the rest of my body, weighing the options while the girls made a semicircle in front of me. I *should* go to Alex's table. I didn't know anything about the first guy, and the handsy one, well, I knew way too well. I hated when guys tried to touch me when I danced.

"Instead of giving me ten dollars, give these two girls five dollars apiece, and I'll go with you." I looked at their semi-satisfied expressions. "If it doesn't pan out, I'll come find you."

Alex handed each girl five bucks, and they went on their way.

"There are already three girls there," Alex said as we made our way towards the table.

I shot her a look, but she seemed prepared for my surprise.

"He likes to have a table full of girls, but he doesn't get dances."

This time, I stopped walking.

"I promise, he always pays well," she said with a pleading note in her voice. "All you have to do is act like you're a party girl and have fun."

I rolled my eyes. "Isn't that what every guy wants?"

"Yes, probably, but he's willing to pay you for it, and I make a ton of money from his tip at the end of the night. Those bottles of Dom go for a hundred dollars a pop, and he usually gets three or four of them."

I liked Alex, and I wanted her to make money, so I nodded. "I'll give it a try."

We got within a couple of feet from the table when the man exclaimed in my direction. "Howdy, January, have a seat, join the party."

I did as he suggested, wishing it was just the two of us. I worked much better in a one-on-one situation. Three women vying for the attention and money of one man could get very messy. I trusted Alex, and it would be great if I could make another hundred dollars before James got here. Maybe this man could afford all four of us.

Sitting down, I glanced around the club to see where the other two waitresses had gone, just in case this table was a bust.

"Thanks for coming over, " the man said. He looked to be in his late fifties, wearing a mocha-colored suede cowboy hat and matching jacket. His gold belt buckle was larger than my hand. "I saw you on stage and knew right away I wanted to get to know you."

As he smiled at me, I felt his hand hit my knee under the table and then the unmistakable scratch of money against my skin. I brought my hand down to take what felt like several bills but kept my facial expression neutral. If he gave it to me under the table, it was supposed to be a secret.

"Thank you very much," I said, hoping he understood I was thanking him for the invitation and the money—especially the money.

"Whatcha drinking?" he shouted.

His Texan accent was strong, so I answered with a similar colloquialism.

"I'm as thirsty as a horse. How about a glass of water to start?"

"There's plenty of water in champagne," he bellowed out. "Get this split-tail a glass."

Alex looked at me for confirmation. I glanced down at my hand to see that the man had given me three crisp hundred-dollar bills.

I grabbed one of the other girls' glasses and held it in the air. "Champagne for everyone!"

"That's the spirit!" he shouted. "I knew you'd be a fun one."

I folded the money and tucked it in my purse with the rest of my evening's stash while Alex poured me my own full flute of Dom. It was a relief knowing I had made enough money to make Frank happy *and* to sit with James for a while, but how in the hell was I going to pretend I was drinking this much bubbly?

I knew fostering these thoughts about James was a bad idea, but they made me feel so alive—a different kind of alive than I usually felt. For the first time in a long while, the jittery excitement in my stomach was coming from something besides worrying about disappointing or upsetting Frank.

I took a sip of champagne and then, at just the right moment, turned my head and let it flow back into my glass.

Time was crawling. James and his enthusiastic feelings for me were building an anticipatory excitement that was making it hard for me to sit still. I looked over at the door and Rich's bar every chance I got, but I hadn't seen him yet. I wondered if it was possible to be both spiritual and have a friendship with someone not on "the path."

Whenever our customer placed his attention on one of the other girls, I snuck my glass under the table and carefully spilled most of its contents onto the rug.

I wished I'd get called for the stage. That would be a good way to burn some of this frenetic energy off. My cheeks hurt from fake smiling, and my brain was getting anxious about finding new and clever ways to dispose of this liquor.

"I need to use the lady's room," I said with a pretend slur in my voice. I stood up, rocked back on my heels, and pointed at everyone at the table. "I'll beeee right back."

I walked into the bathroom and abandoned my drink on the sink.

Sean called my name to go onstage while I was washing my hands. Relief flooded my senses. In total, that gregarious man had secretly handed me five-hundred dollars, and I appreciated it. But I couldn't sit with him anymore.

"What would you like to dance to?" Sean asked as I stood next to him, peering out of the booth looking for James.

I squinted into the crowd. "How about a couple of songs from INXS?"

"Who are you looking for?" he asked, holding one of his hands up to his brow like we were at sea.

"No one," I said, distracted by my search. Maybe James wasn't coming. Maybe he forgot. I half-hoped he did; nothing was even going on between us, and I was already this conflicted.

"You're on in ten seconds."

I nodded my head in agreement but wasn't fully listening. Wait, was that him? I thought that was him over by Rich's bar. A burst of butterflies let loose in my stomach. This was definitely a different feeling than the one I had when I first got here tonight.

"Jan-u-ary," Sean sang, "now we only have five seconds."

"Shit..." I stared at him. "I'm sorry. Both songs INXS. First song 'Suicide Blond,' second song, 'Never Tear Us Apart.'"

"Okay, good job, you did it!"

I snorted out a laugh, ran from the booth, and walked onstage.

I dropped my things on one of the clean tables and headed to the back bar to tip out. Adams, the night manager, oversaw collecting ten percent of the money each dancer made for the door guys. The other ten percent we gave straight to the DJ.

"How was your night, January?" he asked, counting out the stack of one-dollar bills I gave him.

"It was all right," I said. "The money was good."

"Forty-two, forty-three, forty-four, forty-five. You don't have bigger bills you could give me, instead of all these ones?"

"Sorry, I hate trying to spend them in public, and the teller at my bank is starting to look at me like I'm a drug dealer."

I couldn't give them to Frank either. If you only had to give him eighty-five dollars for your tithe, he would still expect you to give him a hundred-dollar bill. He'd always say, "You can never give too much. The extra money might even give you good karma."

I looked over at Rich. "Was I just seeing things, or was your friend James here this evening?" I shifted my weight from one foot to the other. "I mean, he said he was going to come in, and I think I saw him, but then he disappeared. I didn't see him again for the rest of the night."

Rich looked at Adams, and then they both looked at me.

"January," Rich said like he was about to tell me someone died, "James overheard a customer tell someone you were in a cult."

I closed my eyes to hide my shock while Rich gave me the rest of his news.

"He didn't take it very well and left."

I looked towards the door where eight of my supposed cult girlfriends were impatiently waiting for me for our nightly caravan back to the house. We definitely weren't a cult, were we? You'd think we would know if we were in a cult.

"I see," I said, my voice a little shaky. I looked up at the ceiling, rapidly blinking to keep the tears from falling. The disappointment of losing something I never had oozed through me. Even if he was a minor distraction, I was looking forward to getting to know him better.

"I'm so sorry, January," Rich said while wiping down the bar. "I didn't know what to tell him."

I opened my mouth to suggest he could have told him I wasn't in a cult, but heard "January" from a couple of the girls.

I was sure they were tired and unaware of the situation I was attempting to stifle. I patted my eyes with the cuff of my sweatshirt and clocked a look of concern move across Adams' face.

"Follow me," he said, which I did without question. I just needed a minute without all the girls watching me to get my bearings.

I flashed them a grimace while Adams held the door open to the office. "I just need a minute and she can go home," he called over to them.

Adams' towering height and calm expression blocked the cheap light fixture on the water-stained ceiling. We had been working together almost since I first walked into the club. The first time we'd met, he tipped me as a customer, and then the following week, he showed up in a nice shirt and dress jacket to begin his new job as a bouncer. Three months after that, he was promoted to manager.

"How many strippers does it take to screw in a light bulb?" he asked me.

I closed my eyes, trying to keep my tears at bay and find an answer. He was the king of bad jokes. "I have no idea," I said, dropping my hands.

"One hundred," he said, "one to change the bulb, and ninety-nine to ask if they can go home early!"

I bent my head as my chest gave way to a string of breathy laughs. "That's so true...and the best bad joke you've ever told me."

"At least it made you laugh."

"At least? Thank God." I changed my tone to something more sincere. "Thank you for always being so nice to me."

"Look, January, I'm pretty good friends with James' boss, we play high-stakes poker in tournaments all around town. I know that he thinks he's a good, hard-working guy."

I shrugged, not interested in debating his point at the moment. "Why do people think we're in a cult?"

"You know, you guys have an interesting situation, one the people around here can't figure out, so they assume the worst. Or at least the most interesting."

"I agree it's unusual, but it really helped me out," I said. "I'm not sure where I'd be without it." The backs of my eyes began to sting again, but I kept going. "I'm not sure what normal looks like anymore. I'm either in the group, where I'm learning and improving myself, or I'm here at the club."

He grabbed a flyer off a congested countertop. "The Pecan Street Festival is next weekend, and I need a dancer to represent the club. Maybe it could be you? Perhaps it could be a way for you to see if the world is still as scary as you remember it. I'll be there, and you will be working—not for money, but for a good cause. Maybe Frank would let you do it."

"I doubt it. I'm pretty sure Frank won't think that's the best way to facilitate my spiritual growth. I've also never been a big fan of dressing like a hooch in public."

He shook his head. "Comments about your spiritual growth in a strip club may be one of the reasons people think it's a cult and...*hooch* is what I'm trying to avoid.

"I promise it's for a charity organization called Clubs Care. All the bars and clubs in town get together under one name to help raise money for single mothers. We're a sponsor, so the Tulips logo will be on the back of the t-shirt, but it will be there with the other twenty businesses taking part. Everyone working the tent will be wearing one of the shirts. You can wear shorts, jeans, or a nice skirt, whatever makes you feel the least hoochie or that Frank will allow."

"I'd like to do it. Really, I would," I said, looking at the flyer. "I'm just not sure Frank will see it that way."

"I get it. If you can, great, if not, I'll understand."

There was a knock on the door, and Victoria leaned her head in, looking wearily heavy-eyed. "The girls are getting restless, January."

Adams changed his voice into something more authoritative. "You're one of my favorite employees, I'm just asking you to follow the state rules, so you don't get arrested for dancing too close."

He shot a quick look at Victoria. "That includes you too." Victoria pinched her lips together and backed out of the room. Adams winked at me.

I grinned, appreciating his finesse. "I really will do my best to help with the event."

"There are directions to the best parking lot down there and a map where the tent will be located."

I flipped it over for confirmation and jammed it into my bag.

"Don't count on me," I said and headed for the door. I gave him a weak smile. "Time to return to my *cult*."

Chapter 6

Under Pressure

Jewels

I'd been sitting on my futon writing affirmations when I heard the tiny bell ring. Liz and Tracy had been cooking lunch for the past hour, filling the house with smells of barley, tabbouleh, steamed vegetables, and roasted chicken.

The bell had a dual purpose: it let everyone know the food was almost ready and told me it was my turn to do my job in the kitchen.

After many years of failed attempts to teach me how to cook, Frank gave me the title and position of expedition chef-in-training. I now oversaw table-setting, food distribution, clean-up, and occasional food prep when needed. I think everyone at the house was relieved they no longer had to worry about eating my burnt food or being accidentally poisoned.

I checked my notebook to ensure I'd finished the affirmations Frank told me to write this week.

I am a money magnet.

The more money I make, the more energy I have.

I love everything about making money.

The more money I give to Frank, the more money I make.

I double-checked to make sure I didn't accidentally write *the faster I stopped thinking about James, the more at peace I would be.* I'd never wanted to get to know anyone I'd met at work on a personal level. He made me curious about life in the real world and wonder if I was still on the right path.

I used to feel good here, like I was healing and had a purpose. But over time, things had changed; Frank had changed. If this was no longer the place for me, then where was? Did I want a normal life again? I wasn't even sure what a normal life looked like.

Maybe Adams was right, and volunteering at the Pecan Street Festival could help answer that question. I was assuming the people that went to the festival had regular lives. Perhaps if I could get a peek at life outside the group, I could get it out of my system, then get back to life before I met James.

I closed my notebook, placed it on my shelf for Frank to check later, and headed into our disproportionately small galley kitchen.

"It smells so good in here," I told Tracy and Liz.

"Thank you," Tracy said, "it's all about the love."

That was her go-to feel-good saying. Tracy was a year younger than me and had been living in the house for a couple of months before I arrived. Most people here fit into two categories: under twenty-five or over thirty-seven. I liked her tranquil demeanor and quiet strength. She was also a fantastic dancer and one of the few girls in the group that didn't dance under a stage name.

I grabbed the heavy stoneware and utensils from their respective cupboards and drawers and carried them to the dining room. On the four nights Frank taught classes, up to fifteen people sat at this table. Thanks to Jodie and Steve's carpentry skills, we had two picnic-style tables that sat together lengthwise, making a perfect square that fit neatly in the small space.

The bench seats eliminated the need for cumbersome chairs. Lunchtime was usually just the women that lived at the house and Frank.

"What's going on with you?" Frank asked while loading his plate up with food.

I looked around the table to see whom he was talking to. His gaze fell on me.

"You've been flat and distracted all morning."

I nodded as I swallowed the whole bite of food I had in my mouth. "I'm going to get my period soon," I said. "I've been tired these past couple of days, maybe a little anemic." I nonchalantly loaded my next bite of food on my fork, hoping he would accept this answer.

"Make sure you take an iron supplement after lunch. Darkness is always waiting for you to have a moment of weakness. You need to be alert and aware of your surroundings at all times."

"Okay." I handed him the information about the event in hopes of changing the subject. I also chose this time to bring it up because many of the girls that work at the club were here, and I didn't want them to think I was hiding something from them.

"The manager at the club asked me if I could attend this festival. He said most of the other girls working there took part in events outside the club. Sounds like a waste of time to me, I won't be making any money," I added so that I didn't sound too eager.

He looked at it for two seconds and tossed it in the middle of the table.

Tracy finished taking a piece of chicken off the serving dish. "Not everything is about money."

He drew his brows together. "What's that supposed to mean?"

Everyone around the table fell silent. He was constantly fishing, always giving us room to sabotage ourselves. I was sure he didn't care about the event. But if Tracy was going to give her opinion so freely, he would use the situation to see if she was hiding any secret yearnings.

Tracy looked at him and said, "There's an us versus them thing building in the club. We," she said, pointing her fork around the table, "are so separated from them that there's an intrigue and growing stigma about us. They've even started referring to us as 'the cult girls.'"

Whoa, I guess I wasn't the only one who'd heard them call us that.

Frank's eyes shot up from his plate; she had his attention now. He stopped fishing through her psyche and started digging for more information. Frank had no interest in attracting attention from the outside world.

"Go on," he said between bites.

"They think we're weird. It was one thing when only a couple of us worked there, but now there are nine. We're officially a group."

"Why would they think our group is a cult?" he pressed.

"I think there's several things. They know most of us live together. They know we don't eat red meat; they know we don't drink. They know we do yoga."

"Yoga?" he asked after taking a drink of water. "How is that a defining factor?"

"Hippies in communes practice hatha yoga and transcendental meditation. Yuppies in Austin do step-aerobics and Jazzercise."

I stifled a laugh as she continued.

"I think the hippy commune terminology was a mouthful, so the word *cult* took its place. We're also a group that doesn't participate in events, doesn't encourage liquor sales, and doesn't help promote their business."

Frank returned to looking bored with the conversation. Everyone at the table ate their food, ignoring the uncomfortable silence ever-present when he considered a subject closed.

I tucked my heart and desires between my remaining bites of food and swallowed them whole. After eating, I grabbed my empty plate and headed into the kitchen to do the dishes.

"How long will this event last?" Frank asked as I set my plate in the sink.

"With drive-time, I'd be away from the house for about six hours."

I hesitated for a few seconds to see if he had further questions while I started soaking the pots and pans. He got up from the table and handed me his empty glass.

"Okay, you can help at the festival. You'll still be able to work that night, so it shouldn't disrupt your ability to make money."

I expected to feel happy about his decision, but my insides were exploding—with fear. Why was I doing this?

I cranked down the window to let the warm mid-morning air fill my truck, and lifted my hair off my sticky neck and rubbed my shoulders.

It'd been four years since I'd done anything non-group-related. Outside of running errands for Frank, I was never alone; one or more group members always went with me.

The people that lived outside the main house had a little more freedom than we did. They often talked about social things they did outside the group. It was generally expected that your commitment and engagement levels were different if you lived at the house.

I hit my blinker and moved into the right lane.

The minute we moved into the house, we silently agreed that our focus would be on Frank and the lessons he gave us. At first, his teachings were firm but benevolent. Somewhere along the way, it had become a living, breathing petri-dish of uncertainty where he meticulously tracked our every move and emotion in order to correct us.

Occasionally he'd say something like, "The ladies that lived in the house are part of the elite team. They're on the fast track to healing." This would do two things: it would make us feel important and more dedicated to our responsibilities, and make the others jealous, spurring them on to do better by giving more of themselves—or their money.

Before leaving the house, I had looked over the map on the flyer but I'd failed to anticipate road closures. I looked down the road and toward my exit. Sitting next to it was an orange detour sign. I downshifted, got off the highway, and pulled into the parking lot of an unopened restaurant.

It was a good thing I was alone. Frank would have used this situation as a teaching opportunity to reprimand me for not being properly prepared. I placed my hand over my heart, willing it to slow down. This was a minor setback—there was no reason to panic. I dug into my glove box for an Austin city map and laid it across my bench seat. I used my pen to scratch out the new route.

I squinted through the glare in my windshield at a sign for the restaurant I was in front of. The top of it said El Arroyo. The message on it read.

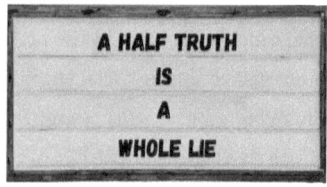

My breakfast shifted in my stomach. How much had I lied to Frank about my doing this event? Was it still a *whole* lie if you only told a quarter truth? I took a couple of breaths, remembered that El Arroyo meant *The Ditch* in Spanish, and returned to the road.

It only took me twenty minutes to find the correct parking lot. Once in a space, I closed my eyes and took a deep breath. The air filled my lungs; I released it with a breathy all is well, all is well.

KNOCK, KNOCK, KNOCK!

I jerked my head toward my window to see a dirt-stained older gentleman calling something out to me.

I cranked my window down a couple of inches and swallowed my frazzled nerves. "I'm sorry, what did you say? It's my first time down here."

He hacked a thick loogie onto the pavement. "Three dollars to park."

I handed him the money as the rancid stench of his body odor wafted into the cab of my truck.

He smirked. "This is your first time downtown?"

I nodded as I reached out to get the parking pass for my dashboard.

He turned to walk away. "Good luck, lady."

I rolled up my window. Why would I need luck? Could he tell I was wigging out or was I in actual danger down here? This was a horrible idea. I was ready to go back to the house where it was safer and more familiar. How would I explain it to Frank? I'd have to tell him another half-lie to get out of this bigger lie.

How angry would Adams be if I bailed on him? I mulled it over for a second and decided that not showing up at all was a shitty way to handle the situation.

Okay, I'd find Adams, tell him I was sorry, I bit off more than I could chew and couldn't do this. Then I'd go home and tell a whole lie about how other people showed up to work the tent, and I didn't have to.

Then I wouldn't tell any more lies. I'd continue doing what I'd been doing until I could do something else without freaking out. I didn't think I'd be this scared since I'd been thinking about having a normal life.

I rubbed my clammy palms on my acid-washed jeans and got out of my car. I checked the parking lot for any suspicious characters and headed toward 6th Street— Pecan Street as it was known during the festival. Back when the city was called Waterloo, all the streets were named after trees and rivers. Now all the tree streets were boring numbers instead.

I wanted to see everything, but I knew the sooner I saw Adams, the faster I could return to the house where the stress was just as intense but at least more familiar.

My eyes widened as I caught my first glimpse of the festival. I didn't think it would be this crowded so early. I swallowed and kept going. As far as the festival went, there were two rows of ten-by-ten tents in the middle of the road. They were connected back-to-back and stretched the entire length of the street, going on for several blocks. It was like having a pop-up book come to life. All the places I'd heard advertised on the radio were here: Shakespeare's, Maggie Mae's, Steamboat, and a sign that said Abrato's on 5th with an arrow pointing South. The girls at work raved about that place.

I was itching to find the club James worked at, but that would be going against my actively letting him go.

The tent directly in front of me was selling BBQ. I swallowed down the extra saliva my mouth had generated due to the aroma of the rotisserie chicken and pecan pie.

"Excuse me, lady," a man barked in a gruff voice behind me. I spun to see him, but he wasn't waiting for me to get out of his way; he was already inches from barreling me over. I jumped to the left to make room for him and the large keg of beer in his arms.

I double-checked my surrounding to make sure no one else was going to run me over. I was standing in front of Ivory Cats. According to the flyer, the Clubs Care tent was across the street, in front of the 311 Club.

I pulled my sweaty shirt away from my skin and headed across the street.

My steps slowed; the booth had not been opened up yet. Did I beat Adams here? Was I too early? I looked down to see what time it was; my heart was beating faster than the second hand on my Swatch.

And then, from behind me, I heard a familiar voice. "January?"

I leaped back. What was he doing here?

Oh God, did Adams arrange this? He'd mentioned he knew James' boss.

As guilt engulfed my brain, I started to speed-swallow the extra moisture flooding my mouth. I barely had permission to come to this event. I absolutely did not have permission to be with a guy, especially one I had a secret crush on.

Turn around, my mind instructed, *walk away, do whatever was necessary to get away from here*. I tried to take in a full breath of air, but I couldn't. It was getting shallower and harder to regulate. My mouth flooded with the acrid flavor of panic. I darted my eyes to the left and right. What was the fastest route out of here? A flash of cold sweat covered my body as the blood drained from my face.

"January, are you okay?"

My fight-or-flight responses were making choices before I could acknowledge my movements. I took a swift turn and walked toward the booth, away from James.

From what sounded like miles away, I heard him repeat my name.

I blinked to clear the fuzz from my eyes. My clothes were strangling me to death. My body was losing the battle to keep me from passing out.

"*January!*" was the last thing I heard right before James caught me. Right before my knees entirely gave out.

"I've got you, you're safe," he said.

I could feel his strong arms wrapped around me and his warm, humid words in my ear, "We'll get through this together."

He slowly walked us backward until we were in the tent, alone. "Breathe with me and know, if I'm getting enough air, so are you."

I did as he said. Our bodies were expanding and contracting together.

As my heart rate slowed and the stress of the moment subsided, my eyes filled with tears. I fully relaxed into James and started to cry. The wetness from my eyes made little dots on his Clubs Care shirt.

Between the tears, I sucked in the surrounding air. Each breath became easier with a deeper level of awareness. My senses were coming back to me. *Inhale, I'm with James. Exhale, he's helping me.*

"Are you okay?" he asked, filling the silence in the tent.

I gazed up at him. "You smell like coffee, bacon, and cologne."

James chuckled but didn't move to separate us. "Maybe I should eat breakfast before my morning shower."

I let out a half laugh. "I think I'm okay now."

He moved his head enough to see my face. His assessing gaze made my heart fizz like I had swallowed a package of Pop Rocks.

James loosened his embrace to test my balance. I gave him a reassuring nod, and he let me go.

"Thank you," I said, wiping my tears off with the palm of my hand. "You were very good at calming me down."

"My sister went through a phase of getting panic attacks during her freshmen year of high school. Do you get them often?"

"It hasn't happened in a while," I said, hesitating, unsure how much I should share with him. "It used to happen every day."

"Every day?"

"Yes," I said, fanning myself with both hands. "It's warm in here."

"I agree. It'll cool down once we open the tent flap. Did Adams give you a festival shirt to wear?"

"No, he didn't. I just assumed I'd get one here," I said with a sigh. My mistakes were adding up fast. I braced myself for James to scold me the way Frank would have.

He walked to one of the tables and lifted the polyester skirting. "That's no biggie, I bet there's one in these boxes."

"It's not?"

"Nah, who cares?" He held up one of the t-shirts, eyeing it for size. "I think this one will fit you."

I took the shirt from him and glanced around the tent. There were no other sections to the small space. Nowhere for a bit of privacy to change. He didn't think I would undress in front of him just because I was a dancer, did he? I know he'd already seen me nearly naked, but not like this.

He must have read my mind. "I'm going to step outside. Just holler at me when you're through."

I shot him a dorky half-smile and took off my shirt the instant he was out of sight. The panic attack left a light sulfurous order on my skin. I used my shirt to wipe it away as much as possible and put on the Clubs Care shirt. At least its aqua-blue color was one Frank would approve of.

Shit, what if Frank came down here? He'd never do that, just like he would never come into the club. He didn't like or endorse these types of activities. He constantly reminded us, "People go out because they don't have what they need at home."

I took a big breath, folded up my shirt, and tucked it into the box.

"I'm done," I told James, opening the tent flap to let him back in.

He looked at me, smiled, and jumped right back into the conversation we had started before I had to change. "Did you say you used to have those attacks every day?"

"Before I joined the group...." I trailed off and gave him a weak smile. "First, I think I should clear something up for you. I'm not in a cult."

He looked down at the ground for a second and then back up at me. "It's not a cult, or you don't hang out with the cult?"

I pointed back towards the tables and suggested we could put everything out while discussing it. "Well, I hang out there and I live there. It's a therapy group, not a cult."

"What kind of therapy?" he asked, pulling the rest of the boxes out and handing me the pamphlets that needed to be displayed.

"The kind that helped me with anxiety, panic, and fear."

He nodded like he understood what I was saying, but I could tell by how his eyebrows pinched together that he was thinking it through.

After we placed everything on the table, we stepped back and looked over our handiwork.

"What do you think?" I asked, tilting my head to examine the display. "Is it okay? Should we move the flyers to the other side of the table? Maybe we should fold the t-shirts a different way?" I took a breath to slow down my brain.

James was staring at me. But then the right side of his mouth curled into a smile. "I promise you, there isn't a right or wrong way. I think, however we want it to look is perfect. We can adjust it as we go."

I looked back to the table, contemplating.

"January," he said, the tone of his voice relaxing and encouraging. "I don't give a shit about the table. The important question is how do you feel? Are you ready for me to open the tent, or would you like a little more time to get your bearings?"

I took in a gulp of air and straightened my posture. "I'm okay. I'm ready."

"Awesome, let's do it." He walked over to the canvas tarp and carefully folded it open, securing it with a thick strap to one of the poles.

It wasn't super busy, but every once in a while, we would get five or six people strolling in at a time. They would ask me questions I didn't have the answers for, but James was always there to help me through it. His instruction style was much more forgiving than Frank's.

I answered one lady's questions correctly, and James gave me a thumbs-up behind her back. My chest swelled with satisfaction, then I heard Frank's voice in my head saying *Pride goeth before a fall.* I slumped and shifted back to a service mindset rather than a boastful one.

Adams showed up around 2pm with more boxes to sort through and items to sell.

"Wow," he said when he saw me. "You made it."

I beamed at him. "Yes, I did."

He gave me a warm smile. "You look good. You look *happy*."

Huh, I thought I always looked happy. I knew for sure I was always *trying* to look that way at least. Had I been pretending for others so long that I didn't notice how unhappy I'd become?

Adams gave me a nudge. "You guys can go now, you're done for the day."

"Great," James said and shook Adams' hand. "This was fun. I'd be happy to do it again next year, especially if I get to work with her. It was a nice surprise."

What did James just say? He wanted to do things with me, even though he thought I was in a cult? Oh my.

"Are you sure?" I asked Adams. "It doesn't seem fair to leave you here alone."

"I'm positive," he said. "A woman who works in the office will be here any minute to help out."

James turned to me and smiled. "Ready, January?"

My cheeks flushed. "Ready?"

"Yes, I'm going to walk you to your car."

"Um, yes," I stammered out, "yes, yes, I'm ready."

Adams smiled at me. "See you at work, kid."

"Okay." I leaned forward, closer to him. "I know you orchestrated James and I being here together."

He lowered his voice. "Can you keep a secret?"

"Yes," I whispered.

"So can I, see you later."

I rolled my eyes.

James was waiting outside the tent. He glanced over at me, put on a pair of Wayfarer sunglasses, and said, "Come with me." He grabbed my hand and pulled me through the crowd.

We went about a block, darted in and around groups of people talking about their purchases and wondering where they were going to eat. This wasn't the way to my car. I was just about to ask him what we were doing when he hopped up onto the sidewalk and stopped.

James let go of my hand and gestured. "This is it! This is the place I want to turn into a bar."

I looked up at the building in awe and wished he hadn't let go of my hand.

He began telling me everything he wanted to do to the building, how he wanted to change the awning from red to navy blue and how he was going to paint *Gellhorn* in typewriter font across the picture window. His arms swooshed through the air attempting through gestures to explain all his grand ideas.

I filed bits and pieces of what he said away for later; what had me enthralled was how alive he looked. I could've run my hairdryer for a month on the energy his excitement was producing. I used to be like that; I used to have ideas and dreams. I couldn't wait to become an adult so I could go to college, get a great job, and go on exotic vacations. All of that changed when the anxiety attacks showed up. Now my excitement came in tiny increments that felt like emotional survival.

I stared at the building and did my best to imagine what it would look like when it was finished. I doubt I'd ever get down here again.

"I have all my hopes and dreams riding on this place," he continued. "If I don't make it happen soon, I'll have to get a real job. I may even have to move back to Dallas."

My stomach dropped. If he moved out of town, I wouldn't ever see him again. He'd never come back into the club.

"I'm sure you can do it," I said. To me, he had everything you would need to do something of this magnitude: determination, drive, desire—all the things I no longer had.

I was desperate to say something encouraging, but who was I to give advice? I gave up thinking I could have the American dream long ago. Now I hung my hopes on being a counselor like Frank. He told us we were all assembled here by the universe to grow and learn how to help people the way he did. But I was beginning to wonder. It felt more like the universe just wanted us to work to death and get fussed at all the time.

"Thank you for showing me your dream," I said while walking by a bench. I glanced at my Swatch; I still had quite a bit of time. *Just go home Jewels, you've broken enough rules today to get kicked out of the house for three lifetimes*. But I wouldn't ever get this chance again. "Umm, I don't have to be anywhere for a while if you'd like to talk for a little bit longer."

"That would be nice," he said and gestured for me to sit down first. He gave me a sheepish grin. "So, you can go out with me if it's not a cult?"

I didn't expect that question. Shit. "No, I'm sorry I still can't go out with you."

"You don't like me?"

My ears pricked with heat. "Umm, I like you, but my teacher—my therapist—doesn't think I'm ready to date yet."

"What do you think, January?"

Interesting question. Even if I thought I was ready, Frank would never let me do it. Knowing I needed his permission to do anything was always in the back of my mind. But I was okay with it because up until now, the only thing I ever wanted was to feel better.

James was charming and an amusing distraction, but he had nothing to do with my purpose. Did he?

"I'm not sure," I said. "I mean, I think I should be able to go out into public without passing out before I try dating."

He took off his sunglasses. "Was today a typical day for you?"

"No," I admitted, "today was very outside the norm. I took a lot of risks to be here."

"Risks," he repeated, more to himself than to me. "I'm glad you did. I've really enjoyed getting to know you better."

I cleared my throat. "I could try being friends with you."

"Do you have many friends, January?"

"None that aren't in my therapy group." The more questions I answered, the more it did sound like I was in a cult.

"Well, I'd love to be your friend," he said, knocking his knee against mine.

Chapter 7

Secret

James

The squeak of a pissed-off grackle snapped me out of the daydream I was having about January. I refocused on Brad, who had been on the tee box for what felt like an hour. His approach was textbook: his grip flowed straight down from his shoulders, his knees looked comfortably bent, and his upper body was tilted forward and straight.

He glanced over at me. "Why is drowsiness listed as a side effect for sleeping pills?"

"I don't know," I said, pressing the heels of my hands into my eyes. "Please concentrate."

He smirked, drew his arms back, and pulled the club through the muggy mid-October air. The beautiful sound of a perfect *swoosh* was followed by a *crack* off the head of the ball, sending it straight into the trees lining the fairway.

"If you were as bad at sex as you are at golf, you'd never get laid," I teased after his shot disappeared in the crown of a pecan tree.

"That's not true," he said, jerking his head back. "I *would* get laid, just not by the same girl twice."

"Ha, good point."

He pulled his tee out of the ground. "I think I've gotten better over the years."

"Yeah, sure you have. What's your handicap?"

"My swing, obviously," he said while we walked to the cart.

"I think you close your eyes when you strike the ball." I took my beer out of the cup holder and checked it for bees. "You should try hitting the ball without being such a pussy."

"Fuck off, old man."

I chuckled as we loaded into the cart and headed for my ball. To be fair, this wasn't the easiest course in town, but it was the least pretentious. They'd let you wear a concert t-shirt here—as long as you could find a way to attach a collar to it.

"How are things going with Ripley?" I asked.

He gave me a sheepish look. "I'm pretty into her. In the past, I've shied away from dating strippers because I thought they'd be too wild for me. But so far, she's calmer, more conservative, organized, smarter, and cleaner than I am. She told me she saw you and January hanging out at Tulips a couple of nights after my birthday."

"Ah, yes, we did," I said, remembering her cold hands, inquisitive mind, and how she knew almost nothing about Austin.

"She said you guys looked pretty cute together."

"I thought so too, and I was looking forward to getting to know her. But that was before I knew she was in that weird therapy group."

Brad shot me a quizzical look but didn't say anything as we emptied ourselves from the cart and walked over to my ball. He dropped his a couple of feet in front of mine. I opened my mouth to say, *that's cheating*, but he spoke first.

"Ripley says she's very sweet."

It hadn't crossed my mind that Ripley would know much about her. "What else has she told you?"

"She said she's always smiling, funny, and caring. There are always other girls around, so she doesn't get to talk to her very often. Ripley said she likes to sit next to them in the dressing room, so she can overhear their conversations."

I held up my hand to stop his train of thought, plus I'd already figured out most of those things. "How long have you known or thought she might be in a cult?"

He shrugged. "Probably since the day I met her. She came to our table, did a couple of dances, and the minute she left, the other girls started telling us all about it. It's just one of the things everyone knows. The drinks are overpriced, the women are hot, and a bunch of them are in a cult."

"Dude," I said while taking a practice swing, "you didn't think to mention it to me?"

"I thought you knew," he said with a hint of an apology intertwined with his chuckle.

"How would I know? I never go to Tulips."

"I thought Rich might have mentioned it. He was the first person you talked to after she unbuttoned your shirt."

"Well, I think he tried," I said, hitting my ball onto the green a couple of feet from the hole. "Clearly, I missed his attempt."

He took his glove off and put it in his pocket. "What's that mean?" he asked, walking up to his ball.

"He said, 'You can't have that one.' I thought he was saying she was very hard to get."

Brad picked up his ball and smiled at me. "I can see you taking it that way, and technically, he wasn't lying."

"I agree," I said with a smirk. "Why'd you pick that up?"

"I figured I'd skip shanking another ball off the course and let you finish in peace."

I nodded. While walking back to the cart, I told him I had worked with her at the festival.

"Whaaat? You didn't tell me that either."

I pushed the pedal down and started driving up to the green. "I didn't mention it because I don't want it to get around."

After I stopped the cart, he took the last sip of his beer and crushed the can. "Who would I tell?"

"I can think of at least ten people, Ripley being the first."

He nodded in agreement as he pulled the flag out of the hole.

"Then if any one of them told anyone else, it would eventually get back to one of the other cult girls. From what I can tell," I said, grabbing my ball out of the hole, "that would get January in a lot of trouble."

He replaced the flag. "So after getting to know her better, do you still think it's a cult?"

"Yes, I do, but she doesn't."

"Ah, that's why you called it a therapy group earlier."

Brad and I stood there quietly for a second before he continued. "I guess I always thought the term *cult* was a bit of a stretch. Like, maybe we were taking what little we knew and building it into something bigger than it was, not a *real* cult."

"I'm not a hundred percent sure, which is another reason I didn't tell anyone. But if you could've heard how she talked about the guy that's her *therapist and leader*, you would think so too. Oh, and how many rules they have to follow, how perplexed she is when making a simple decision. The version of January at the club is much different than when she's out of her element. I'd bet all her friends are that way as well."

"That's pretty deep, dude," he said as we walked to the cart.

"Don't tell anyone, but she said she wants to try to be my friend."

"What does that mean?"

"I think it means she trusts me and wants to see if she can have a connection outside that group. I'm going to start hanging out at Tulips more often."

"Really," he said with an incredulous tone. "You've never been a big fan of Tulips."

"True, but I want to get to know her better. She has very limited personal freedoms. That *therapy guy* knows where she is every minute of the day. The only place I can see her is at the club."

"I'm going in there tonight to bring Ripley Whataburger for dinner. Maybe we can all hang out."

"Yeah, that's a good idea. I'm still worried about you telling Ripley what I've told you."

"Ripley won't tell anyone, she's a mama bear. If she likes someone, she'll protect them tooth and nail."

"Okay, if you trust her, I'll trust her."

"Speaking of tenuous situations, how are things going with your father? Have you told him about your progress with the bar?"

I groaned. "Not yet. I keep dodging his calls and letting my answering machine deal with him."

"Talk about a pussy way to handle something," he said, rolling his eyes. "Just tell him the truth and get it over with."

"Very amusing. I'll tell him once I get a couple more things nailed down." I looked down at my watch. "Oh shit, we gotta go, I'm meeting my banker in an hour."

I heard Bob's labored breathing before he broke the silence. "James, you're right on time."

He plopped what I hoped were my investor packets on the desk and grinned. "Hot off the press, the printer just brought them over."

His blue, poorly-cut suit groaned at the seams as he reached out to shake my hand. He always had a friendly smile, but I worried the fluorescent lighting was turning his skin grey like his smoking had yellowed his fingernails.

"I was downtown the other night," he said, sitting down and catching his breath. "My wife and I were grabbing a bite at Paradise Cafe. Great food for a bar," he went on while resting his hands on my packets.

I sat upright, leaning halfway on my chair, hoping he would hand me one. I stifled the urge to interrupt his story and snatch one from him. I just wanted to feel it, weigh it, and analyze it.

"After eating, we walked to the bookstore to check it out."

I settled into my chair and gave up the urge to speed up the process. Plus, now he was talking about my building and anything having to do with it was worth listening to.

"We were at the back door in the alley when my wife asked me about the tiny metal door about two feet off the ground."

"Oh yes," I interjected, "the one that's too short for milk, and why would they deliver milk to a business?"

"Keen observation," he said, his eyes glowing with excitement. "That door is too small for milk, but it's perfect for a shovel."

"A shovel?"

He gave me a couple of seconds to think it through and then pounded his hands on my packets, twice, once for each word. "For coal."

I palmed my forehead. "Coal delivery, of course, That makes so much more sense, I'm a little embarrassed I didn't put that together myself." I shifted my body a little closer to his desk.

His mouth spread into a full smile. He wasn't kidding when he said he loved old buildings. "Let's take a look at these," he said, finally handing me one.

The weight of it made the hairs on my arms stand up. I raised it to my face and inhaled as much of the smell as I could. I looked up to see Bob giving me a quizzical look.

"It's an old habit from grade school," I said. "I used to smell all the loose-leaf assignments the teachers handed out."

He laughed, "The ones that came off the ditto machines."

"Yes, I swear that fresh purple ink gave me a little contact high."

We spent a couple of minutes double-checking the figures and paperwork inside. "You said you were from Dallas, right?" he asked, cutting into my concentration.

"I sure did. North Dallas, to be exact."

"I was finishing up your paperwork from our first meeting and remembered there were a couple of customers named Sullivan in the downtown Dallas branch. I think one of them was named Tim?"

My father's name was Tomas; his friends called him Tom. Perhaps my friendly banker was confusing the two. My father worked downtown and deposited his checks in that bank for almost twenty-eight years; they might have known each other.

I didn't want to encourage the connection, though. "My sister and I tried to count all the Sullivans in the Dallas Metro-Plex when we were in grade school. We gave up that idea when we opened the phone book and saw at least five pages of them."

Bob nodded, and we moved on without any further family questions.

"Each investor will have to put in a minimum of twenty-five hundred dollars," he said as he read and fiddled with his lighter. "There is no maximum. You can have fifty investors or one, it doesn't matter to us. If we factor in closing costs, inspections, and the like, you'll need to come up with almost three hundred and thirty-seven thousand dollars.

I let out a long whistle. I'd run the base numbers but forgot to add in all the extra expenses. "That's a chunk of money" were the only words I could get out of my mouth.

"You're sure you don't want to ask your parents? This is going to be a lot of work."

"I am one hundred percent absolutely sure."

He slid the folders across the table in my direction. "Okay, this is your homework. Get some investors and let's get this bar of yours opened."

When I arrived back at my car, I placed the stack of investor packets on the passenger seat and started the engine. This was it. This was the beginning of my turning a very long dream into reality. I knew half the drinking population in this town; I couldn't imagine it would be that hard to find a couple of handfuls of investors.

The valet guy gave me a wry smile as I handed him my keys. I just went ahead and answered the question I was sure he was going to ask. "Park it anywhere you want. I'm going to be here all night."

I walked in, paid, and there was Alex.

"Hey," she called out. "You're here again. How ya doing?"

"Great," I said, giving her a hug and sidestepping the remark about being here again. I was sure she had figured out why I kept coming back.

"How about you? How's your other job going?"

"Not bad," she said, beaming. "I got a call back for a movie I really want to be a part of." She spun her empty tray around like it was an oversized Frisbee. "Who knows, maybe I'll get it."

"I hope you do. I think you'd be a fabulous movie star."

"Ha, I'm not sure movie star is my goal, but an actor that's making most of my money acting instead of waitressing would be a great start."

I could relate to that. I didn't have to be the biggest or best bar owner in town either but making my money as a bar owner instead of just a bartender would be nice.

"You meeting someone?" she asked with a bit of mischief in her voice.

I blushed. "Yeah, Brad. Have you seen him?"

"Yeeeep, He's hanging out with Ripley at a table between the back bar and the second stage." She batted her eyelashes at me a couple of times and deadpanned, "with January."

I looked at the floor and scratched the back of my neck.

She stopped spinning her tray and playfully hit me with it. "What kind of beer do you want tonight?"

"How about a Miller Genuine Draft."

"You got it. One ice-cold MGD coming up. I'll see you over there."

I stood there for a beat to see if she was going to say something or warn me about January being in a cult. Maybe she didn't know. Ha, that was impossible, that girl knew everything.

I walked down the stairs, listening to my new favorite song "Give it Away." A guy in the corner was celebrating his birthday with five girls giving him a lap dance at the same time. They'd tussled his hair and untucked his shirt. I could hear him laugh out, "Oh, no, don't take my shoes off."

Just past the second stage, I found Brad and Ripley sitting at the table. Just like Alex had said, January was with them, bending over, talking to Ripley.

Undetected, I had the luxury of gawking at her. She wasn't a big person, but she looked very strong. She had nice broad shoulders and a curvy, athletic body. Her legs weren't long, but they looked like they could crack a lesser man in half.

She was wearing a short red fringed dress that clung tight to her body and swished with even the slightest movement. Her shoes matched her outfit, red leather with a gold metal heel. How in the hell did she walk and dance on a 6-inch heel made of *metal*?

January was the first one in the group to notice me. She gave me one of her smiles that made the sides of her eyes crinkle, and hurried over to greet me.

"Hello, friend," she said while closing the gap between us.

My insides ignited. I was her friend now, and not just any friend but her first friend in years. She was so adorable that I wanted to toss her over my shoulder and run right out of there.

I reached out to shake her hand, but she cracked up. She bypassed my indecision and stepped into my arms.

"Is it okay if we do this? I mean, I know we've hugged and sat together before, but it feels different now, and I don't want to get you in trouble with the girls in your group."

She stopped embracing me. "I'm going to tell anyone who asks that you're a really good customer. We always give them more attention, so the girls won't be suspicious."

I raised one eyebrow. "Does that include hanky-panky stuff?"

I'd heard of dancers that do other things for money, in and outside of clubs. I was pretty sure it was more popular in places that had darker corners and private rooms.

She stepped back. "I'm a stripper, not a Hooters waitress."

I roared.

January was holding in her laugh wagging her finger. "I really shouldn't say things like that, but those girls are always talking shit about dancers. Like they have the moral high ground because they don't take off their clothes for money. Well, most of us dancers think it's a little inappropriate to wear their uniforms in broad daylight, in front of *families*."

It was nice to see her back to her normal self. Maybe someday she would be this way in her whole life and not just at the club.

She straightened up, wiped under her eyes, and made a gesture for us to go over to the table. She pulled out the chair next to Brad, suggesting I sit. I shook my head no; I wasn't going to sit down before her.

She patted the back of the chair and shot me a warm smile. I sat. That smile could get me to do a multitude of sins, most of which were probably illegal. She walked in front of me and sat right on my lap. This was an unexpected bonus.

"Wow," I said after she sat down. "You are lighter than you look. How much do you weigh?" All three of them shot me a look. January's look was accompanied by a giggle that shook her body enough to vibrate my leg.

"Oh shit, that's not what I meant. You're just so strong, I would think all that dense muscle would weigh more. You're actually very light."

Without missing a beat, she said, "I'm one-hundred-and-three pounds, five-feet-four inches tall, 34-24-34."

"You rattled that out fast."

"I get asked that question about ten times a night."

Ripley nodded in agreement.

"I've condensed it down," January continued, "so I can spit the answers out quickly."

I squinted, doing my best to understand.

She continued. "It's about money and timing. I have to fit everything I do and say into the song that's currently playing, so I can ask for a dance when the next song begins."

"Ah, that makes sense."

"It's stripper math," she went on. "The average song is about four minutes long, which goes into sixty minutes, fifteen times. If you make an average of fifteen dollars per song, that gives you the base opportunity to make two-hundred twenty-five dollars an hour.

"Now, deduct the time you need to get from one table to another, redress between songs, make light conversation, and order a drink. That leaves you nine songs an hour. You typically get on stage three times a night, which takes about thirty minutes each—that's a deduction. You'll also have to feed yourself, take bathroom breaks, and freshen up—all deductions.

"The hard facts are, if you're going to spend the evening trading dollars for dances, you're going to end up exhausted and not have much to show for it. The most efficient way to make actual money is to starve yourself, limit your liquid intake, and luck into a big tipper."

We all sat there slack jawed.

Ripley was the first to break the silence. "No wonder I don't make as much money as you do."

Her strategic brain was so hot. I'd bet having to survive had taught her how to be acutely aware of her surroundings.

January smiled in Ripley's direction, and she returned the gesture by moving her chair closer. They spent several minutes chatting and laughing while I talked with Brad.

I leaned toward him. "Did you tell Ripley about January's situation?"

"I did, and she promised she wouldn't tell anyone."

"Not even Misha? I know those two are close, and Misha is dating Rich and...."

"Not even her," he said while mindlessly clinking the ice in his empty drink. "Besides, everyone already thinks it's a cult, which makes it an easy secret to hide."

We made plans to go to a Longhorns football game the next Saturday and then talked about finding investors for my club.

"Dude, you know tons of people that would want to be a part of the bar," Brad said.

I looked at him, disbelieving. "I thought that too, until I started reaching out to people. All of a sudden, the amount I needed and my potential failure had me second-guessing myself. My father called me last week asking me if I had started applying for a real job yet. I feel like I'm being squeezed from all sides."

"I bet my parents would be interested," Brad said, breaking into my downward spiral. "My dad is always going on about how Sixth Street has so much investment potential. I would ask every friend you have, their parents, and the other bar owners in town. Hell, I'd even ask some of the dodgy drug dealers that drive up to the club in their shiny new Porsches."

"Are you trying to get my legs broken?"

"They only break your legs if you don't pay them back," he said, and then thanked Alex for bringing him another drink.

"Do you want anything else, James?"

"No, I'm—" My mind was hijacked by the feeling of each of January's butt cheeks flexing, one at a time, on my leg.

I gave January a small poke in the ribs and finished what I'd been saying with a laugh. "But let's see if the girls need anything."

January squealed, "I don't need anything," as she popped six inches off my lap.

Ripley ordered another drink, and she and Brad started canoodling, giving me and January a sense of privacy.

She sat back, moving her hands around in a defensive motion, anticipating another poke.

"I won't do it again," I promised. "Won't the girls notice you're not working?"

"Nah, I have lots of customers that pay me for my time rather than for dances."

As she answered my question, she reached over and touched my watch.

"My parents gave me that as part of my gift for graduating from UT," I told her.

She bit her lip and rolled my hand over. Her cold fingers unbuckled the thick leather strap. "Wow, it's much heavier than my Swatch."

She examined it like it was a precious commodity.

"I like Gucci," I said. "They make beautiful dress watches that don't scream, 'I'm a rich asshole' the way Rolexes do."

"I like the red and green stripes on the face. It's a beautiful preppy detail."

There was a hint of longing in her words. As if, at some point in her life, she had lost things that meant a lot to her.

Chapter 8

Under the Milky Way Tonight

Jewels

I lifted a large waxy leaf and stuck my finger into the soil to check the moisture level, then placed the hose above the plant and squeezed the nozzle.

Watering the plants had become my new favorite lesson. Frank was teaching me how to care for something besides myself. I loved how responsive they were to attention. The added bonus was getting to be outside. The minute I pulled the sliding glass door shut, I felt a little separated from the growing tension inside.

Four giant Boston ferns hung in the corners of the large square porch. They were accompanied by every imaginable shape and size terracotta pot. Among other things, we had Chinese evergreens, spider plants, philodendrons, and a huge asparagus fern named Botticelli.

During the summer, these plants had to be watered twice a day, but in fall and winter, I could stretch it out to every third day. Regardless, if they needed watering, I still came out as much as possible to hang out with them.

I looked up through the large patio doors to find a very worried Liz standing there. She quietly pulled the heavy door open, walked past me, and nodded at me to follow her.

Why would she want to talk to me in private? I watched her walk down the steps to the tall hedges in the middle of the yard, and waited until she was out of sight before following. Between steps, I could hear my pulse roaring in my ears.

"Am I in trouble?" I choked out when I reached her.

"No, why would you think that?"

Because I had a very cute, secret friend I liked at the club, and I was terrified Frank knew.

"I'm just kidding," I said with a smile as I waved it off.

She pinched her forehead and pressed on. "I was just talking to Steve; he said a new woman had come to class last night."

I reached over and swept a stink bug off the hedge, waiting for why that mattered. New people came to classes all the time.

"And," she said, waving her hands, "he also mentioned she was beautiful, French, and Frank was giving her a lot of attention."

"French?"

She nodded indifferently as if her being French wasn't very remarkable or her point.

"Okay, that's interesting, but I'm sure it's nothing. He was probably making her feel at home. Right?" I asked, almost to myself, not wanting it to be true. "He's not ready to replace Dylan, is he?"

"I don't know," she answered while looking around the yard to be sure we were alone. "He sent her to the club very early in their romance, and now he's flirting with this new chick."

"Did Steve say *flirting,* or did he say *giving her a lot of attention*?"

She gave me an exasperated look, "He said *giving her a lot of attention* in a way that made it seem like he was trying to suggest Frank was flirting with her."

I rocked back on my heels. "Well, he can't have another girl. We don't have room."

I said this as a halfhearted joke to mask what I was thinking. I didn't want Dylan to be hurt by him. I knew it wasn't any of my business, and if Frank heard me talking about it, he'd be pissed. I'd get the "you can't assume you know what lessons I'm teaching Dylan" speech, and then I'd be ostracized until I learned to stop meddling.

I let out a labored breath. "Does Dylan know any of this?"

"I'm not sure."

The patio door swished open, and we froze. I pointed to the side of the house, suggesting Liz go in that direction to get back inside. I peeked around the corner and saw Steve inspecting the plants.

"Hi there," I said while walking up to meet him. Steve was a delightful man and one of my favorite people in the group. His laid-back attitude and calm demeanor made him very approachable.

"These plants look great," he said.

"Thank you, we have a pretty good thing going. I tend to them, and they keep me grounded."

"I can feel it. Plants are very reflective of the energy from the people around them."

I looked at the plants closest to me. Were they starting to show my confusion and guilt?

"I dropped by to take measurements for a wine rack Frank wants me to build. I was checking to see if you needed anything or if there was anything I could do for you."

I busied myself with turning the plants a quarter of a turn so I wouldn't ask him about class last night. "I don't need anything at the moment, thanks for asking."

"Anytime. How are you doing, by the way? I haven't seen you around lately."

"I've been working a ton. But maybe now that you're building a wine rack, I'll see you more often. Did Frank mention where he would get the wine to fill it up?"

"He's adding it to our weekly offerings."

My eyes darted from the plant I was inspecting up to Steve. "We, the main group, are buying the wine? How large is the rack?"

"Yes, and not just your run-of-the-mill table variety. He wants hard-to-find vintage wines and expensive champagne. The rack holds up to two hundred and fifty bottles."

I took in a slow breath so I wouldn't choke on the information. We wanted Frank to have what he wanted. But I thought that was what he got with all the money we gave him for our tithes and the *extra* donations, which, by my calculations, was at least nine thousand dollars a month. Now we would be giving him all of that, and the expensive wine also?

"Jewels," Tracy said, pulling open the door, "Frank wants to see you downstairs."

"Okay," I said and shot Steve a smile and a quick goodbye.

I stopped in the kitchen to wash as much dirt and guilt off me as possible. *Breathe; you're not in trouble. Frank knows nothing about your tiny friendship with James or what you wish that friendship could turn into.*

I tapped on the door and found Dylan, a tense mess standing in the middle of the room while Frank was pacing. Shit, what in the hell was going on, and what did it have to do with me? Had I done something to upset her?

"Jewels," Frank snapped in my direction. "I want you to help Dylan move her things into the room with you and Jodie."

"Okay," I said, as the tension between my shoulders began to unwind. The tension was about Dylan, not me. *Shit*—if this was about Dylan, maybe Liz was right.

I refrained from asking the question burning through my mind. *And then what?*

"Let everyone upstairs know there will be some changes around here."

I nodded. "All right."

Holy shit. What was going on? Was I the only one that saw it? Expensive wines, intriguing French women, and the never-ending pressure to make more money.

Frank left the room to head upstairs, and Dylan fell to the carpet in a puddle.

I grabbed a tissue and joined her on the floor. "Are you okay?"

She took the tissue and did her best to wrangle in her emotions. She hadn't been here very long, but she knew just as well as anyone else that crying was something done sparingly. A little was all right, but more than that was deemed dramatic and overindulgent.

I suggested we start moving her things. Frank might have gone upstairs, but he would be back soon. It only took us a couple of trips to get her stuff into my room, but it took much longer to find a place to store it all. Now there would be three of us using the closet and the bathroom.

I could tell by looking at her she was still gutted, but she was holding her own better than I thought she would—better than I had.

She grabbed her pillow off the counter. "Where am I sleeping tonight?"

Good question. Was he just moving her things up here, or was he fully separating them?

"You'll be sleeping with me until he gives us more information."

"That doesn't seem fair to you." Her chin puckered. "What did I do wrong?"

"Nothing," I answered. Then I repeated the words Jodie had once told me when I asked her the same question. "The people closest to Frank get the most attention and heal the fastest. He must think you're at a point where you don't need as much one-on-one time."

Was this true? Was it *ever* true? Jodie had told me because she believed it, and I was now telling Dylan because I believed it. Didn't I?

"It's a queen-size futon, there's more than enough room for the both of us." I lowered my voice. "Let's go to work a little early tonight." She agreed with a solid nod, and we went about our separate chores.

Dylan and I drove to the club in silence. As I parked the car, I said, "Take as much time getting ready tonight as you need, don't worry about the money. Just enjoy the space out of the house to get your bearings. That's what I do."

"You do?"

I wanted to tell her I'd spent many nights here, hiding my emotions in plain sight and in the comfort of strangers, but couldn't. I didn't want her to know I wasn't always full of unbending gratitude for how Frank taught his lessons.

"I think we all do it, but probably in different ways. Sometimes you just need a little time to integrate new ideas. Let's go in and see if the atmosphere helps."

Walking up to the door, I proposed we split a quarter's worth of candy. "The endorphins you get from the chocolate and boost from the caffeine might cheer you up."

She laughed at me. "Split them? Tonight, I need a whole quarter's worth."

I told her to sign in for both of us, and I'd go get it from the machine. I went into the dressing room from the back bar entrance with two shot glasses full of M&M's.

"Damn, these are good," she said, giving me a sheepish grin. "Do you ever wish we could drink?" She immediately covered her mouth with her hand.

I didn't want her to feel bad about what she had said, so I answered quickly. "Every fucking day."

She snorted. "Just one glass of wine, that's all, just one."

I agreed and wished I could suggest we have one now, but logistically it would be another secret I'd have to lie about. At least all my James secrets were private. Having a secret you shared with someone else was more complex, and impossible to control.

She moved her gaze to a spot just behind me. I turned to see what she was looking at. "Oh no, that's not a good idea."

"Come on, we're the only ones down here. No one will know."

I closed my eyes in disbelief but couldn't hide my smile. "We don't even know whose glass that is."

She got up and snatched it off the counter. "Who cares," she said and dumped half its contents into her mouth.

"Holy shit!" I said as she handed me the glass.

"Our little secret."

"This is way bigger than a little secret."

She grinned at me, and I took a sip. The sweet liquid slid down my throat, leaving a bittersweet residue in its wake. I wanted to savor the moment and the wine, but I was afraid someone would see us, so I guzzled down the rest. She took the glass from me and put it in the bus tub.

We took our time finishing our chocolate and putting on our makeup. I felt like I was on vacation. The warmth from the wine had taken the sharp lines out of our earlier situation.

"Where did you grow up?" I asked her, my words round and soft on the edges. "I mean, of all the people in the group, I know the least about you."

She gave me a tipsy grin. "I'll tell you, but it will be the second secret you'll have to keep."

"What, is it a real secret? Is there something salacious about where you grew up?"

"Sadly, no, I'm from South Carolina. It's more the fact that we're sitting here talking to each other about personal things that could get us in trouble."

She was right. I was going to change the subject when Ripley and Misha walked in. "Hey girls, mind if we join you?"

Dylan was the first to say, "No, be our guest."

It was only a couple of minutes before the dressing room filled with women from both shifts coming in and going out for the night.

"January, are you down there?" Alex called from the top part of the dressing room.

"Yes," I said, and then added after seeing her, "You look naked without your tray."

"I call it the appendage. It's making my left arm twice as big as my right."

She took a Bonnie Bell lip gloss out of her pocket to apply to her lips. "Clifford Antone and James Sullivan are both asking for you."

Adrenaline coursed through my veins; James and Clifford were here, at the same time. Clifford was a dream customer. He had the best stories about the Austin entertainment scene and was very generous with his money. But James was here, too.

Dylan looked at me. "Clifford Antone, the owner of Antone's on Burnet Road?"

I turned to her. "Yes, and you're going to sit with him tonight."

"What? Me? Why me? He's your customer."

"True, but James is also here, and he gives me more money." A huge lie, but I kept going. "I can't sit with them both at the same time."

"James brought food," said Alex turning to lean on the counter. "What should I tell them?"

"Please tell them both I'll be there ASAP." I turned to Dylan. "You're going to love Clifford. Get dressed."

"Why will I love him?"

"Because he's perfect for you tonight, and you'd be doing me a huge favor. I make a lot of money sitting with James." Ripley, Misha, and Alex gave each other a smirk, probably because they knew it wasn't true.

Ripley jumped into the conversation. "Clifford's wonderful, I've known him for years, he'll love you. You guys will get along great."

Dylan went to her locker to pick out what she was going to wear. I looked over at Ripley, and she gave me a little smile. Did she help me—on purpose?

I returned her smile and collected my makeup off the counter. I pulled a full-length satin spaghetti strap shift dress over my head and told Dylan she looked adorable in her naughty schoolgirl outfit.

Walking through the club with Dylan, I felt like a supermodel. Our tandem stride and take-no-prisoner attitudes were electrifying. This is what I imagined it would feel like to be a strong, beautiful woman.

I enjoyed watching James' reaction when he saw us coming toward him.

"He's cute," Dylan said. "He's young to be a big spender."

"You know," I said casually, "he's one of those guys that own a bunch of that Dell computer stock that keeps splitting. What do they call them?"

"Dellionaires."

I snapped my fingers. "Yes, that's it." It was getting way too easy to spit out these lies.

James stood up, gave me an unexpected peck on the cheek, and extended a hand to Dylan. "You ladies look lovely this evening. I'm James."

Dylan took his hand. "Thank you, it's nice to meet you."

"James," I said with a question in my voice. "I need to go talk to someone really quick. Will you entertain Dylan for a couple of minutes?"

A flash of confusion crossed his face. "Absolutely, I would love to," he said, smiling. "Please, Dylan, have a seat. Can I get you something to drink?"

"How about a glass of wine?" she said.

My mouth dropped open.

"I'm kidding, it's a joke," she said. "I don't need anything to drink."

I stifled a laugh and refocused my attention on James. "Thank you." I went in for a hug to whisper in his ear, "Group friend."

"Take your time," he said, giving me a quick squeeze that I hoped meant he understood what he could tell Dylan.

I hustled to the other side of the club and flung myself into the chair Clifford had waiting for me. "I need you to do me a favor and help my friend. She's had the worst day ever."

At first, he scowled at me, but quickly replaced it with a smile. "I'll miss you," he said, "but if it's important, I'm happy to help."

"Thank you, thank you so much! I'll go get her."

I led Dylan to his table and leaned in to speak softly to her. "He'll be awkward at first, but it passes quickly."

"The king of the Austin blue's scene is shy?"

"He is, it's quite endearing."

Clifford didn't stand when I introduced them. At first, Dylan looked a little put out, but she let him look her over.

"I love your shoes!" he said, pointing his chubby finger toward the floor.

Her lips broke into a smile as she approached him. "Thank you. They're impossible to walk in," she said, climbing into the chair. "But I love them so much."

I took in a deep satisfying breath. He would treat her well, and she wouldn't have to worry about making money tonight. I left them to it and headed to the DJ booth so I could hand Sean forty dollars to put me farther down the list. He winced but spared me the lecture.

I was completely free for the next hour and a half.

When I returned to James, I gave him the longest, closest hug I could without drawing attention to us.

"Oh my," he exhaled into my ear. "The fabric of your dress is so thin, you feel naked!"

We pulled away as a wave of warmth rolled through me. He took my hand and led me to my chair.

"You're making it hard for me to be a gentleman, January."

"Sorry about that," I said, fanning myself.

"I wanted to bring you something, but I wasn't sure if that was ok, so I decided on something digestible. You know, leave no evidence behind."

I grinned and asked him what was in the box.

He flicked his finger on the side of the container. "Fish, of course."

"So, you remembered that sarcastic comment I had quipped the first night I met you about the girls at The Candy Store smelling like fish?"

"Oh, I caught it all right, hook, line, and sinker. One of many things you did that evening that made me so attracted to you."

I covered my face to hide the heat pouring into my cheeks.

He wrapped his warm hands around my wrists and gently moved them back to my lap. "Attracted to you in a *friendly* way, that is."

I let out a long relaxing breath as he handed me a plastic fork. We began enjoying our dinner straight out of the box.

While my tongue was tingling from the earthy, mesquite-blackened fish, James rolled his sleeves up. I swallowed and pushed past the urge to reach out and touch his smooth forearms.

"Would it be all right if I got you a real gift?" he asked between bites.

"I'm not sure how that would work. I definitely can't take it home with me," I said, taking a quick sip of my water.

"You don't have a locker here you can keep it in?"

"I wish, but there aren't enough lockers for both the day and night girls. We have to cart our stuff in and out of the club every time we work."

I took another bite and watched his expression while he worked out an idea in his head.

"Maybe you could get me something if it's tiny and easy to hide."

"Okay," he said while waving around his fish-laden fork. "Challenge accepted!"

It was nice being at the table with him alone. Outside the loud music and half-naked women walking around, it was what I imagined a dinner date with an attractive man would be like.

"Do you enjoy being a dancer?"

"Secretly, I love going on stage."

His brows lifted. "You do?"

"Yes, I think it's what it would have felt like to be in sports in high school."

He wiped the corners of his mouth with his napkin. "I would have pegged you for a gymnast."

"I tried that and soccer, but by the time I was in high school, it was too late. I had no raw talent in either sport and hadn't been practicing like other kids my age."

"Why didn't you start them earlier?"

"I got moved around a lot. And by that, I mean I didn't go to the same school or live with the same adults for more than a couple of years."

He put down his fork, giving me his full attention. "May I ask why?"

I gave him the abbreviated version of how as a young child, I hadn't understood the repercussions of my parents' divorces, how I spent large swaths of my young life wondering where various parts of my family were—and if they'd ever come back.

Where were my mother, half-sister, and my stepfather? Where did they go? Would I ever see my aunts and uncles again? Suddenly, I had a brand-new family, but they were also gone a couple of years later. *Why did everyone keep leaving me?*

I took in a large gulp of air. "By the time I was in junior high, I had a horrible attitude. I got old enough to start doing my own moving around, which was the beginning of six more moves with three different people before I graduated from high school."

James reached up and caught a tear running down my face with his thumb.

"I felt like I abandoned them the same way I felt abandoned by the others. I made a promise to myself I'd never leave anyone again."

I stared down at my hands, worried about how far I'd gone in telling him. "Too much?"

"Not even close. Keep going."

I rolled my eyes. "I sound like such a victim. To be honest, by the time I was in my early teens, my predominant state of mind was rage, and my typical course of action was destruction. I started acting out and punishing everyone around me.

"I decided if I wasn't good enough to be loved, I'd be bad enough to have to pay attention to." I breathed past a tightness in my chest. "I incinerated all my relationships, burning all my bridges."

If the look on James's face was trying to convey understanding, it failed; all I could see was pity.

"January, even under the best circumstances, that must have been very difficult."

I swallowed around a lump in my throat. "I think it added up over time. Eventually, I ran out of places to put all the hurt, confusion, and guilt. That's when the anxiety attacks showed up. Frank often quoted Carl Jung's famous saying, 'What you resist persists.' He said he would help me integrate the things I stuffed down, so I could have a normal life."

The second the words came out of my mouth, I considered my surroundings and where I lived. I didn't have anything close to a normal life.

I looked up to see Victoria barreling toward us. Whew, I was ready to talk about anything else. I would have met her away from the table, but she was moving too quickly.

I looked James dead in the eye. "Cult friend, incoming." I corrected myself quickly. "Group friend, I mean."

He shot me a confused look just as Victoria slipped past him.

"Hi," she said, spinning a chair around and plopping into it. "Mind if I barge in for a second?" she asked him and started whispering in my ear.

He leaned back in his chair and took a few sips from his Heineken.

Victoria told me that Tracy wasn't feeling well and wanted to know if she could ride home with Dylan and me. I was nodding yes when Victoria leaned over and opened the box of what was left of our food.

"Oh my God, is that Mahi Mahi from City Grill?"

James pulled his attention away from the table of guys toasting and chanting *Wing defender, wing defender, wing defender, fuck you!* "Yes," he said. "Wish I'd brought more; I'd feel bad offering you our leftovers."

"Don't feel bad at all," she said, as she snatched up the box and walked away.

James grinned and used his beer bottle to point back to the drunken table. "I swear that's the gamer prodigy that works at...." He waved his hand in an attempt to remember.

"Yes, that's him. I'm not sure what the company's name is either. They're rowdy but very kind and generous. They come in after hitting important milestones on their projects. When they get drunk enough, they start talking about making a movie about the game they created." I smiled over at them. "Dorks on Jägermeister."

"I believe we were talking about you before your friend came over."

"I think what we're talking about now is infinitely more interesting, especially since I'm at work."

"Oh shit," he said, enveloping my hands. "you're right. We kind of slipped into the conversation, I didn't mean to pry."

I rubbed the top of his hand with my thumb. "I'm the one that gave you the 'real' answer instead of the blow-off version."

We sat there for a second, staring into each other's eyes, silently letting the shared moment sink in. *I bet he's a great kisser.*

"Sooooo," I said, getting us back on topic, "shall the nerds inherit Austin?"

He took my lead and moved away from the conversation about my past. "Harris and I were talking about that a while ago. The heart of Austin is music, but its revival and financial health will come from the tech companies and the people working for them. They're the ones that are advancing the downtown regeneration projects and that can afford all the fancy high-rises that are proposed to go up in the next ten years."

He got quiet for a second. "That's the other reason I know my bar will do so well. Right now, people have to go downtown to hang out. In the near future, they'll actually live down there. It will be their neighborhood."

I opened my mouth to agree, but Sean's voice crackled through the club. *Christine, Jennifer, Dawn, and January, you're next on stage.*

I scrunched my face as tight as I could.

"What a look!"

"I'd rather stay here with you."

Chapter 9

Avalon

I lifted the receiver off the cradle, pulled up the antenna, and dialed the first number on the day's list. While the phone rang on the other end, I took my breakfast plate into the kitchen and poured myself another cup of coffee. I wouldn't say that looking for investors was going particularly well. As it turned out, asking people to trust me with their money was much more complicated than I thought it'd be.

Besides the obligatory ten minutes of small talk each call took, I also had to answer a plethora of hard questions. The toughest one was how long would it take to get their investment back.

This was an impossible question to answer. If the club did well, they would get it back soon; if it didn't do well, it would take a lot longer. If it failed—if *I* failed—they would never see their money again.

I slouched into my chair while fidgeting with a golf ball. The number I dialed rang ten times before I hung up. *It's 1991, people, get an answering machine already.*

I placed an asterisk by their name to call them again the next day. The next couple of numbers were family acquaintances, so I removed them from the list. They'd eventually mention it to my father, and then he would know I was actively going against his wishes.

The following two calls were very polite, but they were unable to invest. They both said something along the lines of, "Please let me know when you open; I can't wait to see the place." That was encouraging at least. If they couldn't invest, they could still be customers.

I flipped through my Rolodex for a friend's number who worked at Jeffrey's on West Lynn. He made the most money of all the people I knew in the service industry. Jeffrey's high-end gourmet prices and ten-percent tips added up to a hefty chunk of change.

"Hey, Sullivan, what's up?" I pulled the phone away from my face and stared at it, puzzled. "James, are you there?"

I laughed at the receiver while putting it back to my ear. "Yes, I'm here. How in the hell did you know it was me?"

"I got one of those caller ID boxes. I can tell who's calling me before it hits my answering machine. It's a whole new level of screening."

This new box could be a better way to avoid my father's calls.

"Word on the street is you're opening your own club."

My muscles tightened; the news was spreading fast. Shit, if I failed, everyone was going to know. I could just see the look on my father's face if that happened. He'd give me that *you tried your best, son. Time to give up this immature dream and become a man.*

My friend told me to call him back in a few months. By that time, I wouldn't need investors; it'd be too late.

I wished I could call January. Besides the fact that I didn't have her number, I didn't think calling a cult would be a very good idea. But, I would do anything to hear her sensual melodic voice at a normal volume instead of half-shouting over the loud music at the club.

I plugged away, calling everyone I knew. I might as well be a telemarketer. How did anyone do that job day in and day out? Sales of any kind were challenging for me. As were advertising, event planning, purchasing, and bookkeeping, all of which I was going to have to master until I made enough money to hire people to do them for me.

I picked up my golf ball and began pacing my apartment, letting out a small huff. My father was in sales. Not telemarketing, per se, but *Technical Sales Representative* was on his business card, under the Southwestern Bell logo.

During summer break, he and I would leave the house at the same time. He had been heading to work; I had been spending my day on the course. There were golf memberships, lessons, practices, clubs, and even clothes, all of which were funded by my father.

I used to think he was too uptight to appreciate the finer things in life. That was before I understood how expensive everything was. He worked his ass off so we could do anything we wanted.

We were too obstinate to see the other's point of view until the day he got replaced by someone with half his experience. He never thought it would ever happen to someone with his dedication and seniority in the company. He was only three years away from his fat pension and a gold watch.

That experience didn't make him an instant believer in ditching corporate shackles, but it helped him see that job security wasn't what it used to be. He ended up taking the shitty severance package they offered him and then an early retirement.

I had no interest in putting all my energy into a company and waiting for them to decide when I'd retire or get discarded altogether. Besides, I'd heard them say computers would soon take over everyone's job. Well, we'd have to see how that turned out. Either way, people would always want to drink and be social. I intended to be there when they got thirsty.

As the deep bass from the song *Billie Jean* pulsed through the club, I shook my head. "You don't have a big nose," I said to January, darting my eyes around the club. I pointed to someone a couple of tables from us. "That guy," I said, wagging my finger so she would look at him. "Now, he has a big nose."

She folded her arms across her chest and looked at me, unimpressed. I loved how mischievous she was being this evening.

I pinched my brows together and did my best to look stern, but I couldn't keep the grin off my face. I covered my smile with my hands, but my body shook from the laughter I was trying to hold in.

"Honestly," I said. "You don't have a big nose."

"I can prove that I do."

"Ha!" I doubled over, attempting to relieve the ache in my ribs. "You're ridiculous. Okay, go ahead, be my guest, prove it."

She turned, so I had a perfect shot of her profile. She stuck her tongue straight out, as far as she could, bent it upward, and touched the tip of her nose.

"Tada," she said, with her chest all puffed out.

"That only proves you have a long tongue."

She put her fists up. "That's it, we're going to the mattresses."

"You're the hottest geek I've ever met."

She rolled her eyes. "I bet you say that to all the girls."

That was an interesting comment. I wanted to tell her there were no other girls besides her, but I was afraid to upset the delicate balance our relationship was teetering on.

Her attention drifted to a table near ours.

I rolled my chair closer to hers. "What's going on over there?"

"I've noticed Victoria sits with that customer a lot." She leaned closer to me like she was telling me a secret. "More than how much she sits with him, it's the look on her face."

"What kind of look?" I asked, waiting for the punchline.

She reached up and moved an unruly cluster of hair off my forehead. "It's one of adoration."

Her eyes had a softness to them that I hadn't seen before. I leaned in a fraction closer. "I got you a gift this week."

She looked under the table as if I had hidden it there. "You did not!"

"It's in my pocket. You told me it had to be small."

"Yes, I did," she conceded.

"I couldn't wrap it," I said to lengthen the moment. "It's tiny like you instructed."

Her eyes widened with each crumb of information I gave her.

"Jeez, January, it's just a little trinket. I promise it won't be the last gift...." I let my sentence fall away as I watched her face go from curious to excited to anxious.

I took her hand and turned it upward. Her fingers twitched with anticipation. I laid a small red crystal Swarovski heart onto her palm. Her eyes closed for a couple of seconds. I sat there watching all the excitement drain out of her. "Shit, did I get you the wrong thing?"

"It's absolutely perfect," she said as she closed her hand and held it close to her chest. "It couldn't be any better."

"I doubt that. It's not even close to what I wanted to get you."

She grinned. "It's perfect for a couple of reasons, one being that I would have bought it for myself, so I won't have to hide it from anyone."

I watched her lips as she spoke. I wanted to kiss her, even if it was on the cheek. I leaned in to make my move when she spoke.

"I'm going to dance for you."

I jerked back. "You are?"

"Yes, a gift for a gift. Or maybe it's a performance for a gift? No, that's not what I mean." She sat up straight. "Dancing is a physical way to express my appreciation without anyone in the group noticing. Plus, it would strengthen our ruse of you being a big customer."

I swallowed. "You're going to take your clothes off?"

She gave me that pirate's smile. "No, just a playful dance. I'm not getting naked."

I let my shoulders drop and let out a sigh. There was no way I could handle her ninety-percent naked, dancing for me. I'd seen her do it on stage, and I'd seen her dance for numerous other men. But I couldn't handle it right now.

She waggled her brows as she placed her heart next to my Shiner Bock and stood up.

Moving in front of me, she bent over, grabbed the back of my knees, and jerked my body forward, forcing me to recline further into my chair. Her lips pulled into a devilish smile as she spread my legs so she could dance between them.

"Oh God," I breathed out.

She steadied me with her eyes. Placing one hand on the tops of both my knees, she slowly walked them up my body, one on my thigh, the other on the opposite hip, and the next in the middle of my chest. Her weight was perfectly balanced like a cat.

"I can feel your heart pounding under my hand," she purred with hooded eyes.

I nodded dumbly, unable to use words.

She turned, folded her body in half, and dangled her head between my legs, close to my right foot.

What the hell? Was she trying to give me a heart attack? As she dragged her head up against my calf, her hands went into the bottom of my pants. She rested the side of her cheek on the top of my knee. The hairs on my legs rose as her chilly fingers moved across them. I swallowed as she flattened her palms against my leg and slowly pushed my sock down like she was taking off my boxers.

The look in her eyes exuded sex as if she was going to fuck me like a porn star. I wrapped my arms around my waist and chuckled. She was a master at being both arousing and silly at the same time. I was in so deep.

She pulled my pant leg back to its appropriate place and rolled the weight of her body to a standing position, one vertebra at a time. The laser lights from the stage peeked through her disheveled hair.

Somewhere, I heard the DJ introduce another girl, and the music changed to Don Henley's "Boys of Summer."

Her chest rose as she breathed in the song. She put her foot on my knee and arched her back. I gazed at her perfect silhouette as she lifted her foot straight into the air, making her dress cascade down her leg. I covered my eyes. I couldn't take anymore.

I heard her giggle over the music as she sat on my lap. She separated my fingers as she peeked in at me. All I'd have to do to kiss her was move my hands.

"Hi there."

I exhaled. "Holy shit, January."

"Jewels. My real name is Jewels."

I repeated it like it was a newfound treasure.

She moved closer to my ear. I prayed for that kiss, but she told me a secret instead. "My last name is Heart."

Her name was Jewels Heart. She trusted me with her real name. I reached over and picked up the token gift I had gotten her.

She took it from me again. "I told you it was perfect."

Chapter 10

West End Girls

Jewels

"You okay, January?" Ripley asked as I rifled through my Caboodles case in search of my blush.

I wanted to answer, *I don't think so*, but instead I lied. "I'm fine. Why do you ask?"

"I just told you something, and you didn't respond."

"You did? Oh Lord, I'm so sorry. I think I'm going to get my period; I can't concentrate on anything." I frowned. It was another lie; I was nowhere near that time of the month. There was just no way I could be honest about the news I'd received earlier.

I spun my mascara wand in its tube while she commiserated with me. "I do the same thing, like days before and after. As if the act of bleeding somehow makes me incapable of holding a single, rational thought in my head for longer than, like, a millisecond."

It was so sweet; I was counting lies, and she was counting coincidences.

"What I was saying," she said, starting again. "This is my friend from Corpus Christi. She works at a club there called Crude."

"Wow, I'm a little off my game tonight," I said, standing up. I extended my hand to her and twisted my face into an apology. "I'm January. It's very nice to meet you. What's your name?"

I covertly assessed her as was customary in any competitive topless bar. High maintenance is how I would have best described her. She was tall and tan, with long highlighted bleach-blonde hair and perfect fake breasts. She was Barbie on steroids.

She shook my hand using only her fingertips. "My name is Trixie."

"What a fun name," I said, looking at my hand to see if it was dirty. "Is Crude nice?"

"It's not bad. There's a lot of military and oil refinery money in Corpus."

Ripley pointed at me with the same hand her cigarette was in. "January has making money down to a science."

Trixie looked me up and down. Her bemused gaze gave away what she was probably thinking, how could someone as short as me, with pasty white skin and natural breasts, make money?

I would have welcomed a new girl on any other night, but I didn't have it in me this evening. I took the top off my lipstick, waiting to see what she'd say. After a moment, I finally pointed at myself. "January is a workaholic, so it just seems like she makes a lot." I'd ended up saying more to Ripley than her friend.

Trixie nodded in what looked like understanding. She didn't strike me as overly friendly.

Just past her fancy department store makeup was a strange-shaped, light gray object that resembled a phone.

My mind reached back to a conversation I had had with James the last time he was here. He had told me he was going to buy one of those Motorola *brick phones*. I wasn't sure what it was.

"It's like a car phone," he had told me, "but you can carry it around with you."

"Ha!" I had laughed. "Whatever! There's no way that even exists!"

He'd nodded. "They totally do. They're about the size of half a brick." He'd motioned with his hands. "It has a thick antenna on the top, like a walkie-talkie."

I'd looked at him like he was crazy, and he'd looked at me like I lived in a cave. "Really," he'd laughed. "I plan on getting one if I close on the loan for the bar. I think having the phone will be much better than using a pager. It will help me keep in touch with all the contractors, liquor distributors, permit offices, and such. Plus," he added with a sparkle in his eye, "I can write it off on my taxes. I'll bring it in when I get one."

I lifted my hand and pointed my finger toward the object. "Is that a phone?"

Ripley's face lit up at my recognition, but Trixie merely looked at me like I'd finally learned how to use two-syllable words.

"Yes," she said, picking it up. I thought she was going to show it to me, but she turned and placed it in her locker.

Ripley gave an apologetic smile.

January, you're next on stage.

I shrugged my shoulders, gave the girls a wave goodbye, and headed to the booth to pick my music.

Sean was adjusting the music volume when I walked through the curtain. "Ah, great, you're here."

"Yes, I am," I said, sagging up against the wall of albums.

He stopped what he was doing. "What's going on, January?"

"Nothing."

He tilted his head. "You look very put together, but I'm not sure you're.... Are you positive you're okay? Is there something you want to talk about?"

Yes, there were lots of things I wanted to talk about, but not to my empathetic DJ. I was waiting to talk to James.

"Ugh, I've been working too much. You pick my music tonight."

"Really?" asked Sean. "Anything?" He pronounced *anything* carefully to make sure we agreed. Having a weak set on stage could ruin your night. It was the only way to advertise yourself, so you had to make the most of it.

"Yeah, sure, anything." Who knew, maybe something he picked would help. "Make me a star!" I said, making *jazz hands* while walking back into the dressing room.

The song playing came to an end, and Sean encouraged the crowd to give the beautiful Victoria a round of applause. He continued over the mic with drink special information as she exited the stage, all sweaty, clutching her clothes and smiling.

"How is it out there?" I asked. "It doesn't look very busy."

She plopped into an empty chair, catching her breath. "Not bad, really. There aren't many people, but they're tipping."

A slight grin crept over my face as I heard the song "Just a Touch of Love" begin to play.

Victoria bobbed her head. "C&C and the Music Factory, very nice."

"Yeah, I let Sean pick my music," I said half-heartedly and walked onto the stage.

It was a lovely song, and he followed it up with "Keep on Movin'" by Soul II Soul. But I was still in a funk. I gathered my clothes off the floor and headed for the second stage. According to the TABC rules, the only place we were allowed to walk without our clothing on was between stages. Even then, we had to hold our outfits in front of our chests. We followed their rules because they occasionally monitored and raided the clubs. If they busted you while you were doing a table dance, both you and the customer got arrested. The club would bail its dancers out of jail, but we had to pay them back and got suspended for a week.

There were no handrails on the second stage, so it was expected that you would assist the dancer who was coming down after her finished set. I reached for Victoria's hand as I stepped up a couple of steps, and she stepped down, meeting in the middle.

"Be careful on the back corner," she said, pointing at the one directly across from us. "Someone must have had a ton of lotion on, it's very slippery over there."

I nodded and tried to let go of her hand. "Is everything all right?" she asked over the sound of frat guys singing along to the beginning of Def Leppard's "Rock of Ages."

"Yes, I'm fine, just a little tired tonight," I shouted over the music.

She gave me a prolonged look and then finally let me go. I dredged up the stairs telling myself I only had to pretend to be happy for two more stages.

I got off the third stage and forced myself to visit as many tables as I could before James showed up. At the last table, I said my goodbyes while putting on my skater-style dress, turned a tight circle to leave, and ran straight into James's chest.

"Hello, beautiful friend," he said, grinning down at me.

I closed my eyes and let the relief of seeing him loosen my shoulders. He gave me a questioning glance. "Let's find somewhere to sit. You look like you have something on your mind."

He took my hand and led us to a table in a quiet corner. I sat right on his lap. I had things I wanted to tell him, but this wasn't the place, and I had a customer waiting for me.

Once situated, I let the full weight of my body rest against his chest. I took a couple of deep breaths when he asked, "Are you smelling me again?"

He placed his Michelob on the table and wrapped me up in his arms.

"Yes," I said, burying my face into the crook of his neck. "Most of the men I dance for—and Frank—are forty or older." I took in another deep, satisfying breath. "You smell like youth and possibilities; they all smell like old age and disappointment."

His body rumbled underneath me. "Hah... I know you don't have much time. Are you going to tell me what's wrong?"

"No, not now. I have one more table I have to visit before I can take a break."

"Are you sure?"

"Yes," I said, worrying my upper lip.

He pointed towards a large table near the second stage. "I'll be right over there, waiting for you."

As I walked across the club, I looked over to the table where James was headed. About half the guys were getting dances, and the rest were drinking and chatting.

They always looked like they were having so much fun. Their heads were held high, shoulders back, and always laughing at something. I recognized several of James' friends: Parker, Ryan, and Brad with Ripley perched happily on his lap. I didn't just want to go over there; I wanted to be one of them.

"Hello there," I said after reaching my customer. "How are you?"

He stood up to give me a hug. "I'm great, you look fantastic."

I thanked him and wished I felt half as good as he thought I looked. He was in his late sixties and the type of person that made friends everywhere he went. He had been one of my favorite customers for the last six months.

Following the very first rule of the conscientious dancer, I kept my attention on him. "What have you been up to?"

"Not much, really," he said with a mischievous twinkle in his eyes. "Just hanging out, watching the *Future Titty Dancers of America Contest*."

"What?" I asked, following his line of sight to a big-screen television by the third stage. He was watching the National Cheerleading Competition. He might be on to something. More than half the girls I worked with had been cheerleaders in high school, along with twirlers, glee club, theater, and band. There weren't many here who excelled in Quiz Bowl or were closet mathletes. But we always had a handful of girls putting themselves through college.

"I love this song," I said, nudging him, anxious to get back to James. I felt a little guilty rushing my customer, but I'd make it up to him the next time he came in.

He tapped my leg. "Great, dance for me."

I wouldn't say I liked the song, but that was irrelevant. You could find something redeemable about almost every song. This one was good because it was only four minutes long.

I did my best to pretend I felt sexy and went through all my typical movements. The music dictated the flow and attitude of my moves, allowing the bass and drums to tell me when to be soft and when to be aggressive. I used the lyrics to tell me when to look someone deep in the eyes or when to ignore them. I did it all, but I couldn't feel a thing.

The song was so short that I barely had enough time to get my dress and bra off. He shook his head. "Don't stop now."

I grinned and pouted and did everything I could to feign happy-go-sexy stripper. I just wanted to get back to James so I could lean on him more. During the song, while my back was towards the customer, I stole a glance across the club and glimpsed James lying back in his chair, smiling and enjoying a dance from...Trixie!

Oh my God! No, he was mine. He was my friend. She couldn't have him. I wasn't ready to let him go—quite yet.

Since I'd known him, I'd never seen him even smile at another woman, let alone get a dance. I had always understood that James was a whale in a vast ocean. I mean, he could have whomever he wanted, and there were plenty of women available. I just never thought he would find one in here, right in front of me.

I peeked back over there, hoping to see something different. He sure looked like he was enjoying himself.

I spun around to face my customer, doing my best to regain my come-hither demeanor, hoping his kind expression would help erase what I had just seen.

It didn't. I hadn't realized how much I liked James until this moment. I guess the plastic Barbie doll was his actual type, not me. I finished my dance, gave my customer a quick hug, and jetted off to the dressing room.

By the time I got there, I was already bawling. There were a couple of girls in there, but they weren't group girls, so I flew past them. Crying at work wasn't a rare sight. With this many people pushed into a small building for hours at a time, the mixture of menstrual cycles, alcohol, and competition was enough to push at least seven girls a night into tearful frenzies.

While trying to open my locker, I remembered James's caring instructions from the festival. *Breathe in, breathe out. Know that if I'm getting enough air, so are you.* I begrudgingly did as he had instructed so I wouldn't pass out. He had also said, *I've got you, you're safe.* Looked like he *had* her now. I bet he'd never have to say things like that to picture-perfect Trixie. Shit, they'd even have matching phones.

I kicked off my heels and stepped into my high tops. I snatched all my stuff out of my locker and jammed it into my bag. The sound of hollow metal echoed throughout the dressing room when I slammed it shut. I put my coat over my dress and headed out.

Four wide stairs from the back dressing room door led to the back bar. I only hit one of them on the way down before pushing the door open. The small room was crammed with shelves full of unopened liquor bottles, the popcorn machine, and the only other way out of the club besides the main entrance. I kicked the industrial-grade door open, ignoring all the Fire Exit Only signs.

The chilly November air hit my face like a bucket of water. The thin layer of sweat and tears on my face began to tighten. I stopped for two seconds, looking back towards the club, remembering that the eight group girls I work with would eventually notice I'd left.

I kept going.

Chapter 11

Let Me Go

James

11 Let Me Go James Parker placed his beer on the table and, while staring at a girl on the stage, asked me, "Did you hear the news that Magic Johnson has AIDS?"

I threw him a confused look, trying to figure out how the beautiful woman he was looking at reminded him of something so sad. "Yeah, I saw it on ESPN this afternoon. I'm completely bummed out about it."

"I've been watching him play since he was at Michigan State, and now he's going to die? The things they're saying about him in the press are disgusting. There's a big part of me that's afraid to have sex anymore."

Parker was one of my newer friends. He grew up here in Austin but had gone to Illinois State University to get his degree in biological sciences. After graduation, he'd been offered a position with the DeKalb Agricultural Association, but he wasn't ready to move to the Midwest straight out of school. He came back for a couple of months to party and say his goodbyes, but ended up staying here and taking a job with the Texas Parks and Wildlife Department.

"Is that why I haven't seen you with anyone lately?" I asked him, shifting my body to see if January was still with her customer. She wasn't there; hopefully, she'd be here any minute.

"Yes, that's one reason. I also just like taking a break occasionally," he said, grabbing some popcorn and popping it into his mouth. "Also, it feels like every chick I have a drink with is trying to figure out if I'm marriage material. It really takes the fun out of it."

"Yes!" I laughed in agreement. "I've noticed that as well. Most first dates have turned into an interrogation rather than a casual getting-to-know-someone. They pelt me with questions like *what kind of car do you drive? Do you own or rent?*"

"*Do you have a good relationship with your mother?*" Parker jumped in. "*How much student loan debt do you have?*"

I stopped laughing long enough to take another swig of my beer, when I noticed January over by the back bar. She was wearing her high-tops, had a coat over her short little dress, and was carrying a bright purple duffle bag. In a flash, she opened and slipped out through the door.

"What the hell," I said, putting my beer back on the table.

"What's going on?"

"I don't know," I mumbled, heading in January's direction.

I stopped just short of trampling one of the waitresses. "What's behind that door?"

"Not much, kegs, bottles, coffee maker, popcorn machine, and the fire exit. Is everything okay?"

"Thank you," I said in a rush, and headed in the opposite direction to the front door to see if I could catch her. She'd have to go up a small driveway to get to the front of the club parking lot before she could leave.

I burst out the door and scared the shit out of the valet guy, who jumped back from me. "Do you want your car?"

Desperate to save time, I waved him off while running down the stairs toward the side of the building. I only saw one vehicle coming from the back lot.

I squinted into the headlights but couldn't tell if that was her. I stepped into the crunchy gravel driveway and waved my arms. The car's brakes squeaked, kicking up a plume of dust. January's makeup-streaked face and puzzled expression stared back at me. I went straight for the passenger door and got inside.

"January, are you okay?" I asked her, trying to catch my breath.

She shook her head and gasped into a small paper bag. "I'm having a nuclear-sized meltdown."

"What happened? Does this have to do with what you were going to tell me?"

She tossed me the bag and turned right onto Lamar Boulevard.

I didn't know what was happening, but I was glad to be with her. She drove a couple of blocks down the street and pulled into Threadgill's restaurant. An oversized Howdy Stranger sign bathed the parking lot with an ominous orange light.

I turned toward her. "January—Jewels, please tell me what's going on. I want to help you."

There were pools of tears under her eyes. "You... can't ... help ... me," she said, each word coming out as a cloud of condensation into the cool night air. "*You* are part of the problem."

While taking a moment to think, I reached over and turned on the heater. The crystal heart I had given her was sitting on a piece of cloth in her unused ashtray.

I grabbed it and flipped the heart around in my hand, trying to piece things together. "Okay, I'm part of the problem. I came in, got a beer, and stalked you around the club."

She sat there as I talked, her chin quivering and her breath coming in deliberate slow puffs.

I pressed on, feeling like a confused detective. "I sat with you, watched you walk away to give that guy a dance, and I..."

As I strained to remember what I did next, she sobbed. "And you got a dance from that glamazon, Trixie!"

"Oh, no, no, no," I said as realization dawned on me.

Jewels covered her face with her hands, her body shuddering as she cried. *Damn it*, I never meant to hurt her. This was horrible.

"I don't even know that girl," I said. "I didn't ask or pay for the dance or anything. I swear to you, Parker bought the dance for me. The girl told him she was new in town and not making much money, so he said, 'dance for my friend James.' I couldn't say no and hurt her feelings; she was already having a bad night and—"

She wiped at her face. "There's more."

"Oh shit, I did something else that hurt you?"

"No, it's not something you did."

Whew. My shoulders dropped back into place. "Then what was it?"

"I didn't realize how much I'd grown to like you until I felt how jealous I got."

Relief washed through my body as I took in her words. *She liked me.* She liked me on a territorial level.

I beamed at her, but she frowned back at me.

"Would it help if I stopped coming in to see you?" I didn't want to ask the question, but I wanted what was best for her, even if it would be hard for me.

She slumped a little. "I have to move out of the house."

I agreed with her. She did need to move out. The farther away she got from Frank, the better.

She shook her head and continued in a long, confusing burst. "Frank has been acting so strange lately, maybe longer than lately. And poor Dylan, she doesn't know what's going on. I think he'll break her heart the way he did mine. Now he's moved her into my room."

I pinched my eyes together and tried to concentrate. Did she just say "the way he did mine"? I'd never seen her this upset. She reached over and took the paper bag off my lap. But even though she got it ready to use, she kept talking instead.

"I thought sharing a room with her was fine, but Frank thinks it's time for me to move out. I'm so scared. I've never lived alone, and I'm afraid I'll wake up every day with an anxiety attack. And on top of all of that, now I have all of these feelings for you."

I tried not to smile at the part about her having feelings for me. "If you're so afraid, why is he making you move out?"

"Well," she said, sounding defeated, "I'm always scared. He told me he thought I was ready. He said I've been in a learning stage for many years, and it's time for me to graduate to the next level. But I think it has to do with that French girl."

It all sounded a little suspicious to me, but I wasn't sure this was the best time for me to question her group leader's intentions. French girl?

She took a deep breath, "I have no furniture, no cleaning supplies, no towels, no linens, no dishes, or a phone...." She looked up at me as if remembering I was still in the car with her. "I think *Trixie* has one of those mobile phones you told me about."

"Ugh, that chick," I said and gave her a wry smile. "I told you they existed."

The sides of her mouth began turning up a tiny bit. She let out an enormous sigh and nudged her dance bag onto the floor before folding her paper bag and placing it in the glove compartment. "I don't think I'm going to have a panic attack."

"I don't either. You did an excellent job handling all that stress."

She scooched and little closer to me. "James," she said, her voice weak, "I'm not saying everyone is right, but if I'm being honest, things have been transitioning for a while. It seems like Frank has gone from helping us mentally to helping himself financially."

I ran my hand along the back of my neck. She'd just dropped an iceberg in a full glass of water. No wonder she'd wanted to talk earlier. This made the first things she'd mentioned seem trivial, but they hadn't been at all.

She stared out the windshield. "My whole life could be a lie."

"I think that guy is a douchebag, but that doesn't negate the good things you've learned while you were there. Some of his training has really benefited you. Now you can leave the group and utilize those things the rest of your life."

She shot me a look. "I'm not leaving."

"What?"

"Frank is the only one that can help me. I can't leave the group; I don't have anyone else."

"You have me," I said gently.

She gave me a half smile. "I can't transfer my dependency from him to you. I need a little time to get stronger, to ensure I'm right and not just projecting, transferring, or even hallucinating."

I bit the side of my cheek to prevent myself from saying that I was sure that place was a cult. She was right about the dependency part, however. She needed to find her own footing in the world.

We sat there for a minute in silence before she gave me a searching look. "Too much?"

"No," I said, shaking my head. "I'm telling you. It's never going to be too much."

She reached over and tapped my hand. I had forgotten I was still holding her heart; the point had left a dent in my palm.

131

She took it from me. "I don't know what to do about my feelings for you."

"We'll take it slow, but I must admit that I enjoy knowing you like me enough to get jealous."

She laughed. "I like you enough to have almost killed that Barbie bitch."

"What will you do for the rest of the night?" I asked, hoping she'd say anything that included me.

"After you kiss me, I think I should go back to the club."

My eyes bugged out. "Are you sure?"

"It's the only thing I'm absolutely positive about right now."

She was so daring and delicate at the same time. I placed my hands on her tear-stained cheeks and kissed her forehead carefully. I pulled back, looked into her beautiful searching eyes, and then kissed them both. Each one dampened my lips with what was left of her tears. I placed three more small kisses down her cheek and planted my mouth on her swollen lips.

A groan rumbled out of me as she pressed her lips deeper into mine. I opened my mouth to taste her when a sharp squeak of the restaurant door opening pulled us apart.

It was followed by a man saying, "That was the best chicken fried steak I've ever had," while rubbing his watermelon-shaped belly.

Jewels smiled, placed the heart back in its ashtray home, and drove us back to the club.

Jewels parked, took her keys out, and stared at the building. "That door is a fire exit. It can only be opened from the inside."

"You're kidding." She wasn't kidding, the door didn't even have a handle on the outside. "Maybe Alex could help us? I'll be right back."

I ran back into the building and smiled at the door girl. She gave me a questioning glance but didn't ask me what was going on or why I had rushed out earlier. Alex was near the main stage, heading toward the back bar.

I passed by the table with all my friends. They were too busy getting dances to notice me, including Parker, who was mesmerized by a stunning full-figured girl.

When I reached Alex, her tray was overloaded with half-empty glasses. "Hey," I called out, "can I ask a huge favor of you?"

"Sure, as long as it's quick." She looked down at her tray to point out the obvious. She was busy.

I gave her a five-second account of my needs. Her mouth dropped, and her body shook from giggling. She handed me her tray and told me she'd do it. I watched her walk through the door and, seconds later, come back in with January in tow.

"You're the best," I said. "Man, this tray is heavy, and I promise to tip you well." She gave me a knowing grin and walked off.

I dropped my shoulders, exhaled, and went to sit down next to Brad and Ripley. January joined me a few minutes later, her face freshened up and her hair not entirely combed out but less of a mess than it had been in the car.

"How did it go back there?"

"Not bad. I got stuff crammed back into my locker seconds before Tracy walked through to go on stage. She asked me where I'd been and I told her I tweaked my back and was upstairs in the office looking for some Tylenol."

We spent the next hour enjoying each other's company and talking to the people around us. I was still trying to understand her past better and why that Frank guy had so much power over her.

"Did you say you've never lived alone?" I asked during a quiet moment.

She nodded. "I moved eight times in three states in the year and a half between graduating from high school and the time I met Frank. But I never lived alone. I always had a couple of roommates."

I took in her answer as she looked around the table. She'd told me a while ago that she had also moved a lot as a kid. And, during that time, she had destroyed or complicated most of her family connections. So I bet she was doing a lot of that moving fairly untethered. I only went from my childhood home to a dorm with my parents at my side, and even that had been pretty stressful.

A look of deep concentration had taken over her face.

"Whatcha thinking?"

Her mouth split into a full smile, and she leaned back onto my chest. She moved her arms to signify the scene in front of her. "Is this what normal life is like for you?"

I chuckled. "Outside the half-naked girls fawning all over my friends, this is pretty much what we do most of the time. We hang out, make plans, eat, and drink. While that's happening, we try to figure out what to do with our lives, and we watch out for one another. We don't have all the answers, but we have goals, and we're enjoying the ride. Why do you ask?"

"When I think about moving out, my mind gets flooded with all the things that scare me. The loneliness, fear of being on my own, and the possibility of having anxiety attacks. But sitting here with you and your friends, I realize I haven't considered some of the good things that may be part of it."

I enjoyed watching her figure out what a normal versus group life would look like. I wanted to do whatever I could to help her find the answers. "When do you have to be out of the house?"

"Generally, Frank wants everything he asks for done as soon as possible."

"Let me help you find an apartment. I know all the decent neighborhoods. I can be your personal chauffeur, and you can be the navigator."

"Won't your helping me use up the time you need to spend finding investors?"

"Nope, not even a little."

"Okay, then let's do it. How about Thursday late afternoon, around three-thirty? We can look for a bit, and then I'll come to work afterward."

"January," said a dancer as she stepped in front of us. "Sean is in the booth panicking and wants to know if you can go on stage next. He says he's desperate and would call it even if you could help."

January thanked the girl and waved to Sean to let him know she would be right there. "I have to go, but I'll do my best to come back."

"It's okay, really. I have a bunch of things I have to do tomorrow, and you probably have to make some more money. I'll go home after you get off the main stage."

January. Faith?

She gave him a thumbs-up, and the organ music for the George Michael song started to play. "Shoot, I guess I'm up right now."

"Go, I'll come up there and see you."

While she danced to her first song, I went to find a piece of paper and something to write with. Ten other men were waiting their turns to give her money, but this beautiful creature liked me. She had chosen me over all the other men she knew.

After she finished her customary five-second mini dance for me, she pulled out the side of her bottoms and whispered to me. "Thank you for everything."

I placed the money in her t-back. "My address is folded up in this money. You're not alone, Jewels."

Chapter 12

Running up that Hill

Jewels

"Wow," I said, breathing in through my nose and out through my mouth. "It smells like you in here."

James looked at me and grinned. "You're doing an excellent job trying to relax. Does it feel like you're going to have an anxiety attack?"

"Almost," I said, concentrating on his face. "New situations definitely raise my stress levels and increase the chances of an attack—sometimes."

"But not always?"

"I think of it this way. A plate is my mental capacity, and food is stress. If my plate is empty and somebody gives me a heaping load of food, it's okay. I can usually handle it. But, when it's already full, and I get even the smallest amount of new food, the plate will tip."

"How do you know how much food is on your plate at any given moment?"

I rocked back on my heels. "I haven't figured that part out yet."

The tension eased a bit as I looked around his place. He was much tidier than I expected; I assumed all men were slobs until they got married.

"Would a distraction help?"

"Yes, giving my mind something to do besides worry is always helpful."

"You said the apartment smelled like me. What does it smell like?"

I took a big breath. "Like Irish Spring soap, spaghetti, and some kind of cologne." I looked toward the bathroom. "May I?"

"Of course, be my guest."

I passed by his well-worn, cozy couch on the way to check out his cologne collection. There were a couple of opened Blockbuster cases and a stack of John Grisham books sitting on the floor. A poster of Einstein on the wall above the toilet, sticking out his tongue, startled me. I jumped backward, laughing, and looked over at James.

He shrugged. "It's a holdover from college."

Something about having such a prestigious man appear as if he was poised to lick your bottom was very inappropriate and hilarious.

"I love it, especially in the bathroom." I grabbed several cologne bottles off his counter and started smelling them. "Oh, wow, this is the one you wore the night I met you."

"No way, you can't remember that far back."

The bottle said Calvin Klein, Obsession. I remembered that night very well. I had thought he was really cute and I couldn't believe he had followed me and was going to give me a tip. When I got closer to him, he had smelled so fresh and clean; I couldn't get enough of him. I had rubbed my face and hair all over the front of his shirt, hoping I'd be able to smell it for the rest of the night.

I bit my thumbnail. "I definitely remember this faint hint of citrus."

He nodded. "You're right; that's the one."

"But that's not what you smell like now." I sampled a couple more colognes and picked the dark green Ralph Lauren bottle. "This is the one you've been wearing lately."

"Ha, I wear that one a lot, especially this time of year."

I smelled it again and placed it back on the counter. "And the spaghetti?"

"Dinner last night. You do have a very good sense of smell."

"It's the big nose thing," I said, pointing to my face.

He rolled his eyes. "You can have good olfactory senses without a big nose."

I gave him a playful nudge and became suddenly aware how small a space we were in. After a brief moment of awkwardness, he backed out of the room.

I followed him into his main living space and pointed at a pile of paperwork on his dining room table. "Is that all the stuff for your club?"

"Yep, it sure is."

"How's it going?"

"Not as well as I'd like, I've only found enough investors to make up half of the money I need."

A pang rattled around my chest. If only I could be an investor, but there was no way I could skim money off what I gave to Frank.

"And all these?" I asked, pointing to the ten-plus golf balls all over the table.

"When I'm concentrating, I like to fidget with something. Come with me."

I followed him into the kitchen. He had a map and the classified sections of *The Chronicle* and the *Austin American Statesmen* on the counter. Several of the listings had big red circles around them.

"Wow, this is impressive."

"I like doing this kind of meticulous activity. I could do it all day long and not get tired. If you ever need anything edited, I'm your guy."

"I'll keep that in mind. I can't even spell, let alone edit."

He laughed and gave me a nudge. "There are about six apartments here. I figured we could eliminate a couple and see the ones that are left."

I agreed, and he gave me a basic rundown of each one.

"Some of these are in Hyde Park," he continued, "which is a great neighborhood, but kind of far away."

"Far away from what?"

"Me."

A wave of heat spread across my cheeks, and I fanned myself.

"Sorry," he said, giving me another little nudge. "Do you think you'll have more time for yourself if you're not living at the house?"

"No, probably not. I'll still have my lessons and therapy to do there."

"Lessons?"

"Yes, tasks Frank thinks I need to do to grow, learn, and be of service."

He tapped the pen on the counter. "I see. Like what kind of lessons?"

"Well...um...right now, I'm taking care of the plants, a conscious activity that teaches me to focus on others instead of myself. It's also quite physical, so I can move more and think less. Frank thinks I think too much. I am also learning to follow directions by running all Frank's errands."

James was listening to me and nodding, but the look on his face was giving me the impression that he didn't like Frank very much.

I took the marker out of his hand and scratched out the places east of I-35 and the studio apartments. "This may sound funny, but the thought of living in a four-hundred-square-foot apartment makes me feel claustrophobic."

"I don't blame you. I think something about the same size or a little bigger than my place would be perfect for you."

I agreed. He called the four places left on the map, and we took off. The first place we pulled up to looked rough, but I thought it would be all right. I wasn't excited about it, but I just needed a place to sleep between work and being at the house.

James put the car in park and grabbed my arm.

"What's wrong, James?"

"You can't live here."

"Why not?"

"Jewels, this place is a dump," he said. "I know you feel pressured to get the first place you can find, but this is going to be your home. You get to decide what is right for you, what makes you feel safe, secure, and comfortable."

I'd looked from his face to the view out the windshield, taking in what he just said. *You get to pick. You get to decide.* It was a huge jump to go from not making any decisions for myself to having to decide something this big.

"I'm used to doing whatever Frank tells me to do. I don't trust myself to know what's best for me."

"I understand. But he didn't tell you to live someplace unsafe, did he?"

"No."

"Okay then," he said, kissing my hand, "stay here. I'm going to tell the people in the office we don't need it anymore."

I blushed and spent my time looking around his car. There were even more golf balls, and a used ticket for a UT basketball game against Texas Tech. His ashtray was full of coins, and there were some interesting wires running from his tape player into the glove box.

I placed my hands under my legs to prevent myself from looking inside.

He popped back into the car, grabbed the map off my lap, and we headed to the next place.

This place was much better than the last; it had a nice common area and was close to a laundromat. We parked, he opened my car door, and as I got out, he gave me a quick peck on the cheek.

"For luck," he said, winking at me.

Goosebumps quaked down my arms.

The apartment was the size of a postage stamp. We thanked the lady for showing it to us and went to the next one.

This time after he helped me out of the car, he gave me a quick peck on the lips.

"For bigger luck," he said. "Man, that last place was small."

He reached for my hand and held it all the way to the office, through the apartment tour, and back to the car. He'd held my hand in the club, but this was different, like we were together.

"What did you think?" he asked me once we got inside. "Did you like it?"

"I did, it was huge."

He put his key in the car door. "It's decent, and I like the location, but you'll hate it when it's hot out."

"Really?"

"All those big west-facing windows will make your electric bill astronomically high in the summer."

I grimaced. "I hadn't thought of that."

"It's one of those things you learn living in Texas your whole life. Let's look at the last place before you decide."

James parked the car on the street and again gave me his hand to help me out. I raised up on my tippy toes and kissed him on the lips first. He let out a little moan while placing his hands on my waist. We stood there kissing for a couple of delicious minutes before he slowly stopped.

"Your luck didn't seem to be working," I said, catching my breath, "so I thought we'd try mine this time."

He placed his hand behind my neck, carefully tilted my head to the side, and kissed a hot trail from my ear to my collarbone. "If we keep this up, we'll never find you a place to live."

I let out a fluttery, "Okay."

"Come on, beautiful, let's go test your luck."

As it turned out, my luck sucked. From the outside, it looked very nice, but there was only one window, and James found large mice droppings in one of the kitchen drawers.

"You look a little defeated," he said once we were back in the car. "Don't give up. I promise we'll find you the perfect apartment. I'll ask around, maybe someone at work knows of a place."

"Thank you," I said, my voice weaker and less confident than it had been earlier. "I'm okay, I'm just nervous. There's the actual time things take to get done, and then there's Frank's expectation that it will get done immediately."

James gave me a smile that looked more like a grimace he was trying to hide.

"Holy shit," he said as he cranked the wheel into an apartment complex a couple of blocks from his place.

"Wow, I didn't see this sign here the first time we drove by, did you?"

"No, I would have said something."

"Let's go in." I opened my own door to hurry up the process. We caught up with a guy, mallet in hand, going into the office.

"Excuse me, sir, can we look at the unit you have for rent?" James asked, startling the man.

He jumped and half-laughed. "That was fast, I just put the sign out." He grabbed the keys off his desk and let us into the apartment.

It was perfect. It was large with lots of windows, central everything, and no rodent excrement anywhere. There was a pool and on-site laundry. I liked how calm it made me feel. I could see myself here.

"I'll take it." Then I checked myself and asked, "Can I have it?"

"Yes," he said, "You can have it if you have the money for the first and last month's rent."

I wrote out the check while he called my bank to make sure I had the funds in my account. What a relief...I'd done what Frank had told me to do; I found an apartment. Now all I had to do was find the courage to live here.

The smell of food woke me up thirty minutes before my alarm went off. Jodie stumbled out of bed around 4:30 to cook everything for today's lunch. Many of the women in the group were superb cooks, but none were as good at cooking a turkey as she was. Thanksgiving was Frank's favorite holiday, and the only time we ate food that would be considered traditional. There would be no tabouli or couscous today. Instead, the table would be full of mashed potatoes, candied yams, green bean casserole, cranberries, and both pecan and pumpkin pies.

I stepped into the shower with a dream of never having to come out. The water was just a tick past hot, my skin danced with goosebumps, and all the muscles in my body began to loosen.

Now that the three of us were sharing the bathroom, we went with a pared-down approach of sharing as many products as possible. Frank preferred blondes, so we all spent a small fortune at the salon, lightening, bleaching, or highlighting our hair.

He told us to use Aveda, Blue Malve shampoo, and conditioner because he liked the earthy smell. We bought it by the liter, along with Dr. Bronner's castile soap and Alba Botanical lotion.

Jodie had built us a sturdy shower caddy, and we'd purchased pumps for all the bottles, so we wouldn't have to lift them or worry about misplaced caps. Three women, four products: the science of minimalism.

The congestion caught up with us when adding accessories like luffas, body brushes, and razors. Dylan and I burned through a twelve-pack of razors a week.

After turning myself into a prune, I put on my fuzzy fuchsia robe and headed into the closet to get dressed. I opened the door to find Dylan hunched over her safe, counting her earnings from last night. I couldn't hear her crying, but her bloodshot eyes and wet face gave it away.

"You okay?" I asked quietly, not wanting to intrude.

She shot me an icy look, so I stepped back to shut the door and to give her some privacy.

"Don't leave. I'm not upset with you." Her words stumbled over a crack in her voice.

I sat down beside her. "You look upset. Should you talk to Frank about it?"

"No, definitely not."

"Are you sure? It's going to be a long day, and the club isn't open, so we can't use work to escape," I said, giving her a little wink.

Our secret closeness had grown a lot since the night we'd shared that glass of wine. The guilt about our bond was just another thing I had hidden away from Frank, a list that was growing by the day. It was scary keeping things from him, but I enjoyed having someone to commiserate with. So far, we'd steered clear of discussing anything to do with Frank and the way he ran the group. Or was it a cult?

Ugh, everything I thought about this place was skewed right now. I couldn't tell if I was imagining what I was seeing or if I'd been blind to it this whole time.

Dylan put her money down and let out a soft sigh. "How did you do it? How did you deal with being pushed out of Frank's orbit?" She cleared her throat. "When I became his new favorite?"

"Are you kidding? I was a total bitch to you the first three months you were here."

"You weren't that bad."

I reached into my drawer, grabbed a pair of purple socks, and started putting them onto my feet. Dylan was right; I hadn't been *that* bad outwardly, but inside, I had been raging and terrified. She was beautiful and intelligent, and I could tell by how he'd looked at her that he thought she was special. I'd never seen him behave that way with anyone but me; I didn't know what to expect, so I had anticipated the worst.

I spent the first month doing the exact thing she was doing now, emoting in the shadows.

It wasn't easy getting through something when the only person you could talk to had iced you out. Frank only gave us a week-long grace period to integrate new situations. After that, he would cut the cord and let you work it out on your own.

I wanted to help her as much as possible without crossing the line. I gave her a conspiratorial look. "I must have written thousands of affirmations about the situation, things like the farther I am from Frank, the more love I feel. The more love Frank gives to Dylan, the more love I get from Frank. And my favorite was there is always enough love for me, no matter how much I want to push Dylan off a cliff."

Dylan let out a little laugh. "You did not write that last one?"

"You're right; I didn't, but only because I was afraid Frank would see it. I tried to focus on the good things, which made it easier. Eventually, I could see the benefits of being just outside his direct orbit."

"Could you give an example? Frank just told me Fanny will be here in an hour, and I want to pee in his coffee and watch him choke on it."

My eyes popped out. "What?" I was not used to someone saying something blatantly negative about Frank.

She held her finger up to her lips like it was a secret.

"I've lost count, how many secrets does this make now?" I asked her, not really wanting to know. I knew one was too many, and at this point we had several.

She began to giggle, but a yawn quickly overtook her. "I'm so tired."

She did seem more tired than the rest of us, or in a different way. We didn't have dark circles under our eyes or the hollowness she had in her cheeks.

"More privacy," I said, going back to her question. "Living up here is like living in a laboratory. Being down there with him is like living directly under a microscope."

"Would you ever want to be the favorite again?"

"No, never," I said while silently comparing my new experience with James to my four years with Frank. "The price I paid to be his favorite was more than I could afford. I just didn't realize it while it was happening."

A brief look of possible agreement crossed her face before a rapping on the door disrupted our conversation.

Dylan clutched her money again to look like she was counting it. I wasn't worried. I knew it wasn't Frank; he would never knock.

Liz came in with a clipboard checking off things while spewing out information. "Tracy and I moved the dining room tables in an L-shape to set up the buffet, and the other girls moved the furniture out of the living room. The purple tablecloths are in the dryer to get the wrinkles out, and the guys will be here in about an hour with the extra tables and chairs we rented."

She took a breath and leaned against the door frame. "I also went down to ask Frank if my friend could come to dinner, and he told me Fanny was on her way over." She looked at Dylan but didn't say anything.

Dylan perked up. "Oh, yes, he mentioned that to me also. I'm looking forward to meeting her."

Holy shit, she just lied to Liz right in front of me.

"What friend?" I asked, a little confused. Maybe it was a recruit, and she used the term *friend* as a catch-all?

Liz's eyes darted in my direction, but she side-stepped the question. "Can you guys give us a hand?"

We were on cleanup duty, but the pressure to get everything done on time was always an issue, so of course we would help.

"Okay," Dylan said, "I'll be right out."

"What friend?" I repeated, undeterred.

"Kevin," she said.

"Kevin who?" asked Dylan, looking just as curious as I was.

Liz let out a little huff. "The quicker you can get out here, the better."

"Great," I said. "We'll be there as soon as you tell us who Kevin is."

"He's just a friend."

I blinked up at her. "Do we get to have friends now?" I asked, praying it was possible.

The closet door swooshed with a flurry. "What's going on in here?"

I couldn't tell if Frank was in a good or foul mood. Days like these usually started well but ended badly. The expectation that everything should go smoothly would get mowed over right after the first thing went wrong.

"Ah!" Liz, Dylan, and I shrieked, and Frank's look went from mildly amused to suspicious.

Liz straightened her back and with the tone of a businesswoman said, "Dylan is getting her tithe together for you. Jewels just got out of the shower, and I came in to ask the girls to help us prep the food for lunch."

"Have you started packing yet?" he asked, staring down at me.

I nodded and pointed to a large lawn-sized garbage bag in the corner. Thank goodness James had helped me find that apartment.

"When is moving day?" he asked while Liz and Dylan tried to fade into the scenery.

"The apartment is vacant, so I can move any day now."

"Great. This Saturday, between the group meeting and work, would be perfect. I'm sure Dylan is looking forward to having her own space."

"Yes," I agreed, holding my breath. "I'm sure she is."

"See you guys in the kitchen," Liz said, squeezing past Frank to get out of the closet. He followed her.

Dylan put her paperwork back in her safe. "I feel like I'm forcing you out."

A couple of months ago when I'd viewed her as my nemesis, I would have thought this as well. Now that I'd gotten to know her better, I would give her anything of mine she wanted.

"You're totally not, and I trust Frank. If he thinks I'm ready, I know it will be fine, and the lessons I learn from it will strengthen me and make me stronger."

Though I wasn't sure if that was true, I was comforted knowing I could still spit out what I thought people wanted to hear.

Fanny was older than Dylan and me. Early mid-thirties, I guessed. Liz had told me she had long legs, but she hadn't mentioned she was well-educated and fluent in three languages. Nor did she say anything about her perfect skin and *naturally* blond hair.

Tracy and I were filling serving dishes to put out for the buffet. "I love her accent."

"You have such a warm heart," I said, smiling at her. "If it weren't her accent, you'd find something else you'd like about her."

I reached over and hugged her, smelling her identical hair products, and took a look around the room. We all had similar clothing, hairstyles, and mannerisms. Were we all doing our best to be precisely what Frank wanted us to be?

Before we ate, Frank stood up to give his yearly speech about how grateful he was to the universe for keeping us all safe and prosperous. Absent from his speech was any mention of the thousands of dollars we handed him every week.

I winced. That was a very negative thought about someone who had helped me so much. I had to get my brain in check. Frank was only a conduit, as he would remind us, not the *actual* recipient. We gave to him so he could bless us.

Dylan and I were doing the dishes when she caught me staring into the living room. "What are you looking at?"

"I was watching Frank talk to the friend Liz had invited." I lowered my voice and went on. "Do you think he knows that guy is Liz's super-rich customer?"

She set the plate she was drying onto a stack next to her. "Of course he does."

Now that I was looking at Frank like he might be a cult leader, I was thinking the same thing. But I saw the way Liz looked at Kevin in the club. I knew she wasn't pretending how she felt about him. Maybe Frank was allowing it because the guy had so much money?

Dylan took the plate I had just rinsed out of my hands. "I overheard him tell Steve he worked for a computer company."

I lifted my eyebrows. "A computer company?"

"Yes, he said he was an information technologist."

"What's that?"

"I don't know, but I saw him pull up in a huge BMW. I bet Frank gets him tithing right away."

Did she just suggest out loud what I'd been starting to think? That most of the choices Frank was making seemed more money-motivated than anything to do with healing the people in the group?

I turned to hand her another plate when Steve walked up.

"I hear you're moving into your new place this weekend," he said as he handed me more dirty dishes.

"Yes, Frank wants me to move on Saturday between our group meeting and work." The minute I said it, I wished I could take a night off, soak in my new tub, and unwind. At the same time, and maybe because Steve was standing in front of me, I remembered Frank's new wine hobby and how expensive it would be. The thought of that expense bounced to all the household items I would need to buy for my new place. Moving out didn't mean I was leaving my financial commitments behind.

"Is there anything I can do for you?" I heard Steve ask, like a fresh breeze, pulling me back to his cheery face. "I have a bigger truck than yours. We can use it to move your futon and storage cabinet."

"All the furniture belongs to Frank and will stay here. I'm only taking my clothing and personal items."

"Ah, okay, well, if you ever need anything, give me a call. I'm happy to help."

"Thank you," I said and kept doing the dishes.

Chapter 13

Silent Lucidity

James

I lifted my hand to knock on Jewels' apartment door, but she opened it before I had a chance.

"You going to stand out here all day?" Jewels asked with a sparkle in her eyes and wet tear tracks on her cheeks.

"Is everything all right? It looks like you may have been crying."

"Oh, yeah, these are happy tears. I was talking to my grandmother on the phone. Are those for me?"

"No, I brought myself for you, the flowers are for your apartment."

She snorted. "Where did you come up with that cheesy line?"

I laughed with her. "I honestly don't know. It just popped out. Here, take your flowers and give me a kiss."

She gave me a small peck on the cheek. "Come on in," she said, stealing the flowers from my arms. "These are gorgeous. I haven't gotten flowers since prom."

My mouth dropped. Thankfully, she was already making her way into the kitchen. I didn't want her to have to over-explain or defend everything about her life that surprised me. I made a mental note to make sure she had flowers at least once a month.

Her apartment looked exactly as it had the day we found it, which is to say *empty*. The space had a great floor plan, and was much bigger than mine, with an L-shaped combination living/dining area with the kitchen off to the side. A wall with a giant cut-out and a countertop divided it from the rest of her apartment.

Shuffling noises in the kitchen were followed by the thud of a heavy vase being put on the counter.

She held up a Solo cup. "Would you like some water?"

"No, thank you, I'm good for now. But I'd love a tour."

"You've already seen my apartment."

"But I've not seen it with your things in it."

She gave me the side-eye and took hold of my hand. "This," she said, in her serious tone, "is the living room."

I rolled my eyes. "Yes, I can see that."

We walked a little further through a doorway that led into a hall. It had a built-in vanity, a linen closet, and doors that led to the bathroom and bedroom.

She was using a clear plastic liner as a shower curtain. There was a small grungy towel draped over the rod.

"Jewels, is that a bar towel?"

She gave me a toothy grin. "It is, but I promise I'll return it to the club as soon as I have time to go shopping."

"I have tons of towels and things you can borrow or have, whichever you're more comfortable with. My mother loads me up with that stuff every time I go to Dallas. I'll bring some over for you."

"Thank you. I feel weird asking people for help."

"I get that, and I understand your hesitancy. Maybe you could practice with me. Get used to asking for what you need."

She pointed at the linen closet. "Don't open that door. My club clothes are in there, and they smell like a wet, full ashtray. I need to get a vapor lock for that closet like the one they had in the *Aliens* movie."

I leaned against the vanity. "Frank lets you go to movies that may scare you and worsen your anxiety?"

"Lets me? He *makes* me. He told me it would help desensitize me."

I didn't know much about anxiety, but when my sister had similar issues, her doctor had told my parents that scary movies would keep her nervous system on high alert. He had suggested she avoid them for a while. "How often do you watch them?"

"A couple a month. It's the war ones that really kill me, movies like *Platoon* and *Full Metal Jacket*. Anything having to do with mass casualty overloads my plate. But after the movie is over, Frank gives me affirmations to do so I can move through the pain."

My body tensed, and I used all my will not to let my jaw drop. I wanted to ask her if she thought he was purposely doing that to keep her plate full, but I didn't think she'd know, and I didn't want to freak her out, so I changed the subject. "Wow, I had forgotten how big your bedroom was."

"It's ginormous. I think I could fit five of your king-sized beds in here."

I walked over to the patio door and looked outside. It wasn't beautiful back there, full of scrubby oak trees and dirt, but it brought in a lot of natural diffused light. The only things in the room were an ugly dark pink blanket and a purple pillow, both of which were on the floor.

"What the hell?" I turned and took her hands in mine. "Jewels, you're sleeping on the floor? When you told me the other night you didn't have anything, I didn't realize that included *furniture*."

"Trust me," she said, brushing it off, "by the time I get home from work, showered and rehydrated, I'm so tired I could sleep in the kitchen sink." She shrugged, "I'm just glad I have carpet; it makes all the difference."

She said it as if she were an expert at both options. I was curious but didn't want to interrupt the smile in her eyes, so I let it go. "So, you talked to your grandmother today?"

"Oh, yes," she said as she sat and lied back on her makeshift bed. Floor or not, I wasn't going to pass up an opportunity to be close to her. I lied down, and when she snuggled into me, I instantly wanted to kiss her.

The thought must have washed over my face because she gave me a knowing smile. "Are you thinking naughty thoughts?"

"No," I answered with a look that suggested I was lying. "Yes, I am, but I really want to hear about your conversation, so let's start there and finish with kissing."

She nudged closer to me and started telling me how relieved her grandmother was when she called.

"I don't blame her. Most of the times I've talked to her lately, I was standing close to Frank and didn't feel like I could be myself. I had to be very careful about what I said to her to avoid getting in trouble. She'd always ask me, 'Are you sure you're okay?'"

"I told her I had my own apartment. She seemed very happy to hear that." Jewels contorted her face into a pained look. "When she asked me about my job, I lied to her. I told her I was a hostess at a very nice restaurant."

I kissed her forehead.

"I'm still lying to so many people," she said, looking up at me.

I grimaced. I was in a similar situation with my father. The only difference was that I avoided him, so I didn't exactly lie.

"Hopefully, a day will come when you won't have to lie, and you can apologize for deceiving them."

When she was done sharing all her information, I gave her another kiss. "I want to take you out to dinner to celebrate."

"I'd like that. I'll have to come up with a good reason and ask Frank's permission."

"Ah, yes, permission."

"Sorry, the girls will panic if they don't see me at work tonight. But if I call him and tell him I don't feel good, that might work. He may let me take a night off."

Don't say a word, I implored myself. *This is her battle to fight. You are a support person, not the captain.*

"A penny for your thoughts," she said, looking into my eyes.

"I'll see your penny and give you five bucks for a kiss."

"Deal," she said, laughing, and covered my face with quick kisses. She planted the last one on my lips, and our mood went from silly to sensual.

"Jewels," I said, letting out a small moan, "I want—"

A pounding at her front door echoed through her empty apartment, shocking us both.

"Hello," someone called from outside the front door, "anyone home?"

Jewels took in a breath of air that cleared the room of oxygen. "Holy shit, it's Liz!"

"Who's Liz?"

"Victoria, sorry. Victoria's real name is Liz. She can't see you here."

Her face turned several shades of red as her blood pressure clearly spiked. "Shit, shit!"

"Jewels, say, *be right there*," I told her, and which she did, somehow calmly despite the panic I could see in her eyes.

"Good job. Now, run into the bathroom, turn on the shower, and answer the door."

Her messy blond hair swayed as she nodded in understanding. "What about you? What are you going to do?"

I walked over to the patio door and released the lock. "I'm going to go out this door and back to my apartment." I turned back to her. "Come over when you're done."

But she was already walking out of the room. The shower turned on, and Jewels sprinted past the bedroom, taking her shirt off as she went.

"Liz," I heard Jewels say from the living room, "come on in."

"Nice bra. Where's your shirt?"

"I was just getting into the shower. Come in, I'll shut off the water and get dressed." I smiled and slipped out, knowing she'd made it through the most challenging part.

I walked home, not sure what was going to happen next. Were we going to dinner tonight? Was Liz popping by, or was this lunch? How would Jewels tell Frank she wasn't feeling well when she was with Liz today?

Unable to answer any of those questions, I decided to do something productive. I still needed to come up with a quarter of the money to open my bar, but I wasn't in the mood to talk people into investing right now. Instead, I opened the Yellow Pages and looked for contractors to help me check out meeting the utility codes and painting Gellhorn's on the front window. I also looked for a company to give me an estimate on switching out the red awnings for navy blue.

Once those things were taken care of, I switched my focus and tidied up my apartment, which led to actual cleaning that reminded me I had some things I wanted to give to Jewels. I opened my overflowing linen closet, grabbed handfuls of towels and washcloths for her, and placed them on the couch. While I was in the kitchen getting some dish towels for her, a knock sounded at the door.

I opened it and smiled at her. "Do you need pots and pans?"

"I'm so sorry," she said, stepping into my arms.

I closed the door with my foot. "What are you apologizing for? You didn't do anything wrong."

We sat on the couch. The warm glow of the late afternoon sun brought out the golden flecks in her worried eyes. "I'm afraid you'll decide I'm not worth the hassle. And to be honest with you, I'm not sure I would blame you."

I went to protest, but she stopped me.

"I spend half my time apologizing to you and half my energy lying to them."

"Jewels, I won't decide you're not worth it. That's not how I'm wired. There's no one I'd rather be with or wait for."

She toed her shoes off and cuddled up to my side. Her body seamlessly melted into the nook of my arm.

"Hopefully. I won't always be this afraid," she whispered. "I need a little time to get familiar with the new things in my life, and gain the confidence in knowing I'm no longer the nineteen-year-old on the verge of taking her own life because I couldn't go a day without panicking and passing out."

The weight of her head rested on my shoulder while I rubbed her forearm.

"It was that bad?" I asked her, doing my best to hide my surprise.

She picked at the loose threads of her floral jeans. "I kept thinking the anxiety would go away, but after a year, the panic got stronger, and the fear spread to despair. I sank further and further away from having faith in life. I already felt dead. I didn't see how killing myself could make it any worse."

My guts twisted. How had she made it this far under those conditions?

"By the time I met Frank, I was down to eighty-nine pounds, living on cigarettes and Dr. Pepper. I'd have two or three attacks a day and had moved permanently into my closet."

"Your closet?"

"It was the only place left where I felt safe."

I did my best to understand how her life used to be, but I had no experience with that level of desperation.

"I can't go back to that," she said in a tight whisper. "I've never had an anxiety attack in the cult."

"Why do you think that is?"

"I think God wants me to be there."

I lifted her chin so I could look into her eyes. "Do you really think that?"

"That's what Frank told me."

I rubbed my hand down my face. I was so pissed at this guy.

"James, I've done some bad things. I haven't always been a very good person."

I went to rebuff her, but she barreled on. "I think it's important I tell you, I used to manipulate people to get what I needed. I've stolen clothing, gas, and food money. I've lied—" her voice broke—"just like I'm lying to people now."

"I think your lies to people now are more for self-preservation, not manipulation."

"How do you know the difference?"

"Honestly, Jewels, I'm not sure. It's not like you were lying purely because you wanted to take something from them. You lied to survive."

She tucked her hair behind her ear. "I also went through a period of being promiscuous. I was looking for someone to take care of me. I thought sex was the way to get men to love me."

"Ugh, I think there should be a class in high school teaching girls that guys don't have to love you to want to sleep with you. Many girls make that mistake, Jewels, but I think you learned that didn't work. I don't feel like you're using sex to manipulate me." I put her hand in mine. "We've barely kissed, and I'm already in love with you."

Her eyes doubled in size as her face turned ghostly white.

"Too much, that was way too much," I said quickly. "I'm sorry. I was trying to make the point that you're a good person and that the love I have for you is a testament to the fact that we have not had sex."

We stared into each other's eyes as still as field mice. This time she was expressionless. Usually, I could tell by the look on her face that she was working something out.

"I don't know." She hesitated as her words seemed to get stuck in her mouth. "I don't know how to be loved. Apologize, lie, and cry. That's all I know right now. I'm sorry."

"Don't be sorry. I'm going to wait for you to become you, and then you can let me know."

She let out a long slow breath. "I'm so afraid of turning back into what I was before. The person God decided needed to be with a man like Frank to get straightened out."

"Jewels, I don't think God works that way, and I promise I won't let that happen to you again."

"I wish it were up to you," she said. "Some things take time and have to be done by me and me alone."

"You may be right, you may have to do them yourself, but I don't think you have to do them alone."

She took that in and nodded. I hoped she agreed with at least part of what I said.

"Jewels, I want you to stay here until you get a bed."

She pulled her head back, "That's very nice of you, but I'm not ready to sleep in the same bed with you—yet," she added with a slight grin.

A smile split across my face. I wanted to ask her what that meant exactly. But I willed myself to stay on the subject. "I would sleep here," I said, patting the cushion, "on my couch. You'll have the whole bed to yourself."

She bit her lip, presumably thinking over her options.

"Jewels," I said, taking her hand. "There is no way I will let you sleep on the floor. If you're uncomfortable with me on the couch, I'll sleep at your apartment, and you can be here alone."

"You would do that for me?"

"Absolutely."

"Wow, that's so nice." She swallowed and fanned her hand in front of her face. "I've got to stop crying so much. What if I took the couch and you kept your bed?"

I pitched my eyes together, pretending to be stern with her.

"Ah," she yelped, "okay, you can have the couch."

"Great," I said, getting up and walking toward the basket by the door. "I got this for you the other day."

I turned around and tossed her a key to my door with a rape whistle attached to it. "I thought this may be handy since you come home so late at night."

She smiled at me, put the whistle in her mouth, and puffed on it lightly. "This is a great idea."

Chapter 14

I Melt with You

Jewels

We hadn't spent much time together in the last couple of weeks, between my working every night and James trying to dig up investors for his club. Last week during a rushed phone call, he said, "Please get out of work next Tuesday night. I want to cook dinner for you, a very nice romantic dinner. You can wear girl clothes."

He was great at picking little bits and pieces out of our conversations and finding opportunities for me to do things I typically didn't get to do. Wearing girl clothes was one of them. When I was at the house, I wore the clothing Frank told me to wear. While at work, I wore hootch clothing. While running errands, I wore trendy clothes. None of them felt like me.

I almost wore out the salesperson at Dillard's, looking for a dress to buy for the occasion. My initial instructions to her were *anything but black*, because Frank taught us black meant we had father issues. She brought me twenty dresses in every conceivable color. It took about twenty seconds before my brain flooded me with the rest of Frank's theory about how to tell where people were stuck by what colors they gravitated toward. Light blue was rejection, grey was anger with your mother, and orange was sex issues. Every dress I tried on led back to a trauma I might or might not be stuck in.

About halfway through the pile, I came across one that made me feel like a supermodel. I walked out of the dressing room to look in a larger mirror.

"That one looks great on you," the salesperson cooed from behind me.

I had to agree with her, but it was red. What I saw more than how well it fit or how sophisticated it made me feel was that it screamed, *You have birth issues.*

I finally said *screw it* and went with the one the salesperson liked the best, a beautiful A-line dress made of a cotton rayon blend that swished when I moved. It made me feel feminine and elegant. It was dark blue—the color of rebellion.

I walked through the mall on auto-pilot, humming along with "I Think We're Alone Now" as it played through the sound system. All the typical stores were here: Sharper Image, The Merry-Go-Round, and Glamour Shots. I stopped walking as soon as I got off the escalator, nearly creating a pile-up behind me. A Victoria's Secret store was tucked between Merle Norman and Crabtree & Evelyn. When did they put one of those in here? I had bought things from their catalogs for a couple of years, but their closest store was at the Galleria Mall in Houston.

Once in the store, I held out my hand to paw at every garment I passed. It was like I had walked into a pop-up book; everything I used to see in the catalogs had sprung to life. This wasn't like the hootch stuff you found at Fredrick's of Hollywood or the old lady things you could buy at Foley's department store; this was undergarment heaven.

After trying everything on, I bought a matching bra and panties in the same color as my dress. The intricate stretch-lace and fresh design made me feel like Stephanie Seymour, my favorite VS model. I heard on the radio that she was engaged to Axl Rose; maybe that was why she kept popping up in the new Guns N' Roses videos.

On my way out of the mall, I made an unplanned stop at Regis Hair Salon, and was sitting in the chair picking at my cuticles when the stylist asked me what I wanted. "Can you take all the frizzy ends off and give me one of those straight cuts with a flip?"

She combed my hair and placed her hand right above my shoulder. "I think here would look nice. It would eliminate the damage but still leave you with a nice bobbed cut with lots of swing."

"Yes, I think that would be perfect."

"Anything else?"

Of course, I wanted to say *yes; please dye it back to brown for me*. But I smiled politely. "No, that's all for today."

I spent the rest of the afternoon bathing, painting my toenails, and pushing Frank and all his ideas out of my head. I wanted tonight to be only me and James.

Since I had given him a call letting him know I was on my way over, he met me halfway up the stairs to his apartment.

"Holy shit, you look amazing!" he said with wide animated eyes.

I looked at him and touched my new hairstyle. "I'm a little out of my element."

"This may be new to you, but trust me, Jewels, this *is* your element."

"Thank you," I said, straightening my shoulders. I was suddenly reminded of the night Dylan and I had walked up to him at the club. Twice now, I'd felt more like an adult around him than I'd ever felt around Frank.

"You must be freezing, come on, let's get you inside."

James wrapped himself around me, and we jogged down the hall to his apartment. "Are we going too fast?"

"Are you kidding? These heels are only four inches tall; I could play basketball in them."

He placed his hand on the doorknob and with a theatrical flourish said, "Ho ho ho, merry Christmas," as he opened the door.

"Wow!" I spun in a slow circle so I could take it all in. "This is the best thing ever."

His apartment was adorned from floor to ceiling with decorations of every variety. There were streamers taped to the walls, tinsel hanging from all the light fixtures, and an oversized banner that read Happy Birthday! He had blown up so many balloons that they made a squeaking noise as we walked through them.

"I figured we wouldn't have an opportunity like this again before the holidays, so let's do Christmas tonight."

"Brilliant plan!" I said, pointing at the birthday sign.

James wrinkled his nose. "I have more birthday parties here than Christmas celebrations, so I just used what I had."

"It looks fabulous."

It was pure James. The ease with which he threw his whole heart into things without worrying about perfection was inspiring.

"I already have your gifts but didn't bring them."

"Your being here is gift enough for me," he said, and then laughed. "It's like you bring the cheesiness out in me."

Cheesy or not, the heat from his words made my skin tingle.

He pulled me close. "You're so pretty when you blush." His hot breath spread just below my newly clipped hair. "Dance with me, Jewels."

He took my hand, and we swayed back and forth to the song "With or Without You" playing softly in the background. The warmth of his body pressed against me, and my mind quieted. When the song finished, James excused himself to check on dinner.

I walked through the balloons to the dining area. I'd never seen his table without investment packets, stacks of yellow legal pads, and golf balls all over it. Tonight, it had a simple cream-colored tablecloth with an array of mix-and-match dishes laid out and a pine-scented candle burning in the middle.

"Your apartment looks great," I said through the kitchen cutout. "Especially the table. I love your dishes."

He popped his head into view. "When my parents first got married, they didn't have much money. My mom turned going to garage sales every weekend into a treasure-hunting game. It made a lasting impression on me and my sister, we're both addicted to it."

I heard the oven opening and a baking dish scrape across the rack. "I made us salmon for dinner. I thought it would be a safe choice since you ate the fish I brought to the club," he said. "Do you eat red meat?"

"I used to, but I haven't had any since I joined the group. I miss it."

He came back into the room and handed me a glass of wine. "Maybe someday we can get you a steak. But I think we should ease you into it. If you haven't had red meat in a while, it might mess up your stomach to have an entire steak or hamburger all at once."

I nodded, agreeing with him and appreciating how protective he was of me.

"And the wine, too," he said, winking. "I'm assuming you don't drink much; I've never seen you have even a sip of alcohol."

"I don't, we don't, we're not allowed to." I bit back my desire to say we could buy but not drink it.

"I wasn't sure if that was the case or if you just didn't partake at work. Let me get you some water instead."

"No, please, I think having a glass of wine and dinner with my boyfriend would make me feel like a normal person."

He took a giant step closer and looked me in the eye. "Jewels. Did you just call me your boyfriend?"

"I did," I said, placing my fingers over my lips, "Is that okay?"

He nuzzled his face to my ear. "Absolutely. Say it again."

"Boyfriend, boyfriend, boyfriend," I repeated as I gave him a shy hug. The kitchen timer rang.

He planted a warm, soft kiss on my face. "I'll be right back."

James had made a wonderful dinner with asparagus and baby potatoes to go with the salmon that melted in my mouth.

I placed my fork on my plate as I swallowed my last bite. "Are you having any luck getting investors?"

"Oh, yes, I am," he said, sipping his wine. "I got a call from a man who heard about my bar from Parker today. His questions were so intense, I felt like I was interviewing for Alan Greenspan's job."

He set down his glass and leaned back in his chair. "He wanted to know if I had a prospectus, a business plan, and an investor buy-out schedule. I was absolutely wasted after the call, but I knew all the answers."

He gave me a halfhearted smile. "All I could think was that my father would be so proud of me. I was doing *business,* the very thing he had always wanted for me. But I wasn't behind a desk or trapped in a cubicle, so it doesn't count. It's not 'real business,'" he said, using air quotes, "unless I punch a timecard or report to someone above me."

He paused and took a breath. "The man said he would call my banker directly to place his twenty-thousand-dollar investment."

He stood up and grabbed our plates. "His contribution may be enough to make an offer."

"That's amazing."

He re-entered the room with a glass of water for me in one hand and a small, wrapped box in the other. "Merry Christmas, Jewels."

I took a deep breath. "Oh, I really want to run to my apartment and get your gift."

"I prefer we do it this way, so it's all about you," he said, moving his chair closer to me. "You can give me mine tomorrow."

"Did you wrap this?"

"Ha, no, the friendly people at Dillard's did that."

The box was heavier than I'd expected.

"Open it," James encouraged, with his warm voice and soft eyes.

"I'm scared. What if it makes me cry?"

"Well, if it does, I hope it'll be because you like it."

I pulled on the bow and took it off carefully before picking at the tape on the sides and bottom. The wrapper fell away to reveal a simple black box with the word *Fendi* embossed in gold across the top.

"I can't." I looked up at James, fanning my face, and put the box back on the table. I was so out of the cool people loop that I wasn't even sure what Fendi made, but I could tell by the box that it was nicer than anything I'd ever had.

"Tell me what you're thinking. Maybe we can work through it."

I let out a puff of air. "Is it hot in here?" I asked, standing up. I walked across the room, my feet ricocheting the balloons into the air. "My God, it's hot as Hades in here."

James looked concerned, but I held up a finger. "I'm okay, I think my plate is tipping, but just a little. I do have questions."

"Yes, good. Questions are excellent, ask me anything."

"Is there any chance that this gift could be anything else? I just...I've been looking at things differently, and I think Frank may have used nice things to manipulate us. I didn't notice it when it happened to me or even Dylan, but now it's happening with the French girl."

"Oh, I see."

"Did you buy whatever's in that box because you want something from me?"

He put his hand on his chest. "No! Absolutely not. I enjoy giving gifts, they're one of the ways I show affection."

"Are you hot, or is it just me?" I asked again.

I did one more lap and headed for James. I turned my back to him so he could do as I asked. "Unzip me, please."

His hands were gentle, and he made quick work of my request. As the zipper descended, I pulled the arms off my shoulders and over my hips. I let it fall to the floor and went back to pacing.

James reached down, picked up the dress, and laid it across the back of his chair. "What other questions do you have?" he asked, grabbing my water off the table and handing it to me as I passed by.

I took the glass and took a drink. I sipped, walked, breathed in air, and began to wind down. "How do I know when a gift is out of love and when it's manipulative? I think I'm missing the gene that helps people stay out of danger."

He gave me a pained expression. "That's the fine art of discernment, and it's a constant challenge. Even the people you trust the most can occasionally deceive you."

I stopped in the middle of the room and slumped. "I hate the gift I got you." I grabbed my chin to prevent it from quivering. "I didn't know what to get you. What do you need?"

"Jewels, I don't need anything. The only thing I want is you and my bar, and like you, my bar is just one of those things I have to get for myself." A warm smile took over his face. "You calling me your boyfriend was the most unexpected, delightful gift I could have asked for."

I made a light trilling noise with my lips.

"How are you doing?" he asked, holding out his hand.

"I'm better." I chugged down the rest of the water as we headed to the table, and picked up the box before we sat down. "I think I'm ready."

"Do you want your dress back?"

"No, thank you. I paid more for this bra and underwear than the dress. Might as well let them have their time to shine."

"You do look beautiful in them, and your gift will match perfectly."

I gave him a curious glance and lifted the top. "Oh my God, it's amazing," I said as happy tears soaked my cheeks. "You got me an adult watch."

I lifted the centerpiece out of the box and eased the watch off the green satin material. It had a heavy gold metal strap with an elegant black face. I stood up and sat in his lap. "It's breathtaking," I said while smothering him with kisses. "Thank you!"

He wrapped his arm around my waist, took the watch from me, and slipped it onto my wrist. "It's a perfect fit."

"I love it. I love it so much." I twirled it around my wrist, watching the light dance off the shiny gold band, and turned to grimace at him.

"What's wrong?" I could sense his concern, but there was a playfulness in his voice.

"What I really wanted to say—" hesitation caught my next words—"I wanted to say I love *you* so much, but I didn't know how. I don't want you to feel like I'm only saying it because you gave me something."

James buried his face in my hair. "It's okay. I know you love me."

"How do you know?"

"Because you trust me."

I took a sip of my water. "Why a watch?" I wondered if I had been complaining about my Swatches too much.

"I wanted to get you something beautiful, something feminine. But jewelry seemed too predictable. I saw the watch and knew I wanted you to have it."

I rested my face against his and whispered into his ear. "You're very good at loving me."

He pulled me closer. An almost indiscernible moan escaped his mouth, raising the hairs on my skin.

"Mr. Sullivan," I said, moving my hand to the buttons on his shirt. "I think you're overdressed."

"I'd been thinking that most of the night," he whispered back, "But when you took your dress off, I knew I was falling behind."

"Let's see if we can even the playing field," I said, letting my lips caress his ear as I unbuttoned his shirt.

His body was firm but soft. It had been carved from years of sports and healthy recreational habits. There wasn't anything sharp, jagged, or prickly about him.

The light kiss I placed on his lips grew deeper as I peeled his shirt off. "That's a good start."

I lifted off his lap so we could stand. He kicked off his loafers, and as I reached out for his belt, he said, "I love your new haircut."

"Thank you," I said, pulling at the thick leather strap and heavy brass buckle. His eyes danced as they gazed into mine.

"Are you assessing me?"

His eyes went hooded as I touched the skin right above the button on his khakis. "Yes," he said, looking like he was doing his best to stay focused. "I want to make sure you're okay."

I unbuttoned his pants and slowly moved the zipper down. "Thank you. I'm doing very well right now."

I placed my hands on either side of his trousers and dragged them to the ground. As I bent over, he rested his warm hands on my back for balance. A rush of nerves fizzed through my body, and I purred a little. I stood up and stepped back to take him in. He was the picture of young male sexuality in his plaid boxers and a golfer's tan.

"It's nice to be the one in the room with the most clothing on for a change," I said, nibbling on my lip.

"Get over here."

I let out a nervous laugh and stood in front of him. "I appreciate how patient you've been," I said, looking into his eyes. "I'm ready for you now."

He reached out and rested his hands on my hips. His mouth found my lips for more kisses. "I can't believe I'm touching you like this. Are you sure you're ready? I don't want to cross a line you can't return from. It will add another layer of lying and complexity to your life."

"I don't care anymore," I said, my breathing staggered and shallow. "You're worth it."

He hoisted me up and carried me into his room. "I think we'll be more comfortable in here," he said, and laid me on the bed. He walked over to the closet, flipped the switch, and closed the door about three-fourths of the way. The diffused light spread across the room like a warm blanket.

I smiled at him. "Oh my, you're a pro."

"In my humble experience, I have found that nothing relaxes a woman more than good lighting."

"I agree."

He walked to the foot of the bed and lifted my feet up while paying special attention to my shoes. "Let's take these off—this time."

I curled my toes. "Do you have a shoe fetish, Mr. Sullivan?"

"Let's call it a deep appreciation," he said, tossing them behind him. He got on the bed and scooped me into his arms. "What do you like, Jewels?"

I thought about it for a second. "I don't know. For the most part, sex has always felt like something that was happening *to* me, not *with* me."

He put his arm under my neck and rolled me in his direction. My legs and arms wrapped around him like it was their purpose in life, turning us into a perfect pretzel.

"I would like to go very, very slow," he said. "Going too fast may make you feel swept away and out of control of your feelings. I'd like you to be able to stop us at any time. I'd be just as happy if we didn't go all the way."

"Really?"

"I mean, my ultimate goal is to get to know you better. Having hours to kiss, explore, and talk to you could be just as gratifying as sex."

"Thank you," I said, pressing my lips against his. "I appreciate that."

He pushed a couple of strands of hair off my face and planted small, thoughtful kisses all around my cheek, over my chin, and down my neck.

I threaded my fingers through his hair. "What if I don't want you to stop?"

"Then don't ask me to," he said through a smile.

Chapter 15

Head Over Heals

James

It was dawn when I felt Jewels' body making a move to leave the bed. My blinds cast a pale, diffused light in a horizontal pattern across her body. I reached over and touched her hand. I think by the way she jolted, she was not expecting me to be awake.

"Hey, beautiful, where are you going?"

"Holy shit!" she said in a loud laughing whisper. "You scared the crap out of me. I'm going to my apartment to get some things done."

Her voice was very playful for this early in the morning. I cleared some of the sleep out of my throat. "Do these things have to happen before the sun fully rises?"

"No, I guess not. I'm just not used to sleeping this long."

I looked over at my clock. We'd only been asleep for about five hours. "I'm not sure how you survive on that much sleep."

"I guess I'm just used to it," she said. "None of us in the group sleep much, there's just too much to do."

"Will you lie down and chat with me before you go?"

Last night had been very eventful, and I wanted to see how she was doing. If there was one thing I'd learned about her so far is that she could act okay and still be a complete mess.

She giggled. "Do I have to?"

"No, as a matter of fact, you don't. You don't have to do anything you don't want to do."

"Well, in that case, I'm definitely staying," she said, snuggling into the nook of my shoulder and throwing one of her legs over my hip.

I tucked in the blankets around us. "Tell me what you're going to do today."

"I have to go to the house and take care of the plants."

"How many plants are over there?"

"About fifty."

"What! Who needs fifty plants?" I asked and then revised the statement, still not wanting to put her in a position of defending Frank. "I mean, I don't have *any* plants, so fifty seems like a ton. I'm sure it's the perfect amount for a large house."

It must have worked because she kept talking. "There are more in the summer. As soon as it gets warm, there will be lots of flowers to plant and a rose garden to tend. After I'm done with the plants, I'll check in with Frank to see if he needs me to do anything. If so, I may end up having to stay for lunch."

The gentle breath from her words rolled across my skin as she spoke.

Since we were done talking about her day, I asked her the question I really wanted to know. "Do you still feel good about us having sex last night?"

She stopped breathing once the whole sentence was out of my mouth.

"Too much?" I asked.

"No, it's a great question. Do you want a partial answer or the whole truth? Because the latter may contain information you don't necessarily want to know."

"If it's about you, I definitely want to know."

"Okay, if that's the case, I'd rather we switch positions. I like to look people in the face when I'm giving them unpleasant information."

She untangled herself, and we rolled onto our sides. "You're the first person I've had sex with since the last time I had to have sex with Frank."

She was right; I didn't want to know it, though I'd suspected it was a high probability. But I thought it was best for us that she knew she could talk to me about anything.

I nodded. "I'm okay with that. I don't know what your relationship was with him—I had a feeling it was sexual." I chose my words carefully. I thought the guy was an opportunistic asshole and no great spiritual guide, and I didn't want that to pop out of my mouth.

"I was such a mess when I moved in. I was being evicted from my low-rent apartment complex off Bull Creek. I was barely working because I was passing out all the time. He told me I could stay at the house as long as I needed to."

She swallowed. "I wasn't attracted to him at all; I mean, he's my parents' age. After hanging out with him for about a month or two, he started being kind of romantic with me. Taking me to dinner, buying me things, treating me special. But I was still shocked when he tried to kiss me one night. He was *so old*. I kept wondering why he would like me. Many of the women in the group were much prettier than me, and most were closer to his own age. Anyway, I pushed him off for about a week, but then he gave me an ultimatum. Either be his girlfriend or move out."

She moved the covers down to our hips and started fanning herself.

I brushed a lock of hair off her forehead. "How old were you then?"

"I was nineteen, a couple of months before I turned twenty. As soon as I resigned myself to his ultimatum, his gift-giving and attention went into overdrive. Couple that with the conversations about how God had a special calling for me and the fear of being kicked out—and here we are." She sighed and rolled her eyes. "This is the first time I've told anyone this. Hearing it out loud makes me feel so foolish. How could I have been that gullible? I got so caught up in all the attention, the gifts, the accolades."

She said that last part with a shrug. Now I understood why she wanted to make sure my Christmas present was only a gift.

Her voice got quieter, "I didn't see what he might have been doing. I don't know, it's all so weird. How can I prove it?"

I didn't answer her; I was fairly certain she was asking herself more than she was asking me. I reached over and grabbed the first thing I could off my nightstand, an undershirt I'd forgotten to toss in the hamper, to wipe a tear off her face.

"I love the way you smell," she said, grabbing the shirt from me and holding it close to her chest. "Can I take it back to my apartment with me?"

"Of course you can, and anything else you want."

She finished wiping her face, cleared her throat, and began again. This time her words came out a little clipped. "I kind of snapped out of it one day. I looked over at him and thought, eww, you're so old. But just because I wanted to stop having sex didn't mean he did, so it didn't stop."

Since I didn't want to interrupt, I looked at her with as much understanding as possible, hoping she understood I was sorry that had happened to her. I was also afraid if I spoke, she'd pick up the rage in my voice.

"I felt so trapped," she said, elongating the word for a couple of seconds. "You know, I saw an anti-rape thing in one of the magazines the girls at the club left on the counter, the one that said, *When does a date become a crime? When she says no, and you refuse to listen.*"

"Yes, I've seen the television version of that ad."

"James," she said, covering her face with my t-shirt. "I never said no."

"Aw, Jewels, your situation is very different from that public service announcement. When Frank tells you what to wear, what to eat, what kind of wine he wants you to buy, do you say no?"

"No. I do what he asks. If I don't, I may miss the opportunity to learn the lesson he's trying to teach me."

I nodded and took in her words. Did she really think it was only about these so-called lessons?

"Yes, but ultimately, what would happen if you didn't do what he asked?"

"Oh," she said as if she was now seeing what I was saying. "I would get punished."

"That's what I was thinking. How would saying no about sex be any different?"

She furrowed her brow and went on. "But if I didn't say no—"

"The word yes is consent, not the *absence* of the word no."

A flash of rage crossed her face.

I handed her my pillow. "Go for it."

She took in a deep breath and unleashed several blood-curdling primal screams.

"How did I let this happen to me?" she asked after exhausting herself.

"Jewels, this guy is a predator. He's a professional con man that preys on people with psychological wounds and limited social structures."

"It's so nice to have someone who I can talk to, someone I can tell the whole truth."

I wanted to be that guy for her, but the more I learned, the less confidence I had in her getting away from him.

177

A couple of hours later, I was woken up by the long *beep* of my answering machine recording a message.

"Mr. Sullivan," a woman's voice echoed through my apartment. "Mr. Bennett would like you to come into the bank this morning to fill out some additional paperwork and talk about the letter of intent he's going to send the 606 East Trinity Street property owners."

My eyes cracked open as I patted the bed next to me. Instead of a warm body, I found a sheet of yellow legal paper. *I'll call you as soon as I can. ~love Jewels* was written in large, nearly illegible writing.

I checked my watch. Holy shit, it was already eleven. I stumbled out of bed and called the bank. The good news was that I was right; the man Parker introduced me to had contributed enough money to move forward.

Bob was waiting for me when I arrived. He had everything organized and ready to sign for the first time since I'd met him. We chatted about our holiday plans, I thanked him profusely for all his help, and I was out the door.

Unable to contain my excitement, I headed to the one place I knew I could get a great meal and some sound advice.

I slid into a booth at El Arroyo, regaling my morning to Ryan. "The meeting was pretty straightforward, and I already knew the astronomical terms of the loan, but signing the paperwork scared the shit out of me."

Ryan nodded while drying his hands on his apron. "I bet you could use a beer?"

"Damn right I could."

"What do you want to eat?"

"I'll have the pulled pork enchilada meal."

"Okay, I'll put in your order and be right back."

I sat there for a couple of minutes while waves of excitement rippled through me. By the time Ryan returned, I'd eaten half the basket of complimentary chips and all the salsa.

"Hungry?" he asked, climbing into the booth across from me.

"Starving," I said, grabbing my beer and sliding the basket to the middle of the table.

"What'd the banker say?" he asked as he watched me guzzle half my Tecate.

"He said I had enough investors and that they would present an offer to the current owners. It's done. Now we wait for an acceptance or a counteroffer." I spun my knife around on the table. "Guess it's time to tell my father his worst fears have come true."

Ryan grimaced, "How do you think he'll take it?"

"Oh, he's going to blow a gasket."

"Here's your food," said the server placing my lunch in front of me. "Do you need anything else?"

"More salsa," Ryan and I answered in unison.

I shoveled the first gooey bite of melted heaven into my mouth. "Damn, this is exactly what I needed.

He gave me a rueful smile and changed the subject. "You want to talk about January?"

I wiped my mouth. "So, you've already heard?"

"Well, the last time you were here, you were meeting someone, and the next time Parker and Brad came in, they told me you were hanging out with a dancer named January, and I put the two together."

"And the cult part, did you know about that?"

"You know, I heard the rumors just like everyone else, but I didn't believe it. I'm not saying I wasn't curious, but the chances of meeting a stripper in a cult seemed pretty unlikely."

I tipped my head back. "Not to mention the eight others that are there."

"Shit, that many?" Ryan said as his eyebrows shot up. "I'm surprised you hadn't talked to me about it sooner."

"It's taken me a while to gather enough information to even know what to ask."

"That's fair. So, tell me what you've learned so far."

I let out an exhausted breath. "I don't know if it's a cult per se, but I do know the guy running the show is absolute trash."

"Here's your salsa," said the waiter and took off.

Ryan nodded. "Go on."

"When she first met him, he bought her nice things, made her feel cherished, and helped her with her biggest problem: anxiety attacks. At that point in her life, she was already suicidal and disconnected from most of her old friends and family."

The bell above the door rang. Ryan glanced up to see if the hostess was there to greet the couple that walked in the door. "Keep going."

I swallowed and went on. "Once she was living there, he started teaching her everyone outside the group was against her. He even has her convinced that because she hasn't had an attack under his guidance, this is where God wants her to be."

Ryan put his beer down. "Setting himself up to be the only one on her side."

"Yes, and he won't let them talk amongst themselves if they have a problem, they can only talk to him." I could feel my face getting red. "He works them to death, doesn't let them sleep much, keeps them busy all the time, and takes most of their money...all in the name of therapy."

"He's the poison and the only antidote," Ryan snarled.

I sat back in the booth. "Everything I want to do to this asshole would put him in the hospital and me in jail for a very long time."

"Sounds like he deserves it. Sadly, it's almost impossible to get the authorities involved. Unless there's a minor or a dead body in his bed, it's just her word against his. What else have you observed?"

"You name it, he's insidious. He knows all her weaknesses, and if she steps out of line, he ices her out until she begs for forgiveness. He uses her like a servant while making her think he's teaching her some mystic lesson. It's all bullshit."

I scooped up a massive bite of food. "It just gets worse from here."

I was unsure if Ryan knew exactly what I was referring to, but I couldn't bring myself to tell him Frank had been raping her for years, and she'd just now figured it out.

"The more she shares with me," I said, swallowing, "the faster I want her to get the fuck away from that guy. So far, she's only said she can't leave or she's not ready yet."

"Of course she's not, he has her completely brainwashed. In her mind, he is the alpha and the omega. Psychologically, he is as important to her as the air she breathes, the umbilical cord to her survival."

Ryan kept talking while I placed my fork on the table. I was suddenly more interested in what he was saying than eating.

"I wouldn't be surprised if she had post-traumatic stress disorder."

"What? I thought that was a diagnosis for combat veterans."

"That's what I'd been taught. But I was in a lecture the other day with a groundbreaking therapist who said she was working on a case study with thousands of people who had tumultuous life experiences. Most of them have the same symptoms as veterans who have been through unspeakable horrors."

"So you're saying he's traumatized her to the same extent as someone who has been to war?"

He shrugged, "Chances are, the trauma didn't start with him. He's just a fine-tuned, underhanded prick who's figured out how to exploit her past to control her."

Based on everything she'd shared with me so far, I knew that Ryan was probably right.

"It's amazing that the version I see of January at work is so different from the version of her outside the club.

"Yep, that's one of the many side effects of people that live through long-lasting or recurring traumatic situations. They turn into chameleons. They emulate the behaviors of people around them that they think are doing well. That way, they can blend in and keep moving forward."

I paid my check, thanked Ryan, and walked through a cyclone of blowing leaves to get to my car. I sat my lunch on the seat and checked for cars behind me. DON'T GIVE UP ON A CATERPILLAR glared at me from the pontificating marquee.

I walked into my apartment and hit the answering machine button to replay the messages. There was one from my mom using the possibility of heavy holiday traffic on I-35 to convince me I should come up a day earlier than planned.

The second message was also from my mom. "Don't forget the casserole dish I sent you home with last month. Oh, please call your dad, he thinks you're avoiding him."

Ugh, my father. I should call him. But I'd be there in a couple of days, and I would rather tell him in person.

The last message was from Jewels. "Hey, handsome. My trip to the house went super fast. Want to come open your Christmas gifts and take me to the mall?"

I heard a long tone followed by her laughing. "Oops, that's not the END button."

I ignored the calls from my mother and called Jewels back to tell her I was on my way. I thought about walking over to her place but knew she would prefer I'd drive us to the mall. Five minutes later, I was at her doorstep.

"That was fast!" she said, opening her door.

"Who would dawdle when being enticed with gifts and a mall date?"

"*Dawdle*, great word," she said, grinning. "Come on in."

She gave me a quick kiss and handed me my present.

We moved into the kitchen so I could put my package on the countertop. Jewels still didn't have furniture that would be considered guest friendly. She saved enough money to buy herself a bed, but that was it. Everything else in here was something I had given her. We talked about going to some garage sales, but Frank took priority in her busy schedule, and there was hardly a time of day he didn't want something from her.

Jewels paced in and out of the kitchen while I worked on opening the gift. "Get in here," I said, laughing. "I'm going to love whatever you got me."

She peeked around the corner.

"I see you, beautiful," I said, holding my arm out, hoping she would come to me. "I'm not opening this without you."

She returned to the room, dragging her feet and worrying her upper lip.

"Honestly, you could have gotten me a box of shit, and I would be happy because it came from you."

Her shoulders dropped as she laughed at my ridiculous remark. "I wish you needed something I could buy or give you."

I stopped trying to break the ribbon she'd triple-tied and took her hand. "I feel the same way. The watch I gave you is pretty, but it's just a trinket."

I'd be happy to take that watch back if I could drive her to the cult house and hold her hand while she told Frank she was quitting. Or ensure that she would never have another anxiety attack. But those things were all out of my control.

"Thank you," she said, opening the drawer and giving me one of the knives I had lent her.

"Yes, that will do the trick." I cut through the curling ribbon and tore off the wrapping. Inside the decorative box, tucked between embossed tissue paper, was a beautiful Hermes tie and dark blue leather Coach dopp kit.

I groaned. "You won't buy yourself a chair, but you'll spend three-hundred dollars on a gift for me?"

She shrugged.

I gave her a crushing hug and kissed her forehead, "Thank you, I love them."

"Really?" she asked, the tone of her voice heavy with relief. "Whew. Maybe next year we can go shopping together for our gifts or travel."

I gave her a questioning glance. "That would be amazing." Placing my gifts back in the box, careful not to wrinkle the tie, I wanted to ask her if that meant she was leaving the cult, but I held back.

I kissed her hard and long and told her again how much I loved them. While kissing me back, she asked if we could go to the mall right then. There was something there she was desperate to buy.

"Of course, we can."

With that, she pulled me out of the kitchen, picked her coat off the floor, and opened the door. She was serious about wanting to leave immediately.

We drove the short distance to the mall, quietly holding hands between my shifting gears. I thought she wanted to pick up something for work or do some last-minute Christmas shopping, but she told me we could park in front of Dillard's to get what she was looking for. I barely got my car in park before she had the door open.

"I give up, what are you getting?"

She beamed at me. "A piece of myself I gave away five years ago." She grabbed my hand and started pulling, laughing, and pleading with me to hurry up.

The store was packed to the brim with last-minute shoppers and displays full of imported fancy lotions, oversized cocoa mugs, and fuzzy slippers that looked like snowmen. Jewels didn't seem to care about any of those things. She gripped my hand tighter and led us directly to the shoe department.

We passed the boots, walked in the opposite direction of the heels, and made a laser-like path to the Bass shoe display.

"You came here to buy loafers?"

"Yes!" she said and inhaled the smell of leather.

Jewels asked the attendant if she could get her a size six, dark brown penny loafer.

"I've only seen you in those high-tops," I said. "I thought you loved those ugly pink shoes."

"I *hate them*," she snorted. And then she told me the fate of her last pair. "The day Frank had them thrown out was like losing part of my soul."

"How do you walk around in shoes and clothing you don't like for years?" I asked her while waiting for the salesperson to return.

"You'd be surprised by the things you'll do if you think death is your only other option."

I let out a quiet sigh. It broke my heart that she knew this.

She bought the shoes and told the saleswoman she didn't need a box, but did need a bag to throw her high tops in.

I sat on the bench next to her and looked down at her hands. "You brought pennies with you?"

"I sure did," she said, flipping the two coins in her hand to show the date. "This one is nineteen-sixty-seven, the year I was born, and the other one is this year, nineteen-ninety-one, the year I purchased the shoes."

She carefully placed the pennies in the half-moon cut-out slot of the leather strip while explaining that her grandfather had bought the other pair for her. "He gave me pennies and showed me how to put them in the holes."

"What year did that happen?"

"Nineteen-eighty-three. The beginning of my sophomore year. I'd do anything to get those shoes back." She swallowed hard and held her finger up. "There will be no more tears today. I have replaced the shoes, and they will still remind me of my grandfather."

"Can we go toss your high-tops in Lake Austin?"

"I wish, but I still need them."

She was making small gestures to put herself back together, but I didn't see her doing the big things it would take to get out entirely. And in the meantime, I was falling harder and harder for her.

Once we reached the car, I unlocked her door, but didn't open it. "Do you think about really leaving the cult?"

I wanted to take it back the second it left my mouth. She let go of my hand and stepped backward. The expression on her face looked like I'd slapped her.

"Every day," she said. "Every hour of every day. But wanting to leave and leaving are so different that they shouldn't be able to share the same root word."

"I'm such an ass, I'm sorry."

"There are so many things that have to happen in order for me to consider it." Her tone was defensive, and I hated that she was using it on me. *Wait*. Did she say she was not even considering it?

"One of which," she continued, "if I quit, I won't be able to talk to my cult friends anymore or work at Tulips."

I leaned up against my car. "You can't be friends with the cult girls if you leave?"

"Correct. Once I'm out, he will punish them if they talk to me. No more Dylan, Tracy, Liz, Jodie, Steve..." Her voice got weaker and weaker as she named more of them.

Okay, that made sense in a cult environment. "Wait, did you also say you'd have to leave your job if you leave the cult? Why is that?"

"Once I quit the cult, I become the enemy. I become the next example of the wickedness he's been warning them all about."

Her expression softened, and she stepped closer to me. "I don't think I can work with eight women I love who treat me like a villain."

"I'm sorry, Jewels," I said, opening the car door for her. "That was very insensitive of me. I've never dealt with anything like this. I just want you away from that guy."

She gave me a resigned smile. "Me too."

Chapter 16

How Soon is Now

Jewels

With the receiver to my ear, I pulled a face and looked at James. He pinched his eyebrows together, trying to figure out who I was talking to. I nodded several times and gave a couple of *uh-huh*s. "Okay, I'll be right there."

"Who was that?" James asked.

I moved my hand over my chest to still my heart; at least it was a whole group meeting, not just me and Frank. Crap, what if it was a whole group meeting—about me?

"That was Tracy," I said. "I have to go to the house."

He gave me an incredulous glare. "Right now? You're sure you have to go right now?"

I considered how good his half-naked body looked wrapped up in my sheets compared to the new edge to his voice.

"Yes, right now." I grabbed my shirt off the bottom of the bed and pulled it on. Crap, it was black. I took it off and went to the closet to find a purple one.

"Right now? You can't wait until we're done with what we're doing?" He moved his hands around to show we'd been in the middle of a feverish make-out session.

"God, I'm sorry, I really am. But this..." I mimicked his motions, "will take another thirty minutes, and the travel time up to the house is longer now because it's so close to Christmas."

I pulled my shirt over my head. "This is a *called-in* group meeting, which is cult speak for *get your ass here NOW!* The last person in the door...." I trailed off, trying to stay focused.

"Where did I put my shoes?" I asked, looking under my bed. "The last person in the door gets a military-grade ass-chewing in front of everyone. I don't think I can handle that right now. I can't be late."

James huffed as I stepped into the hall to find my shoes.

"I promise to make it up to you," I told him.

"How?"

"Um, I could clean your kitchen?" I returned to the room with my shoes on and rummaged through the things I had stacked on the floor. "Have you seen my keys?"

He pointed down the hallway. "I think you put them on the stove, and my kitchen is spotless."

"Ugh, good point." I grabbed my coat off the floor and slid it on. "Dinner out! I will find a way to take a night off, and we'll have dinner at the steak place you told me about."

I patted my pockets to see if my keys were in there.

"Jewels," he said, his voice tight. "Your keys are in the kitchen. Please slow down, you're so frantic."

I took off in that direction, and he followed close behind. I saw the keys as soon as I passed through the kitchen door, and snatched them off the metal surface. The hollow clattering ricocheted off the bare walls.

"When am I going to see you again?" he demanded.

The cold from the door handle spread up my arm. "Oh, shit, when are you leaving for Dallas?"

I could feel disappointment oozing from his pores. "Tomorrow morning."

"Early morning, or James morning?"

"Early. It's a four-hour drive, and I promised my mother I'd get there before lunch."

"You could stay here tonight," I offered, doing my best to look peppy.

"You're working. You won't get back here and into bed until three-thirty. If I have to be up at eight, that only leaves us four and a half hours sleeping together."

I was losing the battle of trying to make everyone happy. "That's the same amount of sleep I get every night."

He took a step back.

I dropped my shoulders. "That wasn't fair of me, I'm sorry." I let go of the door handle, walked over to him, and buried my face in his chest. "I'm so, so sorry."

"It's fine," he said, as his stiff arms half-wrapped around me.

We kissed goodbye, and I walked out the door. I took a cleansing breath of the crisp December air and heard him wish me a merry Christmas just before the door shut.

Shit.

Chewing on my cuticles and trying to get James out of my mind, I crawled up MoPac. He used to be more understanding, flexible with my schedule, and okay knowing Frank, the group, and work were my highest priorities. I wasn't sure what was going on with us.

I grabbed a napkin from my glove box and wrapped it around my thumb to stop the bleeding. If Frank saw that I'd mangled my fingers, he'd know for sure I was hiding something.

I didn't blame James for running out of patience with our situation. Would I be a perfect companion if I was number four on his list and he was number one on mine? Absolutely not.

I could do this, make it work a little longer and be everything for both sides of my life.

I took the makeshift bandage off my thumb, shoved it into my pocket, plastered on a smile, and walked into the solarium. While kicking off my shoes, I glanced through the glass door to see if Frank was sitting in his recliner.

All is well, all is well, all is well ran through my mind as I took the stairs two at a time. I cracked the door and prayed I had cloaked my guilt enough to save my ass. Every eye in the room shot in my direction and then returned to Frank. The Christmas tree was the only thing illuminating the area, but even the warm glow of the twinkle lights couldn't compete with the tension in the room.

Frank was perched on a large floor pillow, Fanny and a box of Kleenex at his side.

She was luminescent. Dylan and I used to look like that. For the first time since she'd arrived, I was compelled to warn her, to let her know that this honeymoon phase wouldn't last long.

I straightened my shoulders, tiptoed into the room, and waited for Frank to grill me about being late. A couple of minutes passed by without him saying a word. I must not be the last one here. Thank God.

Frank wrinkled up his nose. "What is that smell?"

A flush of sweat pushed out of every pore in my body as I struggled to take my next breath. Time came to a near standstill as everyone turned and stared at me. Could they pick up the lingering mixture of James's pheromones and his Ralph Lauren cologne? Frank pinned me with his gaze, seemingly demanding an explanation.

"I was shopping at Book Joy a couple of hours ago," I blurted out. "They were burning four different kinds of incense in there." I plastered the best poker face I had in my arsenal and stared him down. *He only knew the information you gave him*, I told myself. *He can't read your mind. Give him nothing.*

As his eyes drew together, the handle on the door rattled, and Frank and the rest of the group turned their attention to Steve floating into the room—everyone except for Dylan, whose soft eyes were still looking at me. Her lips bent into a nearly imperceptible smile.

Frank refocused his attention in my direction. "I've decided we're going to Hawaii early this year. My allergies are bothering me, and Fanny and I are sick of the rain."

We all nodded dutifully.

"Tracy and Liz checked around and found us great flights on American Airlines. If we purchase companion tickets..." Frank stopped speaking for a second while he grabbed a tissue and sneezed.

"It's a buy-one, get-one-half-off deal," Tracy continued for him.

Frank shot her a look. She shut her mouth.

"Right," he said, taking back the conversation. "Fanny and I will leave the day after Christmas and stay until the end of January. Get together and figure out when you can come and go, making sure we have an adequate number of people in Hawaii at all times taking care of us. You must travel both directions with your companion to get the deal, and you have to buy the tickets today."

Satisfied we had the information needed, Frank excused himself, taking Fanny with him. He left behind the floor pillow and a pile of used tissues. As soon as the door closed, the murmurs around the room began.

You could feel everyone's worry level increasing by the second. Even if the ticket was discounted, it was still time away from doing our jobs and making him money.

Eventually, though, our panic subsided, and we got down to the business of making plans and buying tickets. Steve and I bought ours together. We would leave Austin on January third and come back on the fifteenth. I was going to miss nine days of work and lose out on making at least twenty-three hundred dollars.

There was a palpable flatness to my cult friends and me as we got ready for work. There was no playful banter, no conversation about eccentric customers, and no how-to questions from Dylan.

The short couple of months she'd worked at Tulips had turned her into an exemplary stripper. She had learned all the tricks and started making just as much money as the rest of us.

I was pretty sure we were all still processing the information about our sudden trip, but no one would talk about it. The only thing worse than having trip problems right now would be having Frank problems.

Sean called Ripley and me to the stage next. "Guess it's time to make the donuts," I said, putting my things into my locker.

I opened the drapes to the DJ booth to find Ripley and Sean in a serious discussion about her music choices.

"I love you like a brother, Sean, but I'm not in the mood for something as long as 'Bizarre Love Triangle' tonight."

Sean looked up at me. The expression on his face went from frustrated to worried. "January, what's wrong?"

My mind raced. *Should I say PMS, cramps, heavy flow, or pregnancy?* I could try the truth. "I'm exhausted. Who's up first, Ripley or me?"

"You."

I slumped.

Ripley stopped looking at the album she had in her hand. "I'll go first if it'll help."

"Are you sure? I just need a little more time to adjust my mood from foul to fabulous."

"Absolutely no problem. I'm happy to do it." She put the album back in its place. "Okay, Sean, play 'Bizarre Love Triangle' and one of Depeche Mode's longer songs. Let's give our girl as much time as we can."

"Thank you, Ripley."

"Anytime," she said as she walked past me.

"That was super nice of her," I said to Sean after she went into the dressing room.

"Yes, she's pretty cool, but she's usually only that nice to her close friends. What do you want to dance to?"

"Something sultry. It's a lot easier to pretend I'm sexy than it is to act like I'm happy."

Ripley's set lasted long enough for me to get a glass of water and use the bathroom. I put as much effort into my set as possible, but I didn't get many tips.

By the time I got to the third stage, I was dr-aaaag-ing.

I grabbed the cold pole and flashed back to how James said *Merry Christmas* earlier today. My stomach turned. There was no way he and I were going to work. His patience was running out, and I was too afraid to leave the cult. I was trapped in the middle.

I was so lost in thought that I didn't see the guy standing below me, waiting to give me a tip. Where'd he come from?

He was maybe twenty-two years old. I could see the smile on his lips, but there was no joy in his eyes. I'd seen this on people before, but never someone this young. Frank used to call people like this *the walking wounded*.

Frank, Frank, Frank, I shouted inside my head. I was so sick of thinking about what Frank would say, what Frank would do, and what Frank expected of me.

I gave the guy the minimum amount of sexy, squatted down to take his dollar, and said thank you. He smiled quietly and asked if I would join him at his table.

I couldn't sit with him; he looked more depressed than I did. I needed a regular customer to come in, someone who would pay me even if I wasn't at my best.

I winked at him and said, "I would love to, but I doubt you can afford me."

What a bitch I am tonight.

He fished five-hundred dollars out of his wallet. "Is this enough?"

"It's a very good start." I grabbed my things, jumped off the stage, and followed him to his table.

"My name is Teddy," he said, pulling out a chair for me.

I buttoned my dress as I sat down. "I'm January."

I felt a little bad that five-hundred dollars changed my mood so quickly, but I was going to spare myself the inner diatribe about how shallow a human I was.

Teddy drank his Manhattan while I got situated. "Tell me something I don't know."

I laughed. "Most people start with, is January your actual name?"

I collected weird information just for these occasions. Little bits of intriguing facts to surprise people and help break the ice. "Seventy-five pounds of lye heated to three-hundred degrees will completely dissolve a two-hundred and twenty-pound body in two point five hours, give or take thirty minutes."

He put his drink down and gave me a slow clap. "Well done."

It was a fun game. "Your turn."

"My turn?" he asked, jerking his head back. "Anything?"

"Yep, you can tell me anything."

"A couple of years ago, my parents were on a European trip. They were flying from one country to another, and their plane crashed."

I closed my eyes, absorbing what he said.

"There was a settlement, and I'm their only child. So, now I have no parents and a mega-shit ton of death money."

I looked down at the table and let out a long breath of air. I couldn't imagine what it would be like to lose the people you loved like that.

"That's horrible," I said as my cheeks burned and a small tear slid down my face.

"Oh shit, I knew telling you wasn't a good idea, and now you're crying. Here, I have more money."

I held up my hand, shaking it in protest, and used the sleeve of my shirt to blot my face. "No, please, no more money. I appreciate your honesty and your trusting me with your story. I have a real one as well." I took a sip from my water and gave Teddy a five-minute version of my life in the cult and my love for James.

When I finished, he lifted his drink for a toast. "People talk about our drinking but never about our thirst."

I grabbed my water and clicked his glass with mine.

He put his glass on the table and took my hand. "Can I give you some advice?"

I nodded.

"There are always going to be things you're afraid of. But love for another human being doesn't come around every day. My parents were my best friends, and now they're gone. I can never get them back."

He squeezed my hand for effect. "You have more options than I do, and if it were me, I'd choose love. You can leave that cult and spend the rest of your time enjoying life, or you can stay and give up. I promise you, the cult is never going to get any better. There's nothing to wait for, no fear too scary to hold you back. There is no time that will be better than any other. You only have right now."

I sat back, taking in what he had said. *There is no time that will be better.* Was that true? Could that be part of what I was waiting for? The right time. A time when I would feel safe. A time when I would feel strong. A time when I wasn't afraid of anything.

He repeated himself. "You only have right now."

Everything in my body was buzzing. He was right. What in the hell was I waiting for? Even if I had to be in therapy for the rest of my life for leaving the cult, it would be worth it.

"I have to go," I said, standing up.

He gave me a quick hug. "I was hoping you'd say that."

"Thank you, I hope I see you again."

"I'm sure I'll be back. The faster I blow through this settlement money, the happier I'll be."

Darting through the DJ booth, I handed Sean a hundred dollars. "I've got to leave. Please give half of this to Adams."

I collected my things and drove to James' apartment. I knocked lightly on his door, and dug through my bag to find his key. I couldn't located it, so I knocked again.

"I'm coming," I heard him grumble from the other side of the door. "Who is it?"

"It's me, Jewels. I don't have your key with me."

He opened the door, hair askew, in his dark blue boxer shorts and a white t-shirt.

God, he looked good. "I'm so sorry. I'm sorry that I left this afternoon. I'm sorry I keep choosing the stupid cult over you."

I wrapped my legs around his waist as I climbed into his arms. As he held me, the tension between us dissipated.

He gave me a light kiss on the neck. "Will you do me a favor and please attach my key to your key ring?"

"Yes, I will, I promise, I'll do it first thing tomorrow. I'm so sorry that I've been such a chicken. But I get it now. I'm ready to leave the cult. Ready to have my life back. Ready to do whatever it takes to get over my fears and start trusting myself."

"Good for you, Jewels. I'm very proud of you, and I'm sorry I overreacted today."

I kissed his entire face. "You're so good for me. Things will be even better for us as soon as I leave the cult, which I'll do as soon as I get back from the trip to Hawaii."

James' arms went limp, leaving me with only my own strength to prevent me from falling. "What trip to Hawaii?"

Chapter 17

Christmas Wrapping

James

17 Christmas Wrapping James My mother's shrill singing in the kitchen and my father snoring on the couch beside me was making my brain hemorrhage. "Mom, please, Santa came and left two days ago. Could you stop singing Christmas songs?"

"Oh, yeah, sure I can." The next thing I knew, she was hovering at my side, nudging a small plate with two cookies into my hands. I took it from her while the fresh gingerbread aroma flooded my nose.

"Thanks, Mom."

Her voice was almost a whisper. "I'm proud of you, James. I know it wasn't easy to come here and tell us what you've been up to." She pointed toward my father, indicating he was the hard one to tell. We shared a knowing smile, and she went back toward the kitchen.

I'd told her and my father at dinner the first night I got here about the bar. I'd expected him to lose his shit, but he didn't. At first, he'd pelted me with questions; I'd thought he was trying to assess how far I was in the process.

"Have you gotten your Tax ID yet?"

"Yes, Father, I have an LLC under the acronym BBC&F."

"What's that stand for?"

I'd given my mom a little wink, knowing she would appreciate the use of my grandfather's favorite saying. "Nothing gets you through a problem like beer, booze, coffee, and friends."

He'd given me a skeptical glance. "Where'd you get the capital?"

"The money came from friends, friends of friends, parents of friends, associates of friends."

The loud full-sized grandfather clock ticked away the minutes. "Pass me the potatoes, please," my father had said. "At least we'll have a decent place to get a drink when we come to visit."

He'd given me a nod, and it was done. There would be no further discussion until he was ready. He didn't indulge in oversharing his feelings or thoughts. He preferred to mull things over in solitude.

I'd spent the afternoon running errands with my mother and most of the evening talking to Jewels on the phone. The conversation with her had started tenuously. I had been thrilled when she'd told me she was leaving the cult, but pissed when she said she was going with them to Hawaii for almost two weeks. She had left my apartment in tears, and I was embarrassed to admit I didn't chase after her.

I'd tried to call her the following day before I got on the road, but she didn't answer. I couldn't talk to her about it at the time. I had just woken up; I was nervous about coming up here to face my demons, and maybe, like my father, I occasionally needed a moment to reflect on things by myself.

"I don't understand. Why are you going on vacation with them?" I asked her while pulling the hall phone into my old bedroom.

"It's not a vacation," she said. "It's the same old hell with prettier birds and waxier flowers. I have to go. We all bought discounted tickets in pairs. If I don't go, Steve can't go."

"Why is that your problem?"

A prolonged silence echoed through the line. "It's an integrity thing."

"Didn't you tell me you were telling dozens of lies a day? How will one more lie save your integrity at this point?"

"This is different from a lie. I can't leave with a clear conscience while simultaneously stabbing someone in the back. This would put Steve on the hot seat, and that's not fair to him."

"I guess," I said. "It seems like everyone's integrity is a different shade of gray." It was a crappy thing to say, and I wanted to take it back as soon as it came out of my mouth.

"I've been on the phone with the airline for an hour," she said, her voice a little shaky. "I've done everything outside of offering them my life to get out of these tickets, but they are non-changeable, non-transferable, and non-refundable."

"What about canceling the tickets you bought together and buying him his own ticket?"

"I asked about that; seventeen hundred dollars is the price for that change. All single, non-companion seats are booked except for a couple in first class. Had I not spent hundreds of dollars on Christmas for twenty-five cult members.... I wish I could do it, but I don't have the energy to make more right now."

A twinge of guilt echoed through my gut; the present she gave me wasn't cheap. I was part of the problem.

"Look, no one wants to take this trip less than I do. I'll have to spend the next thirteen days with an emotionally full plate, pretending to be *Cult Girl of the Year*. It'll be a miracle if I don't get busted by Frank."

"Okay, okay, you're right, I'm sorry. I just don't want you to go."

What she was going to go through was horrible, but I had my own selfish reasons for not wanting her to leave town. I knew Jewels and my ex-girlfriend Gracie were two women in very different situations, but what if Jewels went to Hawaii and didn't come back? Not literally, I knew she lived here, but what if she went and Frank re-brainwashed her? She'd come back and not want me anymore, just like Gracie.

"I know I'm being an asshole," I admitted. "I'm just scared, you know? I have no idea what the hell goes on in Hawaii. I don't know if you're going to…" I trailed off, my voice losing its conviction, and I started over. "I don't know if you'll want to stay with them and choose them over me."

"Trust me," she said. "Nothing in the world would make me want to stay in the cult. I'm done. It's over. One more commitment to fulfill, and I'm out!"

When I'd hung up the phone with her, I had felt a little better, but not much. I hoped she meant what she said, but deep down inside I didn't feel confident in her answer.

"*Rudolph the Red-Nosed Reindeer had a very shiny nose,*" my mother's tinny voice bellowed out from the kitchen, bringing me back to the present.

"Mother, please stop singing," I called out.

"James," said my father from the couch. "Stop shouting."

"Sorry," I said, meaning it. "I think I've been cooped up in this house for too long."

"Me too," he said, sitting up. "Let's go for a drive."

My father and I made an excuse to leave the house and slipped out the back door to get into my car.

"What's this?" he asked after opening the passenger door.

"It's a Walkman that plays compact disks," I said, unsure if he'd ever seen one.

"Yes, I know that. But what's it connected to? What's this wire?"

"Ah, it's attached to a cassette tape. Check this out." I ejected the cassette from the player. "You push this blank tape in, and the Discman will play through my car's audio system, so I don't have to drive around with those goofy orange spongy headphones."

"Why is it sitting on a towel?"

"Oh, that helps it from skipping when I go over bumps. Just put the whole thing in your lap for now. I'll play you something."

I started up the car and hit *play*. The words *Jump around!* erupted repeatedly through my vehicle. I grabbed my rearview mirror so it would stop vibrating, as the thunderous sound of House of Pain pushed out of the speakers.

My father's face contorted into a look I'd never seen before. It was as if his body thought it could make the sounds stop coming into his ears if he squished his face tight enough.

"Oh my God, that's horrible!" he shouted over the music. "Why in the hell would you want to listen to it anywhere, let alone a place as small as your car? Please, James, turn it off."

I turned the music down while stifling a chuckle.

"What was that, rap music?"

"No, Father, they call that hip-hop."

"Let's go get a beer," he said after recovering from my music. "We can talk about the bar."

As we drove around, my father gave me the rundown of all the pubs and places he liked to hang out at in the neighborhood.

"I've been scouting them out since I retired a couple of years ago," he told me as I parked the car. "Besides the garage, they're the only safe place to hide from your mother."

I peered up at a sign that read Welcome to The Happy Medium. "Why do you have to hide from her, and what's in the garage?"

He opened the door to enter the pub and swept his arm to gesture that I go in first. "Retirement is a cruel mistress, son."

"What?"

"Hey, Tom, how's it going!" called a man as we walked in.

We found a place at the bar, and my father introduced me to the bartender and some other people nearby. Apparently, many men my father's age were hiding from their wives. Once situated with beers in our hands, I asked him again why he had to hide from my mom.

"You spend your entire life working, waiting for your long-deserved break, just to realize you're now trapped in your house listening to someone sing Christmas carols two months out of the year." He took a swig of his beer and stared up at a Miller Lite sign. "Don't get me wrong, I love your mother, and I have a couple of hobbies that interest me, but every segment of life takes a different strategy, and I thought this part would be easier. Now, tell me about the bar."

I nodded, contemplating what he had said. I was genuinely interested in learning a bit more about him, but I figured he was ready to give me a hard time about my life choices, so we might as well get on with it. I started by giving him the basic rundown of my vision. I told him how I wanted it to be more than just another grungy frat bar on 6th Street.

It was nice watching his expression change from annoyed to curious. He loved the idea of my focusing on coffee and other drinks during the day. He even said he would go to a place like that here in Dallas if he could find one. I agreed with him and went on about how I got the idea while talking to people about investing. Many of them had asked if this was the type of place their knitting group could meet or where they could play cards and have a cup of coffee, and it got me thinking. I wanted to find ways to bring people together, things like game nights, group guitar lessons, and nights where we played the number one hits from other countries. Family-friendly by day, a little more mature at night, only loud and annoying on drinking holidays, New Year's, St. Patrick's, days like that.

"Absolutely, you have to take advantage of the people that are already down there for those events," my father agreed.

"Exactly," I said, impressed that he understood that. I grabbed a cocktail napkin off the stack by the peanuts and said, "The more liquor I get from the distributor, the better the price, especially on kegs of beer."

I drew a rough layout of the club. "So, I'm going to take a little space out of the back bar area to add to the cooler."

"Interesting idea. Is it wise to have that many kegs in storage? How long do they last?"

"About four months," the bartender said. "Ready for another round?"

"Sure," we both answered.

He poured us a couple more Guinness and continued. "I think the kid's right. We've never had a beer keg go bad, but we've run out of beer on many occasions." He lowered his voice. "Squeezing a couple of extra people over the fire code limit is easier than running out of beer on a busy Friday night."

My father's eyes widened. "Don't pollute his young mind. Geez, he doesn't need you telling him how to break the law before he even gets his liquor license."

"Just trying to help." He tossed his bar towel over his shoulder and shuffled away.

"Have you looked into the license yet?" my father asked. "How long does that take?"

"Forty-five to sixty days, depending on what county you're in and how backed up they are. Austin has a considerable turnover of places that sell liquor, so I think it will be on the longer side of that time frame."

My father asked me a lot more questions than I thought he would. He was interested in even the most minor details, which surprised me.

"Where are you going to get tables and chairs?"

This conversation was going much better than I had thought it would. We hadn't spent this much time together since I started college. "I've not looked into those yet. The only thing I know for sure is that I'm not interested in the 'Texas ranch look.' I want lightweight pieces with a simple, clean design, things that are easy to move around, stack, and have a modern feel. At first, I'll probably get most of what I need at sales."

We had another beer, played a round of dominos with a couple of his friends, and finally meandered back to the house.

I had a couple of turkey fold overs so I wouldn't get hungry on the way home. My parents helped me load my car with my leftovers and a couple sets of double-sized sheets for Jewels. I hugged Mom goodbye and shook my dad's hand.

"Thanks for everything," I said as I waved goodbye. "I'll talk to you soon"

It was nice to actually mean that for a change.

Bumper-to-bumper traffic on I-35 the entire way to Austin had me itching to get out of my car and desperate to use the bathroom. The door opened without my key, and I found Jewels waiting for me on my couch.

"I'm glad you're here," I said, rushing past her. She was curled up in a blanket, watching MTV and eating candy corn. "I see you finally used the key I gave you."

"I did," she said, giggling at me. "Do you have to pee?"

"Yes, so bad. It took me almost five hours to get here."

Once I was done, I pulled her off the couch for a hug and kiss. "Let's lay back. I need to stretch out and have you near me at the same time."

After we got situated, I covered her in kisses. "I've missed you."

"I've missed you too," she said. Her hair tickled my neck as she inhaled a large breath. "You smell so good."

"Impossible! I've been in my car for hours. What do I smell like?"

She took in another breath. "Like cookies, the inside of your car, sweat, and your aftershave."

"Wow, that's pretty good. At first, I thought you would say cologne, but I didn't put any on today." I readjusted my body, so I was more on my back than my side. "The older I get, the less I like my car. I need a sedan."

"That's funny, I was just thinking, when I quit the cult, I'm going to trade my truck in for one of those new Mazda Miatas."

"Perfect," I said while squeezing her. "We can drive my car when we go to dinner, so we don't get our fancy clothes and hair messed up, then drive your car with the top down to Lake Travis for a day in the sun."

"I've never done that before."

"You've never been out to the lake?"

"No, not really. A long time ago, we went out to Hippy Hollow before we started dancing. Frank thought it would be good for us to get comfortable with our naked bodies. He hadn't anticipated all the naked men peeking at us from the bushes and touching themselves. We never went back."

"So," I asked to clarify, "you've never gone out there to hang out at Carlos and Charlies, driven around on a boat with all your friends, gotten stuffed on tacos and margaritas?"

"No, but I've always wanted to. I hear the girls at the club talking about it all summer long."

"Aw, Jewels. Your life will open up so much when you leave that cult."

"Yes, I can't wait!" She gave me several kisses on the neck while she chatted away about how she had spent her morning. Her words warmed my ears as she drew languid circles on my arm. I let out a little moan as sparks shot through my body. I turned my head to find her sweet mouth while she shifted and climbed on top of me.

"I know you're upset about the Hawaii trip," she said, covering my face with kisses, "but I'm very excited."

I opened my mouth to say I wasn't as upset as I was a couple of days ago, but she filled it with her delicious candy corn-flavored tongue.

She sat up, her body straddled over me and took her shirt and bra off.

"What's happening?"

"Makeup sex."

My mouth split into a grin. "I'm not sure we fought enough to have makeup sex."

"Hmph," she said, shrugging. "Then screw the makeup part, let's just have sex."

"Great idea," I said, grabbing her by the neck and pulling her down on top of me. "I'm not sure this couch is big enough for us to have sex on."

Her hands grabbed at my t-shirt. "It will be if I'm on top."

A zing of electricity pulsed through me. "Let me help you with that," I said as I lifted my upper body so she could get my shirt off. "You want to be on top?"

She jumped off the couch for five seconds so we could both take our pants off. "I think so," she said while climbing back on me. "I've always had to be on the bottom. It's the whole submissive woman, dominant cult leader thing."

I took her face in my hands and looked into her eyes. "You never have to be submissive again, Jewels. You can be on top, on the side, standing up; we can do anything we want to, and none of it has to be me controlling you. We can just have fun and enjoy each other."

"That would be very nice," she said as she bit her bottom lip. Her eyes turned soft and hooded, and she bent down to kiss me. "How rough can I be?"

I laughed out. "As rough as you want...."

An hour later, I glanced up at the clock. "Let's go out for dinner," I told her naked, taxed body as she lay on top of me panting. "Let's go have steak."

She pulled her head off my chest and looked up at me. "Makeup steak?"

"No, we didn't fight enough for that either. Frank's already in Hawaii, right?"

"Yes, he and Fanny left yesterday. I'll call Dylan and tell her I'm not going in. Do you think I'm ready for a whole steak of my own?"

"I think so, we've taken you on plenty of test runs. But I'm not thinking porterhouse, I'm leaning more in the six-ounce filet direction."

"Where?" she asked, playing with the hairs on my chest.

"I mean, if it's going to be your first steak, I think it should be Ruth's Chris. Unless you're too tired for girl clothes."

She jetted off me and rifled for her things. "Tired? Are you kidding me? I'm a well-trained athlete in heels, I don't get tired." She grabbed her coat. "Is it far from here?"

"No, It's on Guadeloupe, a couple of miles away."

"I'll be ready by seven," she said, whisking out the door.

Looking across the table, I could see the woman Jewels would someday mature into, a woman no longer ruled by her fears but one full of life, compassion, and quiet convictions. While munching on the complimentary bread, I asked, "What do you think you want to be when you get out of the cult?"

Her shoulders dropped and she let out a sigh. Just when I thought she would give me an answer, she grabbed her wine glass and took a sip. Her brow tightened the more time I gave her. She was more of a feeler than a thinker, so I changed my tack. "Don't answer that. Instead, tell me the feelings you have about the question."

"I feel like I have amnesia. Like I was in an accident years ago, and that's why I don't know the answer to the question. I feel the feelings that tell me I should know the answer. I feel the pressure I put on myself to know an answer. I even think I should be able to come up with a fabrication of an answer, but all I have is a void, an emptiness."

Her mouth twisted into a contemptuous smile. "Ask me what my purpose is."

"Okay, I'll bite. What's your purpose, Jewels?"

"My purpose is to work on myself. To cleanse myself of negativity and to remove all the trauma from my mind and body so I can assist others to do the same. To elevate the group and the number of people we can affect so we can raise the planet's consciousness."

"Is that what you want?"

Her eyes closed, she took in a breath of fresh air, and she continued. "It's what I've been trained to want. It's what I feel guilty for not wanting. I know that Frank has systematically taught me to want what he wants, not to dream of a future he'll never let me have." She opened her eyes, drank the last swallow of her wine, and reached across the table to find my hand. "I can't wait to get out of the group and start over. It's time for me to get back to living again."

"I'm very proud of you," I said as her eyes grew. It took a moment before I heard our server bringing our sizzling steaks from behind me.

Jewel's voice sparked with delight. "Who knew steak could be so loud."

The server moved in front of us. "These plates are extremely hot, please don't touch them. Napkins up."

I grabbed my elegant cloth napkin off my lap and held it in front of my shirt. "It will prevent your clothes from being splattered with shooting drops of butter and meat grease."

The server waited for her to follow my directions and slipped our plates onto the table.

"Could we also have another glass of wine for her and another Carlsberg for me?"

"Yes, sir, I'll be right out with those."

"Thank you for this," Jewels said after the server had left. "Thank you for all of it. For being a friend to me, giving me time to figure things out, and showing me the life I can have."

My heart swelled. "Thank you for trusting me. I had no idea when I first met you what a leap of faith that would be for you. Hell, I just thought you were sexy and wanted to take you out."

Jewels spent every bite of that steak moaning. It wasn't a loud, deliberate exultation of passion—just a quiet overflow of her mouth's reaction to pure culinary pleasure. Once we couldn't eat another bite, we shared a Bailey's coffee and paid our bill.

Jewels put her arm through mine on our way back to my car. Her steps had a languid quality from the two glasses of wine. "It's nice out here."

"I think we should go to your place and have makeup sex again," I said, drawing her closer and kissing her nose.

"My place, who can wait that long? Let's make up in your car."

I peered into her soft glistening eyes, but I couldn't tell if she was serious or kidding. I leaned her body against my car and pressed my thigh between her legs. "Do you have a thing for cars, Jewels?"

"Yes," she breathed out. "I think I might."

I gave her a crushing kiss.

"I'm very flexible and a little double-jointed," she moaned, her cheeks turning light pink from the conversation. "Let's try it."

Heat crawled through my body as I surveyed the parking lot's privacy level. Feeling mischievous, I decided to test the water and see how far I could take it. "Is that what you want?" I asked, bending down to whisper right into her ear. "Do you want to fuck me in my car?"

"Oh my God!" Her body sprang forward as a thunderous laugh came out of her mouth. Her once-pink cheeks were now a deep crimson. "Ba-haha, that was both shocking and hot. I think I like dirty talk as well." Our combined laughter bounced off the buildings around us, making it feel like we were in a crowd.

I removed Jewel's hands from covering her face. "This parking lot is lit up like a high school football field. There is no way we could do it here, now. I'll make you a deal. Let's take this to your apartment tonight, but I promise to find a safe place to live out your fantasy on New Year's Eve."

She stiffened. "But I can't on New Year's Eve. I have to work."

"What?"

"I have to work," she said, her face sharpening out of its warm, amorous state.

"When were you going to tell me?"

"I thought you knew. I assumed you would work as well. Isn't New Year's Eve the busiest money maker for alcohol sales of the year?"

"I took the night off after you told me you couldn't get out of the trip to Hawaii, so we could be together before you go." I turned and walked away to get some air and space.

"Oh, shit, I'm so sorry, James—just three more weeks," she called after me. "One more trip from hell, and it will all be over. I will spend every Thanksgiving, Christmas, New Year's, Valentine's Day—all of them and more, with you."

I rubbed my face with my hand. "Okay, three more weeks. Promise you'll come back to me."

"I promise," she said. "Nothing he can do will keep me in the cult."

Chapter 18

Tainted Love

Jewels

My bedroom floor looked like the last day of a seventy-five percent off sale at The Gap. Clothes were everywhere. Clothes that needed to be washed were in a pile next to the door. Things I would be taking to Hawaii in cult-approved colors and summer styles were with me on the floor.

I brought a stack of things back from James' place on the bed. He insisted on giving me half his dresser and ample space in his closet. He also had suggested I throw my dirty things in with his laundry several times, but I felt weird about having him wash my delicates. So I carted my clothes back and forth, switching them out occasionally.

Steve and I were leaving tomorrow morning. I was eager to start Phase One, Survive Hawaii, so I could get to Phase Two, Begin My New Life.

I stopped filling my duffle bag for a moment and reached over to turn down my boom box. I held my breath to hear better; was someone at my door?

I was staying at Frank's tonight for our flight in the morning. The neighbors next to the cult house already hated the extra traffic our presence had increased on the cul-de-sac. So parking my car there while I was in Hawaii was problematic.

I checked the time then took off my beautiful watch so I wouldn't accidentally wear it to Hawaii. It was earlier than I thought. I walked over to the window in my living room and looked out at the rain. Dylan was standing there crying, soaked to the bone.

"What's wrong?" I asked her, opening the door. "Are you okay?"

"I'm early," she said apologetically. "I was in the neighborhood."

In the neighborhood? Why would she be in this part of town? "Come on in."

I shut the door and turned on my desk lamp on the floor. "Come sit down. Tell me what's going on."

She turned towards me, her face slick with rain and tears. "I'm okay," she said, hyperventilating.

"Oh my God! Dylan, what's going on? Please sit before you fall."

She sat where she was standing, a foot away from the door, as if she didn't have enough energy to make it any further into the apartment. I ran into the kitchen and grabbed the roll of paper towels off the counter for her.

In a daze, she spoke to the blank wall behind me. "I just got my results back from the gynecologist."

Holy shit, Frank got her pregnant! My eyes bounced from her to the ceiling as I tried to do the math. How pregnant was she? She wasn't showing. Was he having sex with her and Fanny at the same time?

I could see him doing that, but not Dylan.

She must have seen the thoughts cross my mind because she started shaking her head. "I'm not pregnant."

My mouth ajar, I started rattling out the possibilities. "Do you have a cyst, endometriosis, or ovarian cancer?"

"I have AIDS."

I gasped and covered my mouth with my hands. "No, that's impossible," was all I could say, but my brain was bursting with questions. How was this possible? Dylan was relatively new to the group. I didn't know her as well as I knew the other members. I was confident she wasn't running around having unprotected sex with a bunch of men. When would she fit it into her already crammed schedule?

I placed one of my hands on the carpet to stop the room from spinning. "Have you had a blood transfusion lately?"

She shook her head as a stream of tears flooded out of her. "There was a guy I dated years ago. Way before we started asking people about their sexual or drug history."

Boy, I thought I had things I wasn't sharing during group meetings. I wondered if Frank knew about this part of her past. My poor sweet friend, she was only twenty-three, and she was going to die. Everyone died when they got AIDS. I mean, that was what they said on the news. It was either that or complications due to AIDS, but they all died and very quickly.

She wiped the tears off her face with the palms of her hands. "Jewels, there's more."

My mind seized. "More," I said, folding my arms over my stomach. "How could there possibly be more?"

"The doctor at the clinic told me you need to be tested as well."

My chin jutted forward. "Me, why would I have it? I don't have sex with you!"

For the first time in the ten minutes she'd been in my apartment, her mouth curled up just a little. "No, you're right, we don't have sex, but we share a bathroom."

My pulse was roaring in my ears. "What does that have to do with it?"

"We use the same razors."

"Whaaaaaat?" fell out of my mouth in an avalanche of disbelief.

"The doctor told me I had to talk to anyone that had come in contact with anything that could have my blood on it. So, you and Jodi need to be checked, even though she doesn't shave very often."

I tightened the grip on my stomach while reaching over to pat her leg with my other hand. "We'll get through this," I said and stood up.

There it was, the biggest and most blatant lie I'd told to date. As far as I knew, she would not get through this. None of us would. She and Magic Johnson, me, and maybe Jodi were all going to die. What about Frank? Oh, and Fanny too. The body count was adding up —quickly.

I stood up and staggered to the wall to support myself and stop the room from spinning. My plate was tipping. I ran into the bathroom and started heaving.

"I'm so sorry, Jewels," her tinny voice echoed through a tunnel in my brain. She stepped into the bathroom. "I'm sure you don't have it." She kept repeating it as she moved my hair off my face and placed a cold washcloth on my forehead.

Between retching, fighting back an anxiety attack, and trying to tell her I was okay, I had the most terrifying thought of them all: what if I gave it to James? I gasped for air, leaned farther into the toilet bowl, and wailed. Reaching up, I grabbed the handle and pulled, hoping to flush my puke and fear down the drain simultaneously.

The two of us huddled together on the cold tile floor and cried until we were out of tears.

"I have to take care of something," I croaked out. "It will take me about twenty minutes. Will you be okay here by yourself?"

"Yes, I'll be fine."

I tossed the washcloth into the sink and zipped through my apartment and out the door. I didn't bother with my coat or keys. The cold, drizzling rain was a welcome distraction; it helped solidify my new resolve. I ran the three blocks to James' apartment. Taking the stairs two at a time, I reached his place, riddled with anxiety and out of breath.

Fueled by adrenaline, I scraped my knuckle knocking on his door. "Ouch," I blanched, picking the torn skin off the back of my finger. I watched the small bead of blood collect over the wound in dumbfounded panic. Where in the hell was I going to put it? I stuck the injured finger in my mouth and started to suck. The blood that kept me alive might now be a lethal weapon.

James answered the door with the phone to his ear. "Brad, I gotta go. I'll call you back in a while."

He extended his arm out the door to bring me in. "What's wrong? You're sopping wet, let me get you a towel."

He darted over to his linen closet and grabbed me a clean towel. "Fresh out of the laundry," he said, placing it around my shoulders. "Please, have a seat, you're making me nervous."

"I'd rather stand."

He gave me a double take. "You look like you're going to drop a bomb on me."

I leaned up against the wall. I didn't know where to begin, so I opened my mouth and let the numbness pull me through the information I had to share with him. I hit most of the bullet points: how and when Dylan got it, why he and I had to be tested, and that he couldn't tell anyone. Not a soul.

James pinched the skin on his neck in what looked like an attempt to better swallow the news.

"Wow," he said. "That's horrible for your friend, but I'm sure you and I are okay."

My eyes bulged. "Aren't you worried?"

"Yes, a little bit. But I can't go from worried to freaking out until I have more information."

I wanted to agree, but I was incapable of rational thought.

"Look, Jewels, I'm sure there are cases of shared razors giving someone AIDS, but I bet it's extremely rare. It's going to be okay. We'll get through this."

He just used the exact words I had told Dylan twenty minutes ago. I wondered if he was lying to me the same way I lied to her.

"James, I can't leave Dylan in the cult alone."

"What does that mean?"

"I'm not leaving. I'm stay—"

"You're staying in the cult!" His angry breath hit me in the face. "I knew it! I knew you wouldn't leave; I knew you'd find an excuse to stay."

The weight of his words forced my eyes closed like I was boarding up a house to protect it from a hurricane. When I reopened my eyes, James was peering at me. Anger had replaced worry. A light sheen of sweat covered his face.

"That's not fair," I said, my voice thin but determined. "I wasn't looking for a reason to stay, and I wouldn't have wished a life-threatening disease on my friend to do so."

"That's it. That's the problem. It's not about you and me and what we want and what we're willing to put into our relationship. It's about you and anyone in the cult. They will always be more important to you than I am."

I swallowed back an urge to throw up again. "As a whole, the cult is one bad person ruling over everyone else. *They* have not been controlling or hurting me, only Frank has. So staying for someone I care about, who's never been mean or unkind to me, doesn't seem like that hard of choice."

He peered at me. "There must be a way you can help her and be outside the cult."

"Trust me, I've seen many people leave, and it's ugly. He will never let any of them talk to me. I will have no way to communicate with her. It's all or nothing."

"Why—why do you have to be the one to stay with her?"

"Because I promised myself I would never abandon anyone again." My emotions were fraying. I was shutting down.

"Where are you? Where have you gone? For the first time since I've known you, you have that look in your eyes, the vacant stare of someone in a cult." He placed his hands on my arms and squeezed me enough to get my attention. "Jewels, don't do this."

I threw my shoulders back and moved away from him. "Dylan's going to need all of us by her side. She won't be able to work; we'll help her financially, and Frank will help her emotionally."

He bit his lips together and shook his head *no*.

"This is what the group has been working toward since its inception, raising our consciousness to assist others. Helping the weakest link and providing hope and clarity for people in need. That's what was given to me. It's my turn to give it back."

"No, that's what Frank has programmed you to believe."

"It's part of my bigger purpose."

"I'm not letting you break up with me. I told you before I would wait, and that's what I'm going to do."

I didn't have anything to add. I waited for him to debate his next point, but he didn't. He just stared at me in crushing disbelief.

"I'm not breaking up with you," he repeated.

"I'm not coming back," I said. "I've made my choice."

I handed him his towel and walked out the door.

When I returned to my apartment, Dylan was curled up in the corner of my living room. She was using her coat for a blanket and the roll of paper towels I had given her as a pillow. I tiptoed past her to finish packing.

On my way through the hallway, I spotted my Fendi watch on the makeup counter. Shit. I took another peek at Dylan to make sure she wasn't watching me, and opened the built-in drawer to place the watch inside. I stood there for a minute holding it, letting the smooth metal glide across my fingers, replaying a reel of all the painful facial expressions I had just seen on James' face. I hoped he wouldn't hate me forever, but I wouldn't blame him if he did.

I knew in my heart that I was doing the right thing. When I returned from Hawaii, I would find a way to give the watch back to James. I laid it carefully in the drawer and closed it.

As far as the things I was taking to Hawaii went, everything stayed the same. I still had ample amounts of shorts, tees, and swimsuits. I double-checked to ensure I had my affirmation notebook and something to read. I switched out my earlier book choice of *Siddhartha* with a copy of *The Alchemist*. I was too depressed to read a hundred-fifty-page book about old age, disease, death, and spirituality. *The Alchemist* was much lighter with all its traveling, a beautiful girl named Fatima, and lots of sheep.

Shortly after I started straightening up my room, Dylan came in and climbed onto the bed. Now that I knew how sick she was, a wave of profound sympathy rolled through me. All those nights she'd been working at the club, all the days doing whatever stupid thing Frank was making her do, all the while, her body was quietly being taken over by the virus.

She sat there folding my laundry with me as we chatted. "All done packing?"

I patted the zipped, oversized duffle bag on my bed. "Yes, it's all in here."

"What time is it?" she asked while placing my kelly green Ralph Lauren polo shirt on a hanger.

"It's already six-thirty. We're super late for work."

She pinned me with a tired grin. "We're taking the night off."

"What would we do instead?" My mind started calculating the plethora of ways that could go wrong. But none of them were as horrible as Dylan having AIDS, scarier than thinking I could be sick, or more heart-wrenching than breaking up with James.

She grabbed a baby blue argyle cardigan from the laundry and folded it. "I need an order of moo goo gai pan and a pint of Tofutti ice cream."

I shook my head. "That sounds amazing. Too bad we didn't think of it earlier."

She picked up another shirt. "Do you have the membership card to Blockbuster?"

"Yes, I have it."

"Good, we'll swing by there after our food run. I need a distraction, and I want to watch that *Pretty Woman* movie Frank wouldn't let us see."

I gnawed on my upper lip. "Are you suggesting we're going to watch a movie and eat takeout in Frank's room?"

She nodded like this wasn't an act of pure anarchy.

"What about Tracy and Liz? They'll notice we're not at work."

"I'll call the club and tell Adams I'm not feeling well and to tell the girls you're staying home to take care of me," she said, standing up. "Where's your phone?"

"It's on the cradle on the kitchen bar. But—"

She cut me off to give me the rest of the plan. This side of Dylan was a force. There were no words like *maybe* or *could* in her statements. It was all *we* will *do this*, and *I'll take care of that*. She could run the map with this kind of attitude, be the person that got the corner office, be the leader of a small army. But she wouldn't. She wouldn't live that long.

I was sliding back into my emotional pit of hell when I heard her speak. "We'll be asleep by the time they get home, and I'll be taking you and Steve to the airport before they get up. If they say anything to me when I return, I'll tell them I needed your help. By the time they get to Hawaii and hear I'm very fucking sick, they'll put it all together and blow off mentioning it to Frank."

We lugged my things into her car and headed out. I stared up at James' apartment as we drove by. I should have never dragged him into this. Frank was right; my purpose had nothing to do with being normal. The more I sought it out, the more painful my life would be.

We parked in the middle of the strip mall, and I picked up the movie while she got our food.

Once back at the house, plates loaded to the brim and movie in the VCR, I asked Dylan, "When do you get to Hawaii?"

"On the fifth, Sunday night."

I took another bite of my food and tried to enjoy the savory, woodsy flavor of the shiitake mushrooms.

"Do you think I should call Frank and tell him?"

My eyes darted up to meet hers. I hadn't considered this question yet. "Who else knows?"

"No one. I went to your place right after my appointment."

I let my next bite drift back down to my plate. "I'm not sure if it's instinct or self-preservation," I said, "but I think you should wait and tell him in person."

"I think you're right."

"Plus," I continued, "by the time you arrive, there will be several of us there, and as a group, we can help Frank jump-start your therapy. You're going to need massages, aromatherapy, breathing exercises, and an enhanced diet. I'm sure he'll also want to give you in-depth, personalized sessions to help you balance your intellectual stress with your chakras."

Just listing out the things that could help her situation gave me hope—unless Frank had it, too. In which case, we were all fucked.

I moved past that thought as fast as I could. "Do you think you'll be okay here with no one to talk to about it for a few days?"

"Yes," she said. "Do you think you can lie to everyone until I get there?"

I lifted my fork back up to my mouth and nodded. I thought she'd be shocked to know what a proficient little liar I'd become.

I spent most of the time I should have been sleeping staring into the darkness of my old room, listening to Dylan talk in her sleep from Jodie's bed. I had the thin comfort of not knowing if I had AIDS or not. I couldn't imagine how her mind was handling the certainty of her diagnosis.

I got out of bed around five and studied myself in the bathroom mirror with a critical eye. Was I starting to show the kind of fatigue Dylan had been exhibiting? If I had the virus, how long would it take before I started showing the symptoms?

I couldn't remember ever looking at her and not thinking she looked tired, even through her beauty. I moved around to see if I had darker-than-normal circles under my eyes. Did *I* look tired?

I decided this line of questioning was futile, brushed my teeth, and popped into the shower. I came in here to clean my body; instead, I was staring down my enemy. I gathered all the razors, opened the shower curtain, and tossed them in the trash. They clattered and ricocheted off the plastic garbage can, giving me quiet strength. I didn't care if I ever shaved my legs again.

I finished my shower, sprayed in some leave-in conditioner, and dressed. It was only fifty degrees here, but I'd rather be cold for the couple of minutes outside in Austin than be hot after we landed in Kauai. I wore a pair of long jean shorts and a boxy dark purple t-shirt that said Surf's Up, which I had bought the last time we were there.

Dylan and Steve were outside putting his things in the trunk of her car when I came out to join them.

I dragged my bag across the driveway and handed it to Steve. "How are we doing on time?"

"We're doing great, we still have thirty minutes. Plenty of time to drive to Mueller Airport and get to our gate." Steve flashed me a carefree smile. "It's going to be a glorious trip."

I returned his cheerful gesture with a half-hearted hug and turned to Dylan. "Thanks for driving us to the airport."

"I'm going to miss *you*...guys," she said. Our friendship had grown to the point that we now shared not only secrets but hidden facial gestures.

Steve clapped his hands together. "I think we're ready!" he said in a sing-song voice.

I wasn't ready. Sure, my things were in the car, and I had my ticket with me, but I was not emotionally prepared to begin the farewell trip, which had changed into my welcome-back stay.

Dylan and I did our best to keep up with Steve's enthusiasm, but small talk was something neither of us seemed to be capable of at the moment. I didn't want to say goodbye to her. She was now the only person that shared even half of my pain, and I felt vulnerable without her.

I usually loved everything about airports. The smell of jet fuel had always given me a heady buzz, but not today. Instead of joyfully watching families and friends reunite on the concourse, I was deconstructing a daydream I'd had about running into James's arms after this long trip was over. I kept hoping that the more I slashed away at the what-could-have-beens, the quicker I'd get to the quiet resignation stage.

We crossed the threshold into the plane and exchanged terminal air for the smell of stale cigarettes and bad plane food. I fastened my belt and closed my eyes, hoping to fall back to sleep.

Steve, on the other hand, was ready for a heart-to-heart chat. "I'm worried about you," he said as the flight attendant droned through the safety demonstration.

Had Dylan told him anything this morning while they were outside? "Me? Why are you worried about me?"

"Your spark is gone."

I let out a breath. "I'm just tired. It's been an interesting couple of days." I closed my eyes, hoping he would decide that now was not the best time for this conversation.

"Yeah, but it's been a couple of months, not a couple of days."

Steve and I had a very good relationship, but I could no more tell him than I could tell Liz, Tracy, or Jodie. From what I'd learned, secrets were a euphemism for burdens. They were pretty packaged bombs that the person receiving them would have to eventually deal with by deciding to keep them and let them rot their soul...or tell Frank.

I gave him a quick pat on the arm. "Maybe we can talk about it on the beach." I was hoping we would not have time for this conversation before Dylan got to Hawaii, not unlike the impending conversation that might come up with Tracy and Liz about our skipping work the night before. I needed everyone to give me a little psychic space until Dylan could reveal her diagnosis. Would life ever go back to a time when I didn't feel the need to tell lie after lie?

He gave me a simple nod. "I understand. I know the proximity you guys have to Frank puts a strain on all of you...." The roar of the engines nearly drowned out Steve's voice, but he kept going. "Sometimes the flame that warms your soul can also singe your spirit."

I gave him a quick eyebrow lift to confirm what he said, and turned to look out the window so he couldn't see the tears welling up in my eyes. My spirit currently felt incinerated to the core, but I couldn't blame all of that on Frank.

Chapter 19

Gone Daddy Gone

James

The past eight days had done nothing but suck. There was an endless movie of Jewels' and my greatest moments playing nonstop in my brain, whether I was awake, asleep, or taking a dump. I could not get her out of my mind.

Inactivity was crushing me from every direction. I already had enough investors, so there was no one to call. I couldn't bring myself to do laundry, clean my apartment, or clip my toenails.

I opened the phone book to get the number for Planned Parenthood so I could schedule an AIDS test. The woman who answered told me they closed at three and suggested I make an appointment for next week. I picked an available slot early Tuesday morning.

There were a couple of hours of good daylight left, but I had no idea what to do with them. The only thing I knew for sure was that I couldn't stay in my apartment. A movie, maybe? There was one called *Rush* that came out a couple of weeks ago. But after reading the review in the paper, I decided now wasn't a great time to watch a show about two cops going undercover and turning into drug addicts.

I was getting a glass of water in the kitchen when I peered through the cut-out. My golf clubs were resting against the wall in my dining room. Yes, that was what I'd do; I grabbed my new driver and a couple of irons and headed to the range.

After parking my car, I bought a large bucket of balls and walked over to the tee line to work on my swing. The sun was set low in the sky, casting a diffused yellowish orange light across the course. Because it was so late, it was only me and the golf ball picker out here.

I placed my tee in the ground and set up for my shot. I smashed the ball, skipping the practice swings. The ball made a full-bodied pinging noise as it sailed through the air, and a rush of pleasure surged through my body.

The next several balls pulled left of the target, and I took a moment to stretch and recalibrate my shot. The next one landed near the flag.

Besides the satisfaction of the shot, the fact that some of my choices were affecting the outcome was very gratifying. It gave me a sense of control. It occurred to me that none of this perceived control existed in my relationship with January.

Frustrated, I placed more balls on the tee. I hit them, thinking about all the times she had said she couldn't do something with me because she would have to get permission from Frank.

Then I thought of all the hours January had spent at the club making money for him instead of buying herself any furniture besides a bed. *Thwack, thwack*, another ball sailed through the air, and then another.

I rolled yet another ball in front of me and remembered her telling me how she would never abandon anyone ever again. *Well, she left me*. I hit the ball so hard that I thought the plastic cover would peel off it.

I kept this up for a good ten minutes until I had only one ball remaining. When I set up this shot, I thought of the day January came to break up with me. She hadn't shed a single tear. I'd watched her cry so many times, but that day—the day she was breaking up with me—not a drop. I lifted my club and obliterated the ball.

I didn't understand until that moment how angry I was with her. Sadness had been my overwhelming emotion for the past week. Now I realized that underneath that sadness, I was pissed—and underneath pissed, I was heartbroken.

I picked my other clubs off the grass and walked to my car. By that time, I was the only one left in the parking lot. I sat on the trunk and watched the sun drop below the horizon. I was mad as hell at that woman, but I'd still do anything to get her back.

I opened the door to my apartment, and the smell of January permeated my senses. I hadn't realized that my nose had grown used to her scent while I'd been cooped up in here. Maybe that was why I couldn't stop thinking about her. I headed straight to the kitchen for a black, thick plastic bag to put her clothes in. I dug everything out of the drawers she was using. Everything of hers got shoved it into the bag, which I tied up and placed in the corner of my linen closet, where I wouldn't see or smell January's things daily.

There was one message on my machine. I hit the play button. "James," said my banker in an ominous tone.

I let out a painful sigh.

"I have some bad news. Your twenty-thousand-dollar investor has backed out. Without those funds, your deal is dead. I'll be at the bank until six this evening. Call me as soon as you get this message."

Of course it was dead. The girl I loved had returned to her cult, and my chance to prove to my dad that I was competent enough to build my own business had evaporated.

I must have woken up three times the next morning and decided to go back to sleep. As far as I could tell, there was nothing to get out of bed for.

The conversation with my banker last night was a basic rehash of the message he had left me. The guy Parker had introduced me to had changed his mind at the final hour and pulled out of my deal. Without his cash, there was no bar, thus no reason to get up.

I checked my watch; it was two-thirty in the afternoon. Late, even by my standards. I got up to use the bathroom and stood there relieving myself looking face to face with Einstein. This time, his tongue sticking out felt personal. I finished my business, flushed the toilet, and tore half the poster off in one rip across the center. The rest hung on by the remaining tacks.

I shuffled into the kitchen to make coffee, but I was out of Folgers, cream, and sugar. I checked the cupboard for a glass, but they were all in the sink. I turned on the water and took a few gulps from the tap.

The phone rang from somewhere in my couch. I leaned up against the wall and let the machine get it.

"James, it's your dad. Could you call me as soon as you can? It's important."

I banged my head lightly against the wall. I wanted to pick up the call, but I couldn't tell my dad what was going on just yet. I needed food and aspirin first.

The phone rang a second time. I let the machine answer it again. This time it was Brad. I scrambled to unearth it from deep within my couch.

"Pick up the phone, old man. I know you're there feeling sorry for yourself."

I had told him about my deal falling apart last night at work. "I'm not feeling sorry for myself," I said after hitting the answer button.

"Really?" he asked. "I might be if I were you."

I sighed into the phone. "I'm so frustrated. I've never felt this helpless in my entire life."

"Let's go grab a beer."

"Eh, I haven't even had coffee yet. Plus I've been around stupid drunk people for days, so I'm not sure a bar is where I want to spend my Friday afternoon—" I lowered my voice for emphasis—"and I'm definitely not interested in going to a strip club."

"Me either," he said. "I was thinking something chill, like food and a pint at The Dog and Duck."

"Sounds good. I'll pop into the shower and meet you there in thirty."

Brad was already sitting at a table in the back, as far away from the nerdy Trivial Pursuit players as possible, when I arrived. I took off my jean jacket, tossed today's paper on the table, and sat down across from him.

He shook his head. "What in the hell is that for?"

"It's time I look for a job."

He barked out a laugh and flagged down our server. "You just need a stiff drink and a good pep talk. I'll take the want ads. If anyone is going to get a real job, it'll be me. I love working with you, but I'm tired of bartending. I'm ready to sign up for a nine-to-five work week and benefits."

Our server came over and placed menus on the table. "My friend here needs two cups of coffee with lots of cream and sugar."

Nobody on the planet knew me as well as Brad did. Those years we had spent smashed in our dorm together turned him into the brother I had always wanted.

I gave the waitress a nod and added a Reuben to the order.

I wasn't surprised Brad was ready to get a job; he'd been talking about it forever. He would have done it months ago if he had not started seeing Ripley. I couldn't say I envied their situation. If he did get a job, they'd have conflicting schedules. But that was their challenge to sort out.

"I love this place. It's very eclectic."

He was right. The Dog and Duck was unique with its green panel walls and brass ceiling fans. My favorite thing was how the bar sloped a good ten percent from one end to the other, as if the owners had decided they didn't have to impress anyone. It was good enough the way it was.

I thanked the server as she placed my two cups of coffee on the table.

"All right, let's start with January," Brad said to me. "She's a stripper in a cult. Surely you knew going into this deal that it was a long shot."

"Knowing the chances of something not working out doesn't prevent you from being disappointed when it ends."

"I'll give you that. So what happened?"

I gave him a sidelong glance. I didn't want to lie to my best friend, but I couldn't be honest with him, at least not with the parts that didn't involve me. There was no way I could say anything about Dylan having AIDS. I trusted Brad with my life, but not with a secret, especially now that he was dating Ripley. Her connection to all of January's cult friends was too close and too big of a temptation.

"She got spooked," I finally answered. "She has many valid reasons for staying in the cult: stability, relationships, a family-like environment, emotional support. I can't offer her any of those things, I don't even have a real job."

He rolled his eyes.

I barreled on. "I think I get that. Part of my brain gets it. The other part is a petulant child, and it wants what it wants."

"So, what *do* you want?"

"I want her to choose me. But she didn't, and now that part of my brain is going through the constant gymnastics of trying to figure out if there was something else I could have done."

Brad nodded, "I do that too."

"Right! We all do it. I can tell I'm moving into the calculating, manipulating stage."

"What's that look like?"

"You know, I think of ways to get her to come back to me. Like, maybe if I hold the shit she left in my apartment hostage, she'll come over to pick it up, see me, and change her mind. Or, if I go to the club every night, I can wear her down. Do the boom box over my head at her apartment complex like in that movie with John Cusack."

Brad snapped his fingers. "Oh yeah, *Say Anything*, total chick flick. My sisters killed our VCR playing the shit out of that movie."

Our server dropped off our food, and I asked her for a Coke.

"The good news is after that stage, I'll roll into the 'I wasn't that into her' stage," I said. "Then I can move on."

"How long do you think that will take?" he asked.

"Hopefully, not very long."

"You can do what Parker does."

Just the idea of doing something Parker did was sketchy. He was a great friend and he always had my back, but I didn't really trust him when it came to the intricate dealings with a woman. He was more of a love 'em and leave 'em type. His longest committed relationship lasted about eight days.

"What does he do?" I finally asked.

"He moves on as fast as possible, snatches up the next girl that smiles at him that he thinks is pretty. He says it takes the edge off, cuts down the recovery time."

I nearly choked on my soda. "Ugh, that's horrible. He's using that chick to get over the last chick? I can't do that. I could never do that to a woman."

Our conversation paused so we could stuff some more food in our mouths. Brad started things up again after taking a drink of his beer. "Let's talk about the bar."

"Do we have to?"

"Come on, old man, stop pouting and get your shit together."

"I'm not pouting."

"Look, I absolutely think you can do this."

"I can't take another challenge right now," I said and then mumbled one of January's aphorisms. "My plate is too full."

"What? It's not another challenge, it's an extension of the original challenge, and you need to get it done."

"I'm out of people to call."

"Bullshit. Have you called my dad? I know you haven't," he said, holding up his hand. "Get back on the phone, press the flesh, sell your soul, do whatever it takes to get the money."

We finished our meal and went outside. I thanked him for getting me out of the house.

"Sure, thing, dude, I'll see you tonight at work. Go find the money."

Chapter 20

Love Will Tear Us Apart

Jewels

Disappointment oozed through me when Frank didn't choose me to pick up Dylan and Tracy from the airport. I wanted to talk to Dylan to see how she was doing without other people around.

Instead, I was told to go to the grocery store with Steve. We were instructed to pick up ahi tuna steaks for tonight's dinner.

The store was one of the oldest on the island and had been run by the same family since the early nineteen-hundreds. The owners always remembered us, probably because of the insane amount of fish we bought the two times a year we inhabited the large house half a mile away. A tapestry of their family heritage spread across the bamboo walls in black and white photographs. I enjoyed examining the pictures; they gave my mind something to do so I could tolerate the pungent smell.

"Mahalo," said Steve reaching out his hands to take the eight pounds of fish.

The man crinkled his leathery-tanned face into a smile. "Mahalo, and welcome back to Kauai. We are expecting a large delivery of your favorite fish in the morning."

Steve bowed his head. "Thank you for the tip; we'll be here first thing tomorrow to pick some up."

I was curious to know if he was bowing out of deference to the older man or if he was just used to being submissive. Either way, it was a kind thing to do, and I needed to put all those prickly thoughts back through the looking glass. I wouldn't survive here long with that type of dualistic thinking. I'd made my choice, and it was time to embrace it. Though our schedules were staggered, there was a point in the month when our visits all overlapped. Almost fifteen of the core group would be here within a few days. Before someone noticed, I needed to solidify my convictions back to the group ideology.

Steve turned down the gravel cul-de-sac that led to the house. "Hey, looks like the new group has arrived."

Dylan and Frank were out on the lawn. I squinted through the windshield while a pit in my stomach developed. From this distance, all their hand gestures and body language could have been perceived as typical conversation, until Frank stooped over, shaking his head in disbelief. Dylan rested her hand on his hunched back, but he recoiled and moved out of her reach. She dropped her head and ran into the house.

Steve pointed down the road. "What do you suppose is going on up there?"

Answering his question with an *I don't know* was too big of a misrepresentation, so I said, "I'm not sure."

By the time we pulled the rental car under the stilt-styled house, Frank had become a statue. His vacant gaze made him look trapped in a storm of unwanted thoughts and terrifying options.

The girls were peeking down from the living room window, no doubt trying to figure out what was happening.

"Steve, will you please take the food upstairs?" I got out of the car and made my way to Frank. I wasn't being stealthy in my approach, so it surprised me when he didn't acknowledge my arrival.

I was very familiar with the expression on his face. Both Dylan and I had matching ones several days ago. His relationship with her had been much deeper than mine, so the information might have hit him harder. Instead of standing in front of him, I stood at his side just in case he puked like I had.

There was no way to soften the blow her information had delivered. He was incapacitated. We were already at the triage stage, so I prepared myself for his next reaction, hoping it wasn't rage.

He blinked at me. "How long have you known?"

"She told me the day before I arrived."

He tipped his head, and I braced myself. "What do we do first?"

Was this a test? Why was he asking me what we should do? He'd never asked me a single action question that wasn't rhetorical.

I took in a breath and tested the water. "We should sit down and tell everyone and get tested. The sooner we know who has it, the faster we can start helping everyone."

"Ok," he said, turning toward the house. "Round 'em all up and let them know. I'm going to meditate. Find a place to put Dylan. She needs a room of her own to keep the others safe."

What was he talking about? Now I was the one standing dumbstruck in the middle of the yard. How did I get put in the "person in charge" position? I *wasn't* that person. I was the comic relief, fly-under-the-radar, follow-directions person.

The daily gray, heavy clouds in the distance began choking out the sun. The mood in the house was thick with confusion. Frank gave Fanny a look, and they headed straight for their room. Once he was out of sight, everyone's attention turned to me.

I told them the only thing I knew at the moment. "We're going to have a meeting in about five minutes. Please get everyone together."

I walked into the bedroom I shared with Tracy. Dylan was sitting on our bed, staring at the floor.

"Are you okay?" I asked. "How was your trip?"

"He didn't take it very well."

"He'll be fine. I'm sure he's overwhelmed right now. It'll pass."

She gave me an apologetic smile. "Now what do we do?"

"He wants me to tell everyone. I've asked them to meet in the living room so that I can give them the information all at once. Would you be up for doing that with me, or would you rather wait to answer some of their questions later?"

"Yeah, I'll come."

We walked down the hall into the open kitchen, dining, and living room area. The rain made light pitter-patting noises against the awning that covered the wrap-around porch.

Dylan and I sat together on the couch and told our friends what had transpired. To my great relief, everyone was very supportive. None of them panicked like I had or retreated the way Frank did, and everyone confirmed their endless solidarity for Dylan.

"What should we do next, Jewels?" Liz asked.

I pinched the bridge of my nose. For starters, I reminded them I was not in charge. "Who wants to find a place so we can all get tested?" I asked reluctantly.

Tracy raised her hand. "I'm happy to take care of that."

"Great, thank you."

I asked Liz and Jodi about food prep and schedules. They assured me everything was in order. Others jumped into the conversation, offering to assist wherever necessary. We were doing it; we were fulfilling our purpose, functioning as a single-minded group to administer various therapies to nurture someone in need.

We spent about an hour rearranging everyone so Dylan could have her own space. The bedroom wasn't very big, and the door faced into the main living area, but it was private.

I helped her lug her bags in from the car and unpack.

"I don't need my own room," she protested. "It's not leprosy. I'm not going to ooze contaminated blood out of my pores in my sleep."

"I know, this is just what he told us to do. I'm sure he will feel better tomorrow, and we can return to how it usually is."

About an hour later, the door to Frank's room opened, and Fanny came out.

"He wants more privacy," she said, standing in the doorway to my room.

I patted a place for her to sit on the bed. "Come on in. How are you holding up?" She might have been new to the group, but she was Frank's current girlfriend, which put her in the top tier of people most likely to be infected.

"I'm okay," she said with her soft French accent. "I dislike the contraceptive pill, so we always use plastic things."

We sat there delicately talking around the awkward situation. Her broken English somehow made her more vulnerable and charming. I couldn't help but wonder how long it would be before Frank asked me to train her at the club.

Both Frank and Dylan had their dinner in their rooms. After everything was cleaned up and put away, I went onto the porch to find my own piece of momentary solitude. I spent it crying and thinking about James.

The sound of Frank asking Tracy to make coffee woke me up. As soon as she left the room, he grabbed the covers on her side of the bed, pulled them across where she'd been sleeping, and sat beside me.

"Jewels, are you awake?" he whispered.

I guess he didn't know the golden rule: if he was awake, we all needed to be awake.

I rubbed the sleep out of my eyes. "I sure am."

"I'm having a lot of strange dreams. Can I tell you about them? Maybe you can help me figure out what they mean."

Who was this next to me? *Can you? Will you? Should we?* I'd been with Frank for four years, many of them intimately. He'd never used these words with me before or with anyone else, as far as I knew.

He told me about his dream, which was more of a nightmare than I'd expected. Frank used our dreams to analyze us often, so I didn't think he needed my help to decipher this one.

"You've always taught us dreams about drowning represent the fear of losing oneself or control in general."

He agreed, and we sat there for a bit in silence. Finally, I told him I would get his coffee and soaked almonds so I could have an excuse to leave the room. I went straight to check on Dylan and was happy to find her still sleeping.

Fanny, who'd ended up crashing on the couch, was rising when I tiptoed into the living room. "I didn't wake you, did I?"

"Non, je me réveillais juste," she said, immediately shaking her head. "I was just waking up."

I smiled, and my nurturing side urged me to care about her more than I was ready to.

The smell of ripe papayas from the trees in the front yard floated in through the open doors and windows. People had started milling about in the house while Jodi and Liz were making breakfast. Steve asked me if

Frank was going to be joining us, and all I could do was shrug. Up until twelve hours ago, I knew his every mood and reaction, but now he was a complete mystery to me.

I grabbed Frank's coffee and almonds off the counter. "I'll go ask him." I was praying he would say yes and leave our room.

Unfortunately, his answer was, "I'll have it in here with you." *Crap.*

That was how my entire day went. We talked a little, we meditated, and we wrote our affirmations. I made occasional trips into the living room to check on everyone and answer their mounting questions such as would it be all right for them to leave the house or could they go for a walk or to the beach. We were all used to getting our directions from Frank, and not sure what would be appropriate under the circumstances.

The next day I said to Tracy, "Frank, Fanny, Jodie, and I are going to get our HIV tests. I think you should move the shared clothes to a different room until we figure out what he's going to do." Swimwear, tunic dresses, watches, and certain t-shirts were all shared items among the girls. It was nice when you or someone in your room was the designated caretaker of the items because you had close access and first dibs on anything you wanted to wear. It wasn't so great when people were streaming in and out of your room all day and night to pick out what they wanted. Right now, it was complicated because my room had become Frank's emotional bunker, and there were five women in the house who no longer had access to anything.

"All of them?"

I smiled at her. "No, just the ones people want to wear."

"Sorry," she said. "That was a silly question."

"And yet, somehow appropriate. And please get the watches out of there as well. The ten of them together are very loud," I said, tripping on the memory of the quiet watch James gave me.

There wasn't a Planned Parenthood on the Island of Kauai, so Tracy found a private doctor willing to test us. She told me the office would be very accommodating and only asked that we come in groups of four so we didn't overwhelm their staff. They suggested that the people at greatest risk be the first to get tested. The results would take a little longer than on the mainland, but we were already familiar with the concept of *island time* and grateful they could help us.

Our rental was at the very end of the north shore, near the Ha'ena State park entrance. The doctor's office was on the south shore. There was only one main road that made a seventy percent loop around the island. The remaining thirty percent did not allow cars so it could be preserved for the many state parks and the Waimea Canyon. This meant we had to backtrack often.

After our ninety-minute, dead-silent drive to the doctor's office, we were greeted by the kindest people and the smoothest experience I could have wished for. They ushered us into a private office, required minimal paperwork, and asked us very few questions. It took us longer to get to the office than it did to give our required tube of blood. I was hopeful that starting the process of getting my results would help me feel better, but it didn't.

"Where should we go now?" Frank asked when we got back into the car.

I needed some fresh air and suggested a quiet stroll.

We pulled over to the nearest beach, took our shoes off, and started walking. Frank and I stuck to the beach while Fanny and Jodie walked a couple of feet into the surf, looking for shells. The air was thick with humidity and the lingering scent from last night's rain. Even though this beach was public, there weren't any big hotels on this part of the island, so the majority of beachgoers were locals and the occasional tourists like us were in small, palatable doses.

Here among the wind, sand, and sun tanners, Frank told me he was sorry he had put our lives in danger. "I'm supposed to be the healer," he said, "the guru. I let my guard down and let evil come into our group."

I didn't think that was true. I wasn't that big into the dark-versus-the-light theory.

"Maybe it's not evil," I said while the sand mushed between my toes. "Maybe it's just a different, more intense level of learning. Something to prepare us for what's coming. Who better to help people through this crisis than someone with experience? Maybe more will come to us for help. Maybe Dylan is the first of many."

I waited for him to tell me how naïve I was, but he said nothing. We walked up and down the beach until he got hungry, and then we drove back to the house.

New people arrived. Those who had been here a while explained Dylan's condition; they got tested, and Frank returned to my room every morning. Dylan mingled, but her nature was always more introverted, and the pressure of everyone trying to make her feel normal silently fueled her further retreat.

Several days had passed when Liz knocked on my bedroom door. "It's the doctor's office."

Frank gave me a blank expression. "Go see what they have to say."

I swallowed and headed for the kitchen. Each step elongated the hallway like in one of those scary movies Frank made me watch. Half the group was hanging out in the living room, and all of them were watching me.

I put the receiver to my ear and stared out the window. I could hear the sound of my own belabored breathing through the earpiece. Each second that ticked away tipped my plate closer to the edge.

As the nurse gave me the news, my line of sight shifted from outside to Liz's face and then around the room to everyone else. The salty flavor of my tears had made their way to my lips and brought me back to my senses.

"Thank you," I told the nurse. "We appreciate everything you've done for us."

"Negative," I whispered once I'd hung up. "All four of us are negative."

Liz reached out to put her hand on my arm, and I collapsed into her. If the four of us didn't have it, there was very little chance anyone else was infected. Tiny bubbles of contained joy floated through my mind for James and me, but it was impossible to experience complete relief when I was still agonizing for Dylan.

Frank was already standing behind me when I went to tell him the news. There was a familiar sternness behind his smile. Repentant Frank was gone, and Guru Dick Breath was back.

He clapped his hands, hushing everyone in the house. "No more lying around," he said, his usual condescension weaving through his words. "What do you people think this is, a vacation?"

He pointed at me, "Go tell Dylan, but make sure she understands she must stay in that room alone."

I spun away from him so he wouldn't see the *what an asshole* look that was all over my face. Fueled by disgust, I barged into her room and closed the door behind me.

Dylan gave me a wide-eyed stare. "You okay?"

I wasn't sure if she was asking me about my results or the anger I was struggling to contain.

"Not entirely. Our tests came back negative, but I just realized I have to spend the rest of my life with Frank."

She gave me a slow, knowing nod. I didn't elaborate or mention I was staying because of her. That was none of her business.

Chapter 21

Cuts You Up

James

My morning appointment at Planned Parenthood had gone fast and easy. January and I had always used condoms, so I didn't think I had AIDS. I knew her risk was higher living with someone who unknowingly had the infection, but I still felt the chances of her having the virus were low.

After they took down my information and drew my blood, they told me my results would be back on Friday and they'd give me a call.

A ten-minute drive later, I arrived at Swedish Hill, my favorite bakery in all of Texas. I came here to have lunch every couple of weeks, but because of my schedule, I rarely had the chance to enjoy their breakfast menu. I was here today because my dad wanted to meet with me. He had called last night to tell me he would be in town for a couple of things and wanted to have breakfast.

I had yet to tell my dad about the bar falling through, but I figured now would be a good time. I had been calling everyone I could think of to come up with the money, including Brad's parents, who were interested, but only for twenty-five hundred dollars. Other than that, I'd hit a brick wall.

I headed inside and joined my dad at the counter. By the looks of it, he had arrived right before I did. I patted his shoulder and sat on the stool next to him. "How are you doing? It's good to see you."

"Hey, James. Thanks for joining me."

A frazzled-looking waitress walked up to take our order. "Coffee?"

"Yes," my dad and I answered at the same time.

She spun around, grabbed a pot of coffee and two mugs and filled them to the top. I ordered the number three from the menu and steadily answered her questions, which came out like a cross-examination.

"How do you want your eggs?"

"Over-easy, please."

"Sausage or ham?"

"Ham."

"Muffin or toast?"

"Toast." Her lips separated for her next question, and I quickly spat out, "Wheat, if you have it."

She turned to my dad, "How about you?"

He looked up from his menu and said, "I'll have the same thing he's having."

She grinned in apparent approval. "It'll be out in a jiffy."

"What are you doing here?" I asked as soon as she walked away. "And where is Mom?"

"She's in Dallas. She decided to stay since this was such a quick trip. I'll be going back this evening."

I nodded and took a sip from my coffee. I hacked and set it down immediately.

"You all right?"

"Yes, I'm fine. I forgot to add cream and sugar."

He pushed both of them in my direction. "I was talking about you in general. You don't seem like yourself."

I stirred my coffee and told him about January's breaking up with me. The worry lines between his brows deepened. He'd witnessed me going through breakups before, and I didn't remember them making his face contort into such pain.

"I'm sorry to hear that. I know your mother and I never met her, but from our conversations over the holiday, you seemed to really like her."

He was right about that. I missed talking to her on the phone, hanging out with her, and watching her rediscover herself. I even missed watching her cry, seeing her navigate her anxiety and occasional rage toward her situation.

"Here y'all go," said our waitress as she slid our plates in front of us and headed off.

"What else is bothering you?" Dad asked as I crammed my food into my mouth. "Jeez, son, you in a hurry? One bite at a time."

I wanted to give him a look that would convey *Please don't lecture me on how to eat my food*, but his grinning face caught me off-guard, so I softened my expression. "This food is too good to eat politely, and you were right. I've lost the building and the dream of putting a bar together. I've started looking for a stable, nine-to-five job."

Telling him this made the loss feel more permanent, more real. Abject failure was lodging itself in my throat; I did my best to swallow around it.

"I'm sorry to hear that," my dad said, wiping the corners of his mouth. "Can you tell me what happened?"

I shrugged. "One of my biggest investors had to back out at the last minute. His portion was significant enough that I couldn't find someone to replace it."

"Why didn't you ask us?"

"Well, I know you didn't like the idea of me starting my own business. I didn't want to put you in a position of having to reject me. That didn't seem fair to you."

"Yeah, I made it pretty clear this wasn't what I wanted you to do. For quite a while, that's exactly how I felt. You know, my parents grew up in the depression and were terrified something like that would happen again. So they pushed me to save, save, save and plan for the worst. Now I can see how I did the same thing to you."

He took a quick sip of his coffee and went on. "I also didn't want you to have to work that hard. Running your own business, especially a bar or restaurant, is a 'round-the-clock, every-day-of-the-year commitment. When you came up for Christmas and showed us all the progress you'd made, I not only realized how much you wanted it but how capable you were at getting it. And honestly, who am I to stop you? I want you to do more with your life than work at a boring job just so you can save for a rainy day."

I reached for my toast. "Well, either way, what's done is done."

"Yes," he said, "What's done is done, which is why you and I need to finish our meal and head to the bank."

"Why would we need to go to the bank?"

"Because Bob Bennett is waiting for you to sign all the documents so you can be the next owner of the property of 606 Trinity Street."

I jerked back and shot him a curious glance. "How do you know my banker's name and the property address?"

A sly smile spread across his face. "I knew Bob when he was just a teller. He gave me the address."

I *knew* it. I knew the minute Bob brought it up the second time I'd met with him he might know my dad.

"But..."

"He called me shortly after the man who was going to invest the twenty-thousand backed out. He knew you didn't want to ask us to co-sign, but maybe you would be okay with us investing. He believed in you enough to stick his neck out and call us. Your mother and I talked it over for about three seconds, and that was that. We signed all the paperwork up in Dallas yesterday."

I sat there with my mouth hanging open, looking around the restaurant to see if any suspicious people were around. Was I on *Candid Camera*? I'd had two days of horrible news in the past two weeks. To have something this fantastic coming from the one person I thought was the least supportive of my choices in life was—miraculous.

"Look, we want to be silent investors. It's not our intention to tell you how to run your business. We just want to put some of what we have saved—into you. We think you're a good investment."

"I don't know what to say. I'm in shock."

He gave me an awkward punch in the arm. "Better eat up, Bob's expecting us at ten-thirty."

As we were walking into the bank, I caught a glimpse of my dad. He looked happier than I'd seen him in years. The permanent scowl he usually wore had been replaced by deep crinkles at the corners of his eyes. Where I was used to seeing tightness in his jawline, he now had faint smile lines.

Knowing my grandparents had instilled a fear of running out of money in my dad helped me understand him so much better. He was taught that profound concern for a loved one's financial stability was how you showed you cared for them.

I expected my experience at the bank to be the same as all my other visits. But this time, Bob's assistant was waiting for us in the lobby, and instead of taking us to his office, we were escorted to a conference room. She opened the heavy doors, and there was Bob, along with several other men I had never seen before.

This room was completely different from the rest of the bank. It was more in tune with this decade. All of the late seventies decor had been replaced with dark cherry wood-paneled walls, rich blue suede curtains, and a ten-foot-long granite conference table.

"Come on in, Mr. Sullivan," one of the men said, and I looked over to my dad, who gave me a nod.

"He's talking to you, James."

"Oh, so he is," I mumbled, walking over to the head of the table and sitting down in one of the many high-back leather chairs.

Bob instructed my dad to take a seat beside him.

"Mr. Sullivan," a man with a black well-tailored suit and steady expression said, "the past owners were here an hour ago to sign everything we need to transfer the title to you."

I nodded and did my best to follow along with his explanations. But my dad's beaming smile was making it hard to concentrate. I had no memory of him ever being this proud of me, not even when I graduated from UT.

The gentleman to my left got my attention by patting a two-inch stack of documents. "Shall we get started?"

Forty-five minutes later, we had completed all the paperwork. I stood up to stretch my legs, and Bob came over to give me the keys.

The minute they landed in my hand, the melancholy of January's absence hit me. I was flooded with little snapshots of her while going through this journey. How she had asked me what a Gellhorn was and how embarrassed she was that she didn't know it was a woman's name. How I would see her over by my kitchen table curiously peering at all the paperwork. And how I explained this whole process was a little disappointing because my dad hadn't been there to witness it.

Well, now *he* was here doing business—with me—and *she* couldn't see it.

Bob's assistant came back into the room with a camera. She herded people in and out of the way so she could take a picture. I was only half-paying attention, talking to one of the other men in the room. Suddenly, Bob had thrown his arm around my shoulder.

"Say *cheese*," his assistant said.

I held my finger up to stop her. "Dad," I called across the room. "Come here! You have to be in this photo with me."

Once we were finished at the bank, my dad drove us to the bar to look around. We parked in the one spot in the alley designated for my building.

I jacked with the key for a bit and added *new lock* to a mental list of things to change or fix. When the door made a painful whining noise as I pushed it open, I added *WD-40* to the list as well.

We couldn't find the light switch anywhere in the room. Decent light came in from the large windows and door in the front of the building. The switch must have been in the office, which was completely dark. We walked a couple of feet into the room, my dad's hand on my shoulder so he wouldn't collide into me. I hit what felt like a piece of wood with my foot that scraped across the floor, and we both startled.

"I have a flashlight in my car," my dad said. "I'll be right back."

I added *a flashlight* to my list.

It was a little weird standing here by myself in the dark. Of course, the first thing I thought about was January. I guessed I wasn't quite ready to stop thinking about her after all.

I heard the back door open, and a stream of light bounced off the walls from the flashlight Dad was wielding.

"Aha, there it is," he said, walking past me.

A second later, the lights were on. I was instantly grateful we hadn't come any farther into the room. An old metal desk and beat-up filing cabinet were only inches in front of me, with a bottle of champagne on the desk next to a note that read *Congratulations, James. You are the proud owner of a piece of Austin history. —Bob Bennett.*

I added his name to a list of people to invite to the grand opening and then added *an organizer* to my list of things to buy, so I had some place to keep all my lists.

We shuffled around the office and adjoining storage area for a while, figuring out the upgrades I'd have to make on the electrical box to accommodate a much larger air conditioning unit, the walk-in cooler, and outlets for amplifiers and band lighting.

Once back in the main room, I spotted a chair sitting a couple of feet from the door.

I looked over at my dad. "Where'd that come from?"

He gave me an unassuming shrug, "The trunk of my car."

"What? Wow, it's exactly what I told you I was looking for. Where did you find it?"

"Is it? I should have asked you for more details. I know you wanted it to be lightweight and modern, so I thought this would be a good place to start."

I walked over to the chair and picked it up. It was a little wider than your typical kitchen chair. The frame and spindles were lathed thinner than chairs I usually saw, and it had no ornamental details or embellishments, just a simple ladder back with a slight bow for added comfort.

I flipped it over to look for the manufacturing details, but there were none. I turned it around several times and finally sat on it. "Where did you find this?"

"I made it," he admitted.

"What?" I asked, popping up.

"I went to the library and did a little research on what you were looking for. I found something similar to this in a book about Scandinavian furniture. I haven't put any stains or paint on it yet. It's just a prototype."

"It's amazing!" I said, grinning at him. "So, this is what you've been doing in the garage?"

He nodded. "I met a man at one of the pubs I frequent that told me he's been a woodworker for years, and I'd been looking for something to do, so he showed me his place and started teaching me. I went over there several times a week and we made a couple of things together. After I was sure I enjoyed it, he helped me buy some of my own equipment."

"I can't believe you didn't mention it."

"Well, we haven't had much to say to each other for a while."

I remembered all the times I had let his calls go to my answering machine. "I'm sorry, Dad, that's my fault. I should have called you back."

He waved me off. "If I wasn't always shoving my ideas down your throat, you might have wanted to talk to me more often. Anyway, when you told me what kind of furniture you wanted, I thought I'd take a crack at it."

"It's perfect. Can you make another thirty of them in the next few months?"

He scratched the back of his head. "Aaah, I'm not sure I can have that many so quickly. Maybe half and then a couple more every ten days or so."

"Can you do tables too?"

"Yes. I don't have one finished, but I have a sketch of one in the car we can discuss."

"Fantastic," I said, staring at the chair. Eventually, I pulled the napkin from my pocket that I had drawn for him over Christmas and described how and where I would put the bar.

"You going to keep these floors?" he asked, toeing a piece of the old tile that had broken off.

"I'm not sure what to do with the floors. They're hideous."

His stomach rumbled. "Let's grab a bite to eat and talk about it. I've seen something up in Dallas that you might be interested in."

We locked the place up and headed over to Paradise Café.

Chapter 22

Love is a Stranger

Jewels

I'd only been in Hawaii for ten days—ten of the longest, strangest, most eye-opening days since joining the group. Now that Frank was no longer drifting through an existential crisis, his teachings had a renewed energy and purpose, one that didn't include compassion or understanding. He had replaced skulking around with prowling for people to insult and ridicule.

It wasn't the first time we'd seen him like this. We had all become adept in the strategy of duck-and-cover, and had been doing this rather successfully until lunchtime the day after we got our test results. "We need some exercise," he commanded once Liz had removed his empty plate from the table. "Set up the volleyball net."

Volleyball was the game Frank had started making us play after a documentary we'd watched about Carl Jung a couple of years ago. The film showed how Jung used physical games to intensify feelings and reactions in his patients. Frank's eyes had sparkled as he'd watched Jung's patients struggle through a myriad of complicated emotions. Shortly after that, competitive hostility became his favorite perversion.

Had I been able to read people's minds, I was sure everyone at the table was secretly screaming—*no*.

Steve was the first to spring into action, placing his plate by the sink and walking out the patio door to the backyard. Like well-trained seals at the circus, everyone followed his lead.

Frank watched the room clear. "Jewels, go tell Dylan she's not allowed to play, but I want her to participate as the referee."

I knocked on her door, the hairs on my neck tingling from the weight of Frank's stare as he evaluated my actions.

"Come in," I heard her say, and I cracked the door just enough to slip through and shut it behind me.

Dylan put her book down. "Ugh, now what?"

"We have to play volleyball; he wants you to be a linesman."

Nodding, she got off her bed. "Sure, I can sit on the sidelines and tell him he's right. I've been doing that for months."

Dylan and I walked through the house and out the door together. By the time we got to the balcony, they had already erected the volleyball net. The court had been placed in the middle of the backyard. Jodie and Steve had been marking the last boundary with twine and tent stakes. It fit snugly against the bamboo and banana trees planted along the property lines. The plumeria, hibiscus, and bird of paradise flowers had a courtside view for Frank's version of psychological sports terror.

He only cared about two things when playing the game: winning and making people cry. He used an obvious outcome like missing the shot to illustrate our weakness. It was a clear sign that we weren't ready if we didn't return the volley correctly.

The first game went well for Frank's side. He had several taller players on his team, and they were winning. The most challenging part of playing against Frank was when he would spike the ball. Those of us on the opposing side did our best to return it, but all we got for our efforts were severely red and bruised arms.

Seconds after his spike, the ball slapped haphazardly against our raw arms. "We'll take the point while you enjoy the burn," he shouted.

I knew this was part of the "lesson" inside the game, but he was being particularly brutal this afternoon.

He moved from the front of the court to the back. "Oh good, now I can practice my jump serve." He launched the ball at our side for five unanswered serves in a row. Each of them ricocheted painfully off different parts of our bodies.

Frank's team won twenty-one to ten, and I was grateful we were finished and ready to go back inside. The darkening sky warned that the afternoon rains would be here soon.

I had started making my way toward the house when Frank said, "I think these girls need me on their side so they can see firsthand what a player does to win the game." He switched with one of the girls on my team, and we began another game.

Steve shook his head. Even from this side of the net, I could see the pity in his expression. My frazzled nerves were making it hard to keep my lunch down.

The first couple of volleys went well. Our team did a decent job setting up quickly and hitting the ball to our teammates or, when lucky, over the net. A menacing layer of mist began glazing everything in the yard: the net, the ball, our bodies, and the grass. The other team served the next ball over the net straight to Liz. She returned the lobbed ball, but it was a poorly executed shot.

Frank scowled at her. "You do know there's a one in six chance they will hit the ball to you, correct?"

"Yes."

"Then why can't you be ready?"

There were no good answers to his question. "I won't let it happen again."

"What a joke," he said, tossing the ball back to the other team. "Wanna win? Hit it to Liz, she's the weakest link."

I tugged my wet t-shirt off my skin, anticipating the ball's arrival. It was nice and high, and there was plenty of time to get below it. I took my stance but underestimated its path. Instead of bouncing off my forearms, it smacked against my elbow pits. A dull thud from the awkward connection was followed by a momentary numbness in my fingers.

Frank howled out a laugh. "I take that back. Liz is not the only weak link on the team. They all suck equally."

I wanted to chuck the ball hard enough against his smug-ass face that I could see the name Wilson tattooed across his cheek.

The other side served the ball again. This time, it went to Tracy. She hurried to get into position, but slipped and crashed to the ground, her ankle twisting in the process.

"You're not concentrating!" Frank barked, instead of asking her if she was okay.

The mist turned to rain as she stood and rubbed the grass and mud off her legs while I prayed for lightning. The ball kept heading straight toward her. Though she attempted to return the serve correctly every time, she was unable to do so. I glared at the server. I didn't think he was sending it to her intentionally, but he could have done a better job at cutting her a break.

The rain thrashed against the banana leaves. The next ball rocketed across the net, straight into Tracy's arms. Relief flooded through me until the ball popped sideways, hitting Frank on his shoulder.

He thundered across the court. "Get your head out of your ass and play the game!"

The whites of her eyes doubled. "I'm sorry! I'll try harder."

"'I'll try harder, I'll try harder,'" he mocked. "Trying implies failure. Just get it done, *do* better. As a matter of fact, you will stay out here for the rest of the afternoon, *trying* to do better. Until then, get off the court."

"I can do it, I can do better now, I promise."

He pointed to the other side of the twine. "Get off the court!"

She stared at him, not moving.

"*Get off!*" he demanded again, lunging toward her.

She jumped over the boundary line and dropped into a squat position with her hands above her head. "Please don't hit me, I can do better."

The veins in his neck bulged. "All you have to do," he shouted through the downpour, "is what I fucking tell you."

Dylan took a couple of slow steps and stood in between them. I could tell that she was playing her "I have nothing to lose" card to protect Tracy. What a rock star. That was exactly what I wanted to be someday, a person strong enough to stand up to a bully to help someone who had lost their footing in life. But who was I kidding? That lesson was not in Frank's curriculum.

"Game over, we win," he said loud enough for everyone to hear before he walked away.

The following day at five-thirty in the morning, Frank woke us up by walking down the hall, banging on our doors. "Up and at 'em, you've had more than enough sleep. It's time to make me breakfast."

Tracy and I looked at each other through half-open eyes. I waited to see if she would say something about his ridiculous behavior, but she didn't. Within five minutes, everyone in the house was either preparing food, cooking, or setting the table.

Frank walked into the kitchen after his shower, and we all sat down to eat. No one said a word. I didn't think anyone wanted to be the first person he chided this early in the day.

He finished his meal and asked for more coffee. "Get all the gear loaded up; we're going scuba diving. Who's in charge of dinner tonight?"

Jodi put down her fork. "I am. We have ten pounds of mahi mahi ordered for pick up at four-thirty."

"Good. Everyone get ready, we're leaving in twenty minutes. Fanny will use Jewels' gear, she'll be staying behind with Dylan." He stood up and walked out of the room.

Checking the gear and loading up the car for this excursion took more time than he gave them. Frank would have a fit if they forgot a wetsuit, mask drops, dive cards, or clean regulators.

"Just leave all of this and go get ready," I told everyone. "Dylan and I will take care of it."

Most of the gear was stored in large containers in a built-in room in the parking area under the house. Steve and a couple of the other guys went outside to gather all the towels off the railings and load up the van. Once everyone had filed out, I helped Liz get snack bags together for the ride back on the boat after the dive.

Frank walked around shouting orders and reminding people what had to be done. As he left, he turned to me. "You and Dylan need to clean the house, especially my bathroom. It's a mess."

I nodded, and he shut the door.

Once they had pulled away, Dylan walked out of her room. "I'm sorry you have to stay behind with me."

"Don't be. I wouldn't want to be anywhere around him today, and I hate diving."

"You're kidding."

"I've never liked it. Being thirty to ninety feet underwater and sucking air out of a straw from a tank strapped to my back is not my idea of a good time."

"The things we do to get and keep his approval." She shrugged. "Look, I need to get out of this house. Let's get the place in order and go down to the beach."

"That sounds good. Are you up for cleaning? It's not going to drain you?"

"I feel good today. My immune system is probably very low, but I can vacuum, dust, and do laundry if you can do all the toilets, dishes, and mopping."

"Deal," I said, and we got to work. I was in Frank's room when Dylan turned on the built-in sound system. Warmth cascaded through my chest. I would have never been bold enough to play music while I did my chores.

It took us four hours to get everything done. We opted not to change into our suits because we didn't think it would be a good idea for her to swim, and I just wanted to walk and sit on the beach for a while.

We strolled down the private walkway at the end of our cul-de-sac, the sound of our flip-flops echoing off the houses that sat on either side of the path.

Dylan pointed to a No Outlet sign. "Do you think it's a coincidence that the two houses we lived in throughout the year are both on dead-end roads?"

"Probably." I let out a half-laugh, and we kept walking until we reached the sand. "So how are you holding up?"

"I'm okay, you know, the fear comes and goes in waves."

"I'm so sorry. I feel responsible for the way he's treating you. Maybe we should have told him you were sick over the phone. It might have helped."

"No, Jewels, there is no way you could have predicted his reaction," she said. "It's okay. At first, the isolation crushed me, but it's nice to have a place of solitude to deal with my thoughts and feelings."

We padded over to the shoreline, and I took my shoes off and walked by the water's edge. She left hers on and stayed on the beachside. We weren't too worried about her getting splashed by the water, but were very cautious about her getting cut by a broken shell or piece of glass.

"So," she said in a flirty voice, "we know what's going on with me, now it's your turn."

"Not much, really," I said, "just doing my best to stay out of Frank's way."

She gave me a hip bump. "Come on, Jewels, I mean, you've been different since I told you, sure, I get that. But then your test came back negative, and you're still not yourself."

"Huh, I'm not sure what 'myself' means anymore. I look back at all the things I've done and I've said, and I'm not sure which ones are me. Which ones do you think I'm not being anymore?"

"I don't know," she said. "Mostly, I miss your dry wit and humor."

"I'm using too much of my brain staying on Frank's good side to be funny. He's dangerously unpredictable right now."

She agreed. "Okay, I have another question. Want to tell me about all those preppy clothes in your apartment?"

I stopped walking.

"Jewels, it's okay. I won't tell anyone. I'm leaving."

What did she just say? She was *leaving?* But, *wait*—I'd left James to stay in the group *for her*...and she was now leaving the group? I would be stuck here with Frank—alone. *Shit, shit, shit.*

I worried the bridge of my nose. "You're leaving?"

"Absolutely. I'm not sure what the rest of my life will look like, but I know I don't want to spend it locked away in a bedroom. I need to find resources, doctors, and to reconnect with my family. I only came on the trip because of the damn companion ticket."

I rolled my eyes. "Me too."

"Where did you go the other day, the day I told you I had AIDS?" She paused, changing back into her flirty voice. "And where did you get that seven-hundred-dollar watch?"

I walked a foot farther out into the water. *Craaaap!* I should have been more careful. Things happened so fast that day; I couldn't believe I'd left my watch out.

She reached over and pulled me closer to her. "I won't tell him or anyone else. I'm leaving the group." She shot me a sly smile and lowered her voice to a whisper. "Or is it a cult?"

I stood there in a stupor. "So you've heard the rumors at work?"

"Oh yeah, Mr. Clifford Antone and I had many conversations about it. I'm sorry I didn't tell you what I thought, it was just too risky. I couldn't take the chance of you saying anything to Frank or Tracy or Liz."

"I get it," I mumbled, my brain hamster-wheeling through all this new information.

She waved at me to get my attention. "So who gave you the watch?"

I took a small breath. "James."

"James?" she repeated. "The young, cute Dellionair? The guy I sat with at the club for a couple of minutes the night you introduced me to Clifford?"

"Yes, he's the one." I was still calculating. As far as she knew, he was just a customer with a crush on me.

She whistled. "That's a very generous gift. I haven't seen him at the club in a while."

I was just about to say, *you know how it is, they meet other girls and move on*, when she spoke again.

"I haven't seen him since you moved out."

I stared into the Pacific Ocean, wondering how long it would take me to swim to Japan.

"Oh, my God," she yelled in a playful tone. "Are you seeing him? Please, *please* tell me you're dating that young, gorgeous guy."

I cleared my throat. "I left my apartment that day to break up with him. We are *not* together; those clothes are no longer necessary." My voice cracked. "I'm returning the watch as soon as I get home."

"The hell you are!" she said and then stopped. "Wait, why did you break up with him?"

I scooped up a small pile of shells and pitched them, one at a time, back out into the water. Why did I do it? At the time, it had felt like the right thing to do. The love I had for James was selfish compared to the love the whole group and I shared for Dylan. I couldn't have both.

I tossed the last shell. "Because I realized working on myself and being a part of the group was more important than having a friend."

She took that in and placed her hand on my arm. "Did you leave him because of me?"

"I don't know, kind of. I couldn't leave you here. I couldn't just say, sorry you're sick, but I'm going to go hang out with this guy."

I pointed up to the beach and suggested we sit down. After running my hands across a patch of sand to check for sharp objects, we took a seat facing each other.

"At that time I thought the group and I would take care of you," I said, "that Frank would use all his resources and knowledge to make sure you had a fighting chance to survive. I didn't expect him to lose his fucking mind."

"Well, he did, and I'm not staying—and neither are you!"

I appreciated her enthusiasm, but without someone on the outside to help me, I didn't know how I'd ever leave the cult.

"Jewels, I realize your work with Frank was useful when you first got here. But I think things have changed since then." She took my hands. "At this point, the only thing he's doing is running a stripper ring. I mean, what's next, placing happy-ending massage ads in the back of the *Austin Chronicle* and moving us into full-blown prostitution?"

I knew she was right. We were no longer here to heal ourselves and help others. We were here to make money and take care of Frank. -

"Don't stay for me, and don't leave for James. Leave for Jewels."

Leave for Jewels. It sounded so possible and elegant when she said it. Like it was something I could actually do. Before, when I was still dating James and thinking about leaving, I had him to help me through it. Now, I only had myself.

I looked up from our connected hands. "You're really not staying?"

She shook her head. "Yesterday morning, when everyone went on a walk, I called my cousin. I only had a few minutes to tell her I was sick and needed her help. She told me she would do anything to help me, including putting money into my bank account. Once I get back to Austin, I'm going to leave the cult and go home."

"Holy shit, you have family, money, and a plan. You're so lucky."

"I also have AIDS."

I winced. "I'm sorry. Shit, I'm so self-centered."

"No, you're not, you're just scared. I feel bad that I can't stay and help you."

"I'll be fine," I promised.

But I wasn't convinced at all.

We stood up and started making our way back down the beach. Once we were back at the path, I wiped the sand off my feet and stepped into my flip-flops.

"When are you going home?" she asked.

"In two days. Steve and I fly out Wednesday morning."

"Jewels, that gives you two weeks away from Frank to figure things out. That's an eternity for a resourceful twenty-five-year-old girl working in a strip club."

I scratched the back of my neck. "Okay, to buy myself some time, I'll get back to Austin, still water the plants, show up at the house, do everything I normally do, so no one suspects I'm planning to leave.

She nodded. "Exactly. You'll be working and making money, which always comes in handy. Speaking of which, I would also go check out some other clubs to work at in case it gets weird working with the girls from the group after you quit."

The other best club in town was The Candy Store, the place James hung out before we met. I pushed him out of my mind as fast as possible. I couldn't deal with that part of my life right now.

"Good idea," I told her.

"Yes, see, you can do this. I'll be back in Austin on Friday. I'm going to grab a couple of my things, say goodbye to you, and go home to South Carolina."

"Say goodbye," I whispered as the words hit the pit of my stomach. How would I prepare myself for that?

We strolled back to the house. For the first time in thirteen days, I felt like I was *in* Hawaii. I could finally see and smell and hear its beauty. Dylan told me her brother was going to Georgia Tech and that her mother had won several beauty contests when she was in high school. She didn't mention her father, so I didn't ask.

She picked a pink hibiscus off a bush and put it behind her ear. "I'd like to come back here someday.

"Me too, but without Frank."

She gave an agreeing smile that changed into worry. She pointed down the road. "Oh crap, they're back already."

"What? They're not supposed to be back for another couple of hours."

We ran to the house. At the same time we had gotten to the top of the stairs, Frank pulled open the heavy teakwood door from the inside.

"Where have you girls been?" he snarled.

I flinched, but Dylan looked him in the eye. "We were at the beach."

His eyes pinched into little slits. "Get in here, there's been a change of plans."

We passed through the doorway, where we saw the entire group sitting prostrate on the living room floor. I searched their eyes for a clue about what was going on, but they looked just as confused as I was.

Frank gave us an impatient arm wave. "Have a seat."

We did as we were told.

"I'm not sure what's going on with you people," he said as he paced back and forth. "Ever since we got here, you've been walking around with your heads up your asses. Every one of you is behaving like you've forgotten your purpose. How many times do I have to remind you? This is not a vacation. We do not come to Hawaii to vacate our minds or our responsibilities. We are not here to numb ourselves with beautiful scenery and forget about doing our work. Most of you can't seem to remember to have gratitude for all the things I have made possible for you."

He looked at Jodie. "I asked you this morning about dinner. You assured me it was taken care of. Why didn't they have our fish?"

"Yes, um, I think I said we could pick it up at four-thirty. It's only two. The daily catch hasn't come in yet."

"'The daily catch hasn't come in yet,'" he repeated in a mocking tone. "What are you going to cook instead?"

"Well, I don't know off the top of my head, but I'm sure I can find something to put together for you."

He stopped pacing and started tapping his foot. "I don't understand why we have to keep going to the market to get fish every day."

Jodie cleared her throat. "This refrigerator isn't big enough to hold enough food for fifteen people and more than one day's worth of fish."

"Are you going to blame it on the refrigerator instead of your gross incompetence?"

Steve's soft voice glided through the room, "I don't think you're being fair. This refrigerator is half the size of the one in Austin. And they didn't say they weren't going to get the fish, they just said we were too early. We can go back at four-thirty and get it then."

Frank dragged his gaze in Steve's direction. "Oh, are you going to rescue Jodie today? Save the damsel in distress? Does she remind you of your emotionally neglected mommy?"

My guts twisted. I'd never seen Frank strike a woman, but he'd told a couple of stories about physical altercations with men in the past. Would he hit Steve?

"I'm not trying to save anyone. I'm clarifying the situation, so we can solve the issue and get dinner on the table by six."

Frank lifted his hand and dismissed what Steve was saying. "Fanny and I are going out to dinner. Liz, get on the phone with the airlines and get the two of us back to Austin on the next available flight. You people are unteachable. At this rate, you'll never become healers." He reached for Fanny's hand and walked her out the front door.

Thank God he left. My plate was way too full for a physical

altercation right now. I gave Dylan a questioning glance. How in the hell would we execute our plan if Frank was in Austin? How were we *ever* going to get away from him?

Chapter 23

It's My Life

Jewels

After placing our luggage in the trunk, Steve and I jumped into our taxi and headed to the house. He shot me a sour face and whispered, "It smells like an ashtray on wheels in here."

I rolled down the window a bit. "At least we're home and not stuck in Hawaii." Changing Frank and Fanny's tickets for their next-day departure cost a fortune the group had to pay for collectively. This expense made it impossible for anyone else to change their tickets, especially since they were all companions and had to change both tickets to make it work.

Some arrived only a few days ago and would stay until the end of the month. They would spend at least two weeks there worrying and stressing about how much Frank would punish them when they finally got back to Texas. They were paralyzed in paradise. Liz, Tracy, Jodie, and Dylan would return in two days. He'd be decent to them.

Exhausted from the seven-hour flight, I relaxed in my seat and mindlessly watched the city go by. It wasn't until we exited onto Anderson Lane that I remembered my car was at my apartment. Shit, we were way too close to the house to double back. I'd have Steve take me home. That would work; his car was at the house.

I'd panicked the night Frank told us he and Fanny were coming home early. Dylan had reminded me that my plan to leave the cult would still work even if Frank were in Austin. The only change was that he would be at the house when I came to do my chores, just like he always was. Whatever his mood might or might not be, I would be safe and sound in my apartment.

The heartbreaking part of my plan was that I couldn't properly say goodbye to everyone. I wouldn't even get to see Dylan again. I wanted to tell everyone in the group that I loved them. We'd been through so much together.

Steve and I tipped our driver, dropped our things in the solarium, and went upstairs. Frank and Fanny were in the kitchen cooking dinner. He was at the stove sautéing vegetables, and she was standing close by, drinking a glass of wine. They looked like an average couple doing everyday things.

Frank placed the spatula on the counter. "Oh look, it's Steve, the resident knight in shining armor."

"Sure smells good in here," Steve said.

Steve had more game than I had given him credit for. He didn't take the bait, he didn't defend himself, and he complimented Frank's cooking.

Frank took a sip from his glass and told me the plants looked thirsty. I agreed with a simple nod and headed out the patio door. Once I clicked the door closed behind me, I reached out my hand and started caressing the plants. Man, I had missed them.

"How's everyone doing?" I asked, my eyes welling up the moment I whispered the words. Watering those plants was an enormous responsibility and a chore I initially considered a huge burden. I could now see how they'd taught me about resilience, beauty, and patience. I wished I could take some of them home with me.

At this very moment, the plants were sheltering me from having to be in the house during a heated discussion. I bet I'd be the next person in line to be yelled at. I turned on the hose and started watering. By the time I finished, dusk had eaten up the remainder of the day. I told the plants goodbye and walked back inside. I stood there for a bit, looking around the house.

Where was everyone?

I tiptoed a couple of steps to the kitchen. The dishes from Frank and Fanny's dinner were piled in the sink. I wiggled the faucet to stop a slow drip.

The only thing I could hear was my shallow breathing and pounding heart. Where was everyone? More importantly, where was Steve? He was my ride out of this hell, my bridge to freedom. I crept to the other kitchen doorway and looked down the stairs to Frank's living space. His door was closed, and no light was coming from the bottom of the door.

I wrung my hands and went into my old room, I pulled the blinds apart and looked into the darkness. The single streetlight cast enough light on the driveway to confirm my greatest fear: Steve had already left.

"Jewels," a voice said from far away. "Jewels, wake up."

I pulled the comfy white comforter around my neck and smiled, hearing James' voice. "Ooookaay."

"Jewels, why are you sleeping in the closet?"

I sprung to life like a marionette being picked off the floor. I grabbed the hanging clothes as blood rushed to my head and the closet spun.

"Fanny and I need coffee and almonds," Frank snarled and walked away.

Once he was out of sight, I fell back to the floor, clutching the blanket I'd grabbed off Dylan's bed last night. I brushed at a small mascara stain on her pillow from crying myself to sleep.

Shortly after realizing Steve had left without me, I took Dylan's things into the closet. I went in there because I didn't want Frank to hear me crying. I took her things because they smelled like her, and it soothed me. It hadn't been my intention to fall asleep.

I rubbed my eyes and hustled into the kitchen to make coffee and get the almonds Frank had asked for. While the water for the French press heated on the stove, I cleaned up the dishes from last night's dinner. My stomach rumbled; I hadn't eaten since yesterday's breakfast on the plane.

I was bummed that I'd dreamt about James. A part of my mind was clearly having a hard time letting him go.

Slow and steady, I trudged down the stairs. Frank and Fanny were sitting on the loveseat. Warm light from the solarium poured into the room from the French doors that connected the two rooms. Fanny was filing her nails while Frank sat next to her, reading a book called *How to Turn Others' Work into YOUR Abundance*.

"Here you go. Do you need anything else?" I asked, placing the tray on the coffee table, hoping I would appear devoted and not rude. I was sure that once Frank had his breakfast he would have Fanny take me home.

"Our bed needs to be made, and I want you to go to the store and buy some food for us," he said, and I nodded. "Fanny and I will come up with a list while you clean up our room. You can take my car."

I said okay, primarily to Fanny, since Frank had still not looked at me.

I made the bed, grabbed the list, and headed to Whole Foods on the corner of Research and Burnet Road. It was chilly out, but the only clothing I had with me were shorts and t-shirts. I looked ridiculous in my neon-colored summer attire, but I didn't care. Once I entered the store, I made a beeline to the prepared foods department and got myself a medium-sized container of brown rice and broccoli. I covered it with Tamari, devouring it while picking up the items from Frank's list. Between bites of my food and placing things in the cart, I tried to figure out how to get to my apartment.

271

I paid for the groceries and headed back to the house. I rounded the corner at the top of the street, disappointed there were no other cars parked in the driveway. It would be just me, me alone, to deal with Frank and Fanny.

I snatched a bag out of the car and went inside. The tray I had brought down earlier was in front of his door.

There was a note on the kitchen counter written in perfect block letters. WE WILL BE READY FOR OUR LUNCH AT 12:30.

My shoulders dropped as I let out a quiet, desperate sigh. I pushed my frustration away and returned downstairs to get the rest of the food. Little waves of panic ran up and down my nervous system. I could do this, I told myself. I could put a decent lunch together, and then he would let me go back to my apartment. He and Fanny had food in the house. She was a great cook; they didn't need me here.

I finished putting everything away and walked into Liz and Tracy's room. A hint of ginger from Liz's favorite lotion made the back of my throat tighten. I scooped Tracy's favorite earrings into my hand and put them in her drawer in the bathroom. Liz had a stack of books and tattered journals strewn across the floor next to her futon. I placed them in a pile and stowed them neatly in her cubby. They probably thought they would be home weeks before Frank, and it wouldn't matter. Now that he was back, he would throw them away the minute he saw them.

I stopped in the middle of the room to take one more look. I was going to miss these girls so much.

I spent the next couple of hours over-mothering the plants and spooling my emotional issues onto their delicate leaves. While doing so, I decided I'd attempt a simple chicken vegetable stir-fry over brown rice for lunch.

I walked inside, confident I could efficiently execute my plan because I could cut the vegetables and cook the rice beforehand. In the kitchen, though, I stared at the pressure cooker. It was the weakest link of my brilliant plan; I could feel it mocking me. Everyone who knew how to use this appliance without blowing up a house was in Hawaii. Or were they?

I whirled out of the kitchen, grabbed the laminated list of group members, and dialed Steve's number.

"Do you know how to use a pressure cooker?"

Well-aware of my culinary challenges and the fact that I was cooking for Frank, Steve launched straight into the instructions. "It's not as hard as you think. Once you close the lid, set—"

"Okay, hold on...." I grabbed the cordless phone base off the table and dragged it into the kitchen. I needed to get a look at it to get a better understanding of the pressure valve and gasket.

"Once you close the lid, set a twenty-one-minute timer," he instructed. "When the timer goes off, take the pot off the burner and let it sit until that valve has gone down completely."

"Okay," I said. "How long will that take?"

"About twenty more minutes."

"Shit, I better go! Thank you for helping me."

"Let me know if you need anything else?"

I hesitated for a bit, wanting to add, could you come to pick me up? But I couldn't bring myself to ask him to piss Frank off even more than he already had. I curled both lips into my mouth and used my teeth to keep them in place. I shook my head and heard Steve ask me if I was still there. "Yes," I said, releasing my lips and wiping a tear off my cheek. "I think I'm good, thank you."

"Okay," he said. "Let me know if you chan—" was the last thing I heard him say before I slammed down the receiver and got to work.

After I had followed Steve's instructions to the letter, I turned my attention to the vegetables. I diced mushrooms, bell peppers, zucchini, and carrots. I cut the chicken into bite-sized squares. I was crying over the cut onions when Frank walked into the kitchen. He placed two pounds of ground turkey meat, which he must have dug out of the freezer in the garage, onto the counter.

His brows set as he surveyed the disaster I had turned the kitchen into. "We want spaghetti for lunch. Fanny says she's in the mood for Italian."

My heart hit the floor. I searched for the strength to push out a simple *okay*, but the kitchen was filled with the overbearing buzz of the timer. I headed to the other side of the kitchen to silence it. When I turned back, Frank was gone.

I went to the stove and took the pressure cooker off the burner. What in the hell was I doing? I'd rather be alone staving off anxiety attacks than be treated like a dog. *Think, think, think, there must be someone.* Who else could I call besides Steve to come get me? I picked up the phone and dialed 411.

"Southwestern Bell, what city, please?" a woman asked me in a clipped monotone.

"Austin, Texas."

I heard her punch the information into a keyboard.

"Okay, Austin, Texas, what number can I find for you?"

"Yellow Taxi, please," I said, creeping over to the junk drawer and taking out a pen and paper. I kept my eyes trained on Frank's door while I wrote down the number.

I thanked the operator and called the cab company, but the dispatcher told me it would be a forty-five-minutes to an hour wait. There was no way I could stay at this house that long.

"I'm at the Randall's on the corner of Mesa and Spicewood Springs," I told the man and gave him my name. He gave me the cab number to look for and reminded me to call back if I had to cancel.

Standing at the door connecting the living room to the solarium, I questioned my insane plan. I'd have to gather up all my things in Frank's full view, then walk a mile in beach shorts, a neon pink shirt, and flip-flops.

I grabbed the door handle and walked down the stairs. Frank and Fanny immediately looked in my direction. I told myself that I was not going to pass out.

Frank watched me grab my bags. "What are you doing?" he yelled.

"I'm leaving," I said through my cotton mouth.

"Where in the hell do you think you're going?"

"I'm going home," I said, heavy with luggage and tears in my eyes. "I won't be back."

I walked out the front door and raced towards the street while talking myself off an anxiety ledge. I couldn't breathe; my heart was pounding so fast. *All is well. All is well. All is well.*

I made it to the street, and a sense of relief filled me—right before I felt his hand on my arm.

"Where do you think you're going?" he asked, yanking me around to look at him.

His bulging, fire-engine-red face made me gasp. "I'm leaving the group," I said, jerking my arm out of his clutch and taking a step back.

"Why?"

"Because it has turned into something unrecognizable."

He sneered at me. "You're just going to run away when things get difficult?"

I hoisted my bag back onto my shoulder. "I'm not running. I'm choosing to go after careful consideration."

His expression softened. "Jewels, you're too close to completing the hardest part of your lessons. Don't give up now."

I pinched my eyebrows together and let out a huff. "What a joke. You've taught me enough to know when someone is lying and trying to manipulate me. Thank you, I appreciate it. I'm not coming back."

The rage flared in his eyes, and the air around us pressed against my skin. I took another step back and reached into my purse. As he lunged toward me, I whipped out the rape whistle James gave me and held it close to my mouth.

I squared off and stared him in the face. "Get. Away. From. Me!"

"We're not finished," he said, holding up his hands and walking away.

I walked backward until I saw him turn up the drive. I turned and hurried away. *All is not well. All is not well. Shit is hitting the fan.*

That was when I saw Steve driving towards me. *Crap.*

"Hey!" he said through his passenger window. "Need a ride?"

"Nope, I'm good," I said, trying my best to jog.

He parked and got out of his car. "Jewels, wait, what's going on?"

I couldn't keep running. I owed Steve the truth and wanted to say goodbye to him. I dropped all my shit on the ground and tried to catch my breath.

Steve and I looked toward the house and then at each other. I shook my head. "I'm not going back there."

He smiled. "Good. Neither am I."

Chapter 24

The Killing Moon

James

James Some alleys on 6th Street were cool. They had that "Speakeasy vibe." This alley, my alley, smelled like one-hundred-twenty-year-old cat piss and garbage from the pizza place next door.

I went inside, placed the new locking mechanism and can of WD-40 on the floor, and looked around. I expected the building to have hints of the bookstore that had been here, but all traces of it were gone, which left me with an unexpected, eerie feeling. How could something have been here so long and leave no residual feeling in its absence? That idea was in stark contrast to the relatively short amount of time I had known January. I could still feel her in every inch of my life.

The heels of my loafers echoed off the empty walls and ornamental tin ceiling. I leaned down to grab the chipped-up piece of tile my father had noticed the other day.

"Nice floor," I heard Brad say from behind me. "Are those tiles asbestos?"

"Hey," I said, looking up at him and Parker. "The inspector said no."

Parker came over and handed me a cup of 7-11 coffee. "You going to keep them?"

"I don't think so. My dad told me about this restaurant in Dallas that stained and sealed their concrete floors, and now I want to do it to this place."

"Interesting," he said. "That's pretty high-cotton for Sixth Street."

"I agree, but there's zero upkeep, which I'm a huge fan of." I walked over to the middle of the room and put my stuff down. "Let me give you the official tour, or at least an idea of what it'll look like."

Brad pointed at my things. "Old man, what in the hell is that, a leather Trapper Keeper?

"No, douchebag, it's called an or-gan-izer. All the yuppies have them now."

I told them about my dad showing up at the eleventh hour, surprising me with his last-minute investment, and showed them the chair he had made. I also explained that I was going to paint the rough-hewn limestone walls with clear polyurethane paint with just a smidge of gold-frosted color. I left out the part that it had been January's suggestion. *Like my nails*, she had said. *They still look natural but have just a hint of shimmer.* I pushed her out of my head.

"How long—" Parker started to ask me when my phone rang.

All of us snapped our attention to the middle of the room where I had left it on the floor.

I jogged over and answered it. "Mr. Sullivan, this is Planned Parenthood. Do you have time to talk?"

"Yes, I do," I answered, walking out the back door for a little privacy.

"Mr. Sullivan, it looks like we got your results for the HIV test you had requested. Would you like the results over the phone or in-person?"

I cleared my throat, more nervous than I'd expected to be. "Over the phone would be great."

"Okay," she said. I could hear shuffling of papers through the receiver and I silently implored the universe to speed this woman up. "It looks like—it looks like your test came back negative."

A rush of relief washed over me. I stood stock-still as she explained I needed to come in every six months to be retested for a year, and then hung up. The call filled me with half-hope. There was still a possibility that January didn't have AIDS. I took a moment to let that sink in.

I headed back inside, where the guys were still standing right where I'd left them. "What were you going to say?" I asked Parker.

He knocked his knuckles against his forehead. "Oh yeah, how long do you think it will take before you have your grand opening?"

"I'm not sure. I think permits, logistics, and build-out will take about three, maybe four months. And then I'll do a week of soft openings and invitation-only nights to work out the kinks and show my appreciation to all the investors, friends, and my family."

"That's a good idea." Brad nodded. "This place is going to be great."

"I agree," Parker said, patting me on the back hard enough to force out a cough. "Hey, Brad and I are going to The Oasis for lunch. Come with us."

I considered their invitation. The Oasis was a restaurant out by the lake that had been converted from a Spanish-style ranch house. The drinks were stupid expensive, and the menu was a fraction better than bar food, but I loved it anyway. The best part about it was I'd never been there with January. Hopefully I wouldn't think about her while there. "Sounds great, I'm in."

I locked up the bar, and we piled into Brad's Nissan Maxima, a gift he had gotten from his parents for graduating on time from UT.

"Your car still has that new car smell," I said, thinking that was exactly what January would have said.

He rolled his eyes, and we took off.

We got off at the right exit but turned in the wrong direction. "Dude, the lake is west. You're going the wrong way."

"We need to stop off at Tulips, then we'll head out there."

"What the…. We're going to Tulips? Why? Are you crazy? I'm not going there. You left that part of the plan out."

Brad held his hand up in the air to slow me down just as Parker started pelting me with questions about my mobile phone.

"It's just a pop-in, I promise," Brad said. "Ripley left her dance bag at my place last night, and I told her I'd drop it at the club for her. Besides, it just opened, so the place will be empty."

"Hello?" Parker said into the phone, pretending to be talking to someone. "Was this thing expensive?" he asked while pushing all the buttons.

"Yes, it was very expensive, and it costs a fortune to make a call, but the time I've saved having it has already made a big difference."

"It's heavy," he said, tossing it from one hand to the other.

"Please put it down, it's not a toy." I winced as I thought to myself, "Maybe I *am* an old man." Then I returned to the question of stopping at Tulips. "Fine, we'll go, but we aren't staying long."

I used generic conversation to distract myself from the feelings I was trying to avoid. I'd said yes to this outing to get away from thinking about January and her return today, and now we were going to walk right into the building where half of our relationship took place.

We pulled up, parked, and turned off the engine. "I don't think I've ever been here during the day," I said, eyeing the empty parking lot. "It's kind of sad looking, like an old woman with too much makeup on."

We piled out of the car, and I felt the strangeness of not tossing the keys to the valet and the void of not hearing the thumping of the bass from the club. We walked up the stairs and opened the door. There was no door girl to greet us yet, and the club was still all lit up. The sound of a vacuum cleaner humming by the main stage caught my attention, and I heard a familiar voice.

"Sorry guys, we're not currently taking auditions for dick dancers." Rich was standing in front of the bar, wiping down the chairs.

"Hilarious," said Parker. "How about better-looking, more capable bartenders?"

Rich flipped him the bird, and we all chuckled a bit. "What brings you guys in this time of day?"

We walked towards Rich as Brad held up Ripley's bag and explained. The DJ was doing a quiet sound check, and then "God Only Knows" by the Beach Boys filled the room. As I dragged my finger across the top of a nearby table, the corners of my mouth turned up involuntarily. I'd always found it amusing that one of the best love songs ever written started by suggesting they may not love a person forever.

"Yeah, sure," Rich said. "I'll make sure she gets it." He looked over at me and smiled. "I haven't seen you in a while."

I gave him a grin while wondering if he knew that January and I had broken up. I hadn't been in here since she moved out of the cult house.

"Is that the new Motorola brick phone?" he asked.

Saved by the phone, I thought, exhaling.

"Sure is," I said, as I closed the gap between us and handed it to him. He asked me the same questions Parker did, but then added some additional ones about billing areas, roaming charges, and reception. I told him to take down my number and call me sometime while I was driving around, and we could test it.

I didn't enjoy Austin in the summer as much as I appreciated it in the winter. The summers were hot as shit, and by the middle of September, I was sick of the sun and the one-hundred-degree temperatures. But the winter was wonderful. The winter was what people up north experienced in the fall. We had our cold days, and we got rain when most others were getting snow, but most of the time spent from October to March was warm and sunny. Today was one of those days. Perfect for jeans, a polo shirt, and Ray-Bans. No jacket required.

After arriving at The Oasis, Parker told us he was working out later, so he would just have a Coke and drive us back to town. I decided a frozen margarita with an upside-down Pacifico beer floater would be just the ticket. I was going to be tired and in need of a nap in a couple of hours, but if that was the price for a short emotional vacation, I was okay with it.

We chatted back and forth, burning time between getting our drinks and waiting for our food. Brad told us he had gotten a job at Dell. "The company is really growing," he said. "According to the *Austin Business Journal*, they're up to twelve-hundred employees. I think there's still some potential for growth."

Parker held up his Coke, and we toasted to Brad's decision to enter the adult workforce. Then Parker looked at me and asked when I was going to snap out of the January fog.

"I'm not in a fog," I protested, shaking my head. "I'm fine."

"You're not fine, you're in a funk. I have some advice for you."

I groaned and sucked as much of my drink into my mouth as possible without giving myself brain freeze. "I'm good, really. Besides, Brad told me how you bounce from one chick to another to get over the other. It's just not my thing."

Parker threw his head back as an amused chuckle rolled out of him. "Dude, that's not what I was going to suggest. As a side note, a chick taught me that trick."

Out of the corner of my eye, I saw Brad pinching his brows together in a sign of disbelief.

"I'm serious!" he went on. "She said the best way to get over one man was to get under another."

My jaw dropped. Brad muttered an incredulous *Whatever!*

"I'm not kidding," Parker continued. "I mean, this woman is older and not into bullshit. She's the type that says what's on her mind." He took a breath. "I never go into something intimate with a woman unless I tell her what I'm capable of. I tell them I'm not looking for anything long-term."

I continued drinking, not interested in getting his advice or contesting how he negotiated having sex with women.

"This is what I was going to suggest," he said. "Do three new things a week. Things you've never done before. Like, go to museum, hike Walnut Creek, take up macrame or some shit like that."

Huh, I wasn't expecting this type of advice from Parker. He was more of an "if it feels good, just keep doing it" kind of guy.

"Three new things?" Brad asked.

"Yes, it's the best relationship advice my father ever gave me. If you do it, you stay busy, you won't keep running into old memories of the two of you, and, as a bonus, you get to learn and have more experiences." He sucked the last bit of Coke out of his glass and looked me in the eye. "Working on your bar does not count as a new experience."

I opened my mouth to protest, but he was right. Everything about that place led to a thought of January.

I wanted to share everything with her. I wanted to tell her how well my dad and I were getting along and that he was now an investor in my bar. I also wanted to show her the amazing chairs he was going to make me, and what he suggested I do to the floors.

The sound of Parker shaking the ice around his glass got my attention. "See, you can't even help yourself, you're thinking about her right now."

My friends knew me way too well.

Chapter 25

Genius of Love

Jewels

Steve drove me to the nearest pay phone so that I could cancel my taxi before we headed to my apartment. He parked behind my truck, grabbed my bags, and followed me inside.

"Just drop them anywhere," I told him and opened the blinds to let in what was left of the afternoon sun.

Walking past my answering machine, my heart ached when the display showed I had zero messages. I didn't realize until just then that I was holding out a sliver of hope that there would be a message from James—anything at all from him so that I could play it back and hear his voice.

I filled two Solo cups with water, and Steve and I sat on the floor in the living room and talked. He admitted he had been thinking about leaving the group for a while, but knew it was inevitable when he saw how Frank treated Dylan in Hawaii.

He picked a sequin from one of my work dresses from my carpet and handed it to me. "I knew I couldn't quit while in Hawaii. Frank would have kicked me out of the house, so I guess I was waiting to see what Dylan would do, see how I could help her." He paused for a second. "I guess I was thinking if she was staying in the group, I'd stay, and if she were going to leave, I'd leave. Either way, it'd be easier to help her if we were both on the same side of the fence."

He let out a puff of air. "Then I got your call this afternoon and realized you were there by yourself and headed over. Jewels, I'm so sorry I left you there last night. Frank told me he wanted you to stay so he could thank you for helping him and stepping up when the group needed you. I should've known better."

I reached for his hand. "How would you know? We trusted him. We were trained to trust—in all things, at all times."

"I was so happy to see you walking down the street. I knew instantly you'd left the group, and now was the right time for me to leave." He took a sip of water. "I'll find a way to help Dylan from the outside."

I nodded and smiled at him. "Dylan isn't staying in the group either."

"Oh thank God," he said, dropping his shoulders.

"She's contacted her family and is going back to South Carolina. They will help her decide what she wants to do with her remaining life." I said this last part with regret. No matter who left the cult or what happened to me, Dylan was still completely hosed.

After we chatted for a bit, Steve called the house in Hawaii. He told Dylan that he would pick her and the girls up from the airport and go with her to the house so that she could get her things. "I don't want you to do that alone," he told her. I could hear her crying and thanking him through the receiver.

We gave her the option of staying with either of us, but she said she would feel safer at a hotel where Frank couldn't find her. There were several by the airport where Steve could take her, making it easier for her to catch a flight into Myrtle Beach on Sunday morning. It was a good plan, and having one more person on our team was nice. We were not alone.

I was not alone.

We ended our call, and Steve went home. I locked the door behind him and quickly looked around my apartment for something to barricade the door. Unfortunately there was nothing. I went into the kitchen, grabbed an empty soda can off the counter, and placed a couple of dimes inside.

It took me a few minutes, but I got the can to balance on the doorknob. If someone turned the knob from the outside, the can would fall off the handle and make enough noise to wake me up. I could then run out the sliding-glass door in my bedroom. It was a ridiculous plan, but I needed to feel as safe as possible.

I walked over to my vanity, opened the drawer, and took out the watch James gave me. After placing it on my wrist, I held it close to my heart. Today had been so full of emotional upheaval, I didn't think it was possible to feel anything more. I laid down for a nap, letting my pillowcase soak up my tears.

My eyes opened before the sun rose, so it took me a while to realize it was the following day. I went back to sleep. For the first time in five years, I had slept longer than five hours.

After waking up the second time, I was ready to start my day. I grabbed a handful of nuts out of my desolate cupboard and began the process of checking my finances. I opened my safe and dug out the three stacks of paper-clipped bills, each containing one-hundred dollars.

I took the clips off the money and spread it out on the floor. All of it was mine—every single penny. Ten percent would not have to be tithed to Frank. No percentage would go to buying fancy bottles of wine or funding his expensive hobbies.

Three hundred dollars had never felt like so much money.

I set aside fifty for groceries and put the rest back in the box. Today I was going to get lost in self-indulgence instead of self-preservation. I would start with a long soak in my tub, a conditioning balm on my hair, and a pedicure for my feet.

Before I started treating myself like a human, though, I'd do a load of laundry. I dragged my duffle into my bedroom and emptied the contents onto the floor. Everything still smelled like sweat, sun, and sand. I ended up with three piles: purple, fuchsia, and turquoise. I didn't want any of this stuff; I would rather launder it and give it away.

But why stop with these things? If I was going to purge correctly, I needed to get rid of everything. I started digging through my closet. The clothing that was still in good condition would go to Goodwill, and personal stuff, like undergarments, would go in the trash.

From there, I moved to office and household items, file folders, Post-it notes, and pens. Everything in those three colors, including the purple desk lamp I'd been using on the floor—the only thing I had to light up my living room—was going.

Now for the hard stuff. I pulled out all the linens, towels, pots and pans—everything that I had borrowed from James. They all had our memories tied to them, and I couldn't deal with those haunting me every day; I'd replace them as soon as I made some more money.

I turned the watch around on my wrist. Even though it had been a gift, I didn't feel right keeping it. He could return or sell it and get most of his money back. I would pack it up along with everything of his and give it to Ripley so she could return it to him. I appreciated him lending me his stuff, but I had no right to keep it. I'd return it myself, but I was not ready to face him yet. I was sure he hated me.

In the meantime, I was going to wear the shit out of this watch. I would sleep, shower, shop, and work in the thing. I would enjoy the freedom of not having to hide it from anyone.

My apartment looked as bare as it did the day I had moved in, but that felt okay now. This was the beginning of me figuring out who I was without Frank breathing down my neck.

I didn't want to go to work, but eventually, I wanted something to sit on in my apartment besides my bed. Facing the girls from the group was going to be uncomfortable, but most of them were still in Hawaii, and only Liz and Tracy would be coming in. If I had to stand my ground, it would be better to do it with a couple instead of eight. I hoped they wouldn't hate me as much as James did. I didn't know what Frank had told them or what they thought about Steve, Dylan, and my leaving.

I thought about Dylan, who'd left for South Carolina this morning, several times throughout the day. I was curious if I'd ever see her again. I didn't get her number, but she had mine. Hopefully, she would call once she was settled.

I grabbed my dance bag and headed out the door. I wasn't going to spend the rest of my life avoiding confrontation. I took the long way to work but was still the first one there. The girls' car was not in the parking lot.

"Hey, January," said Sean when I passed through the DJ booth, and then I had to figure out where to sit to put on my makeup. Shit, I should have done that at home.

"Hey, Jewels, how was your trip?" Ripley asked. Misha sat a stool away from her; their stuff was spread out on the counter between them.

I exhaled. "Do you guys mind if I sit up here with you?"

They scooped all the things in front of the available seat into their own spaces. "Absolutely, please, sit down."

"Thank you." I sat between them, holding my bag on my lap like a child on the first day of school.

Misha finished lining her lip and looked over at me. "How was Hawaii?"

"It was interesting," I answered, trying not to cry. "I'm no longer hanging out with the girls in that group."

Ripley put down her blush brush and placed her hand on my arm. "Oh my God, are you okay?"

I shook my head, "'I... I don't know. I'm scared, but I think I'm okay. I hope in the long run, I'll be better off."

"January," said Misha, "if you need anything, please let us know. We can help."

My eyes glanced between the two girls as I wondered if I should share my biggest fear with them. I took in a deep breath and decided to plow ahead. "I struggle with anxiety occasionally, and I think that's the thing that I'm the most worried about." Tears rolled down my cheeks. I kept checking the curtain close by, afraid the cult girls would arrive and see me crying. I mopped up my tears with my jacket sleeve and gave Misha and Ripley a nervous smile.

Misha handed me a tissue. "Aww, so do I. One of my customers is a doctor, he gave me the name of a wonderful psychologist who's really helped me. I'll give you her number."

"Anything you need," Ripley jumped in, "just ask. You're not alone. I think you'll be surprised to know more than half the people in this club have been rooting for you, hoping you would find your way out of that group."

Misha patted the counter. "Come on, get your stuff out, let's get ready."

"Okay," I said, and unloaded my makeup from my dance bag. The three of us got ready and chatted for the next twenty minutes. I was surprised how accepted I felt around them. Maybe tonight wouldn't be too bad after all. I strolled into the booth to put my name on the list for stage rotation when Liz walked in the front door.

"Shit."

Sean gave me a quick glance. "What's wrong?"

"It's a long story," I said while mentally rifling through my options. There was no way I could make it through the long hallway section of the dressing room before she got to the curtain. She would definitely see me scurrying away. *Crap.*

"Oh God," I said just as Liz opened the door to come into the booth; I crouched down and hid under the sound panel behind Sean's legs.

"What the hell?" Sean said to me, and then, "Good evening, Liz. How was your trip?"

"Eventful," was all she said as she walked through the room.

After she passed through the curtain, Sean burst into laughter. "What's going on, January?"

I crawled out from underneath the mixer, and he reached down and helped me stand up. "I quit the group a couple of days ago," I said, righting myself and watching his eyes bug out.

"Whoa, that's intense. Good for you."

I let out a long, slow breath. "They weren't back from Hawaii when I did it, so things are really awkward right now, and I panicked."

He grinned at me. "Yes, you did. Honestly, I probably would have done the same."

I straightened my shoulders. "I won't do it again. I'm stronger than that."

He gave me a quick hug and agreed with me. "You're up in about five minutes."

I left the booth and headed for the bar to get a glass of water and find a customer to sit with later. Sunday nights weren't very busy, and I didn't see anyone I knew. Sheesh, I forgot about the 6th Street crew; I hoped they didn't come in tonight.

My water and a shot glass were sitting on the bar, waiting for me. I pointed at them. "What the hell is that?"

Rich beamed at me. "I heard you're no longer a cult girl. It's half a shot of vodka to celebrate or give you courage. Whichever you need most."

I placed my hand over my heart. "Misha must have told you."

"Yep, she and Ripley were just over here. We're here for you if you need anything."

I fanned my face. "I have too much mascara on to cry again." I picked up my water. "I'm going to skip the liquid courage and use my own strength to make it through the night. But thank you for thinking of me."

He lifted the shot glass and toasted. "Fuck 'em if they can't take a joke," he said, and we drank.

The audience clapped for the girl leaving the stage, and I booked it through the dressing room to do my set. Liz was still getting ready down in the lower section, where we used to all hang out. She gave me a slight nod. I returned the gesture and was grateful she had broken the ice. Even if it was just a tiny crack, it was better than nothing.

Later, back in the DJ booth, I was flipping through the albums to pick a song for my second set when Liz busted through the door and grabbed my arm.

"Oh, thank God," she said, out of breath. "I'm so glad you're in here."

My mouth fell open. "What's going on?"

She let go of my arm. "I was standing over by the third stage with Alex and Misha when Frank walked in," she said between breaths.

I stopped what I was doing. "What? You saw *our* Frank walk into this club?" I wanted to correct what I'd just said. He was no longer *my* Frank. But now was not the time. "Then what happened?"

"Well, the girls saw the look on my face and asked me if I was okay." She took a quick breath. "Damn, my heart's pounding. Anyway, I hid behind them so that he wouldn't see me; I explained he was the leader of our group and then came to find you."

"He's still out there?"

She nodded as we inched toward the window, crowding into Sean's space.

"See," she said, pointing, "there he is."

I watched him stroll through the club. He was dressed in crisp jeans and a dark purple dress shirt, not his typical yoga lounge wear. I never thought he would walk into this building. "Shit," I finally said. "What is he doing here?"

Dread blanketed Liz's face. "I think he's here for you."

"For *me?*"

"Well, I don't think he drove over here for the stale popcorn."

I shrugged. "What's he going to do, grab me by my hair and drag me back to the cult?"

Liz tipped her head. "Cult?"

The door to the booth crashed open. "Oh my God, is it true?" Ripley asked. "Is that him?"

Liz and I nodded.

"Four minutes, January," Sean said, eyes wide with intrigue.

"She's not going onstage," Liz said, looking at Sean like he was insane. "Ripley, can you take her turn?"

"Yeah, sure, whatever I can do."

"Thank you, Ripley, but I'm going on," I insisted. "I won't let him intimidate me like this. I mean, I'm not even a hundred-percent sure he's even here for me."

"What?" asked everyone in the booth.

"Holy crap, this is crazy!" Alex said, coming in through the dressing room curtain.

"Duck, girls," Sean said. "He's heading in this direction."

Everyone ducked—everyone but me. I wasn't going to be afraid of him anymore. I was done with it. He could go ahead and make a scene; I didn't care. Secretly, I'd love to watch the bouncers toss him out.

He turned and sat down at a table close to the stage entrance.

I grabbed an album from the rack and handed it to Sean. "Please play number two for me, as loud as you can. I'll leave the second song up to you."

"You got it, January."

The three girls stood in front of me, aghast. I walked past them and headed to the dressing room. They followed, spouting their protests. Liz leaned against the locker beside me, her eyes pleading. "Jewels, you can't do this. It's nuts."

"I left the group fair and square. He can't come in here to force me back in. If I don't make a stand now, then when?" I felt like I'd been asking permission to take my next breath for the past five years. It was time for me to stop living in fear and to finally trust myself.

"Alex," Adams called out from the lower part of the dressing room. "Your customers are looking for their beers."

"I can't help them right now. January needs me."

"So I've heard," he said, walking up the stairs to join us.

"You have?" I asked.

"Yep, half the club is buzzing about it."

"Adams," Liz demanded. "Tell her to skip going onstage so we can sneak her out the back."

He winked at me. "Oh, I'm pretty sure she can get out that back door without our help."

I shot him a look while leaning into the counter to put on fresh lipstick. He knew I had left that night and hadn't said anything about it. I turned around, taking in the scene. Seeing my new friends and Liz rallying around me was amazing; maybe I wasn't as alone as I had felt. But where was Tracy? I saw her go onstage earlier, but hadn't seen her since.

Adams pointed at me. "It looks like she's going out there."

The music faded out as the crowd clapped. "Gentlemen, let's give a warm round of applause for Lucy," Sean encouraged over the microphone.

Lucy came through the curtain, her hair tussled and a wad of money in her hand. She took one look at us and stopped on her heels. "Oh crap, are we being raided again?"

Adams told her everything was fine and to head over to the second stage.

I wiped my palms on my skirt as the intro to my song played.

The sides of Alex's lips curled up. "'Freedom!' This is one of my favorite George Michael songs."

"Me too," I agreed. "I'm pretty sure it will become my lifelong anthem."

I walked over to Liz and hugged her. "I love you. I don't know where you are with all of this, but I'm pretty sure this'll be the last time we can talk openly. My door will always be open, and I'll forever hope you'll knock on it someday and say, 'I got out.'"

She cocked her head like she wasn't sure what I was talking about, so I left it at that. It wasn't my place to interfere with her life choices.

I stepped back and smiled at everyone. I wished Tracy were there; I wanted to say goodbye to her as well.

As soon as the first words to the song hit the club, I threw open the curtain and walked out. Sean did as I asked and cranked the sound system to its fullest potential; each bass pulse shook the stage floor.

The song's words boomed through the club, not all of them saying exactly what I was feeling, but close enough. Just hearing George Michael belt out the word *freedom* repeatedly in the chorus was magic. I'd watched the video for this song a hundred times; now, it played effortlessly through my mind with the original supermodels lip-syncing their lines with perfect precision. Linda, Naomi, Christy, even Cindy Crawford, who was born in my hometown, were all singing *freedom*, and it felt like it was just for me.

I spun, my skirt corkscrewing tight around my body.

I dropped into the splits.

In between beats, I crawled around on stage.

I stood up, spun twice to get back to the pole, and just as I was whipping my leg in a perfect circle above my head, the song hitting the pronounced piano key slide, I saw Frank walk up to the stage.

His face and neck were blood red. There was a single dollar bill in his hand. Good God, maybe he would grab and drag me out of here.

The song kept belting out *freedom*.

I took another quick spin, trying to figure out what to do next. Adams walked up to the stage about a foot away from Frank. Arriving seconds later was Ripley and one of her best customers. I kept dancing. I knew they were only up here in solidarity, not to tip me.

I squinted into the stage lights, watching people make their way to the stage. Everyone was there. Old and new customers of mine, girls I barely knew, Misha, and even Rich, who must have left the back bar deserted.

Beyond the throng of bodies crowding the stage, I finally spotted Tracy. Relief ribboned through my body. I waved at her, trying to convey how much I loved her, and was sorry I didn't or couldn't tell her I was leaving the group. She returned my wave by pointing to a spot behind me, toward the DJ booth. I wrapped my arms around my midsection, trying again to convey that I loved her. This time she pointed at herself, put her hand on her heart, pointed back to me and held up two fingers. I was sure she was saying *I love you too*.

I clapped, believing we understood each other. She pointed behind me again, this time more vigorously. I didn't think she was talking about Frank; he was on the other side of the stage. I could see him out of my peripheral vision.

I held out my hands to indicate my confusion, and she laughed at me while pointing again. This time I turned to see what she was trying to tell me.

There was my James, my number one support person standing there smiling at me.

I stood there in shock. What was he doing here? I had assumed he hated me; however, his smile could have illuminated a dark cave. I walked over to him, shaking my head, and squatted in front of him.

"I got here as soon as I heard the news," he yelled over the song.

I looked up at Sean, and he turned the music down. Everyone in the club hushed.

"What news?" I was curious to know if he was talking about me being back from Hawaii or Frank or what. No one had seen me until tonight. How would he know that?

"The news that you left the cult and that Frank was here giving you a hard time."

My mouth dropped open. "How did you hear that news?"

"I was in the drive-through line at McDonald's, and that asshole," he said, smiling and pointing to Rich, "called me."

I looked over and Rich, who was beaming with pride, and then back to James. "Called you how?" I asked, my face pinched in confusion.

"On that new mobile phone I told you about. I got one a week ago."

"You got your club?"

He raised his arms to help me off the stage. "Yes, I got it!"

"Oh my God, I'm so happy for you!" I hugged him on my way down. "I'm sorry I chose my friend over you. I'm not sorry I wanted to help her, but I'm sorry I hurt you. I'm sorry I didn't think things through, and I'm sorry I didn't include you in the decision-making process."

"It's fine, I understand," he said. "I mean, it hurt like hell, but I would have done the same thing."

"Yes, probably. But you would have handled it so much better than I did. I was such a mess...."

He shook his head and kissed me. The crowd erupted into cheers.

"Hey!" yelled Frank over the din from the other side of the stage.

James released me. "Let's get out of here!"

"Yeah, great idea!" I said, laughing. We turned toward the door, and the crowd of waitresses, customers, bouncers, and dancers cleared our path. Tracy was holding the door to aid our escape. I opened my mouth to protest, knowing it would get back to Frank that she had helped me, but she waved her arm as if to say *hurry*.

"I quit this afternoon," she said as we headed through the door. "I'll call you tomorrow!"

A rush of cool winter air and silence greeted us on the other side where the valet was holding James' car door open for me.

"Well," James said with a smile. "Now what do you want to do?"

"Everything!"

Epilogue 1

This Must be the Place
(Jewels)

4 Months Later

I wiped the tears off my face and tossed my purse into my new Miata. I wished I could say that once James and I had walked out of the club the night Frank showed up, all my problems melted away, but they didn't. Not only did they not vanish, but new ones appeared.

I had my first full-blown anxiety attack within the first three days; the second one came hours later. I spent that night sleeping under James' bed. It was the only place I felt safe. He slept on the floor next to me, holding my hand.

Misha gave me the name of her therapist the next night at work. "January, you will love her. She's a great listener and will teach you how to deal with things. I'm sure she can help."

I was skeptical and afraid of letting someone else get inside my head. "Has she ever been in a cult?"

Misha shook her head. "I don't think so, but she was lost in the ocean for days on a life raft."

I gave her a double take. "She sounds perfect, I'll call her." I figured anyone that had been through that much would be able to help me.

I rang her office the next day to get on her schedule. For a couple of months, I saw her twice a week. The first thing she suggested was the last thing I wanted to do—go on Prozac. But then she asked me a question that changed my mind: "If you broke your leg, would you choose not to use crutches?"

"No," I said incredulously. "I would use them."

"I'm suggesting a very low dose so the tsunami of emotions hitting you all at once will feel more like manageable waves. Once the onslaught has passed and you have more tools to help you understand and cope with your feelings, we can wean you off the medication."

I gnawed on the inside of my cheek. "I have days when I think being in the cult seemed easier than being out here in the *whole* world."

"I understand," she said, "and to be honest with you, that might never go away. PTSD is the gift that keeps on giving. Our goal is to learn to appreciate what it's offering us."

"What's that?"

"It's the gift of feeling bad. An indicator to let you know you still have work to do."

I shot her a look. "It feels more like a curse than a gift."

"Yes, at first it does, but after a while, you'll start to trust yourself and your feelings. You'll learn that they're showing you where you have a little more work to do, work that we're going to turn into games."

I was skeptical at first, but it was starting to work. One of the games was a notebook with a line drawn down the middle of a page. There was a minus sign on one side and a plus sign on the other. The objective was to systematically move things from the negative to the positive side. We used every tool we could come up with to circumvent the multiple layers of brainwashing I was dealing with.

My newest and most unexpected challenge was something I never had the luxury of experiencing in the cult—depression. But we had a game for that as well. It was a suggestion that Parker had once given to James: try three new things a week. We altered it to four new things a month. I did many of them myself to begin finding my own autonomy.

One of my new favorite things to do was take long drives out to the lake, which I was doing now. I had the top down in my car so the sun's warm rays could spread freely across my face and body. It would take a bottle of conditioner to get the nest of knots out of my hair later, but I didn't care.

I had also joined a knitting group that met at James' club Monday afternoons. I had already made him three of the most misshapen scarves on the planet, but he swore he was going to wear them that coming winter. I was determined to replace them with better ones as my skill level increased. Sewing was next on my list I wanted to try.

The other game we devised was the gratitude game. This one took a while to embrace because so much of the concept was similar to ideas Frank often talked about—and usually used against us. So we changed the name to "appreciation activity." It was two-parted. The first part was to find something I could appreciate, no matter how small, even in the worst circumstances. This took a lot of imagination, but I was starting to see how even the shittiest times could be strangely beneficial. The second part was easy. Every night before I went to sleep, I listed all the things and people I appreciated.

James was always on the list. Most of the time, he was there for multiple reasons. My family was also there. I was fortunate to have reconnected with all of them. Some weren't open to forgiving me immediately, but most were just very happy I was back.

Dylan was also high on my list. I wouldn't have gotten out of the cult without her. Tracy and I called her cousin a week ago. She told us that Dylan couldn't take AZT and had moved to San Francisco so that she could participate in cutting edge clinical research for development of experimental medications, and hopefully one day a cure."

I had lots of appreciation for my new friends. Ripley started calling me "little filly" because I was curious and cautious. Between her and Misha, I developed a much deeper relationship with many other girls at the club. They had become part of my extended family and were full of good information. The other day I'd asked the girls in the dressing room if they knew the number of a good gynecologist. I had ten different referrals in five minutes; most of them had been written in lip liner on the side of a tampon box.

On crappy days, when my new tools or games didn't make me feel better, I allowed myself to cry because I knew things would eventually improve. On my good days, I could see that life was a crazy, scary, magical, tragic thing, and I appreciated all it had to teach me.

Epilogue 2

This Must be the Place (James)

8 Months Later

I pulled the tap and slowly poured Rich and Misha a couple of fresh Lone Star beers. Across the bar, my mom was fussing with the black plastic tablecloths and decorative floral centerpieces. My dad was happily ensconced in the corner, talking about carpentry with Jewels' ex-cult friend Steve.

My parents had moved to Austin a couple of months after I'd opened the bar. They were a little bored in Dallas, especially after my sister and her family had moved to Waco. My mother told me she had been planting the seed for years, waiting for my dad to retire and take the bait. I assisted her by giving his number to anyone that asked about the furniture he'd made for my bar. It was a little manipulative, but I could see that they were happier here.

It took Jewels awhile before she was ready to meet them. The afternoon I told her they were relocating, she said, "I can't start my relationship with them lying about my job or the cult."

I agreed with her. After deliberating, we decided I would tell them first and see how they took it. If they didn't freak out, Jewels would happily meet them and answer their questions.

My father had a *Playboy* subscription for most of my childhood, so I suspected he was a little more adventurous than he portrayed. I wasn't surprised when he didn't blanch at her being a dancer. The part about her being in a cult piqued his curiosity more than anything else.

My mother's reaction was a bit more trepidatious. She didn't know enough about either subject to know what questions to ask. I assured her Jewels would be happy to start from the beginning and tell her everything she wanted to know.

Once they closed on their house and moved in, they had us over for dinner. Jewels was a nervous wreck on the drive over, but it was instant camaraderie when she and my mother met. My mom was the kind of person that had never met a stranger, especially one as open and vulnerable as Jewels.

As it turned out, my mom was great at everything Jewels was interested in. They often went garage sale-ing on weekends. They found her a sturdy dining room table that my father insisted on refinishing and making chairs for. She also came across a matching tartan plaid sofa and chair set she had to have. My mom was also helping Jewels with some of her more complicated sewing projects. Occasionally they tried cooking, but more often than not, my mom just made twice as much as she and my dad could eat and filled Jewels' freezer with the extras.

The persistent squeak from the back door caught my attention; Parker and Ryan had arrived.

Parker pointed up at the Happy 50ᵗʰ Birthday! banner I'd hung up. "Ha, Brad is going to hate that."

There was a Reserved for a Private Party sign on the front entrance. I had told all the invitees to use the back door—or cat-piss passage, as Jewels liked to call it. Shortly after Parker and Ryan walked up to the bar, several of Ripley and Jewels' friends from work arrived. All the drinks were being poured at cost; it would have felt weird making a profit on my friend's celebration.

Almost everyone had arrived. Even Brad's family was already there. We were only waiting on him and Ripley.

Rich walked behind the bar and suggested I take a break and mingle. I was giving him a pat on the back when Jewels entered. She had been here earlier today decorating with my mom, but that had been a totally different woman.

"Holy shit," I said to Rich, "look at the stunning brunette that just walked in the door."

He laughed. "Wow, dude, she's hot, but I don't think you can have—"

I pushed him out of the way. "Oh yes, I can. I can, and I *will* have that one."

I jogged over to greet her at the entrance. She was staring at the floor while wringing her hands. I lifted her chin so I could see her eyes. "You look magnificent."

"I probably should have told you, I've been thinking about it for a while but didn't know I was going to do it until I was at the salon."

"I love it."

"Really?"

"Yes, but stay away from Parker."

We looked over at him. He was giving her two enthusiastic thumbs up. "Since I've known him, he's told me blondes are pretty, but brunettes are beautiful." I took her in my arms and gave her a semi-inappropriate kiss. "You're gorgeous, inside and out."

"Thank you," she said, biting her lower lip like a bashful child. "I'll put my coat in the office and help you out." She rose on her tiptoes to look over the crowd. "Where's your mom?"

"She's in the corner talking to Adams. I'm sure he's trying to talk her into learning to play poker. You rescue her and I'll hang up your coat."

She gave me a peck on the lips and trotted off. I went to hang her coat up in the office before checking to make sure that none of the kegs needed changing.

Brad and Ripley came through the door as I returned to the room. I started singing, "*Happy birthday to you*," and everyone joined in.

Brad rolled his eyes, his face turning beet red. He was halfway through the line that had formed to hug him and wish him happy birthday when he hit me on the arm.

"What's up?" I asked him.

He pointed up at the banner. "You're such a dick."

I flipped him the bird. "I love you too, buddy. You and Ripley have an open tab, so make yourselves at home."

He nodded, and I went to find Jewels. She was talking to Tracy and her new boyfriend Sebastian. I sipped my beer and waited for a more opportune moment to interrupt. I was so proud of her; she had come a long way in the eight months since leaving the cult. I knew it would be hard for her, but there was no way I could have known how complicated it would be to extract Frank's ideas out of her head. I admired her perseverance.

Ryan helped me with my anger and frustrations dealing with Frank and what he had done to her and her friends. I wanted him to pay. I'd never hit another human being, but I was itching to make an exception for Frank. Ryan kept reminding me that those choices were up to Jewels and the other people that had been in the cult. My job was to love her, not to punish him.

Once her friends dispersed, I leaned in so my lips were close to her ear. "Want to help me pick out music?"

I had purchased a ten-rack CD changer for the club to play one disc after another without interruption. We put both fast and slow songs in the player to have an excuse to do what Jewels called cuddle-dancing as much as possible.

We sang to Brad again while we brought out a sheet cake my mom had made for him. As the night went on, Jewel's friends from the club were great at getting everyone to dance.

Around twelve-thirty, the last of the revelers had left. Jewels and I were cleaning things up a bit when I gave her a poke in the ribs. "Come with me."

"Where are we going?"

"I have something for you in the office."

"Something for *me*?"

"Exactly. Now, close your eyes." She did as I asked. I led her there and turned on the light. On my desk was a vase bursting with pink tulips. "Happy anniversary, Jewels."

She gasped. "Aww, thank you, they're so beautiful."

I took her hands. "Can you believe it's been a year since I walked into that club?"

"I can't," she said. "Thank you for not giving up on me."

I opened my mouth to say I would never give up on her, but she placed her finger on my lips.

"And...thank you for supporting me and giving me the encouragement I needed to learn how to trust myself and how to find my own strength." She lifted her finger. "Now, together, I think we should explore one of my fantasies."

My eyebrows lifted to my hairline. "Which fantasy is that?"

"Sex with my boyfriend—at his bar."

I laughed. She was so daring after a couple of glasses of wine. Jewels gave me flirty eyes as she began unbuttoning my shirt. "Oh shit, you weren't kidding."

She flashed me her pirate smile. "Too much?"

I smiled back. "It's never going to be too much

Please, please take a moment to leave a review on Amazon (and Goodreads if you have it)! If writing reviews isn't your thing, no worries—just leaving a star rating helps more than you know.🩶

Spotify.com- https://tinyurl.com/yn2uj96w
AppleMusic - https://tinyurl.com/mms3s3zz

James & Jewels Mix-tape

Chapter 1 She Sells Sanctuary / The Cult

Chapter 2 Blue Monday / New Order

Chapter 3 Whisper to a Scream / Icicle Works

Chapter 4 Every Rose Has Its Thorn / Poison

Chapter 5 When Love Breaks Down / Prefab Sprout

Chapter 6 Under Pressure / Queen, David Bowie

Chapter 7 Secret / Orchestral Manoeuvres in the Dark

Chapter 8 Under the Milky Way Tonight / The Church

Chapter 9 Avalon / Roxy Music

Chapter 10 West End Girts / Pet Shop Boys

Chapter 11 Let me Go / Heaven 17

Chapter 12 Running Up That Hill / Kate Bush

Chapter 13 Silent Lucidity / Queensryche

Chapter 14 I Melt with You / Modern English

Chapter 15 Head Over Heels / Tears for Fears

Chapter 16 How Soon is Now / The Smiths

Chapter 17 Christmas Wrapping / The Waitresses

Chapter 18 Tainted Love / Soft Cell

Chapter 19 Gone Daddy Gone / Violent Femmes

Chapter 20 Love Will tear Us Apart / Joy Division

Chapter 21 Cuts You Up / Peter Murphy

Chapter 22 Love is Stranger / Eurythmics

Chapter 23 It's My Life / Talk Talk

Chapter 24 The Killing Moon / Echo & the Bunnymen

Chapter 25 Genius of Love / Tom Tom Club

Epilogue(s) This Must be the Place / Talking Heads

Also from the Author

Continue the Love Takes the Stage series with Lucy's novella. Plus, six more Romantic Shorts are on the way—each packed with passion, drama, and unforgettable moments!

Book 2

A Novella
Available in
Kindle Unlimited,
Kindle, or Print

March 17th, 2025

Books 3 - 8

"Romantic Shorts"
Available individually on
Kindle Unlimited or as a
compilation book in KU,
Kindle, oand Print

June 2025

A Love Letter to Neurodivergents

My fellow neurodivergent friends,

I want you to know how much you mean to me. You are an amazing person, and your unique perspective on life is a true gift. I admire the way you navigate the world with your own set of rules, and the way you think about things in ways that others may not even consider.

I know that life can be difficult for you at times, and that the world may not always understand or appreciate you. But please know that you are valued. Your quirks, your passions, your struggles - they all make you the incredible creative person that you are.

I understand the resilience and strength it has taken you to have learned to adapt and thrive in a world that often feels overwhelming and challenging. Please never give up on your dreams, desires, or creative pursuits. You're a shining star in this world and your contributions are immeasurably valuable.

With all my compassion and admiration,
Julia

Acknowledgments

I have organized this cray journey into sections:
The naive drafting period.
The "will it ever end" middle?
The do-or-die, final push!
Publication and beyond...

The naive drafting period

Thank you, thank you, thank you, **Robin Reed**, for all your encouragement. You could have said one-hundred negative things to me the day I told you I was thinking about writing a book, but instead, you told me you thought it was a great idea. I would have never written this book without your initial belief in me. Also, thank you for reading the first ten chapters and helping sort out my tense issue. What a game-changer!

Crystal Traver, what the hell is NaNoWriMo (National Novel Writing Month)? Had you not told me about this organization and method for drafting a book, I would still be writing my characters into corners and never finishing the story. Thank you for continually teaching me how to do just about everything. I'm lost without you. I mean, like, REALLY lost.

Hillary Rose, you were the very first person to show gushing interest and unabashed curiosity in my fledgling project. I'll never forget the day

I read you the first four scenes while we were DoorDashing —during that crazy blizzard! It's a memory I'll cherish forever. Months later, you volunteered to read my first whole shitty draft. Honestly, I don't deserve you!

YOLO!! **Lindsey Karnuth**, you were the second person that listened to my writing. That was also when you talked me into doing the 'recycled guitar art' project with you (which I loved doing after my silly fear passed). Thank you for continually supporting everyone's artistic side and being a beacon to those who think they're on the fringe. You use your unending compassion to make everyone around you feel treasured. Love you, Toaster Girl.

Bill Cox, I'm sure I talked your ear off about the book for eight hours straight. Thank you for allowing my excitement to use up all the oxygen in your truck. Also, thanks for being one of the most decent humans I've ever met.

John Clementson, you're such a trooper. Thank you for reading my book back to me one chapter at a time, every day, so I could get it in good enough shape to send to the professional developmental editor. Your continuous encouragement was sometimes the only thing that kept me going. This book is better because of your tender care during my most neurotic moments.

Thank you, **Sue Porter,** for taking my call and reading my book to me when John had to tap out due to a work conflict. It was courageous of you to help. Also, thank you for giving me a place to live, and..., and..., how can I ever repay you for all you've done? I Love you, Auntie!

Jamie Gifford The veracity with which you devoured my book was like gasoline to my flame. You filled me with so much hope thinking someone outside my circle would want to hear the story. You'll never know how much your input and desire encourage me to continue. From the bottom of my heart, thank you!!

I want to give a special nod to all my **friends and family on Facebook**. You guys quickly answered questions for me, like: 'What's a great name for a bar?' or 'Where in Austin was a particular business located thirty years ago?' And, 'Can someone tell me something unique about being a bartender in Texas?' You were my human encyclopedias of memory, resources, and creative ideas. I can't thank you enough for all the love and support you gave me. Especially, <u>but not limited to</u>, **Ted Burris, Tex Mazel, Kent Conlan/Mr. Clean, David Cody, and Bill Andrews**.

The "will it ever end" middle?

The joyous day I received the constructive critiques from my developmental editor was the beginning of almost two years of self-defeating writer's block. No one could have predicted that her advice would make me think, 'Oh, I can't make her suggestions; that would take a *writer*. I'm not a *writer*; I just spat out a story. I'm not smart enough to fix the issues.' This part of the journey was the time when I cried the most. I woke up daily hating myself because I couldn't figure it out. I couldn't find the words, I couldn't fix the plot, and I couldn't revise the book I had told everyone I wrote. For all the people who were therapists for me, who listened to me bawl when I couldn't go on, I want to express my unending gratitude to **Crystal Traver, Bill Callahan, John Clementson, Tammy Flahive, Britany Ott and Linda Stewart.** A heartfelt thank you to **Bill Callahan & Peanut** for allowing me to live with you while my grandmother was passing. You made one of the most challenging times of my life bearable. It's a debt I'm not sure I will ever be rich enough to repay.

Pat Callahan, I can't believe you volunteered to read my book **twice**! Once as a bad draft and once as the proofreader. Having your perspective was critical in helping me better handle my male characters. Thank you for taking the time to make my book a more pleasurable reading experience. I can't thank you enough...you mean the world to me.

Michelle Christensen, I think of you as "the hawk." Nobody found inconsistencies in my book more than you did. What a gift! Thank you for helping me weed through thousands of words to identify where I had mentioned something twice or given it the wrong name. I also want to express my gratitude for your significant help to Bob Bennett's character. My inspiration for writing him well came from wanting to impress you. I'm your biggest fan.

I learned along the way that "positive pressure" was the best possible motivator for me, and that's when **Claudia Burris** & by proxy, **Ted Burris,** jumped in to read the chapters I was revising. It was a great system, and I can't thank them enough for being there for me. **Claudia**, could you be a better cheerleader? No, you are, in fact, the very best!

During this section of the book, outside of crying and hating myself, I also set a path to learning how to be a "writer" and fix my many "writing" issues. I would be remiss not to thank the following people and institutions. Alessandra Torre and her fantastic Inkers Conference. Start with her if you want to write, publish and market a book. She is an amazing resource of knowledge and compassion for Indy Authors.

To "**Liz**" for turning me on to Alexandra Stein's book *Terror, Love and Brainwashing - Attachments in Cults and Totalitarian Systems.* This book helped me understand and show in my story the one question that came up the most in its early editions. Why doesn't Jewels just leave? Thank you, **Liz!** You, **your pup**, and _____ (redacted for legal reasons) are the cake, the frosting, and all the sprinkles. I'm so happy y'all are a part of my life.

Every iteration of the "Save the Cat" books, videos, and blogs. That Cat saved my Ass! (If you know, you know.)

I am incredibly grateful to all the **TikTok** self-published writers and editors for the tips and tricks you taught me. **AuthorTok** is a loving and giving community I am proud to be a part of.

I would also like to express my gratitude to **BookTok** and all the readers who take a chance on indie and self-published authors. Thank you for taking the time to read my book. I am deeply honored.

The do-or-die, final push!

Connie Worden, I couldn't have finished this book without you! There, I said it, in writing. You are my "ambassador of Quan." You are the total package: a listening ear, a confidence builder, and a grammar wizard. You were the person I could bounce ideas off of in real-time, which gave me the freedom to move forward. I'd also like to give a shout-out to **Larry Worden** for taking the time to talk to me about music, Hiawatha history and "forcing" me to enjoy some evenings out for dinner with him and Connie. I genuinely appreciate feeling included.

To my fabulous critique partners, **Megan Wheless** and **Sara J McAllister**, I don't even know where to begin. Whenever I needed more from you two, you gave it to me. Every time I needed extra attention, you said, "Absolutely." Thank you for being such an essential part of my writing journey and mental well-being. Having you two in my corner was invaluable. I vote that we never break up the band and continue helping each other with many more books to come.

To my fantastic beta reading team, **Claudia Burris, Kellie Currier, Mark Ivins, Tina Bulk, Helen Davis, Linda Callahan, Sheri Stout, Bobbi Moore, Carrie Bemis, and Hannah Nelson**, thank you for reading the book in its "not quite mature yet stage." I'm sure for those of you with solid grammar backgrounds, it was maddening. Your perseverance, questions, and suggestions gave the book the magnifying glass of attention needed for the final revision. Your hard work is woven into the words and sentences of every chapter. I truly appreciate all of you!

To my shy developmental & line editor, **A.S.**, you are the bringer of sparkle. Thank you for making my words shine.

Publication and beyond...

I'd like to express my eternal gratitude to all the individuals whose lives may or may not be depicted in this book. For legal reasons, I am unsure of the exact way to phrase this... I want to convey that if you recognize yourself as one of these characters and were a part of my life during that time, thank you for allowing me to capture the essence of our relationship and transpose it onto paper. It takes a great deal of finesse and grace to blend history into an enjoyable and entertaining narrative. I hope that the parts you recognize, perhaps of yourself, bring a smile to your face.

*If you think you may be Frank in this book, you're NOT.

To all the people who played a critical role in my real-life story but couldn't be included in the book, please know that your character's absence does not diminish the significance of our connection. Even though you may not see yourself portrayed in these pages, you are never far from my thoughts, and I cherish our bond deeply. The truth is, I love you with all my heart.

To all the kind-hearted individuals who innocently asked me a simple question about my book and patiently listened to me ramble on for 30 minutes or longer, I want you to understand how valuable those conversations were to me. Your willingness to engage and discuss my book helped me navigate plot problems, identify areas needing refinement, and encourage me to delve deeper into subjects I didn't realize people would be interested in.

To all the individuals who have graciously agreed to be part of the Advanced Reader Copy Team, or as we fondly call it, the ARC Team, I extend my heartfelt gratitude. As an Indy author, garnering reviews and ratings are crucial for establishing trust with a new audience.

Your willingness to accept a complimentary eBook in exchange for an honest review is immensely appreciated. I apologize that your involvement in this process occurs after the book's publication, preventing me from including your names in the physical copy. Please know that your role is vital, and I am incredibly grateful for the love and honesty you provide. Your dedication and contribution are deeply valued.

To all the beautiful people that support Indy Authors!!!

All right, everyone, group hug!!!!

About the Author

1991
Photo credit: Tracy

2023

Julia Heart grew up in the Midwest, Lived in Austin for twenty-eight years, Mexico City for three years, and Longmont, Colorado, for five. She loves to knit, crochet, listen to books, play bags (corn-hole), travel, and take long walks. She HATES to cook, is painfully dyslexic, neurodivergent, and a self-professed introvert.

You can get to know her better on social media

 .julia.heart   @juliaheart

 juliaheart   juliaheart.com

#igot**out**

Freedom of thought is a universal human right.

Tell your story.
Impact lives.
Change the world.

The Mission —

HEALING • EDUCATION • PREVENTION

The mission of #igotout is to inspire survivors of high demand environments who have experienced cultic, religious, or spiritual abuse to tell and share their stories - *if and when it's safe to do so.*

The hashtag, the igotout.org website, and associated social media platforms are intended to provide an inclusive online space in which to heal, learn from each other, prevent further harm, and educate the public about the harmful effects of coercive control and undue influence.

We believe the simple yet profound act of safely sharing our stories can help lessen the burden of shame, stigma, and isolation while also correcting widespread misconceptions about cultic involvement. Our stories can help the general public better understand complex cultic dynamics and how they impact us all today.

We tell our stories. We change the world. igotout.org